Born in Scotland, Andrew worked as a research scientist for almost a decade, on projects including DNA synthesis, forensics, and drug development. His short fiction has featured in several anthologies published by Fox Spirit books and his fantasy novel serial on Wattpad amassed nearly 175,000 reads.

The Hunter is his debut novel.

Praise for *The Hunter*:

'Reid's debut hits like a spin-kick. *The Hunter* is razor-sharp action from start to finish.'
James Swallow, bestselling author of *Nomad*

'Non-stop action all the way, packed with graphic violence and mayhem, hi-tech chicanery and suavely dangerous villains bent on taking over the world.'
Irish Independent

'This is top drawer stuff, and should give Lee Child and Simon Kernick a few sleepless nights.'
James Oswald, bestselling author of the Inspector McLean series

'*The Hunter* is an exhilarating, action-packed, gripping tale. Andrew Reid has written a real page turner that thrills and entertains from start to finish.'
Adam Hamdy, author of the Pendulum series

THE
HUNTER

ANDREW REID

HEADLINE

First published in 2018 by
HEADLINE PUBLISHING GROUP

First published in paperback in 2018 by
HEADLINE PUBLISHING GROUP

1

Cataloguing in Publication Data is available from the British Library

ISBN 978 1 4722 5635 5

Typeset in Adobe Garamond by Avon DataSet Ltd,
Bidford-on-Avon, Warwickshire

Printed and bound in Great Britain by CPI Group (UK) Ltd,
Croydon, CR0 4YY

HEADLINE PUBLISHING GROUP
An Hachette UK Company
Carmelite House
50 Victoria Embankment
London EC4Y 0DZ

www.headline.co.uk
www.hachette.co.uk

For Lisa

. . . there is an area of town for degenerates and an area of town for the working class. There is nothing positive gained from having them so close to us. It's a burden and a liability having them so close to us. Believe me, if they added the smallest iota of value I'd consider thinking different . . .

Silicon Valley CEO, 2013

Chapter 1

On the highway, the snow is already thick enough that Cameron can't make out the center line. There are tracks where other cars have been – trucks, maybe, from the width of them – but they're fading fast into the static fuzz of the blizzard. About a mile back, they'd passed two cars pulled over, the syncopated orange blink of their hazard lights soaked up by the falling snow. The barrier is still there, the white-crested strip of silver just visible on the right-hand side of the car, and Cameron can't help but think about what happens when a car hits it. They're built to break, to take an impact, bolts popping free and a few hundred feet of steel bending like a weighted rope as it soaks up the force needed to decelerate two tons and change without killing everyone inside. Even in the best-case scenario, if you had no choice but to hit it, you want to hit it as slow as you can. Right now, the speedometer reads eighty-two miles per hour.

The whole car lurches forward as Nate puts his foot down, and for a dizzy instant the back of the car feels as though it is sliding free of the road. According to the radio, the worst of the weather was supposed to be hitting over to the east. Either the forecast was lying or everyone due east is digging in right now to welcome in the end times. Cameron's gut goes cold, and she glances across at her brother. Not for the first time tonight, she wonders what the hell his problem is. There's no emergency that she knows of. Just some business opportunity he pitched her a couple of days ago that turned into a dinner meeting. He's always had a good head for that kind of thing. He left a high-paying position with a multinational biotech firm to join her team, taking the computer systems he'd built to track epidemics and using them to predict how brands go viral instead. Ever since, he's been a key player in landing some of her best endorsement deals – but it's late in the year to be thinking about signing something new. She only agreed to go with him because she trusted his instincts. Now, though, she's starting to wonder if there's something else going on.

'You sure you should be going this fast?' she asks.

Nate doesn't answer. He's got a hard-jawed look that doesn't suit his face, and he glances up at the mirror quickly before hunching back over the wheel. He's gripping it in both hands, like a learner driver, his chin thrust forward. He's wearing a big jacket that hides his skinny frame, and even though the aircon in the car is blasting them with heat, he's got a scarf jammed up tight around his neck like any second now he expects to be out in the cold. Cameron clears her throat.

'Nate. Slow the car down. Now.' She can hear her mom in her voice. Something about it always goes south when she tries to sound like a hard-ass. Normally she hates the sound of it, but then maybe it's the kind of push that Nate needs right now.

He swallows hard before he answers. Nervous. Guilty. 'You ever get into trouble, Cam?' He doesn't look at her.

Oh Nate, she thinks, *what have you got into?*

'Enough.' Fighters get into nothing but trouble. Even with a good manager, a really good lawyer, and as clean a promoter as she could find, there had still been a few close moments that she'd rather not have to remember. One time she'd got back from a weigh-in to find a picture tucked inside her kit bag, next to her wraps. It was a picture of her parents' home: cheap paper, a little blurred from the printer, but unmistakable for what it was. There had been a phone number on the back. Cameron had been so angry that she had sidestepped everyone – her lawyer, her manager, even Nate – to get it dealt with quickly. That decision had been a whole other kind of trouble, and it had taught her one thing. 'Enough to know you can't outrun it,' she says.

Nate nods, swallows again. Worries at his lip like he's trying to work something out. Cameron has seen that look before. More brains than sense, their dad always said, but then Nate overthinking every damn detail has saved her career more than once. Clauses in contracts that her manager had missed; a guy in the crowd he'd seen in another fighter's entourage weeks before, waiting to spray oil of wintergreen in her face during the walk-in. His face is blue in the light from the low-beams reflected back through the windshield by the falling snow. 'I'm not trying to outrun it, Cam.'

'Trying to get us killed?' She tries to say it lightly, make it a joke, but it catches in her throat and comes out high and scared.

When he answers, his voice is far away. Like he's forgotten that they're pushing ninety along a skating rink disguised as a highway. 'You ever wonder if it's possible to just . . . disappear?'

3

Don't let him do this. Cameron checks that her seat belt is fastened. She's already running through the options, her brain switching on to automatic. Can't pull the handbrake. Can't fight over the wheel. Both of those would crash the car. She could hit him, catch the angle of his jaw with just the right amount of force to cold-cock him, and get a hold of the wheel. The only thing that stays her hand is that it's Nate. Geeky, dumb, dependable, big brother Nate. In her whole life, he has never once let her down. Not one time.

'Whatever's happening, Nate, you can talk to me.'

Nate turns and looks at her, the long angles of his face softening. It's not fondness. It's like he's relieved. 'You know, I really can't.'

The way he looks at her snaps something inside of Cameron. It's like the last time he'll see her. *Do something*. She reaches down past the handbrake and pops his seat belt, the buckle whipping across his chest and catching under his left armpit. There's a sour twist of triumph, an echo of the feeling she gets when she outmaneuvers someone on the mat. He has to slow down now. The crash would kill him.

Nate nods at her like they've just shook hands on a deal, like this was what he was waiting for, then wrenches the wheel two-handed, a quick swing to the right that takes them on to the verge and then back again, hard over to the left.

The Lexus fishtails in answer, and as their forward momentum suddenly becomes sideways the car flips, driver-side wheels peeling reluctantly off the tarmac then springing skywards as it turns up and over.

It's like a hip throw. Cameron feels the jolt, the sudden violent motion, and in its wake the drawn-out moment of almost weightlessness as the whole car goes over.

Time goes slower when you're upside down. Cameron sees the snow spiraling through the windshield, like it's the whole world turning and not her, and she has more than enough time to recognize that queasy lurch of shock, the dawning awareness that you're no longer in control of the fight. That what comes next is a world of hurt, and there isn't a damn thing you can do about it.

When the car lands on its roof, it's like being hit with a sledgehammer. Cameron sees nothing but sparks, like purple snow swirling across her vision; feels nothing but the impact, a bone-deep jolt that shakes every single joint in her body loose. She's never been hit so hard in her life and then she's weightless again as the car bounces and makes another three-sixty turn about its long axis.

They tumble twice more, or fifty times – she can't keep track of how many it really is – and at the last something in the roof gives way with a shriek and some fucker chooses that exact moment to kick her in the head.

Cameron is eight years old again, and she's just lost her first fight. In fairness, nobody ever wins when they fight gravity. She lay for a long time on the asphalt not daring to move, because moving made her leg hurt more than anything had ever hurt before.

It was Nate who came looking for her, eleven years old and not quite strong enough to carry Cameron's weight but he did it anyway, hauling her crying on to his back and walking her home, step by heavy step. Cameron's crying from the pain and doesn't hear him wheezing, struggling for every breath, doesn't realize what's happened until they get home and the ambulance comes and it's not for her.

She asks her mom why he did it, lying in bed with her bandaged ankle like a hot coal at the end of her leg. She asks why he carried her all that way when he knew it was hurting him.

'Because he's your brother,' she says, almost scolding her, as though she's shocked it needs to be said at all.

Cameron wakes up to blinking lights, red and blue flicker; the crunch of boots on fresh snow; the buzz of radio static and the ticks and creaks of metal under stress. There's a hiss of hydraulic pressure, loud enough to startle her fully awake, and she realizes that she's upside down in the wreckage, halfway out of her seat belt, pinned in place between the buckled seat back and what's left of the glove compartment. She's not sure if there's no pain at all, or just too much of it to process.

'Nate?'

It comes out as a whisper. She tries to take a deeper breath, but there's not enough room for her chest to expand. A couple more inches and she wouldn't be breathing at all. She'll take the whisper.

'Nate?'

There's a wedge of fresh air down by her right arm, cubes of safety glass crusted round the edge of what once was a window like salt round the rim of a cocktail glass. A pair of boots appear, turn into gloved hands as whoever's out there gets down on their knees, and finally a face. Cameron can't make out much of his face – he's nothing more than a pink blur right now – but she knows it's not Nate.

'Ho-ho-holy shit,' he says, and Cameron tries not to panic, tries to keep her shit together enough that she doesn't hyperventilate. Control your breathing when you're in a tight spot: that's what she knows, what she clings to. Make the best of the air you've got. He's looking away now, fumbling for something, and Cameron thinks of the hydraulic hiss she heard. The jaws of life. They're going to cut her out of the car. She's going to live.

The man grunts, sliding down on to his side so he can get an arm inside the car. His forearm presses up against Cameron's, and the contact sends pain coursing through her. Every last scrap of self-control she had is taken from her by it, and she twitches and shrieks in her panic as his arm moves further into the car. He's holding something up by her face, and Cameron turns towards it. Whatever it is – water, painkillers, a bandage to stem some bleeding she hasn't noticed – it has to be important enough that he'd ram his arm into a car wreck to get it to her.

The flash goes off right in her face, and the reflex jerk of her body sends a fresh wave of pain through her. His arm snakes back out of the wreck and Cameron is dimly aware of the sound of him checking the photo and laughing to himself.

'Can't believe he did it,' he says. He's got a deep voice. Not local. 'He actually fucking did it.'

More footsteps, and a conversation that Cameron is just too angry to follow. She breathes slow through her nose, brings it all back under control. She's going to live. She's going to live, even if it's only just long enough to take that phone and feed it to its owner.

Time passes, and another face appears at the broken window. She didn't hear them coming, and she can't be sure she was conscious the whole time.

'Miss? Can you hear me?'

Cameron takes as deep a breath as her situation will allow. 'Yeah.'

'Great. That's great.' He sounds like a trainer complimenting her on a good combination. 'My name's Mike. Can you tell me yours?'

'Cameron.'

'Cameron. Okay. This is going to sound real funny, but don't try to move. We're going to get you out of there.'

'What about my brother?'

'Your brother?'

'My brother.' The confusion in his voice throws her. 'The – the driver. Is he alive?'

There's a long pause before he answers.

'Miss, you're the only person in the car.'

Cameron has questions – was he thrown clear? Have they started a search? – but something tightens in her chest and all she can do is gasp, her hands scrabbling against plastic and metal as though to somehow make up for the fact she can't breathe by grabbing hold of the air. She hears Mike swearing, and a flurry of movement, and with one final thought – *I'm tapping, you bastard, I'm tapping* – she sinks into darkness.

Chapter 2

There's nothing lost that can't be found again. Nothing ever disappears entirely. Money, assets, people: they all leave traces of their existence, scraps that – if you look at them all from the right angle, piece them together the right way – tell you how they passed out of view, and where they went. Like a puzzle. You work at it hard enough and clever enough, then the thing you're looking for will pop up as though you've called it.

That's been the truth of Cameron's world in the eighteen months since the crash. The eighteen months since her brother drove their car off the road and almost killed her. The eighteen months since she woke up and Nate was gone, vanished into a blizzard.

There's nothing lost that can't be found again. Not even Nate.

The light on Cameron's phone is blinking. She can see it in the corner of her eye, because she's been watching for it all along. Waiting for it has been a distraction, which goes a long way to solving the mystery of how she ended up caught in a headlock, side on, with only the frame of her arms to keep it from closing on her. She wants to tap out, to check out that blinking light, but there's such a thing as pride. She tightens her grip on the frame, left wrist in right hand, feeling the tension and the opposition of weight against her forearm. She focuses on it, all her attention now bent on this one, simple motion. Somewhere behind her over her left shoulder, a voice reminds her to breathe, to take her time. That this is easy, that to overthink it is to kill it. Listening to it makes her falter.

Her forearm trembles under the strain, and for a moment all she can think of is the fracture lines that thread the length of her radius, the pins they put in there to hold the puzzle-piece shards of bone in place while her body tried to fuse it all back together again. About what will happen to all those pins when her arm gives way.

Fuck it.

She can feel her jaw twitch, the unconscious acknow-ledgement that this is a bad idea, as she leans her weight into her right shoulder, swings her hips away and pushes up with her arm. They can put the pins back later if they need to. Her opponent is two hundred and fifty pounds and change, and as she pushes the bony blade of her forearm up into his neck all that weight stops working for him and starts working against him. He grunts, tries to force the headlock closed with strength alone, but physics is on her side. The biomechanical connection between arm, shoulder, and neck means that the more he pulls, the further his windpipe turns towards her arm. As he recoils from the sensation of being choked, he falls back and her legs scissor about his neck so that Cameron can reintroduce him to the same feeling from a brand-new angle. She counts to three in her head before he taps her on the leg and she lets go.

10

'Good.' The same soft voice that was telling her to breathe, now louder. Ludo, who runs the gym. 'Good escape.'

Cameron sits up, takes a kneeling position across from her training partner. He's an older guy, heavyset but not out of shape. He's flushed from all the grappling, but his breathing is steady. Ludo brought him along for the session and Cameron has already forgotten his name. She bows, lower than she needs to, and he bobs awkwardly in return. 'Thank you,' she says. 'Sorry to drag you out so far.'

'No, no. It's no problem.' He gets to his feet with surprising speed for a big man. Standing at six-two, he has a clear six inches on Cameron and still manages to look bashful. 'It's an honor to train with you.'

'Anytime, big guy.' She gives him *the smile*, the crooked half-cocked grin that she started off wearing as a shield whenever a camera was pointed at her, which ended up becoming her trademark look. Of all the things she lost, of all the things that have been taken from her, that smile is the one thing she would have missed the least. Figures.

There's a beat as his eyes flick up and look past her shoulder, and she can almost see Ludo nod his permission, before he swallows hard and braces himself. 'Can I have your autograph?'

'Yeah.' Cameron nods, relieved. The last guy Ludo brought had asked her out. 'Yeah, absolutely. You got something I can sign?'

'I-I'll go get it.' He hustles off to the men's room like there's a special offer on. Cameron watches him go, conscious of Ludo watching her.

'It wasn't a good escape,' she says. It wasn't. She can see the phone blinking at her, the urgent flicker of the green light,

11

but she makes herself stay on the mat. Respect is the first thing you learn there. 'It didn't flow. I let doubt creep in. I left a gap.'

'It was a good escape.' Ludo paces round the edge of the mat and into her peripheral vision. He moves like a lion tamer pacing the circus ring, always measuring the distance. He doesn't quite meet her eyes, and she feels something tense up inside of her at that careful avoidance. The feeling that if he looked straight at her, he would see the truth; that he would see every one of her fears. 'You're careful of loading your injured arm. That you finished the escape is good.'

'It was sloppy.' Cameron shakes off the encouragement with a gesture towards the men's room. 'If he'd done the same, you would have chewed him out for it.'

'I would have.' Ludo nods. 'I would. Do you know why I asked him to come train with you?'

'He weighs a shit ton and he's a big enough fan that he'd take a two-hour drive before sun-up to get here?'

Ludo considers it for a moment. 'Well, yes and . . . yes. I chose him because he understands what we're doing here. He gets it.' His eyes lift to meet Cameron's, and she realizes that she was wrong before to think he'd see too far into her. Instead, she can see too far into him. 'That on the mat you're only ever fighting one person. Yourself.'

'Thanks, Yoda.'

He looks away again. 'I was wondering what had happened to the old Cam.'

'She got crushed by a car.'

Ludo's jaw tightens, and though neither of them moves Cameron can feel him pull away. He's not the only one who measures out distances. He lifts his chin. 'You should answer your phone. You've been staring at it since you came in here.'

'Thanks, Ludo.' Cameron bows, quick and formal, before stepping off the mat.

She unlocks her phone and checks the message: it's an automated notification from her computer at home. Cameron might need to sleep or train, but her computer is always working. That was one of the first things she learned after the crash. Sitting in a hospital bed trying to search for any news of Nate online, feeling the pain building as she tried to hold off pushing the button that would flood her system with morphine and send her crashing back into insensibility. The nurse on her ward brought up a guy from IT to show her how to automate it, and Cameron had never looked back. Community college had a bunch of coding classes that ran in the evenings, and the tutors had relished the opportunity to teach someone with Cameron's single-mindedness. Now, she's always connected. Always on.

Always searching.

The message is just an image, a little distorted on the small screen, but even so she can feel the thrill of victory as she recognizes the man pictured. It's a high angle, but his widow's peak and round face are unmistakable. *I've got you*, she thinks.

'Now there's a look I haven't seen in a long time,' Ludo says. Cameron starts, and looks up to find that Ludo has followed her off the mat. He's still keeping his distance, careful to stand so he's not able to see the screen on her phone. Even off the mat, he respects her boundaries.

'What look?'

'You used to get that look in the ring. Like you were about to pounce whether the ref called go or not. Tunnel vision.'

'Something like that.' She holds the phone up so he can see for a second. 'See this guy? He's wanted for a series of high-value frauds across ten states. Anyone that finds him is in for one hell of a payday.'

Ludo frowns. 'Bounty hunting.'

'It's called skip tracing.' Cameron shakes the phone, frustrated by the look he gives her. 'Ludo, this guy's a ghost. Most people when they skip town make maybe one or two new identities. He has hundreds. Similar names, similar social security numbers, all of them spread across the US. Almost all of them have assets. Some of them have jobs. Some even have death certificates. All of them are dead ends. Nobody has been able to pin him down in a year.'

'Until now.'

'Until now,' Cameron says. She looks down at the phone and swipes past the picture to the location details. West coast, of course, because God forbid her travel costs ever be anything less than the lion's share of her expenses. Another thing that's changed. All her sponsors had moved on after the crash ended her fight career, and while they'd been gracious enough to let her down easy by covering most of her hospital bill, Cameron had been forced to severely adjust her 'let someone else deal with it' approach to finances. It had been a crash course, but it had helped her in the end. She'd caught herself on the horns of a whole bunch of dead-end skips early on, and the experience had given her a good eye for spotting bad leads. In this business, *stay hungry* wasn't just some motto to wear on your workout top.

Everyone expected her to get over it, to move on. Everyone else did. Kids, weddings, divorces, the next fight. All Cameron had was the hunt.

The picture has come in from San Francisco, which makes a twisted kind of sense. If you're good with computers and want to get lost, head for a tech hub. Half the skips she's found to date have been guys that made the wrong call and tried to hole up in some tiny Midwestern hamlet with populations that barely scrape out of triple digits. One of them even made the local newspaper's 'Getting to Know Our Neighbor' section. He'd been gone two days before Cameron showed up on his doorstep, the local sheriff in tow.

'. . . find him?'

Cameron snaps out of her reverie and looks up at Ludo. 'Sorry?'

Ludo smirks. 'Tunnel vision. How did you find him?'

'Facial recognition. Got a program hooked up to webcam feeds from all over the US: parks, zoos, city squares.' She doesn't tell him she set it up to hunt for Nate. She doesn't need to. He knows why she retrained, burning through eighty-to a hundred-hour weeks building the rest of the skills she needed. *You're only ever fighting one person.* Cameron has only ever been hunting one, too. The other skips are just practice. It feels like Ludo can see right through her, and she covers by over-talking. 'Lot of local government overspent on kit to keep their budgets from getting cut, so there are plenty of twenty-four-hour high-definition feeds running, and all of them are completely open.'

Ludo's smirk fades as she talks, and before Cameron can say any more he's already shaking his head to stop her.

'I have no idea what you just said, but my son would probably love it.'

'Every family has a black sheep,' Cameron says. Ethan is fourteen and a handy resource. Cameron doesn't want to tell Ludo that his son was the one who hooked her up with the facial recognition software.

He spreads his hands. 'They love what they love.'

'Nate would like him.'

'He loves his computers.' Ludo doesn't specify who he's talking about. A lot of people make a point of using the past tense around her, but Ludo knows it pushes her buttons. He already has his escape lined up. 'You can't force it,' he says. 'Besides, Cleo's got enough fight in her for both of them. She told me she wants to grow up to be you.'

Cameron laughs. Ludo's daughter is five, and wears a permanent scowl like it's her armor against the world. 'With you training her? She's aiming too low.'

'So, you found him. What now?'

'Now I need to go print out a list of all the local aliases that could be him, and check them out.'

'You got a computer program for that, too?'

'I've got feet. Guys like this, you get one chance to catch them.' Cameron checks her watch. Eight a.m. Maybe enough time to build a list and winnow it down to the most likely candidates. 'I can be on a red-eye tonight.'

Ludo frowns. 'Take care of yourself. You need help, you let me know.'

Anyone else, Cameron would blow off. For Ludo, she takes it with a nod. Ask anyone in the Boston martial arts scene to name a trainer, *the* trainer, nine times out of ten Ludo's name

16

would be the first out of their mouths. It had taken Cameron a long time to understand why that was. He didn't have any winners coming out of his club or any titles to speak of. Before the crash, his was the only club that ever turned her down for sessions. Afterwards, Ludo was the first and only one to ask if she'd like to train again. He'd come down to the hospital himself while she was still trying to get used to walking. After that, Cameron got it.

You're only ever fighting one person.

'Think fast, Cam.'

Cameron looks up to see her sparring partner returning, pen and pristine flier in hand. She recognizes it immediately: a promotional handbill from the last bout she fought, a month before the crash: Cameron in the foreground, fists raised; her opponent in miniature over her left shoulder, arms crossed. She can see the watermark, a matte crosshair against the glossy black background, and for a brief moment considers how much it must have cost to print them up like that just to match her brand. If her manager had had his way, they'd have had her in an orange vest and her opponent sporting a pair of antlers.

The big guy has come prepared: he's got a silver marker that will show up nicely against the black. She cracks *the smile* and too late realizes she can't remember his name. *Think fast.* Ludo knows it too, and he's grinning like the devil.

'Hey,' the guy says. 'Sorry I took so long. Didn't want to sweat all over it.'

'No problem.' Cameron takes the flier and the pen. 'You want this made out to you?'

'Please.'

'Just don't let me see this on the Internet going for a hundred bucks.' She shakes the pen to get the ink flowing while he makes vague sounds of protest at both the accusation and the value. Bending down to write, she pauses. 'You know, I've never been the best speller. Could you just spell your name for me real quick?'

There would be a beat of silence if Ludo wasn't coughing into it.

'Well, first there's an A, then there's an L.'

Cameron signs it quickly. 'I'm really sorry, Al.'

Al shakes his head as she hands the flier back to him, both of them taking care not to smudge the still-wet ink. 'No worries,' he says. 'It happens to me a lot.'

Cameron laughs, more genuine this time. 'You ever want to partner up again, let Ludo know. You're always welcome.'

'Really?' His face lights up like it's Christmas, and Cameron almost remembers what it was like to have fans. Back in the day, Al wouldn't have had two seconds of her time.

'Really.' She glances up at the clock again, and feels the weight of all those aliases pressing down on her. It's going to be tight. 'But right now, I've gotta run.' She grabs her bag and offers him a fist bump as she passes. 'See you, Ludo.'

Ludo gives her a lazy salute in answer, and she's out the door.

Chapter 3

The plane's wheels hit tarmac at six forty-two a.m., and by seven fifteen Cameron is on her second coffee of the day. Every part of her body hurts, every fiber of her being crying out for some good, healing sleep. For the moment, it'll have to make do with too-hot liquid caffeine spiked with so much sugar it makes her gums ache to drink it. She managed two hours of shut-eye on the flight: trapped in the zig-zag fold of an economy-class seat, semi-lucid dreaming the tilt of a horizon through half-shut lids, a pulsing, flickering orange glow that followed the curve of the Earth, her dread of it growing strong enough to make her spasm awake before the flight was half-gone. Her neighbor had no such problem. Sagged so deep in his seat it was hard to tell if he was wearing his rumpled beige suit or if it had been laid over him, his breath whistling raggedly through his nose, he was dead to the world. Cameron had shut her eyes and tried her best to get somewhere in the vicinity of sleep, but once her brain acknowledged that it could hear that whistling, it was all she could think about. She'd waved down a cup of water from a harassed-looking flight attendant, beat her neck pillow into something approximating an actual shape, and tried to block it out by focusing on the task at hand.

When Nate vanished, the first thing Cameron had found out about skip tracing was that it was an easy job to get started in. Anyone with a little seed money could sign up to the kind of services that trace cellphones and bank transactions, or websites that scrape all the metadata that people sign away every time they skip the Terms of Service and click *Accept*. It was easy to get started as a skip tracer, but hard to get good at it. Most low-level skip jobs were chasing down years-old debts that had been passed from one collection agency to the next. They usually ended with someone's grandma waking up one morning to a stern letter, or two guys on a doorstep with a van looking to take away a flatscreen television in lieu of what they were owed. Most skip tracing was easy work, the sort of pattern recognition you could do from your armchair, and none of it was any use for finding Nate. He went from living a completely ordinary life to a ghost: no bank activity, no phone calls in his name, no social media, no loyalty cards. Off the grid.

Training herself to find him had meant going after the hardest skips, the sort of people you didn't find while sitting in your armchair. You had to get out in the world. You had to hunt. And even if it meant spending money you didn't have on a last-minute flight across the country, you had to be willing to take a risk.

In the morning press of people taking the BART train into the city, Cameron could almost bring herself to feel good about it. Of the thirty or so aliases that her target had scattered about the Bay area, only one of them struck her as being real. Almost all of them had digital trails – social security, travel cards, phone bills, lists of associates, previous addresses – and once she started looking through them side-by-side, the more obvious it became that what she was looking at wasn't so much evidence of a person as the appearance of a person. Only one of them was different.

Half-complete, lacking a phone or social security, it wasn't even close to a new identity. It was the sort of thing that flagged on her radar as an obvious fake, a rushed job left hanging when fleeing the law was more important than making sure you had submitted all the forms you needed. She'd seen more than enough of them in the past eighteen months: some from the skips she'd taken on, most from the ever-growing list of aliases that Nate might have taken, every Nate, Nathan, Nolan, Noah that had popped into existence since the crash.

Samuel Gorton. Not enough information under the name to pin him down, but it had been a start. Cameron had raced the clock counting down to her flight, printing off a map and sticking pins in it wherever she found an alias that could easily pass as both. As *Gorton*, he had no fixed address, but there was a *Gordon* listed as residing in an apartment near the financial district. *Samuel* had no employment records, but *Samantha* was in high demand as a freelance accountant, finding tax loopholes for the kinds of people who were willing to drop a significant annual stipend on someone who could clear even bigger debts off of their ledgers: more than enough to cover the rent for an apartment in a tall shiny building in the heart of the city.

So, a patchwork person. *E Pluribus Unum.* Hunting down Sam wasn't about finding the needle in a haystack: it was about taking a step back and seeing that he *is* the haystack. Hidden behind a cluster of names, all of them incomplete, he was free to seed a more complete identity in any part of the country and send every skip tracer and bounty hunter off on a wild goose chase. Everyone, that is, but Cameron.

Because she's seen it before.

Six months ago, hunting across the South for a guy with a stolen check printer and enough aliases that he'd turn a corner and already be somebody else. The only reason Cameron found him was because she'd got lucky, had been in the same town the day he lifted a case of ink and paper from the local bank's supplies. Until then, he'd been nothing more than a rumor, a shell game of false identities constantly shuffled and discarded when you weren't paying attention. While the police were arresting him, she cloned his phone and copied everything she could off of his laptop, studied it for weeks until she knew how he had done it. Because if he could hide like that, so could someone like Sam Gorton. Or even Nate.

Cameron waits almost two hours before heading to the address to find Gorton. Timing isn't just about being early. When you've only got one shot to take, you pick your moment and make it when it suits you best. Instead of heading straight there, she occupied a stool in a busy coffee shop, nursing her third tall cup of the day while trying to figure out if the barista who kept staring recognized her or was just giving her the stink eye for not drinking up and leaving. Hard to tell with the beard, and the distracting sight of his lean, muscular arms going through the motions of making coffee with aggressive efficiency. He had good arms. Cameron sighed – *another time, another life* – and went through the notes on her phone one more time. She stayed off the Internet, had turned it off before take-off. You never knew what kind of flags you could trip looking somebody up. She'd met a guy who'd stayed hidden on the grid for almost a decade because he'd rebuilt the front end of a tracing website – a big one – and had the presence of mind to build in a warning system should he ever need it. Could have made a fortune brokering that information to other fugitives, selling it on, but he'd had a weird sense of justice about it. Not everyone deserved a warning.

The morning rush doesn't peter out. It builds, and Cameron starts to pick up a lot of talk about a protest that is due in the afternoon. A protest means crowds, and a lot of chances for someone to vanish. *Better beat the rush.* Cameron buys a pastry to go – half apology for hogging the stool, half recognition that coffee alone is not going to be enough to get her through the day – and makes her way down the street to the address she has matched to Sam Gorton.

The apartment building has a keypad entry, but a van is double-parked in front of the lobby entrance and the door is jammed open, a strip of metal bent double and stuck beneath it. No desk or super in sight, and there are enough scratches and scrapes to suggest it's a common enough event and everyone has given up caring.

Cameron takes her time, makes her way round the back of the building and into the narrow strip of alley that edges past the ramp to an underground parking lot. Unlike the pristine face of the building, the alley side is a cement grey box filled high with shadows. City maintenance obviously comes around semi-regularly because it's not banked shoulder-high in accumulated crap, but from the crunch of old glass and the reek Cameron can tell that they do the very least their job demands. She can't blame them. There's a lot of city to clean. A pile of cardboard boxes in one corner catches her eye, an old comforter thrown over the top in a shape that looks oddly human from the right angle, and Cameron stands silent, waiting to see if the owner is still in residence, or if the hunched-over suggestion of a shape is just her wanting to see it. There's no sound, no movement, no huff of breath. Cameron relaxes. A green reflective plate above the door tells her that this alley is a fire exit. She makes a mental note: there are no ladders, no outside balconies. A runner will have to choose between here and the front door.

Sam Gorton won't be a runner. He doesn't look or act the part. Runners are all young, nervy types, the ones who skip on an uncle's credit card and go to bed every night feeling the heat prickling warm on the back of their neck. Nobody goes to the lengths that this guy has to live their life out of a bag already packed. He lives comfortable. He sleeps well. He won't be a runner.

Cameron doesn't do another circuit of the building. The important part of casing a place is not overdoing it. You can walk the block all day, but when it comes down to it there isn't much of your plan that can change. Knock on their door, confirm their identity, and call law enforcement to follow up with the arrest. Easier to arrange for a deputy to be on-site or nearby, but Cameron prefers to handle the first part herself. When she first started the job, she'd been stiffed on the credit for a collar by a sheriff looking to bolster his department's records in the run-up to re-election. Lesson learned, she doesn't bother calling ahead unless the skip looks like trouble.

Finance nerds don't pack heat. All Cameron has to do is dress smart, look serious, talk a tough game. He might try and buy her off, talk his way out of it, but he isn't likely to have a holdout stashed somewhere close to hand.

Cameron makes her way back round to the front of the building and goes inside. On her way in, she kicks the metal strip out from under the door, picks it up and pockets it while the door swings closed behind her. Straight past the elevator there's a door to the staircase. Through it, she starts down the half-flight and the tight turn that leads to the fire-exit doors at the back of the building. The door opens out on a press-to-open bar. Cameron unbends the metal strip into a right angle and jams it behind the bar. Before it will open, someone is going to have to find the strip and jerk it loose. Twenty seconds of work, which is more than enough to eat up any lead a runner might get on the staircase. He won't be a runner, but Cameron has a row of pins in her arm as a reminder about the value of her expectations. It feels like a shitty thing to do, but then half of the active tracers she knows would have just put a padlock on it and bet on the building never catching fire. She can clear it later once the skip is in custody. *No harm, no foul.*

Cameron goes back to the elevator and hits the button for the ninth floor, then all of the buttons for everything above it. It's a cramped little box for the size of the apartment building it's meant to service, mirrored walls to give the illusion of space, and Cameron wonders if there's a freight elevator somewhere for people to move furniture with, and if she should have cased that, too. *He won't be a runner*, she tells herself.

The corridor on nine is clean and quiet, and built to last: the paint on the walls is the kind of industrial taupe that you could scrub with a brush dipped in bleach if you needed to; the carpet is dark brown and cut-pile, laid wall-to-wall. All of the lighting is recessed, flush with the walls. Aside from the brass door numbers and peepholes, everything about the place is put together with an eye for function over style. *Well, nobody pays more for a fancy corridor.* Cameron can barely hear her own footsteps on the carpet, and she suspects a layer of rubber has been laid underneath. *Not getting woken up at three a.m. by asshole neighbors, now that's a selling point.* No nightingale floor for Sam Gorton. It should be a comfort, but the silence is unsettling. No conversations, no clatter or argument, no sound of kids. No cooking smells. She can feel the hair rising on the back of her neck. It feels like the peepholes are cameras, watching her pass. It's like the tunnel before the fight: there's a feeling of dislocation when you walk down it, of unreality. Like when the lift doors opened, she left the real world behind.

Sam Gorton's apartment is halfway down the hall on the left. Cameron takes a moment to take a deep breath and collect herself – *the place is too new to be haunted, get a grip* – before knocking.

No answer. Cameron knocks again, three smart raps with the middle knuckle, not too impatient, polite and crisp. *I know you're there.* That's the kind of knock it is. *And I hate to insist, but get your ass up and open the door.*

Between knocks, Cameron listens. She can hear something from inside, the low mechanical hum of air conditioning, but no movement, no thud of footsteps. No rush to answer or escape. She knocks again.

Cameron can't say what it is that makes her reach for the door handle – instinct, habit, the urge to rattle it and dispel the tension that's still pressing at the edge of her senses – but when she does it turns in her hand and the door swings open. The apartment is light inside, tall windows letting in the warm morning light.

'Sam Gorton?' Cameron calls from the hallway. The hum of fans is louder – too loud for air conditioning, and she can hear the tick and whir of a computer working – but there's nothing past that. She edges forward and puts her head round the door.

Sam Gorton is not going to be a runner. He's seated at a desk at the far end of the room, a bullet hole in his forehead. A black monolith of computer equipment is set up behind him, still running, completely oblivious to the dead man, and the dried blood spattered across his face.

Cameron pulls her head back out into the corridor. 'Shit.' A skip is simple. You find the thing that's missing – person, object, money – you get paid. A dead body is complex. There will be a police statement, forensics, red tape.

There's no one else here. All she would have to do is wipe her prints off the door and she could walk away. *And leave a paper trail that sees you taking a day trip cross-country, and a barista as witness that you were in the vicinity, dumbass.* 'Fuck.'

There is, at least, the skip. All she needs is a photograph, time stamped, to show that she found him first. That's it. Get a photo, call the cops, let them tidy up the mess while you get your payday. Taking the first step is the hard part. Cameron rolls her shoulders, bows her head, closes her eyes. Like in the locker room before they come in to check her gloves, when it's just her and the glare of white tiles. Like in the cage, with a couple of thousand voices screaming, chanting, trying to rattle her, trying to psych her out. There's only silence here, and it's deafening.

You can do this. Cam bunches her hands into fists, feels the scar that runs the length of her left arm go tight in answer. 'You can do this.' She opens her eyes, and makes her way into the flat.

Chapter 4

Cameron doesn't need to check Sam Gorton's pulse. With half the back of his head missing and most of his brain on the floor behind him, he's either dead or planning a run for Congress. The bullet hole is low on his forehead, and the impact has smashed the bridge of his nose and the orbit of his right eye: both are tilted in towards it, like they're sinking. She can still tell that it's him, just, and she holds her breath while taking a handful of pictures on her phone. She needs a wallet, really, some form of ID to tie him to his aliases, but the police can handle that. She's not touching him. Even with the desk between her and the body, it's still freaking her out.

He's tremendously pale, all the blood that isn't on the floor sunk down inside him without a heartbeat to move it, and the fish-belly whiteness of him puts Cameron in mind of a waxwork. There's very little smell – a touch of something sour in the air, but not enough to catch in the back of her nose and mouth, nothing that would turn her stomach, and Cameron suspects that might be because of the bank of computer equipment that's still running at his back. There are three stacks, each one with at least ten boxes stacked in them, fans running full-tilt as they work. It's noticeably colder at the desk. They've kept the corpse cool, preserved it in a cocoon of HEPA-filtered air, as though performing some kind of final service for their operator.

Cameron isn't a coroner, but she can tell that he wasn't killed recently. He's not dripping, at least. She's not sure how long blood takes to congeal but she's had enough cuts to know that it takes its sweet time clotting. And he hasn't been here a while, either. She has video footage of him at a zoo that's less than two days old, so taking off a couple of hours' travel time to get back to his apartment, sit down, get shot . . . he died sometime in the last twelve to thirty-six hours.

That's enough. Cameron can leave the rest to the cops. She walks in a slow circle, debating whether to call her lawyer first, or 911. She considers checking for another number, one that will get her to the desk sergeant of the nearest precinct, something to start the ball rolling on them seeing her as a professional having a shitty day rather than the closest available suspect. But it means she's going to be sitting on hold waiting for that one line to free up, standing in a room with a dead body trying not to sit on or lean or touch anything, and the low, industrial hum of the fans slowly building in her ears until she freaks out. They're already chewing at her nerves and it hasn't been five minutes. As she makes her mind up in favour of 911, something catches her eye.

There's a gun on the floor.

It's not quite hidden by the corner of the sofa that sits hard against one wall, below the windows on the long side of the room. Just the back side of the grip is showing, the roundedoff corners of the magazine butt. It's like whoever shot Sam Gorton – and they would have been standing not far from where Cameron is standing now – tossed it casually to one side when the job was done, not caring where it landed. Cameron might not have noticed it was there at all, her eyes might have passed over the abstraction of its shape caught in the shadows and just not registered what it was, but for the jolt of recognition that brings the full focus of her attention to bear. The gun is hers.

It's a 9mm Beretta Cougar. There's a piece of grip tape – more than one, a double thickness layer – laid across the top of the backstrap, right where the gun sits snug against the base of the thumb. Cameron knows this because she put it there when she'd first got it and found that apart from being fit for purpose in every other way, it didn't sit right in her hand while shooting.

'Oh shit.'

She goes over, crouches down by the sofa to get a better look. Not touching anything. Conscious that her feet are leaving prints right now, that she's left prints and traces of herself on the door, the lift, the lobby. *Christ, you even blocked an exit.*

It's definitely her gun. The one that right now should be sitting in a locked box in her apartment, on a shelf in her closet next to a holster that she's never once felt the need to put on except to check for the fit. *Get a gun. Get certified.* That was the one thing everyone in the business seemed to agree on, repeated to one another like it was Gospel. Said it so often that Cameron had started to believe it herself. Even if you never need to draw it, it's better that the knowledge is there.

She should have known better. The fighter in her should have known better. You don't work combinations to leave them unused. You don't learn holds without thinking about the counters. You build a bag of tools with the intention of using them, of keeping them ready at all times, because the thing that you do half-assed is one day going to come back and bite you.

Get a gun. Get certified. Get set up.

Cameron picks up the gun, thumbs the safety on. It feels heavy in her hand and she pops the magazine to check. It's loaded. She works the slide and catches the bullet that falls out. Nine-millimeter soft point. They'd been on the shelf marked *Home Defense*, the cheapest ones in the store: hence she'd gravitated towards them. There's a nub of grey at the tip, softer metal designed to bloom on impact, transferring all its kinetic energy to the first person it hits. Minimum chance of it going through them and into someone else, maximum chance of stopping them with the first shot. No wonder Sam Gorton was missing the back of his head. Whoever had done this had been thorough, had put a lot of effort into getting hold of her gun, her bullets. Putting Sam Gorton in front of a camera knowing she would be the one to see it. *Who the hell did you piss off this badly, Cam?*

She thumbs the bullet back into the magazine, slides it into the grip, pushes it home with a click. She checks the safety again before opening her briefcase and putting it inside. Risky to carry without a permit, but there's no way she's leaving it here. There's a whole bay of water out there that will solve this part of the problem for her, at the very least. If she's being set up, there are three things that need to happen for it to stick:

32

means, motive, and opportunity. She can get rid of the first at her earliest opportunity.

Out in the corridor, the elevator bell sounds.

Cameron's gut twists as she revises the count upwards. Four things need to happen for it to stick: she needs to be caught. There's a crackle of police-band chatter, muted by the walls, and the soft tread of feet approaching. *Do something.* Her whole body feels like it has frozen up. It's that helpless feeling, the one where you realize that you've been outmanoeuvered, and the worst part of it is not seeing it until it's way too late. Like the flick of a steering wheel, hard over to one side, and then back the other way. The memory is a cold shot of adrenaline straight into the base of her brain. *Get. The Fuck. Up.* Her hands close the briefcase on automatic, flick the combination to something other than 'spring open the instant you touch the hasps', and she stands, phone in one hand, briefcase heavy in the other. Thumbs the screen. Nine. One. One. Green for go. It rings twice as the footsteps slow in the corridor and Cameron thinks she can hear the pop of a hasp on a holster. Shit. Shit. Shit.

'Nine-one-one, what is your emergency?'

Get a grip, Cam. It takes her a beat, long enough for the operator to start repeating herself.

'Nine-one-one, can I help—'

'Sorry. I've just found a dead body. He's been shot.'

'Where are you calling from?'

'I'm in an apartment building, it's on—'

'Ma'am, I need you to turn around and show me your hands.' The cop's voice comes from the doorway. He says it a little too fast and Cameron's mouth goes dry, like she just bit down on a cotton pad. She can almost feel the gun pointed at the back of her head.

'Is there someone else there?' Cameron hits the speaker button as she turns with her phone hand held up and out, screen turned towards the cop to show him what it is, or – more specifically – what it isn't. The cop is standing square inside the door, gun held in both hands, the muzzle pointed down at the floor. His finger is outside the trigger guard. He's about five-ten, Latino, broad-shouldered in his uniform, and from the way his jaw is working it's almost as if she has a gun drawn on him. He looks terrified, but at least he's not terrified and aiming down his sights at her.

'There's an officer in the doorway.' Cameron says it loud enough that the operator can hear her. 'He has asked me to turn and show him my hands.'

'Can you put him on the phone?'

'I've put the call on speaker.'

The gun barrel goes down a little further and the officer visibly relaxes. 'You're calling nine-one-one?'

'I came up here to find the door open and this guy dead. What else was I going to do?'

He nods, a curt acknowledgement, and holsters his weapon before holding his other hand out for the phone. Cameron can see his gun hand doesn't stray too far from his hip, so she keeps her distance as she hands it over. Every nerve she has is singing, the fight-or-flight response desperate to be set loose, but he's de-escalating and Cameron wants more than anything to keep it that way.

He switches off the speakerphone and exchanges a quick call-and-response verification with the operator before identifying himself as Ray Perada. Cameron makes a mental note of the name.

'There's an apparently deceased male, gunshot wound to the head. One female witness present. Yes. Yeah, he's dead. Back of his head's gone.' He stops and looks Cameron up and down, then sniffs the air and screws up his face. 'Doesn't seem recent. If you can pass it on to the coroner's office, I'll start with the witness. Yeah. Yeah. Thanks, dispatch, will do.' He presses a button to hang up the phone, and gives Cameron an apologetic smile that, for a brief moment, gives her hope. 'So,' he says, 'can you tell me what's going on here?'

'Your guess is as good as mine, officer. I came here to verify an ID for a contract—'

'You're a notary?'

'No, the contract was for a skip trace.'

'Okay.' He nods again, this time with the disapproval that all cops have for part-timers and private contractors. She can almost feel the disdain thickening in the air between them. 'You're a bounty hunter. What'd this guy skip out on?'

'Multiple frauds, with a total in excess of five million dollars.'

'And you get how much for finding him?'

'Flat fee plus a percentage of losses recouped.'

'Hell of a payday for you, then.'

'Recouped, Officer Perada.'

'Which means what, exactly?' She can tell he's just rattling her cage, blowing off the head of steam he'd built up coming through the door.

'I'll cover the specifics when you take a proper statement, officer, but to put it bluntly: he's no good to me dead.' It's clear from the sour look on Perada's face that he doesn't approve. He glances over at the body as she says it, and Cameron silently curses herself for not adopting an old-school respect for the dead man. All cops are Catholic, whether they start out that way or not. All that time spent thinking about other people's guilt puts their minds on to a parallel course. By that measure, speaking ill of the dead was probably about as bad a choice as telling him about the gun in her bag. 'Sorry.'

'It's okay, Miss . . .'

'King.' She doesn't offer her first name. 'Do you know how long we'll have to stay here?'

Perada shakes his head. 'Coroner's office will update us on a—'

Cameron's phone rings in his hand. He starts, like he's forgotten it was there, and looks down at the screen by reflex. 'Nate,' he says, before remembering himself and holding it out for her to take.

Nate.

The shift in her gut – shock, fear – is so sudden she can't hide it. Something in her face or the way she stands tips Perada off that there's something wrong, and it spooks him. He stands a fraction taller, and the motion pulls the phone out of Cameron's reach.

'Officer Perada,' Cameron says, picking her way around the words like she's stepping through a minefield. 'I need to answer that call.'

'Ma'am, the only thing you need to do is stay right where you are.' His free hand is back down close to his hip now, the phone held out like he can ward her off with it. It's still ringing.

Nate. It's been almost two years. No word or trace of him,

36

and suddenly he's calling her. The break on this case, the body, the gun, this call – she doesn't know how, but they feel connected. There has to be a connection.

'Ma'am.' Perada has his hand on his gun now. He looks more nervous than when he came in. Cameron tries to think how long her phone has been ringing. *How long before it rings out? How long before I lose him again?*

Cameron makes her choice. Perada sees it in her face, and pulls his gun.

Kicks used to be Cameron's weak point. It took a couple of losses for her to decide to put that right. She'd worked at them constantly ever since, until her high kick became something she was known for. Drop a hand out of guard, take a step the wrong way, and she would pull the trigger. Someone once filmed it with a high-speed camera, and they ended up checking their kit three times to make sure it wasn't broken. The instant her foot was off the ground, the rest of the kick looked like it was travelling at normal speed.

When her foot hits Perada, his gun isn't even clear of his holster. The shock of impact gives him a slack-jawed look as he goes sideways, and he hits the floor with a boneless thump. Cameron catches the phone mid-air as it falls from his hand and hits green as fast as her thumb can find it.

'Nate?'

There's a pause before he answers, his breath loud on the line. 'Cam. Where are you?'

Cameron can hear the growing thunder of her heartbeat as she processes the question, the long-brewed anger roiling up inside of her. 'Where am I? Where the fuck are you? What the hell is going on, Nate?'

'Cam, this is important. Where are you?'

'Important? No shit it's important. I just cold-cocked a cop to take this call.'

'Shit, Cam.' Another pause. He goes off the line a second, comes back sounding distracted. There's street noise in the background: cars, pedestrian chatter. *He's here in the city.* She doesn't know how she knows it, save for a feeling in her gut. 'Are you sure it's a cop?'

'Uniform and badge says yes.' She looks down at Perada, at the standard issue belt and gear. If he's not a cop, he's gone to a great deal of expense to look the part. A cheap suit and a badge would have been enough to play detective. 'And he identified himself to nine-one-one. Where have you been, Nate?'

'Cam, I left to protect you. I wouldn't call you if it wasn't important.'

'Protect me? You nearly killed me.'

'You're in danger, Cam.' He takes a long, shaky breath. A car horn blares somewhere, and Cameron's head comes up as she hears a faint echo of the noise from outside. *He's close.* 'Cameron, listen to me. Listen carefully. You have to get out of there. Just go. Do you understand?'

'Who did this, Nate?'

'Cam, I'm sorry this is happening.'

'Nate—'

'Don't try to find me. Listen. You have to get out of there. Just go.'

Cameron bristles at the interruption. He won't even let her speak. 'When I find you, Nate, I'm going to—'

'They're coming, Cam. Get out.' The line goes dead.

'Mother*fucker*.' Cameron throws her phone at the floor and tries not to stamp on it. Nate's alive. He's alive, and Cameron is angrier than she can ever remember being in her entire life. A dead body, a cop laid out, and all he has to say is *get out*? Cameron yells, a loud, primal roar, her blood fizzing, and she kicks the wall hard enough that it puts a boot-sized hole in the drywall. She pulls her foot free and stands with her eyes closed, thinking. *Processing*. Getting a handle.

Faintly, Cameron can hear sirens. She knows that they're coming for her.

Get out. She takes a deep breath. Of the building, maybe. Of reach of the police department, certainly. But as for the rest of it, she's going nowhere. Nate is alive – in this city – and Cameron is going to find him.

Chapter 5

Coming to isn't the worst part of Ray Perada's morning. Getting kicked in the head wasn't exactly high on his bucket list of things to do before hitting forty, either, but none of it matches up to the shit-eating grin the desk sergeant has on his face when Perada goes to sign in.

'Heard you had a rough day.' Bulwell is a department legend, and not in the good way. Somewhere in his early fifties he just stopped caring, and now he's spinning out the last few years between him and the two beers per guest tab that will pass for a retirement party sitting at the front desk making sure everyone knows exactly how little he cares.

'Depends on your definition of a rough day.' Ray uses his own pen when he puts his name in the daybook. Everything gets logged on the computer, but the department is still holding on to paper copies. Two years previously some punk kid with a computer got his nose put out of joint over a misdemeanor possessions charge. He hacked in and froze the system for a month, flushed everything from the day of his arrest. Most cops would've found it funny, but in the process he zeroed the overtime of everyone who'd worked a shift that month. Serial killers got less manpower assigned to them.

40

While Ray is signing, Bulwell's smile drops off of his face like hot bird shit down a windshield. Normally Ray would've ignored whatever crack Bulwell had lined up for him – something about wetbacks, usually – but the ache in his jaw has lit a fire in him today.

'How'd you figure?' Bulwell is staring down from on high with a face like a thunderstorm. He can't work out what it is, can't leave it either. Perada meets it with a shrug.

'I dunno, Sarge. Most of the guys here, if they got assaulted by a perp they'd call it an occupational hazard. Guys like you fill out an insurance form every time you have to walk more than ten feet.'

'Least I didn't get my ass kicked.'

'Are you kidding? Anyone trying to kick your ass would lose their foot in it up to the ankle.'

Ray can almost hear the cogs turning in Bulwell's head as he thinks it through. 'Yeah, you're real clever, Perada.' A smile like a grease stain lights up his face. 'Clever guy like you around, I'd better watch my back.'

It feels like an itch scratching at the nape of Ray's neck, the thought of all the talk that has gone on behind his back since the shooting board ruled in his favor. You don't need to be paranoid to think like that. Cops talk, and if you're not hearing it then it's definitely about you. Bulwell can see how much it rattles Ray and nods, satisfied. 'Captain wants to see you,' he says. 'Got some brass in there with him, waiting. See how clever you are once they're done with you.'

Ray sucks in a taut breath and walks off, stiff with embarrassment and rage. They used to play up the brotherhood thing at the academy, that the badge was a promise shared by all that wear it. They failed to mention that the slightest tarnish was enough to see that promise broken. Bulwell's laughter follows Ray all the way into the station house, and not a soul lifts their gaze to acknowledge him.

True to the man's word, Captain Adams is not alone in her office. She answers Ray's knock with a brusqueness and volume that suggests she's not happy with having had to wait for him, and he hustles in as quick as his sore jaw will let him. She's sitting at her desk looking more like a judge than a captain, whip-thin and straight-backed, not an ounce of softness in her. *Yeah*, Ray thinks. *She's mad as hell.*

'Officer Perada,' she says. 'Have a seat.'

'Yes, ma'am.' There's one pulled out ready for him. He sits down, and waits in silence. Adams doesn't acknowledge or introduce either of the people that are in the room with her. One of them is the deputy chief of police: Ray recognizes him, and his heart sinks. The last time he saw the deputy chief, it was at a hearing that had ended up costing him six months of appointments with the department shrink and buried all hope of seeing a promotion. *Just when you think things can't get any worse.* The other is a civilian. Gingham shirt, brown jacket, jeans, enough hair product in play to support a small salon, cleaning his thick-framed glasses to avoid eye contact: everything about him screams Silicon Valley wunderkind, the kind that puts in a complaint whenever the bus drivers strike or they see a homeless person rooting through a dumpster. He gives Adams a look. 'Is this a disciplinary meeting, ma'am?'

'Not as such, Perada.' She looks uncomfortable, but doesn't elaborate. 'I understand you took a hell of a knock this morning. Have you seen a doctor?'

'Yes, ma'am. The EMT wanted to have me admitted for X-rays, but I wanted to file my report as soon as possible.'

'Department policy mandates a full check-up after a head injury. You feel dizzy, you vomit, you let someone know, you understand?'

'Yes, ma'am.'

Adams shifts in her seat, like she's got something jammed under her, and it dawns on Ray that she might be angry, but it isn't with him. She slides a piece of paper across the desk. 'Six weeks. Full pay, any and all healthcare costs covered. Effective immediately.' She says it fast and terse, like she's ripping off a plaster. 'We've cleared it with your union official as acceptable terms.' He looks at the paper. It's exactly as she describes: six weeks of 'administrative leave', full pay, full health cover, no strings. She's signed it, the deputy chief has signed it, his union rep has signed it. There's no space for his signature; giving him eyes on the hard copy is just a formality.

'I don't understand.'

'How are you sleeping, Ray?' The deputy chief has a deep voice. He's a big man, as big as Bulwell at the front desk, but all of his weight is hard-packed, the suet-soaked muscle of a bare-knuckle fighter. The question might have sounded avuncular, even concerned, if Ray's hackles hadn't already been rising.

'I sleep fine, sir,' Ray says. 'My last psych evaluation cleared me for service.'

'I understand it might be difficult for you to accept this,' the deputy chief says, as though Ray hasn't said a word, 'but having an officer involved in another incident so soon after returning to active duty could raise some questions about whether or not we rushed things.'

'Nothing was rushed, sir. I'm absolutely fine.' It feels like the truth right up until he says it. Some things you never recover from. They are fixed points: immutable, unfading. But you say the words anyway.

'I understand that. Captain Adams agrees with you. But we have to consider things from the point of view of the department. We have to maintain . . .' He screws up his face, searching for the word, 'public trust.'

'So you're benching me.'

The deputy chief bristles at that. 'Now look—'

'It could have gone worse for you.' The Silicon Valley wonk talks over him, and while the deputy chief turns the color of a fire truck, he doesn't protest. 'The woman who assaulted you could've taken your gun. She could have decided that leaving you alive was a liability. She has already killed one person that we know of.'

Sitting on the desk is the cop's equivalent of Wonka's Golden Ticket, six weeks of all-expenses paid time for Ray to sit on his ass and not give a shit. It feels like a slap in the face, and while he can't take it out on his captain or the deputy chief, a civilian will do just fine.

'Who the hell are you?' Ray asks.

'I'm a consultant working with the—'

'Start with your name, then we can work to whatever asshole title you've got.' Ray shakes his head. 'How do you know she's a killer? Forensics won't even have finished taking photos yet.'

'It's fairly obvious that she went there to kill—'

'The dead guy in the chair? You been out there to see him? That body was a day old. Dry blood, very little in the way of smell. Perp was in a beige pant suit and didn't have a drop of blood on her. And I still want your name.'

'Perada, stand down.' Captain Adams interrupts, close to shouting in the cramped office. 'He's a representative from Carrington Medical. He needs to be here, and if you've got a problem with that you can take it up with the mayor.'

Carrington. With departmental funding being slashed left and right, having a private medical firm offer to pick up the tab for health coverage was a boon to the force and a PR coup for them. Ray had made good use of it, and had never once given a thought to what strings might be attached. It goes a long way to explaining why the deputy chief and the captain are kissing his ass instead of handing him it.

Silicon Valley gives Ray a smug look. If Adams isn't going to back him up, there's no point in fighting it. 'Understood, ma'am.' Ray stands, and takes the paper from the table. 'I'll get my statement filed before the end of this shift.'

Adams closes her eyes, gives the tiniest shake of her head, like she herself can't believe what she's doing. 'Effective immediately, Officer Perada. Get changed, get those X-rays taken, and go home. Get some rest.'

Ray looks from her, to the deputy chief, to Silicon Valley. Both of his superiors avoid his gaze. Silicon Valley looks straight through him. *No statement.* A dead body, a manhunt for the only potential witness: the whole station should be buzzing with it. Instead, the mayor's office is involved, nobody's saying a word, and he's got six weeks to forget all about it. It stinks, and Adams knows it. 'Yes, ma'am.'

He has no intention of forgetting about it. Benched, disgraced, dismissed. None of that matters. Inside, he's still a cop. Ray double-times it to the locker room to get out of his uniform.

He beats Silicon Valley out to the street by ten minutes. Enough time to buy a hotdog from the stand that does swift business twenty feet from the entrance to the station, and to work through his doubts about what he's about to get himself into. He's heard of guys working off the books plenty of times, but none of the stories ever turn out well. Even firing off a couple of snaps of a cheating husband is suspension material if you get caught doing it. Time was he would have shared the same dim opinion that all cops have for moonlighting, but this is different. A man is dead, and with the only possible witness in the wind someone's got both the interest and the pull to make it all go away. And as much as he suspects he's going to regret it, Ray is going to find out.

Any reservations he has evaporate when Silicon Valley trips down the steps and jumps into a taxi. It's been waiting for him, it seems: he doesn't flag it down, the light is off, and there's no apparent conversation. As soon as he hits the sidewalk, it pulls up curb-side. The instant the door is closed, it peels away. Ray makes a note of the number to check later, but suspects that it will bounce back as legit. He crumples the greasy paper up into a ball and holds up a hand to flag down a taxi of his own.

Chapter 6

Cameron checks the nameplate twice before she rings the doorbell. With the nickname 'Pickaxe', she expected Antonelli to live in a cramped room above a crumbling boxing gym, some brick-and-whitewash relic of the seventies waiting for the inexorable rumble of bulldozers. Instead it's a pretty little box of a place, like a full-size doll's house with a flight of steps leading up off the pavement to a cherry-wood door polished to the color of ox blood. A pair of big potted plants flank the door, and Cameron can't quite bring herself to believe that Antonelli has the patience to look after them. The shortest fighter in the division's history, Sophia Antonelli built her entire career off the back of her singular ring persona. Once she stepped through the ropes (and later, into the cage) she switched on a laser-focus anger that made every other fighter look casual by comparison. She got her nickname early when what would have been an axe kick for someone taller turned into an uppercut as her rising heel caught a charging opponent under the chin and put them down six seconds into their first round. Her promoter spent a year trying to push the Italian angle before he conceded that the name just wasn't going away.

Aside from the location, something else catches Cameron's eye: below *Antonelli*, there's another name. *Jones.*

They kept that quiet, she thinks, and hits the button a second time.

Ophelia Jones comes to the door in sweatpants and a 49ers shirt that hangs loose about her shoulders. She's almost a head taller than Cameron, and she stands with the easy confidence of someone whose arms are long enough to connect a punch without ever letting you get close. She's a fighter, too. No nickname – hard to brand initials with a loaded history – and no trademark style. Just a lot of experience and hard work which might not bring in the endorsement dollars but count for as much, if not more, in Cameron's book.

'Hey, Ophelia.' Cameron tries to smile like she hasn't just fled the scene of a crime. 'Is . . . is Sophia in?'

'Who wants to know?' It's a flat, hostile, *get the fuck off my doorstep* question. Aside from their relationship, there's one important fact about Sophia Antonelli and Ophelia Jones that Cameron has been trying not to think too much about: both of them have lost fights against her. And when the crash put an end to Cameron's career, they were forever denied the chance of a rematch. Ophelia grins, the hostility evaporating. 'I'm just fucking with you, Cam, of course she is. Come here.' Cameron sags in relief into Ophelia's long-armed embrace. The experience is like being crushed in a really happy vice, and Cam grunts out a laugh as Ophelia lifts her off of her feet and carries her inside.

'Hey, Pickaxe!' Ophelia yells, back-heeling the door shut behind her. 'Guess what we just got delivered!'

'Pickaxe?' Sophia yells from somewhere at the far end of the hall, probably the kitchen from the clatter of pans that follows. She storms into the hall with the same quick, short steps that make her so hard to gauge in the ring. 'When was the last time you— holy shit, is that Cameron King?'

'Hey, Sophia.' She almost coughs Sophia's name as Ophelia puts her down and her breath drops back into her in a rush. Sophia is on her before she has a chance to really recover, and all Cameron can do is laugh and weakly pat her old rival's back as her ribs creak under the strain of a second hug.

'What are you doing here? Finally realized there's a whole other coast, decided to come pay us a visit? How are you?'

For a brief, precious moment, their warmth feels right, like she has escaped from the nightmare of her own life. That this is sanctuary, and that if she wanted to she could stay forever. Cameron savors it for the three heartbeats it takes for her to remember that it's the opposite. This isn't sanctuary. It's their home, and by going to them, she puts their jobs – their livelihood – in danger.

'Sophia, I'm really sorry to do this, but I'm in trouble.'

Antonelli's smile falters a little, but she recovers quickly. Cameron catches the look that passes between her and Ophelia, the unspoken communication between them. 'What kind of trouble? You need money?'

It's not an unreasonable question. Once you stop fighting, the money dries up fast. Management and tax make purses a lot thinner than advertised, and the fast cycle of events means that endorsement deals have a lot of exit points baked into their contracts. When she'd been fighting, Cameron had tried her best to pass on as much work – coaching, punditry, teaching – to ex-fighters that were feeling the bite. 'It's not money. It's . . . work. I was meant to be out of here on a flight tonight so I didn't book a hotel. I just need to charge up my phone and laptop and make a few calls.'

Ophelia claps her on the shoulder as she sails past. She has an arm of solid oak; Cameron can recall the time in the ring when she'd tried to break it. 'Shit, Cam. Is that all? I'll even throw in a pot of coffee. Gluten-free madeleines, too.'

Sophia waits until she hears Ophelia in the kitchen. Even then she steps closer and lowers her voice. 'What's really going on, Cam?'

'It's Nate.' Saying it out loud makes it feel like madness, like the whole thing is a bad dream she's waiting to wake up from.

Sophia's eyes widen. 'He's alive? You found him?'

'He's alive, but he found me. Called me. Sophia . . .' She can barely find the breath to say it. 'A man is dead. Nate's involved somehow. And someone is trying to set me up.'

'Set you up? How?'

'The dead guy. He stole money from a bunch of banks, all corporate fraud stuff. I was looking for him. When I tracked him down, he'd been shot and my gun was on the floor.'

'Your gun.' It comes out flat, full of doubt.

'I know how it sounds, Sophia. Someone took it from my house. I didn't even know it was gone.'

'What did you do?' She barely waits for Cameron to answer. 'You called nine-one-one and reported the body, right?'

'I—'

'Cam?'

'It's complicated, okay? I called nine-one-one but a cop showed up while I was on the call.'

Sophia doesn't say a word. She knows there's more, and she can wait it out. *Patience.* That was what had changed since they fought. Sophia of old would have charged in, demanding the rest; now she's waiting, calculating. *Working out if she's going to have to ask you to leave before madeleines and coffee.*

'Everything was going fine,' Cameron says. 'The cop talked to nine-one-one, called in people to take care of the body, holstered his sidearm. Then Nate called my phone. He's here in the city, Sophia. I'm sure of it. If I can just run a check to find the phone he rang from—'

'What about the cop?' Sophia asks.

Cameron swallows. 'He wouldn't give me the phone back. When I saw it was Nate, I panicked.'

Sophia puts her face in her palms, draws them down her face with a weary sigh. 'Don't say it, Cam.'

'He drew his gun, so I kicked him.'

'Oh no, Cam. No.' Sophia's eyes go wide. 'There must be an APB or something out on you now.'

'I don't know.' Cameron shakes her head. 'Look, I know this is bad and if you want me to I will leave right now. I just hoped I could charge up my phone and—'

'How did he take it?'

Cameron stops. 'Nate?'

'Not Nate, the cop. How did he take the kick? You can't just say you kicked a guy and leave it at that.'

'He went down like he'd been darted. Didn't see it coming, might not even know what hit him.'

Sophia grins, her face lighting up as she punches Cameron on the shoulder. 'Still got it, Cam. Arm full of pins, and you've still got it. You should get back in the ring. We could call you the Bionic Woman. How about Cyborg?'

'We could call you Car Crash,' Ophelia calls from the end of the hall. 'From the sound of things, it suits you. Coffee's ready.'

'You heard all that?'

'I heard it.'

Cameron looks at the door as Ophelia vanishes back into the kitchen. 'How could she hear all that?'

Sophia shrugs. 'Beats me. I could live to a hundred, and that woman will still surprise me.'

Their kitchen has the minimalist look of a professional chef's dream workplace. Most of the surfaces are clear space in stainless steel, and everything that isn't stored away is neatly racked along one wall. A coffee machine sits incongruously on the island in the middle of the room, dredged up from the back of whatever cupboard it had been hiding in to serve their guest. The madeleines are on a plate next to it, and Ophelia is wasting no time in waiting: she has a mug already brimming and a madeleine half-eaten in her other hand.

'Cheat day?' Cameron asks.

Ophelia nods, swallows. 'Now you're here, it is.'

'Glad I could help.' She looks around, taking it all in. Both women look really fit. Their industrial kitchen helps explain it. 'This is amazing. You guys got really serious.'

'Yeah.' Sophia looks away, almost embarrassed. 'Cam, when your sponsorship fell through, our managers just . . . you know. It's a business. You've got to take every opportunity you can.'

'Don't worry about it.' Cameron waves the apology away. It's not that it didn't hurt. There's just nothing she can do about it. 'Take every cent you can get. You never know . . .'

'. . . when you're going to get hurt,' Ophelia finishes for her. 'We had a talk after you . . . after the crash. About what we would do if one of us got hurt. We decided to put a few things in place: savings, investments, and this place. Full nutrition planning. Personal physio.' She looks up, gestures at the ceiling. 'Our own gym.'

Cameron won't pretend she hasn't been following their fights. Both women have been winning, and winning with ease. They've taken their training up a notch, and it has shown in their records. The way their careers are going, there's only one conclusion. 'So. What happens when you end up on a card against each other?'

Sophia grins. 'Fight of the decade. We'll keep dodging until the purse is too big to ignore.'

'Do your managers know about . . .'

'Yeah, yeah. Both teams do. Closely guarded secret. Non-disclosure contracts, the works.'

'Still, aren't you worried about it coming out?'

'Nope.' Ophelia's grin is wide enough to match Sophia's now. 'One guy even wrote a blog about what amazing "friends" we had become and how we are role models for good sportsmanship. I swear I could kiss her in the street and people would say it was CPR or something.'

'Amazing.' Cameron takes a long drink of her coffee, the two women watching her closely. 'What?' she asks, eventually.

'Aren't you going to flip out or something?' Sophia asks.

'It's just . . . you're the first fighter that we've really told,' Ophelia finishes for her.

'I just kicked a cop in the head and fled a crime scene. I'm not sure I'm in a position to judge anyone.' Cameron shrugs.

'But even if I was, it doesn't change a thing. I'm happy for you guys. And I'm looking forward to seeing that fight.'

'Would be better if you were still around,' Sophia says.

'I'm still around.' Cameron drains her mug, and takes the offered refill. 'Just cheering you guys on.'

'You're still a fighter, Cam. Even if you don't believe it.' For a moment, it's as though Ophelia is facing her in the ring. Her focus is so complete. 'And while it goes against every instinct you have, you need to let go of this idea that you're going to find Nate. He almost got you killed once, and now this? Walk away, Cam.'

Cameron grips her mug in her hands so hard that she thinks it might shatter. Walk away. It is as easy, and as hard, as that. 'I know, Ophelia.' Her voice comes out small. 'I should.' She feels like anything but a fighter as she says it. 'But he's my brother. I can't just walk away from this.'

Ophelia nods, not agreeing but understanding. It takes a moment for Sophia to break the silence that settles over them.

'So.' She puts her mug down. 'Phone and laptop. I'll put them on to charge. Maybe you should give your lawyer a quick call while you're waiting?'

It's good advice. Cameron feels a pang of guilt for putting this on them. 'You sure you don't want me to go? This probably counts as aiding and abetting.'

Sophia shakes her head. '*De nada*. Besides, we've got good lawyers. All this goes south, we'll say you threatened to kick the crap out of us.'

Chapter 7

It took more money than Ray was truly comfortable parting with to keep the taxi driver on Silicon Valley's tail. He flashed the badge, which had the opposite effect intended: 'this ain't the movies' turned into 'now I *know* you shouldn't be doing this.' He'd fully expected to get turned out on to the side-walk, for the cabbie to blurt his number into the radio and see his administrative leave bumped up to a full suspension, but his luck – or the mercenary nature of cabbies – held true. All Ray had to do was let slip his suspicions about the cab Silicon Valley had taken not being legit, and his driver came on-side, even offering some opinions on what he was going to do to an off-the-books driver when they caught him. Still took the time to lighten Ray's wallet, though.

Silicon Valley gets dropped off a block into the Mission district and starts down the road on foot. Ray's driver pulls up at the sidewalk and drops him off before peeling away so fast that Ray loses a chunk of coat to the door slamming shut on it. Ray stumbles, straightening fast at the thought of losing his mark, then spots him crossing the street further up. Another man – taller, bigger, with a shaved head – steps down from the curb to meet him, offering a handshake and a deferential nod to what is probably a question. He's wearing black shirt, pants, and boots: military fatigues that make him stand out like a bruise. The combination of his outfit and the fact that he walks into the street completely oblivious to hazards set Ray's nerves to singing. *Walking like he owns the place.* He's seen it before. Whenever brass enter a perimeter they like to pace it out, mark it as their territory. If they could piss on all the lampposts, they would. The block might not know it yet, but they are on lockdown.

As he walks, Ray cases it out. Silicon Valley and his pal in the Action Man fatigues vanish into an unmarked van on one side of the street. It has some patched bodywork, but the wheels are in good condition. Surveillance vehicle. No holes or windows in the side, so whatever they are watching is up ahead. When Ray passes, he is careful not to look back, taking his phone out as he walks with the goal of looking too busy to be a threat whilst making a quick call to a buddy in the department car pool. When it connects, his ear is filled with the comforting sound of the shit music that the mechanics blast twenty-four seven.

'Yo Perada. What you want this time?'

'Vin. We got a banged-up van on the books rigged for surveillance? Plate starting five, victor, foxtrot, papa.'

'Hold on. Homeland just got authorization to park what looks like a whole fleet of unmarked vehicles with us. You should see these things, Ray. If federal overfunding is the disease, these bad boys are the symptom. Tinted windows, heated seats, enough kit stowed in the back the rear suspension will be shot in six months. Your tax dollars at work, man.'

'Doesn't sound like my guys. They've got a beat-up Ford, looks ready for scrap.'

'Old school.' He can almost hear Vin nodding in approval down the line. 'Nope, Fed cars are all here, nothing else is out on loan.'

'Thanks, Vin. I owe you.'

'Always, buddy.'

As he makes it to the end of the block, Ray thinks it through. Surveillance sitting down the street looking forwards means that they are probably looking across at his side. None of the houses on the van's side of the street look vacant, so there's probably no one in any of the buildings. No clean view into windows, so they're casing an entrance. The neighborhood is upscale enough that the van might be the only surveillance they have. Anywhere more rundown, they would have put people on the head and tail of the street pretending to be joggers or some shit; here, it was a risk, because strangers standing idly at the end of the block would spook the residents. Black fatigues. Like SWAT. The rest of the team would be at the back of the building, or sitting in vans one block over ready to move.

Ray turns left at the end of the block and dials the precinct again, a different extension.

'Hey, Perada.' A woman's voice, Ray's name almost a sigh of exasperation.

'Kaz! How'd you know it was me?'

'Vin called me. Said you were looking for a favor and I should probably brace myself.'

'The man knows. Look, have we got anything big going down today?'

'Aside from the giant protest that's going through half the city? The one with the mayor and a couple of counter-protests to juggle?'

'Aside from that.'

'Good day to get a paid holiday, that's all I'm sayin'.'

'Hey, I don't like it any more than you.'

'Yeah, you sound real choked up. And no, we've got nothing happening.'

'No busts or agency stuff? No out-of-towners breathing down your neck?'

'None that I know of.' She isn't holding back. The last time the FBI had come in asking for cooperation, they'd stomped around the precinct making sure everyone knew how in charge they were. By the end of it, Karen in dispatch had been ready to commit treason on the next suit-and-tie-wearing asshole she saw. That she wasn't audibly grinding her teeth down the line was a good sign.

'You're one of the good ones, Kaz.'

'Don't I know it. What else do you want?'

Ray grinned. 'How'd you know.'

'You always say thanks when you're done. At least that's what I heard.'

'Uh, yeah.' In the background, Ray can hear someone spitting out their coffee. He sighs and looks at his shoes, feeling the heat climb in his cheeks. He'd dated one of the girls in dispatch for a couple of weeks, back before the fallout from the shooting inquiry had marked Ray as *Do Not Touch*. It never went anywhere, but apparently her supervisor had bullied some details out of her. 'So if you've got a black and white handy, could you get them to just check out a block for me? See if they can find an excuse to take a closer look at a van, make sure there's nothing going down.'

'Okay, Ray. Give me the details. But you owe me.'

'Do you take doughnuts?'

'Yeah, if they're bottle-shaped and filled with bourbon.'

The line goes dead and Ray drops Kaz the details as a text. He's almost to the end of the block and when he walks round it he starts back down the next street, parallel to the one he came from. There are no pedestrians, no cars that seem out of place. A little traffic goes by, but no one seems to be circling. For a moment, it feels like paranoia. His therapist said there might be moments of hyper-awareness, moments where his body would suddenly expect danger, and to try and give that feeling context; mundane events might take on a significance that they did not deserve. It feels like vertigo: that dizziness, that vulnerability; the realization that all of it might just be in his head. *And half the station will know it, when that black and white turns up nothing.* Ray feels like throwing up, and he stops to bend forward, hands on thighs, not knowing if it's to steady himself or just to make sure it will clear his shoes. *Breathe.* He counts backwards from ten. At seven, a faint buzz of static interrupts the count and grounds Ray's nerves, all of the doubt flooding out through the soles of his feet and leaving him listening intently for the source of the sound.

His phone vibrates in his hand. He answers the call, keeping his voice low. There's an alley a little way down that echoes with the sound of a man's voice, and Ray doesn't want him to know he's coming.

'Hello?'

'Ray, whatever the fuck you're doing, get out of there.'

'Kaz?'

'Your black and white isn't coming, Ray. I just got my ass chewed out for trying to send one your way, and the captain is on her way down to find out who asked for it.'

Ray's heart starts pounding when she mentions the captain. 'Shit, Kaz, sorry I got you into this.'

'Don't apologize,' she says. 'Whatever it is you're into, we're not allowed to touch it. If you don't get the fuck out, you're on your own.'

Ray tries to thank her, to apologize again, but she has already hung up. *You're on your own.* Whatever it is Silicon Valley is doing, it has its hooks buried deep into the department, and suddenly Ray understands the reason for his Golden Ticket. They've all read his psych. eval., his resolution to be not just a better cop, but the best cop. *You got that time off because they can't be sure you'll look the other way.*

He could turn around right now and walk away. Whatever this is, there's a world of trouble waiting for him on the far side of it. All he has to do is turn on his heel, and it will pass him by. But being a cop doesn't stop when the uniform comes off, and it sure as shit doesn't stop when other cops start looking the other way. Ray never went looking for redemption, but he knows what the right thing to do is.

When he clears the entrance of the alley, he freezes and backs up out of sight. Halfway down it, there's a guy dressed in black fatigues, kit bag at his feet, radio held up to one ear, and a submachine gun slung on a shoulder strap hanging at his right elbow. Ray can't identify the weapon. From the glance he got, it's a cut-down, space-age piece of kit, but it's unmistakably built like a submachine gun: short barrel, stock, big mag, suppressor. Ray's service weapon is locked up at the precinct, but – against his therapist's advice – he's still carrying. He pulls the snub-nosed revolver from the waistband holster at the small of his back and checks the weapon. It's almost childishly small in Ray's hands, but it's a design that's seen few alterations since the fifties and needed none of them. In an alleyway at short range, all the tech in the world isn't going to change the fact that Ray has his gun ready and the other guy is scratching his ass. He gets his badge out, clips it on to his jacket pocket before taking a quick, deep breath and starting round the corner.

There's no fear in him. There should be. His guts should be doing somersaults, but instead all he feels is anger. His jawline still aches from the kick that perp had hit him with this morning, her foot coming up out of nowhere, and the pain of it focuses all his concentration down to a single thought: this is a second chance. Radio Guy is still focused on the alley, the back of the buildings ahead. Ray closes, finger off of the trigger, gun angled down. No need to escalate. Ray's footsteps echo off the brickwork, and Radio Guy's head comes up in answer.

'Sir.' Polite, but firm. Ray puts his gut into it. *Cop voice.* 'I'm going to ask you to keep your hands in plain sight, and turn around slowly.'

Radio Guy startles a little, hands twitching down, but he's not a dummy. They go out to the sides, palms open, fingers spread, and he turns slowly. He's square-jawed, blond and thinning, and wears a neat mustache above a shit-eating grin that borders on insolent. 'Shouldn't you be in uniform, officer?'

'It's at the dry cleaners. You mind explaining what all this hardware is for?'

'You're interrupting an active op, officer. Walk away now and I might think more kindly when I mention this to your captain.'

'Nice try, smartass. I called dispatch. No active ops cleared with them. You're working off the books, you and your buddies in the van that's the other side of the block.' Radio Guy's eyes widen. 'Yeah, I made them, too. Probably got another van circling a couple of blocks away, five or six guys loaded for rapid response?' Radio Guy says nothing, but the grin evaporating off his face gives it away. 'Yeah. So maybe you cut the shit and tell me what you're doing here.'

Radio Guy relaxes a little, steps forward. 'Look, officer, I can expl—'

He lunges for Ray's gun, taking a long step forward and snapping his hand out snake-quick to knock the pistol's barrel to the side. Ray has been waiting for it, could see it coming the instant Radio Guy grinned at him. A step back is all it takes, and the grasping hand whips the air six inches short of its target. In answer, Ray brings the gun up into line, his finger on the trigger, the sights lined up on the bridge of Radio Guy's nose. Rear sight, front sight, target. A couple of ounces of pressure is all it will take to turn the other man's day to shit and he knows it. His face is milk-white. 'Put your hands behind your head.' Compliance is instantaneous. 'On your knees.'

Ray strips the SMG from the man's side, popping the shoulder strap one-handed. The gun is very light, all plastic and air. Half the weight of it must be just the bullets. 'What the hell is this?' Radio Guy doesn't answer. On his belt he has a handful of plastic cable ties, and a folded square of black cloth that Ray takes a moment to place. It's a black bag, ready to be flicked open and thrown over someone's head. They're not here on a surveillance job. They're here for a rendition. *And that's a two-man job.*

Ray snatches up the SMG and runs, just as the air where he had been standing fills with bullets. There's very little noise – the suppressed gunfire sounds like someone riffling the edge of a deck of cards – but from the crack of impact chewing up the cement and the yelp of warning from Radio Guy, Ray can tell it was close. He hits the enclosure at the end of the alley and dives sideways, getting out of their line of sight. There are some trash cans and a few pieces of old furniture here, but nothing big enough to use as cover. There are a few windows where the houses back on to the courtyard, but all of them are too small and too high to reach. Nobody wants a clear view of their trash cans. The handful of service doors stand resolutely shut. *Trapped.*

A mocking burst of gunfire bounces off the wall facing the alley mouth. Ray puts the SMG down, gets his phone out. There's no bars of signal, but he tries calling it anyway. He should have signal, but there's nothing. *They knew you were coming*, he thinks. *They radioed ahead. Baited you in.* Cut lines of communication, encircle, neutralize. Rendition tactics.

He picks up the SMG, pops the clip, checks it. Loaded. Twenty rounds, give or take. He puts it back, works the bolt, checks for a selector switch. There's a space between panic and madness, an unreal spread of seconds that feels like it goes on forever. Ray has been here before. He puts the SMG down, barrel pointing towards the alley mouth – *front towards enemy*, he thinks – and lifts his back-up.

Five bullets. They might have cut off his phone, but he can still send a message. Ray aims up at the windows, angling his shots high. It's irresponsible, stupid, and dangerous, but he's out of options. There's little hope of back-up, but he'll take an open door if he can get it. He prays that the shots don't hit anyone.

Five shots. One by one, he works his way across the lowest row of windows, a bullet for each. Without a suppressor, even his small gun makes an almighty crack in the enclosed space behind the buildings. The handclaps of a giant, controlled and evenly spaced with the rhythm of long practice.

From the alley, silence. Not even footsteps. Ray figures they have taken cover, made themselves ready for a surprise. *Whatever wins you time.*

The SMG is in his hands now, lighter than a gun has any right to be. He isn't ready. Nobody ever is. He looks up at the broken windows, the last shards of falling glass like an impossible summer snowfall. 'Come on,' he says, to no one but himself.

Chapter 8

Cameron didn't call her lawyer right away. The first number she dialed, her fingers punching it in on autopilot so it was ringing before she had even realized who she was calling, was her mom's.

For a couple of heartbeats Cameron tries to tell herself she doesn't even know why she did it. They declared their son dead when the first searches turned up no sign of him, buried an empty casket when the snow thawed. But she knows why. A year and a half of arguments, of them begging her to just stop looking, to accept that he was most likely killed. She couldn't bring herself to tell them that he did it, that he drove them both out into the blizzard knowing that he was going to crash the car. They don't know that she found out that the scarf that he was wearing was actually an airbag collar, designed to be better than a crash helmet. That chasing its purchase and import details down hadn't found Nate, but had given Cameron the conviction that she hadn't hallucinated the whole thing. That knowledge hadn't helped her in arguing with them. If anything, it had made things worse. Ever since, there had been a wall of silence between Cameron and her parents, all three of them too proud, too hurt to back down.

Nate's alive, was what she wanted to say. And *I'm sorry*.

'Hello?' Her mom's voice down the line, quiet from the four and a half thousand miles of distance. 'Hello?'

Cameron hangs up, then lifts the receiver to dial her lawyer instead. She can't bring herself to drag her parents into it. Not until she knows what Nate is into. Not until she has him there to explain himself.

A few minutes later, Cameron regrets not staying on the line with her mom. Dale Cross is pushing sixty, and with no kids he has a lot of spare energy to spend on lecturing his clients instead. All she can do is nod and throw in the odd verbal acknowledgement to let him know that she is still on the line, experiencing every second of the slow-motion explosion as his disbelief blossoms into straight-up anger. *Tell me everything*, he'd said. *Don't leave anything out*. So she did. *Almost*. She can't tell him about the gun. After she mentions that she's dragged two of her old rivals into it, she doesn't get the chance.

'They don't have privilege, Cam. The first touch of this on them, their counsel will advise them to flip on you so fast it will make your head spin.'

'I—'

'I would give you the same advice, if you were in their position.' He sighs down the line, a long, withering exhalation. 'Jesus, Cam. You couldn't have done something simpler, like running a gym? Or a bar?'

'You know why.'

A long pause. He knows why. He's schooled himself not to say Nate's name, as if by not saying it she will somehow decide to move on. 'Cam. He doesn't want to be found.'

'I don't care what he wants.'

'He almost killed you.'

'Nate called me when I went to the apartment.'

There's a long silence on the other end of the line. Cameron realizes how insane it sounds, all her desperate searching, her obsession, and then it's Nate that calls her. When Dale finally speaks, his reasonable tone is gone. His voice is hard, taut with resolve. 'Cam. I am telling you right now, get your ass down to a police station. Turn yourself in. Call me from there and I will be on a flight this afternoon.'

There is a noise from the back of the house: a crack, the sharp sound of glass breaking, then four more cracks, louder than the first. *Gunfire*. Cameron sits up tall, neck craned as if she can somehow spot danger through a wall, and takes the phone away from her ear. Her lawyer has heard it, too.

'Cam, what was that noi—'

'Dale, thanks for the advice. I'll . . . I'll call you back.'

'Cam, don't—'

She hangs up the phone and it rings in her hand. She hits green and lifts it back to her ear. 'Dale, I'm sorry, I—'

'Cam?' Her mother's voice down the line. Cameron's throat tightens, and it takes her a second to answer. She can still feel the gunfire echoing in her ears. *You don't have time for this*, she thinks.

'Hi, Mom.' It comes out weak, like her mom has just caught her with one hand in the cookie jar.

'Are you out of state? I didn't recognize the number—'

'Mom, I dialed the wrong number. I'm really sorry but I've got to go.'

'Not even two minutes to talk to me? It's been weeks, Cam.'

Cameron bristles at the question and bites down on the instinct to counterpunch, argue back. 'Mom, I promise I will call you when I can.'

A pause. Quiet on the end of the phone. Cameron knows she's made a mistake not rising to the bait. You spar with someone long enough, they know your patterns. 'Cameron, are you in trouble?'

I found a dead body. I kicked a cop in the head. Someone just fired a gun. Just one would be more trouble than Cameron has ever seen in her life, but all three of them are tied to the one thing she can't say: *Nate's alive, and he called me.*

'I love you, Mom,' she says, and hangs up.

Cameron heads for the kitchen, and the back of the house. Antonelli and Jones meet her on the way: Ophelia looks shocked; Sophia looks outraged.

'Do you have a back window?'

'Not anymore, from the sounds of it,' Sophia says. 'It's back here.'

'What's happening?' Ophelia asks.

'It sounded like a gunshot.' Cameron tosses the phone to her as she passes and Sophia falls in behind her. 'Call nine-one-one.'

'Where are you going?'

'To take a look.'

There's a utility room at the back of the house that has very recently lost a window. Glass crunches under Cameron's feet the instant she is through the door – shards cast a surprising distance – and she edges past the worst of it to reach the broken pane.

68

'Where does this look out?'

'Courtyard at the back. Where we put out the trash.'

Standing next to the window, Cameron leans over and peeks out past the frame and the last, clinging remnants of broken glass. A bitter taste catches in the back of her throat at what she sees. In the yard below, a man is crouched by the corner leading on to the alleyway with a gun in his hands. As she sees him, he levels the gun around the corner and fires blind, three shots that – thanks to the squat cylinder on the end of the barrel – make almost no noise at all. He whips the gun back as more shots sound in reply, chips of brickwork spinning loose from the corner as he flinches aside. Cameron catches a proper glimpse of his face, sees the bruise along his jawline. It's the cop from the flat. *Perada*. More shots catch the brickwork, and as they do Cameron sees movement in the alley. Someone moving up, under cover of fire. *He's in trouble.*

'Is there a door down to there?'

'There is, but—'

Cameron barges past Sophia, and all her friend can do is point down a short flight of stairs that lead to the back of the house. As Cameron rattles down the steps she's already working through the questions in her head, the most important ones rising to the top, the words already forming on her lips. *How did you find me?*

She hits the bottom of the steps and works the lock, pushing the door open a hand's width, keeping her body angled out of sight behind the wood. There's a good chance a bullet would go straight through it, but she'll be damned if she's going to offer anyone a target.

'Hey, asshole!' Cameron yells. 'Get in here.' She gives the door a kick and runs back up the stairs, out of the line of fire. Behind her, the door bangs off the wall outside and is answered by running footsteps and a burst of automatic fire. The cop swings through the door, pulling it shut behind him. Cameron watches as he works the lock, ducking on instinct as a handful of shots slap against the door. None of them make it through, which surprises her. He leans his forehead against the wall for a moment, eyes closed, and takes a deep breath. Cameron doesn't interrupt him. There's value in that space, that rest, even if it's just a second's worth. Sometimes it's all you need to get centered. He straightens, collecting himself, and looks straight up at her.

'You.' There isn't a hint of surprise in his voice. 'That figures.'

Cameron feels momentarily embarrassed, then anger at the embarrassment. 'How the fuck did you find me? Who are those guys?'

Perada climbs the stairs, fiddling with the gun in his hands. It looks too small, like a toy gun, but Cameron has no doubt that it's the real thing.

'I didn't find you,' he says. 'But they did. I've been following them. There's two out back and a van out front. They're kitted up to kidnap someone.'

Ophelia's voice rings out. 'Cam! I couldn't get hold of nine-one-one. Something's wrong with the phone.'

Perada is already nodding before Cameron can reply. 'They've cut the line. Mobile, too. They'll wait for their team to get here, then they're coming in.'

Cameron's throat feels dry. *Kidnap*. She guesses this is some kind of back-up plan, seeing as she managed to avoid arrest. The thought comes again: *who the hell did you piss off?* 'Cavalry's coming, though, right?' He just looks at her, and Cameron knows it isn't. 'Shit. How long have I got?'

He tips his head, holds the gun ready across his chest, barrel down, trigger finger flat along the top of the trigger guard. *Letting the training take over.* 'One minute. Maybe two.'

Cameron nods. Cut off, front and back. Nowhere to go. She turns back into the house. 'Come with me.'

Sophia and Ophelia are waiting for her back in the hall. Neither of them startles at the sight of Perada, gun in hand. Sophia looks him up and down once, and from her expression finds him sorely wanting. 'Is this the guy that shot out our windows?'

'Yeah.' Cameron's gut feels tight. 'He's the cop I told you about. Look, I'm sorry about this, but you know how I said I was in trouble?' They nod. 'I've brought it with me.'

'What kind of trouble?'

Cameron looks at Perada, who fills them in. 'Private military. They've come for her.' He points at Cameron. 'They're armed and apparently willing to use lethal force.'

Sophia lets out a low whistle. 'Right now?'

Cameron nods. 'Right now.'

'Cool.' It's not the response Cameron is expecting. She looks at Ophelia, who shrugs in answer, as if to say, *you know how she is.*

Footsteps hammer up the steps out front. A heartbeat, and the concussive thud of a ram hard against the woodwork, a blow that shakes the door on its hinges. Ophelia's face goes flat with rage. 'Do they know how much that door cost?'

'Is there another way out of here?' Cameron asks.

Sophia just laughs at her. She's already on her way to the front door, Ophelia falling in behind her, fists tight at her sides. Perada watches them go with a look of pure confusion, clinging to his gun like it's the only sane thing left in the world. 'What are they doing?'

Cameron knows the look she saw on Sophia's face. Pure, undiluted rage. 'I think they've gone to welcome their guests.'

Sophia flicks the latch open just as the ram hits again, and the door springs open faster than any of the men on the other side can react. Ophelia grabs the ram as it hits the top end of its swing and hauls their point man inside. Sophia slams the door shut behind him and locks it.

What follows is an education in how to beat a man senseless. There's not enough space in the hall for a clean swing, so the two women pound him with elbows and knees, the blows passing him back and forth between them like the world's fastest tennis rally. He tries to get his arms up, but gets tangled up in the bulk of his tactical vest and the sling that his weapon hangs from. He's wearing body armor and a helmet, but Sophia's hits are rising at just the right angle to capitalize on the two-inch gap where his neck is exposed. His attempts to cover up are over in the first three hits: another three and he's a ragdoll sliding boneless to the floor.

'Motherfucker!' Ophelia yells, all calm gone in a flash, standing over him looking for all the world like she's going to finish the job. 'You know how much that door cost?' He groans, and she kicks him, hard. 'Hand planed, you son of a bitch!'

72

'Get down!' Perada yells. Whether it's instinct or a cue that Cameron missed, they hit the floor as the men outside open fire, the muffled sound of automatic weapons and the snare-drum beat of bullets hammering into the door. Very little of it gets through the dense wood, but Cameron still feels the whip of air as a bullet passes overhead.

She can't breathe. There are more outside the door. There are more out back. She wants there to be a way out, some secret route, but there won't be. She can feel it coming: the helplessness, the inevitability, the fear of the pain to follow; two-fifty and change is leaning on her arm, and every single pin is going to come loose.

'Fuck it.' It comes out hard and low. 'You said a van, right?'

Perada is prone, his plastic science-fiction gun held out in front of him, aimed at the door, waiting for something to happen. He's on the defensive, and Cameron knows it is a mistake. The thin blue line, outflanked and outnumbered. 'What?'

'They've got a van, out front. The boss will be in it, right?'

He gets this look on his face, like he's remembering something. 'Yeah, that prick is in there.'

Prick? It's a question to save for later. Cameron gets up into a crouch. 'Come on.'

'Where are we going?'

'Up.' She waves her hand at Ophelia and Sophia, both still prone. 'Grab his radio.'

Sophia hauls the radio off the man's belt, stripping a microphone along with it and Ray takes his gun. Ophelia helps her to her feet, and ducks again to reach for the fallen man. 'He's got grenades,' she says, looking up at Cameron in shock. 'What kind of asshole brings—'

73

There's a crack from the front room, the sound of broken glass and the thud of something bouncing off the hardwood floor. Ophelia's eyes widen in realization as Sophia – quicker on the uptake – barges into her, pushing her towards the staircase. Perada hauls on Cameron's arm and she turns reluctantly, too focused on seeing her friends safe. *You did this*, she thinks. *You brought this down on them.*

'Move!' Perada tries to yell at her, but the sound of it is lost as the grenade detonates, the door to the front room bowing on its hinges and springing free, setting loose a blast of burning hot air that hits them like a fist. A muffled blanket of silence wraps itself round Cameron's head and the sensation fills her with panic. She casts about trying to get her bearings, but she feels unsteady on her feet, seasick, the stairs suddenly treacherous beneath her feet. She has to close her eyes and hold them shut to keep from falling, and the sensation of a hand grabbing her forearm startles her.

'You okay?' Cameron opens her eyes and finds Perada's face, close to hers. A high-pitched ringing fills her ears, her whole body is shaking, she feels anything but okay. 'We need to move,' he says.

Cameron nods. 'Up.' She looks back to see Ophelia holding Sophia upright, her partner's arm held across her shoulders. Blood is streaming from Sophia's ear, and the sight of it brings the world back into focus. 'Come on.'

Chapter 9

Ray hits the first-floor landing with lead in his feet. It's a feeling he knows, one that he's been trained to recognize. That first flush of adrenaline, the fight or flight response – that heart-pounding, ultra-aware state, the hormonal equivalent of a shot of nitrous straight into the intake manifold – is only good for a few minutes before it leaves you high and dry. Every single fiber of your body is going absolutely flat out to keep your ass alive, and there's a cost to that effort. You can't suppress it and you sure as hell can't stop it. All you can do is ride it out, knowing in advance that it's not going to last. They tried it with the army, putting boys into combat on a stomach full of pills that hopped their whole bodies up close to the limit and kept them there, combat-ready, storing up the crash to hit them days later. Years later. Rumor was they'd stocked up in the PD after 9/11, back when the departments had been flush with funding and access to everything the army had, all in the name of safety. Caches of pills in every precinct, enough that if the day came they needed all hands on a quadruple shift, everyone would be too busy grinning to call a union rep. Ray could do with a couple right about now.

Cameron King looks like she's already had her dose for the day. The other two women, the ones who just kicked the ever-loving shit out of a dude whose tactical armor did nothing to protect him, stumble up the stairs in a daze, their eyes on nothing, feet moving on automatic. King pushes past Ray with her head up, eyes bright and alert, like a concussive blast is her equivalent of three shots of espresso. She drags him in her wake through to the front room, where tall windows hang draped with white net curtains, spilling light across an unmade king-size bed. The air in the room is fresh, a sharp contrast to the smoke and panic of the hall and stairs, and Ray goes dizzy with the sensation of having woken from a nightmare.

King snaps him out of it with a tug on his elbow. There isn't much to her, but she's got a grip like a vice. She pulls him towards the middle window. 'Is that the van?'

The van that Silicon Valley asshole got into is still there. There's no driver visible in the front seat, but Ray can just make out something that could be a shoulder, an arm, visible on the far side of it. Someone standing on the sidewalk, watching the street. 'That's the van,' he says.

'Think you can hit it from here?'

Ray starts. 'You want me to shoot into the street?'

'No, I want you to shoot that fucking van, before we get an assault team up our ass.'

He hefts the submachine gun. It's light enough that it feels like it should kick to vertical off a single shot, but having fired it he knows there's virtually no upwards movement on recoil. It's precision engineering, the sort of thing that costs more than his monthly paycheck – *probably why you've never seen it before* – and he is certain it can make the shot. Whether he can make it, though, is a different question entirely. Firing blind down that alley was different. They made the choice for him. Ray swallows hard, feels King's gaze hard on him, and wonders what would happen if he gave her the gun. She looks as though she'd spray the street opposite with automatic fire if she thought it would help. 'I can make the shot,' he says.

Ray moves one window over to angle his shot along the length of the truck. King wants to shift them on to the back foot, make them back off. It's the right call. If Silicon Valley is still in there, the last thing he expects is to be used for target practice. All Ray has to do is scare them. *Shoot into the engine block, the seats. No through-and-through. No casualties.* The stock comes up snug against his shoulder and he aims down the sight at the broad target of the windshield. No need to take off the suppressor. They'll know where the fire is coming from. All he has to do is spook them with the first shot, then rattle the cage until they bug out.

He pulls the trigger. The window in front of him shatters, and across the street the windshield of the van spiderwebs in answer. Ray leans back from the falling glass and aims again, flicking the selector switch to three-round bursts. He puts the first one low into the radiator, then another through the windshield, and another into the engine.

Yells from below – not inside, but below – and the window-sill bursts into a shower of stone chips and dust as answering fire comes upwards. Ray shuffles back from it, taken aback. It's full automatic spray, uncontrolled and sudden. All those bullets that didn't find the masonry are going to come back down in about half a minute's time, and the thought feels unreal, hypothetical, like a question chalked up on the board at the end of a training session. *You put a hundred rounds into the air on a windy day in a built-up area: what are the chances you've just killed someone?*

King steps past him and tosses something underhand out of the window. He sees the lever fly just as he realizes what it is: one of the grenades they peeled off of the point man downstairs. 'What the fuck are you—'

His question goes unfinished as the grenade goes off with a flat *crump*, the sound muted by the open space it tries to fill. There are cries from below – panic, pain – and a shot whips past Ray's head to bury itself in the wall behind him. He ducks, and more shots fly through where he'd been standing a moment before. The big bald guy down by the van has opened up, trying to give his team some cover to retreat.

Ray moves one window right in a low crouch, out of the line of fire, and without needing to be asked pops up over the sill to fire down at the van again. *You're in the fight now, and there's only one way to end it.* There's someone in the driver's seat now, hunched over trying to start it, so he aims low, hitting the front tire and the engine block. One of the shots ricochets off something hard inside the van and shatters the driver-side window, and Ray sees the driver bailing into the back. Steam rises from the hood, and Ray shifts his sights towards the back of the van, the doors still resolutely shut.

King pulls at his arm again. 'They're leaving,' she says, and he glances back at her to see that she's jammed the radio earpiece into her ear and is listening to the frantic radio chatter, wide-eyed and grinning like the devil himself. Ray hears the screech of tires peeled raw on asphalt, and she nods to acknowledge it. 'That's their back-up coming to pull them out.'

Downstairs, a door bangs open and Ray turns, bringing the gun round, but stops short of moving towards the door. He can hear the too-loud voices calling out instructions, gruff and clipped, the sound of defeat and confusion. Three of them are yelling at each other, over each other, as they pull out their fallen man.

A second vehicle brakes hard out on the street, doors slam open, and the ceiling above Ray's head begins to fall around his ears as the assault team cover their retreat with automatic fire. King gets to the door before him, and Ray bundles through after her, half-expecting to feel a ricochet hit him in the back.

Out on the landing, the two women are sitting on the floor, backs to the wall, their eyes closed. The shorter of the two has her head on the other's shoulder, her skin is gray with plaster dust, the blood from her ear set bright against it.

King listens to the radio for a moment, then nods to herself, peeling out the earpiece. 'It's done,' she says. 'They're gone.'

The taller woman opens her eyes. 'Cam. What the hell have you got yourself into?'

'I don't know.' King looks around, lost. *There's the drop.* Ray can see the fight going out of her, her shoulders falling under the sudden weight of fatigue. 'I didn't think—'

The woman laughs, a short, harsh sound. 'They'd send a SWAT team? Seems like they don't know you like I do, Cam. If they did, they'd have sent an attack chopper.'

The gun hangs in Ray's hands like a dead weight. The police will be on their way now, for sure. It doesn't matter how high up Silicon Valley's hold on the department is. Chaos like this can't be ignored. Half the street will be calling 911 and the other half will be live-streaming the aftermath of those grenades on their phones.

He can already guess at what will happen, though. If he sticks around to give his version of events, it won't make it off of the captain's desk. Silicon Valley will slide right out of the picture. Ray doesn't have a single witness to back up his testimony. A couple of rich-ass pro fighters and a murder suspect, the same one he just managed to let escape that morning, and not a single one of the gunmen to prove who attacked them. He can already imagine what the excuses will be: betting rings, gang violence, an Internal Affairs investigation gone sour. He'll spend the next six months suspended while they go over every line of his psych evaluations looking for something to screw him with. Even if they don't find something, he'll still be let go. *It's in everyone's best interests.* He can hear them saying it. *Department morale would suffer. Let's not drag this out.* The only way he's going to get to the truth and have any chance of proving it is if he can find out what they want with Cameron King. And that means leaving before the cavalry arrives. 'We have to go.' The words are out before he realizes that he's even going to say them. 'The police will be here soon.'

'I thought you were the police.' King is wary. He doesn't blame her.

'I am.' He grips the gun, suddenly more sure of himself than he has been in a long time. 'But whoever comes might not be. I was ordered to forget about a dead man this morning, on the orders of someone who ended up here looking for you. Until I find out who he is, who he's compromised, I can't go back.'

'You sound like you're scared.'

You would too if you thought you'd been set up. 'You don't sound scared enough.'

In the distance, the shrill wail of sirens, the insistent brass of a fire engine's horn as it shoulders its way past parade-day traffic. King looks at him for a long moment, sizing him up, waiting for his composure to break. For the first time in a long while, Ray holds firm.

'Okay,' she says. 'Let's go.'

Chapter 10

They walk north towards the sirens, against all sense, but there's a reason for it. They're coming south and west from the Folsom Street station. That isn't far from Market Street, where the protest will be marching soon, and Cameron wants to be there when it happens.

The assault team made their move because they were on a quiet street, away from possible interference. It only took one cop turning up, off duty and in civilian clothes, to disrupt them. The more people she can surround herself with, the less likely they are to try again.

There was something in that that felt off to Cameron. She doesn't have any experience of SWAT tactics, but she knows what a lack of discipline looks like. When Ophelia and Sophia had hauled the guy with the ram inside to beat him unconscious, the look on the faces of his back-up had been one of pure surprise. That they'd immediately followed one of their own with direct fire and a grenade spoke volumes about how little he'd been worth to them. Coming back for him felt less like not leaving a man behind and more like they'd been ordered to remove the evidence.

They'd set her up at the scene of a murder. When she'd gone to ground, tried to find a way out, they had come for her again. Twice she'd tried to escape, and twice she'd handed them the initiative. Cameron could feel her back teeth grind as that thought circled round again. She wasn't going to give them a third opportunity.

The cop Perada – Ray – leads the way. Cameron had been tempted to ditch him, leave him to look after Sophia and Ophelia, but he seems really keen to avoid waiting for other cops, and a little local knowledge made navigating the streets a lot easier. She'd heard of people that could memorize a street map, which was straight-up magic as far as she was concerned. She knows vaguely which side of the city the bay is, which side is the ocean, and after that it has all been guesswork. She'd run her phone's battery almost to zero just trying to find Sophia's house. If they'd been tracking her cell, she'd made damn sure they knew where to find her.

Ray stops, and turns to look back along the street they've come down. A pitiful, stooping figure is heading their way, pushing a cart full of cardboard. They passed him before, on their way here, and Cameron could tell then from how thin he was, from the heavy curve of his spine, that he is no threat. Across the street there's an ATM, and Ray tilts his head towards it. 'You sure we should be doing this?'

'We don't have much of a choice.'

They ditched most of their stuff on the way. When you learn all about how to track people down, you spend a lot of time learning about how not to be tracked. The machine gun and grenades had been wiped clean and left on the doorstep to explain the automatic fire that had shredded Sophia and

Ophelia's home. Getting rid of it had almost been a relief to Ray, but he straight-up refused to ditch his back-up gun. It could be traced to him, for a start. Her pistol had been disassembled and dumped in pieces down a sewer grate. Cameron had pulled the batteries and SIM cards from their phones, smashed the phones, and scattered the pieces. She'd pulled the lining out of her briefcase, found the deadstick that was hidden there, and with a heavy heart plugged it into her laptop. It was an oversized USB stick, custom made to render a laptop useless the moment you insert it. There was a good ten seconds during which she thought it would do nothing at all, before it fired a jolt of current through the circuitry and – with a crisp, fizzing sound and the smell of burnt plastic – bricked it. Now, she made an inventory of everything they had left between them. Clothes, shoes, wallets, keys, cards. Still too many things they could be tracked with.

'This is it,' she said. 'The last step. Whoever was following me before is still tracking me. More likely both of us. They'll follow the trail of broken bits and pieces here, and even if they don't, when we use that ATM it's going to be like I set off a flare.'

Ray frowns. 'Has anyone ever told you that paranoia isn't a healthy mindset?'

'Nobody that didn't want to get knocked out again.'

He goes to the crossing and looks both ways. *Regular boy scout.* 'Ray. I'm saying that you can get off here. You don't need to come with me.'

It crosses his face. She can see it, the same relief that came when he pulled the action of the machine gun to pieces passing across his face before being replaced by something else, something she can't read. 'No,' he says. 'Thanks for the offer, but I'm coming with you.'

'Some of the things I'm going to do aren't strictly legal.'

He does a good job of not looking disgusted. 'I can handle that.'

As he says it, Cameron starts over the crosswalk before the signal. Ray makes a noise of protest, and she turns, walking backwards the rest of the way. 'I'm not saying you can't, Ray, but you're going to need to convince yourself first.'

The lights change, and Ray hurries after her.

Cameron gets to the ATM, puts in her card, hopes that they haven't done anything to her account. If her card is frozen, at the very least it will tell her something about how much reach they have, how much power they can bring to bear in their pursuit. She's been running it over and over in her head, and it feels like everything they've done so far has been about position. You want to dominate someone, you need to control their movement. The body and the set-up sent her towards her friends, the nearest source of help; the assault team putting a grenade through the front window stripped that help away from her. They were herding her, pushing her into the corner. She knows what happens to fighters who let themselves get cornered.

She withdraws a thousand dollars, the largest sum the ATM will give her. It spits out the notes in a thick bundle, and she pockets them before pulling her card and bending it in half. She does the same with her business account, not enough in it after flights to make anything like the full withdrawal, but it's better than nothing at all. She waves Ray forward to do the same as she works both cards back and forth until the plastic turns white and she can start tearing them in half.

'Uh.' Ray's voice interrupts her work.

'What?'

'How much should I—'

'All that you can. We're going to need it.'

There's a pause, then the hesitant beep of keys being pressed. Cameron has her cards quartered now, the chip embedded in the card well and truly beyond repair, and she slings the pieces into the trash can nearby. She hears the whir of the ATM counting out cash, and turns back to find Ray checking the bills, lips moving as he counts under his breath. It doesn't take long.

'Seventy dollars?'

He looks up, embarrassed and defiant in equal measure. 'Give me a break, it's the end of the month.'

'I thought cops were supposed to be careful.'

'And I signed up thinking we got paid more.' He folds the cash and sticks it in his trouser pocket. 'You think I'm not careful? You should see my rent agreement.'

'They bleeding you dry?'

'Hey, don't joke about it. One of the guys in janitorial had a problem making rent three months back, ended up giving blood to make up the shortfall.'

'He told you that?'

'He fainted on a shift. Pretty much begged us not to take him to the ER.'

Cameron still has the smaller fold of bills in her hand, and she holds it out to him. 'Here. Hold on to this. Just in case we get split up and you need it.'

He hesitates on the edge of protest, but takes it. 'So what now?'

'New clothes.'

He shakes his head. 'To go with the tinfoil hats?'

She stares straight at him. 'Wouldn't be more obvious than your cop haircut.'

'I don't have a—'

'Ray, you might as well be wearing your badge on your forehead.' Cameron holds up a hand. 'May I?'

'I don't—'

She reaches out and messes his hair up, her fingers curling in on themselves as she draws her hand back, confirming the unpleasant feel of whatever cheap-ass styling wax sits in a jumbo tub on his bathroom shelf. It looks a little better, but even with his hair a mess he still radiates a cop vibe. 'There.'

Ray does not look impressed. 'So . . . we're going shopping?'

In the distance, Cameron can hear the sound of the protest warming up, overlapping voices rising and falling like the sound of waves. She can imagine the crowds, and all the opportunities they'll offer to slip a tail. It's almost the exact situation she would least like to have to find someone in. Get out of the corner. Take the initiative. Turn the fight around. If she plays it right, she might even get to see who's hunting her. She can feel the smile creeping on to her face just thinking about it. 'Not exactly. Come on.'

Ray freezes with his pants round his ankles. For a moment he forgets the reason he's here, the memory of eight grams of lead fizzing past his face, the involuntary twitch that followed uselessly – like he could dodge bullets – and all he can think of is the embarrassment of exposure. California penal code 314: even though it would only be a misdemeanor charge, it could see his name permanently attached to the sex offenders' register. The thought makes him feel sick, instantly, physically sick, and he squats, reaching for his belt.

'What's the hold-up, Ray?' Cameron is halfway through swapping clothes with a girl called Harmony, who is looking at her new ensemble with an expression that suggests the hundred dollars she's getting for the deal is not nearly enough.

'You're sure we need to do this?'

'I'm sure. Now take your damn pants off.'

Ray grimaces and drops his pants again, steps out of them.

'Your boxers, too.' Even the guy Ray is swapping with, a RayBan-wearing tanning booth advert called Chris, starts at that.

'Guys, if you think two men getting naked in an alley is the wildest thing that's ever happened on the west coast, you've got it way wrong.'

Harmony snorts in disgust. 'Not with this many cops out. Loads of private security too. All the big companies want to protect their assets from people waving cardboard signs.'

Cameron's stomach tenses a little. 'Are they televising all this?'

Harmony shrugs, non-committal. 'There's plenty of news crews out there. Lots of sponsors with banners up so they get airtime.' She says the last like it leaves a bad taste in her mouth, then nods at her friend. 'He got interviewed.'

Chris grins. 'I did! I should call my mom and tell her to look out for it.'

'He's a magnet for TV crews,' Harmony says. 'Straight, white, great teeth. Might as well have had him march by himself.'

'How do I look?' Cameron interrupts before the face of corporate America gets his feelings hurt and decides he wants his 501s back. Harmony's battered sneakers are a tight fit, but her white T-shirt, rainbow flag motif printed as a whole can of paint in mid-flight across the front, feels like it sits perfectly across her chest and shoulders. Harmony's jeans are ripped to shit, and the only solace Cameron has in wearing them is that she didn't go the whole way and make them into a pair of hi-cut shorts.

'Woah.' Chris is the first one to say anything. 'What happened to your arm?'

There isn't enough jewelry or make-up in the world to cover it, so aside from wearing long sleeves, Cameron has never tried to hide it. She still forgets the reaction people have to her scar, though. A finger-thick welt of too-pink tissue, it runs from her elbow to her wrist, criss-crossed and punctured by the tracks of all the pins and drains that it took to put her arm back together again.

'Cat got me.' Cameron doesn't even glance down at it anymore, make apologies for its existence. It's part of her. 'Took her to the vet, scratched the hell out of me.'

'Hey, no offence, but that is one motherfu—'

'Chris.' Harmony's voice is soft as she puts her hand on his arm. 'Put your shirt on.'

'Sorry.'

Cameron waves it away, and catches Harmony's eye before the girl looks down and away. There's something about survivors, something you recognize in one another. Not shared, but acknowledged.

'How about me?' Ray asks, and Cameron winces at how fake the question is. He's not dumb enough to have missed anything, and the conflict resolution hammered into him at the academy is kicking in. It's a safe bet he always plays good cop. Forced cheer, self-effacing. The sort of guy who buys donuts for everyone on the last Friday of every month.

'You look like an off-duty cop,' Harmony says. Ray's face drops.

'A more fashionable one,' Cameron offers, to take the sting out of it.

Chris claps Ray firmly on the shoulder. 'You look good, man. Roll up those jeans and you're set.' Cameron tries her best to keep the grin off her face as Ray stoops to do it and Chris winks at Harmony.

Chapter 11

Cameron ducks out of the alleyway and out into the press of people that line the street. She can feel the lenses already, the cameras turning this way and that, background shots for live reporters, directors scanning for interesting faces. She can imagine what facial recognition can do with those kinds of images. Her own set-up had been crude, a facsimile of a much broader kind of surveillance, a precision tool built to find people. If they can see her, they can find her. She moves light and quick on her feet, weaving through the press of people, making contact briefly if at all, bobbing her head this way and that to minimize the time she spends with her face still and exposed.

And realizes that she's only making it worse.

This isn't a chase. No one is hot on her heels. It's a pursuit, and that kind of hunting is as old as humankind. We don't run after prey, or spring out at it, we have no claws to speak of, and our senses are blunt and crude compared to other predators. All we have is a tendency towards stubbornness, and excellent pattern recognition. It's why everyone sees the cop in Ray, no matter how hard he tries to hide it. Right now,

Cameron doesn't fit, and it wouldn't take a supercomputer to pick her out. Her movements – erratic, quick, evasive – would draw the eye of any decent spotter.

She slows down, smiles, joins in with a group of people whooping and clapping at a witty placard that's attracting a lot of camera flashes and feels the shift in the crowd around her. Nobody does a double-take, their brains flagging up the movement of an outsider and demanding they take a second look. She fits.

Cameron looks back to see Ray already comfortable with the crowd, posing for a photo with a woman dressed as the Statue of Liberty. They talk between clicks of the shutter, and she laughs as he offers her a very serious handshake, which she accepts before demanding he give her a high five. Someone takes a picture of them doing it and it sets the hair on the back of Cameron's neck to prickling. She turns in a slow circle, looking for anyone filtering their way. Anyone that stands out. When she looks back, Lady Liberty is looking straight at her. She gives Ray a friendly pat on the chest before letting him go.

'Old friend?' Cameron asks.

'New one.' Ray shows her a card, handed to him by the woman. 'She was asking if you were okay, and if you were, you should give her a call.'

Cameron blinks for a moment, the thought that there still exists a world where people aren't shooting at her a revelation, and takes the card. 'Thanks.'

'Don't mention it.' Ray is smiling blandly, looking up and out over the crowd at the parade going past. He circles her waist with one arm and steers her forward to stand next to a dour-faced man holding a prophetic Bible verse on it. He's incongruous enough against the crowd that people passing see him and not Cameron. 'Our friends from earlier are here. Up ahead,' he says. 'They haven't seen us.'

Cameron grinds a string of curses between her back teeth. 'You sure it's them?'

'You'll see,' Ray says. He smirks to himself. 'They don't exactly fit in.'

They move past the cover the would-be prophet offers and Cameron picks them up quickly. The big guy with the bald head who'd been by the van is now standing completely still in a sea of people, scanning the crowd for any sight of them. His face and posture radiate rage and disgust, and there's a pool of space growing around him as people actively move out of his way. It wouldn't be a problem knowing where he is, save for the fact that they're stuck on the same side of the street and the natural movement of the crowd will eventually pull them on to him.

'Come on.' Cameron heads for the edge of the sidewalk, where a uniformed cop is nodding along to a beat that no one else is hearing, thumbs hooked into his belt, his gaze distant, apparently not too worried about the tide of liberal elitism that's slowly working its way along the street. She pushes Ray towards him, as they might as well make his aura of cop work for them for a change.

'Hey, buddy,' Ray says. The cop startles, but relaxes when he turns. They give each other *the nod*, that shared moment of recognition that everyone does when they see one of their own.

'Hey.' The cop screws up his face, looks out over the crowd. 'Good day to be off duty.'

Ray scowls. 'Mandatory. Had an op last month, can't go back 'til the stitches heal. No overtime. Medical bills are screwing me.'

Instant sympathy. 'Tell your union rep. They got a deal going with . . .' He snaps his fingers. 'Carrington Medical. Them and the city.'

'Thanks!' Ray indicates the Bullet-Headed Hate Machine with a tip of his head. 'What's the deal with Elite Force Delta? Shouldn't he be off hitting a tire with a hammer or something?'

The cop glances warily at Cameron, lowers his voice as he leans in. 'There's been an attack.'

'At the protest?'

'No, but not too far. They think the protest march was the target, and something went south before they could get here. No fatalities, but shots fired, at least one explosion. Everyone's been ordered to sit on it to keep a lid on any panic, but the city have rolled out some extra manpower.'

'He ain't PD.'

The cop shakes his head. 'Don't ever get sick again, bud. These guys are private military: Trident or Axion or whatever they're called now. Mayor thinks we need the back-up. "In case of an escalation," they say.'

'Shit,' Ray says. 'Can't afford hazard pay, but they'll pay to put mercs on the street? Thanks for the good news, man.'

'For the price of a coffee, I'll throw in this week's horoscope.'

'Stay safe, brother.'

'You too.' They shake hands and the cop turns back to the parade. Ray's face screws up tight as he looks down past where Bullet Head is standing. He lets out a low whistle. 'Private military,' he says, and glances at Cameron. 'How did they find us?'

'They haven't. Not yet. They're fishing. You ever see a guy go into a river to shake off tracker dogs?'

'Sure. On TV.'

'Doesn't work. Guy in the water travels pretty slow. Slow enough that they can put men and dogs the length of the river, walk back and forward until they catch the scent again.'

'The parade is the river.'

'Really big crowd to get lost in.' Cameron tries to put confidence that she isn't feeling into her voice. 'They would have had to come, even just to rule it out.'

'So how do we get past them?'

Cameron gestures towards the parade as it passes. Harmony wasn't joking about the corporate touch. Everything fronting on to the street that can support a banner has sprouted one, all sporting big company names: Warton Technical, Carrington Medical, Syntech. A Coca Cola stand is up and running, handing out free bottles of water and bananas in branded bags. 'How would you get across that street?'

'Without them making me? Sneak across behind a cop car or one of the ambulances.'

'Lot of open space between the curb and the back end of the vehicle,' Cameron says. Pattern recognition again. Even if the cops stationed on the sidewalk let them past without issue, all they have to do is step into the open and they're breaking the pattern, creating an anomaly to catch Bullet Head's gaze.

Ray shrugs. 'We wait for a crossing, then. They do let people cross.'

'Not often enough.' Cameron slips a handful of bills from the wedge in her pocket. She can tell it's a lot more than she would like to be getting rid of from the thickness of the wad, but she needs to be sure it'll have the intended effect. Distractions don't work if you need more than one try to get it right. 'Free money!'

She yells it at the top of her voice and pitches the wad of cash up and out, high enough that it separates in the breeze overhead. Between the placards and the waving, uplifted arms, it seems like there are a lot more bills falling than there really are, and the protest falls apart as a large section of it surges towards the money with a roar of approval. Cameron dodges a few outstretched arms, already grabbing eagerly at the air, and pushes Ray back away from the street.

The reaction from their hunters is instantaneous. Bullet Head's hand goes to the side of his head, relaying orders, while a handful of men swarm past him to make a beeline for the disruption. On the far side, a second team breaks cover and rushes in to cut off any chance of escape. Even Bullet Head forgets to hang back, and his tunnel vision as he charges into the crowd is so bad that Cameron and Ray pass through his peripheral vision unnoticed.

Another block down, the police manning the sidewalk take advantage of the stopped parade to let people cross from one side to the other. Cameron and Ray cross, and head off at right angles to the flow of the parade, making their way back north and towards the financial district.

Chapter 12

Ray doesn't need to ask Cameron where she's headed. They're going back to the crime scene where he first ran into her. She's taking a roundabout route, but he can still tell where they're going because it's one of the first rules of investigation. You get stuck, hit a roadblock, come up dry on ideas, you go right back to the very beginning and go over everything again. And again, until you find out what you missed the first ten times you looked at it. There's always something. Another angle, another clue. It's why cold cases get solved decades after the crime has happened: because someone took the time to go back to the start of the investigation and looked at it with a fresh perspective.

He also knows that it's a dumb idea. It's as obvious as daylight, and if the guys that are after her were to make a list of places they might pick up her trail again, that crime scene is top of the list. At the very least, she seems conscious of that fact, as he can see her getting jumpier with every step they take.

'Hey.' He touches her elbow as he says it, and the speed with which she turns tells him he came close to losing the hand. 'What's the plan, Cam?'

'Don't call me that.'

Ray bristles at the correction. 'Look. We shouldn't be here. You know that. So spare me the etiquette lesson and tell me what we're doing going back to look at the dark spot on a carpet where a dead guy was.'

'It's not what you think.'

'I'm telling you, getting stuck in another building is not on my to-do list.'

'It was a set-up, Ray. There's nothing that can help us. The dead guy, the computers, the gun—'

'We didn't find a gun.'

He can tell she took it from the look on her face. Her jaw works for a moment. 'If it's any comfort, I didn't kill him.' She says it very carefully.

Ray can feel the jump in his chest, that kick of discovery when two statements don't quite line up, or you look at the crime scene photos *just so* and what was once a random scrape reveals itself to be at just the right height to have been caused by the bumper of a car. She tampered with the crime scene. Cameron is standing as far away from him now as she was in the apartment, waiting to see what he's going to do with the information. If he tries to take her down now, it will likely be the last he sees of her. He knows how fast she can kick, and how hard.

'What's your play, Cameron?' It comes out flat. *Give me something. Tell me why I should be backing you up and not calling this in the first chance I get?*

She sighs. 'I need to find a payphone.'

'We've passed a few already.'

'A specific payphone. One close to where Sam Gorton was killed.'

'That's his name?'

'One of them. He was wanted for fraud, but had so many fake identities it made him really hard to . . .' She trails off, frowning. She thinks for a moment, then looks up at Ray. 'Really hard to find,' she finishes.

'What is it?'

'Nothing.' She shakes her head. 'When I . . . answered my phone, I heard something on the line. A car horn. I could hear it in the apartment, too. He was close.'

When you kicked me in the head. Ray bites down on it, finds a name instead. Remembers seeing it flash up on the screen as the phone buzzed in his hand. 'Who's Nate?'

'He's my brother,' Cameron says. 'He disappeared two years ago.'

Ray feels like he is standing on the edge of an open pit, and every question he asks is just falling away into darkness. He can't tell if she's lying, or mad, or both. 'Let me get this straight: you come out here looking for this Gorton guy. How much did he take you for, anyway?'

'He didn't take me for anything. I'm a skip tracer, remember?'

'So you were playing detective. Fine.' Ray can't keep the scorn out of his voice. 'But when you got here, Gorton has a bullet hole in his forehead, there's a gun on the floor – which you decide to get rid of – and then your missing brother calls you on a payphone that somehow manages to show up with his name?'

Cameron's jaw tightens. 'I have a hunch. He's involved with this somehow, enough that he couldn't approach me directly. He called . . . he told me to run, to get away, but he knew that I wouldn't. He's left me something. He wants me to find it.'

'How do you know that?'

'Because I've spent every day since he vanished looking for him.' It comes out quick, like she's ashamed to say it. 'He knew I wouldn't be able to walk away.'

That Ray can believe. He knows what it's like to keep your phone on, to never put it on silent, because you still believe there's a chance that you'll get the call, hear that voice come on to the line to tell you that it's okay, that they're not really gone. That you're not to blame. He takes a long, shuddering breath. He knows that feeling well enough to stick with her. Maybe helping someone else find that kind of peace is just as good as getting it for yourself.

'Can you trust him?' Ray asks.

'What?'

'Your brother. Can you trust him?'

Cameron goes silent and stares at the ground, cradling her left elbow in her right arm as though it's injured. 'Nate always looked after me. Even when I didn't want him to. Even when I didn't realize he was doing it. He has always had my back.' She looks up at Ray, meets his eyes. 'I trust him. I don't know what he's doing, but I trust him.'

Ray sighs. 'Okay. You're not looking for a payphone.'

Cameron's eyes narrow. 'What am I missing?'

'You're not from here. I know what you're thinking. Any other city in the world, he'd call you from somewhere nearby, let you find the phone he called from, leave a message taped under it. Here, nobody ever passes up an opportunity to do things the hard and convoluted way. You ever hear of a dead drop?'

'Sure. It's a spy thing, a way of handing over a message without ever meeting.'

'Not just a spy thing. Tech geeks love them. Think they're cool.' Ray nods to himself. 'Your brother was a geek, right?'

'That's one way to put it, yeah.'

'Then get your money ready. We're going to need a new computer.' He catches himself savoring Cameron's puzzled look. 'Or maybe just a chisel.'

They pick up a mobile phone and an adapter cable from a store they find nearby. The guy behind the counter is chatty, asks them if they've heard about the explosion and crashes any chance they have of answering by continuing with his theory that the government are behind it. Spraying chemicals into the air isn't working like they'd hoped, so now they're drumming up fear and panic with false flag attacks. He's too busy telling them about his online discussion group – *The Cause*, said so deliberately that they can't miss the capital letters – to let Cameron know if the phone is charged, so she opens it right there in the shop to discover that it is. Dropping a sixty-dollar chunk of her remaining funds on an off-brand touchscreen phone is a painful hit, and having to charge it up to full would have been the finishing touch to the icing on a shit-frosted cake. She has forward momentum, a lead spooled out ahead of Bullet Head and his friends, and she doesn't want to lose any of it. She drums her fingers on the counter as Ray talks the guy into looking something up online for him and printing him off a copy, the sheet of paper changing hands with a couple more bills on the way. The store is so dark that walking out of it is like walking out of a cave, and Cameron shields her eyes as she recoils from the glare of the sunlight. Cars and people are rolling by as though it's a completely ordinary day, like she hasn't fled two crime scenes since breakfast. Like there isn't a squad of heavily armed mercenaries out there tightening the net.

'So what is that?' Even as Cameron asks the question, she can see the gray blocks criss-crossed by white lines, a map of the Bay area south of the Golden Gate Bridge. A handful of black blobs are scattered across it. 'Map to the stars?'

Ray grunts. 'Yeah, right. Like anyone famous lives here.' He holds the map out so she can see it better. 'Landmines, from the last time the Packers were here.'

'The Packers?'

'You don't mess with Wisconsin.' Ray gets a pen from one pocket and draws a cross on the map. The crime scene. 'Okay. Your brother calls you here. You say you heard something down the phone that made you think he was close by?'

'Yeah. A car horn.'

'Right.' Ray folds the paper, dropping the area down to a quarter page. 'So he can't be far away. You don't hear a car horn ten blocks away, not during the day. Here.' He unfolds the paper again, checks the scale with his thumb, then leans against the wall to draw a quick circle on the map. 'Ten blocks is about a klick. Put that as our radius around the crime scene, and we have got . . .'

Cameron looks at the area he's marked. 'Three sites.'

Ray nods. 'Rincon Park is a stretch, but it's on the way.'

'We should try the one closer to Sam Gorton's apartment.' A car revs its engine nearby, and Cameron feels the hair on the back of her neck rising. She recognizes that it's the fear that's making her jump ahead, and fights it down. If they stay calm, and work quickly, they can do this. 'But you're right. We should try them all.'

When she sees the first dead drop, she understands why Ray wanted a chisel. It's a USB stick, half sunk into the tree, fixed in place with grainy resin that's been mixed to look like a lump of granite.

'If I can pull the USB key out of the stone, do I get to be CEO of a software empire?' Cameron asks.

'I hear that's how Zuckerberg got started.'

Cameron turns on the phone and unwinds the cable they bought.

'Better start praying this isn't just a bunch of malware and porn,' she says.

'Are you kidding? The porn is the best part.'

'Come for the espionage, stay for the dick pics?'

'Something like that.'

She plugs the drive in the wall into the cable attached to her phone. Nothing happens at first, and the drop in her gut manages to pack a day's work of defeat into a half-second beat before the phone screen lights up and indicates that it has found a new drive. Cameron feels a fleeting moment of triumph before she scrolls through the drive's contents. Pictures, mostly, a bunch of archived files that she wouldn't open even on this burner phone, and a mess of old text files dating back five years or more.

'Well?' Ray asks.

'We should have asked him to print off where the pay-phones are,' Cameron says, unplugging the phone with a jerk of the cable.

* * *

The second dead drop is closer to the crime scene, and Ray can feel how jumpy Cameron is getting with every minute that passes. He can't blame her. He's feeling it himself with the extra police presence on the streets, and every time they pass another patrol car he braces himself for the shout of recognition, for someone to come chasing after him.

They get to the drop and he knows even before Cameron plugs it in that it's going to be a bust. It's a half-assed job, a USB stick glued into a groove that's been gouged out of a wooden facing on the side of a building. A tight-faced woman gives them a dirty look through the glass, and Ray puts his hand out to stop Cameron from even trying to connect.

'This isn't it,' he says. A thought occurs to him, one that he's not a big fan of. It isn't going to be the third one, either. If Cameron's brother is a hard-core geek, it isn't going to be one of the drops you can find online. They're going to have to go and see a specialist.

'Are you sure?'

'You think Mary Poppins here will tell us she's seen anyone using this in the last day or so?' Ray gestures at the window, and the woman inside gives him the finger in answer. Cameron's face falls.

'You're right,' she says. 'He wouldn't risk it. Where's number three?'

'It's not going to be the third one either,' Ray says.

'So we're right back where we started.' Cameron looks ready to drop-kick the mobile phone. 'That's great, Ray. Just great.'

'I know where we have to go,' he says.

'You said that before, remember?'

'Yeah, but this time I don't want to go there.' He takes a deep breath. *Volk. The Ghost.* 'How much money have you got left?'

Cameron's mouth twists. 'Five, six hundred.'

'It's going to cost us more than that,' Ray says.

Chapter 13

Cameron follows Ray down a flight of metal steps that end when they butt up against an eight-foot slab of brushed steel that looks more like the business end of a bank vault than a door. There's a hatch at eye height, and even though there's no obvious camera watching them approach, it snaps open as Ray hits the bottom step. With it open, Cameron can just make out the sound of music from inside, the sort of high-BPM Eurotrash techno they'd blast out pre-fight to fill the arena with noise. It was a great trick for the announcers: too loud to even yell a conversation over, so when they cut it for the main event the crowd would already be silent.

'What is this, Ray, a speakeasy?'

'He wishes.'

'What's the password?' The voice at the door isn't the deep, heavy voice of a bouncer. He doesn't sound American, but that's as far as Cameron can place it off a single question.

'City Health Inspector.'

'You change departments, Officer Perada?'

'They keep asking,' Ray says. 'Are you going to let us in?'

'That depends on what you— hey!' There's a thud as

someone else pushes up against the inside of the door, another pair of eyes appearing at the hatch. Cameron hears swearing, her name mentioned and a brief, enthusiastic argument which sounds like German. The only word she recognizes is *Jägerin*, but that's enough. There's a click and several grating thuds as the bolts in the door retract, and it swings open so fast that Ray has to jump to keep it from hitting him. In the doorway are two very tall young men, both dark-haired, one sporting a neat goatee. Both of them are grinning from ear to ear.

'Officer Perada,' the clean-shaven one says, holding his hand out. 'What a pleasure to see you again.'

'Mister Volk.'

'Please, call me Ghost.'

'Ghost?' Cameron asks. Aside from being pale, he doesn't look very ghostly. He has the sort of build that suggests he either lifts weights or has spent a few years carrying a growing calf on his shoulders three hours a day.

'It's from a computer game,' his friend says. 'He loves computer games.' He thrusts out his hand. 'My name is Pedro. It's an honor to meet you, Cameron King. I'm a huge fan.'

'Oh, cool.' The ground feels a little steadier under Cameron's feet. A fan. She can handle fans. She shakes his hand and tries her best to put *the smile* on her face. 'Nice to meet you, Pedro.'

'If it's not too much trouble, could I ask you to punch me?'

Ray starts next to her, but Cameron doesn't flinch. One of *those* fans. 'If you've got a couple of grand and an insurance waiver, sure.'

Pedro gives her an awkward two-handed wave by way of apology for asking, and Ghost rolls his eyes. 'Well, now that he's got that out of his system, can I invite you both in? I don't like being outside on such an unusually busy day.' He steps back, and when Cameron looks to Ray the cop just shrugs and gestures her forward.

Inside the basement, the techno is a lot louder than Cameron expected. Ghost sees her frowning and gives Pedro a look: he strides off past a stack of computer cases, and a few seconds later the music drops fractionally in volume.

Ghost's basement is big. The door opens on to a mezzanine deck that loops round the upper floor of the room, and it overlooks a space that Cameron could only describe as what happens when someone starts building an office and halfway through decides what they really wanted was an arcade instead.

'Do you know where you are, Cameron King?' Ghost asks, his voice just shy of a yell.

'Neon lights, techno music, and a bunch of pinball machines,' Cameron says. 'All you need is a skate ramp and we'd be in 1995.'

'I like it! 1995!' Ghost laughs, spreads his hands. 'This is my humble home, the center of my empire.'

Cameron notices the way he's standing, square on to them, hands spread like a barrier. Whatever his empire consists of, he's not letting them get any closer to it. 'How do you know this guy, Ray?'

'Ghost is a security consultant. IT and communications specialist. He finds holes in systems that companies don't know they have, and fixes them.'

'For a price,' Ghost adds.

'For a price,' Ray nods. 'He helped the department out a few years ago, found a flaw that gave full access to our computer system. We would have been completely exposed if it got out.'

Something changes in Ghost's face as Ray describes it. His expression hardens, and she knows instantly where the story is going. 'You arrested him for finding it, didn't you?'

Ray sighs. 'Yeah. Not my call, but a warrant was put out for his arrest.'

'And with that arrest on his record, his consultancy work goes down the toilet.' Cameron slow claps it out. 'Well done. I hope whoever thought that was a great idea got a commendation.'

'Actually it got the captain a dressing-down from the DA,' Ray says. 'Turned out Ghost has a lot more pull than she thought.'

Ghost coughs, interrupting. 'Since then, I've tried to avoid the attention of the police. I certainly didn't expect my arresting officer to show his face.'

'We need your help, Ghost,' Ray says. 'This is off the books.'

'That would explain your outfit.'

'I'm serious. I'm in some deep shit here and I'm trying to dig my way out of it. Now, Cameron thinks that someone might have left some information for her on a dead drop. We've tried the public ones, but this is a whole different ball game we're playing.' Ray holds out the map, the circle he marked on it face-up. 'I need to know if there's a drop we don't know about within five to ten blocks of this location.'

Ghost doesn't take the map, but bends forward slightly to peer down his nose at it. 'That cross,' he says. 'Does that mean something?'

'No,' Ray says.

He's testing you, Cameron thinks. *Seeing what you'll hold back, what you'll give up.* 'I found a body there. Shot dead.'

A flicker of a smile at the corners of the German's mouth. 'Lying will get you nothing, Officer Perada. Not when you're out of uniform.'

'I also kicked him in the head,' Cameron says.

Ghost laughs, sudden and loud over the music, and nods. 'I know,' he says. 'I know you did, because Pedro and I have been listening to the police band all morning.'

Cameron can see Ray bristling, his embarrassment turning to anger, and can tell he's on the verge of walking out. She steps in front of him, forcing Ghost's eyes on to her.

'You work in IT, right?' Cameron asks. 'Communications?'

'In a broad sense.'

'You ever hear of my brother? Nate King?'

Ghost's smile vanishes, gone in an instant. When he answers, his face is a mask. 'I knew Nate King.'

'You know what happened to him?'

'A car crash. It ended your career, and killed him.'

'It didn't kill him, Ghost. He disappeared. Until today.'

'You saw him?'

'He called me.' Cameron pulls the map from Ray's hand and points at the crime scene. 'He wasn't far from here when he called. I'm sure of it. He's left something for me, and I need to know what it is.'

Ghost reaches out and takes the map from her. 'Do you

have a pen?' Cameron passes the pen to him and he marks the map, writing something down beside the mark. 'You'll find it in a parking garage, just a block over. First floor up, at the far end. Near the stairs. It's easy to miss, so be sure to look closely.' He folds the paper once and hands it back to Cameron. 'But I can give you some advice, if you will have it.'

'What is it?'

'Forget your brother,' Ghost says. 'And whatever he left behind for you.'

'What's that supposed to mean?' Ray asks, as Cameron weighs the piece of paper in her hands. It feels heavier than when she last held it.

'I mean this: if Nate King had been the one who found your department's back door, then your captain would not have got off so lightly.' Ghost waits until Cameron looks back up at him, and holds her eye. 'Everything he ever did, was to serve his own purpose.'

'Thank you,' Cameron says. She knew Nate wasn't big on making friends, but Ghost's cold regard is something else entirely. 'But he's my brother.'

'I understand,' Ghost says. 'It is always different with family.' He looks past her at Ray, and his face brightens. 'But we are forgetting something. The matter of my payment.'

'Don't look at me, Ghost, she has the money.'

'Oh no, Officer Perada, I didn't expect you to pay me,' Ghost says. 'I was just enjoying the sight of that bruise one last time.'

'I've got five hundred dollars,' Cameron offers.

'Miss King, I wouldn't get out of bed for five hundred dollars.' Ghost smiles as he says it, and tilts his head in the direction Pedro went when they came in, and Cameron gets it.

'Five hundred dollars, and I punch your friend so hard he sees stars,' Cameron says.

Ghost grins as widely as Cameron has ever seen a man grin. 'Done!' he cries. 'Just wait here and I'll get him.'

Chapter 14

It's on the first floor of a parking garage, just like Ghost promised, at the far end from the ramp, embedded in a crack in the wall six feet up. A USB stick, just like the others, set dead center in the filler used to repair the crack, with only the plug left sticking out. Unlike the others, someone has gone to some trouble to hide this drop. They've sanded the metal of the plug with fine-grained sandpaper, and it blends almost perfectly against the grey wall it is sticking out of. If she hadn't known to look for something out of the ordinary, Cameron might never have seen it at all.

The garage is unmanned, almost completely automatic. Sensors above each parking bay show red or green to show which spaces are taken, and there are cameras mounted in the corners overhead, squat little boxes tucked safe behind protective mesh. As far as she can see, the dead drop is sitting in a blind spot between the two nearest cameras. Hidden from view.

'Got it.' Moments after Cameron plugs in, she knows she has the right drop. She taps through the dialogue boxes on the screen, holds down on a folder marked *CAM*. Another dialogue box appears, covering up the folder icon.

Password:

'You're shitting me.'

'What is it?' Ray asks.

'He put a password on it.'

'So? Just grab the files, we can unlock them later.'

'I need to put in a password before I can move the files.'

Ray makes a strangled noise. 'Fucking nerds. Don't suppose he clued you in on what it was?'

Cameron doesn't reply, already running through the options: old memories of Nate, things he would have thought were important, things that he knows she will remember. *Carrying her home on his back. The ambulance outside waiting to take him away. The day he left for college. The night he crashed the car.* The memories settle cold in her gut, and she can feel her concentration falter. 'I don't know what it is,' she says, her lips pressed tight around the words. Scratching the surface of those memories is like prying open a wound. *He never let me down until that night.* 'Give me a minute.'

Everything he ever did, was to serve his own purpose. That was what Ghost had said. Cameron puts a hand to the wall to catch herself, her legs weak. *He crashed the car on purpose. He left you.*

'Cameron?'

'I said give me a minute.' Ray's concern brings Cameron back to herself, to the problem at hand. *This is the way you find him. This is how you get answers.* The password won't be short. Nate had strong feelings about short passwords. He was always keen on telling people about them, his great conversation-killer. Two beers into any event, he'd be there holding forth on how quickly you could brute-force a six-digit password.

That the more characters you added to the string, the harder it got to crack. He was very fond of the word *exponential*.

His second-favorite two-beer rant was on the vast number of people who still default to the word *password* when it came to securing their private information. Cameron chews on that thought. Nate was always a fan of the ironic. There was a time she would have typed in *password* without a second thought and laughed as it opened. It's exactly the kind of joke he would have played on her, but that was before the crash. Cameron doesn't know what's happened to him or where he's been, but the Nate of now isn't playing around. There's no room for jokes in him. It will be a long password, and she'll get one shot at answering it.

Cameron, listen to me. Listen carefully.

He told her. Of course he had. Make it something innocuous, a simple string that you could pass on without anyone ever guessing what it was. *You have to get out of there.* No contraction. He'd done it deliberately. She closes her eyes, tries to hear the sound of his voice down the line again. The pit of her stomach lurches as she reaches for it.

'Cameron,' Ray says.

'Quiet. I have to think.'

'Think fast,' he says. 'We've got company.' She cracks an eyelid, sees Ray leaning over the half-wall that overhangs the entrance ramp, hears the thunk of the barrier lifting. 'BMW. Looks like two guys.' Tires squeal as they turn on the painted surface beyond the barrier and the engine roar echoes up through the levels of the garage.

'How did they find us?' Even as she says it, Cameron knows it doesn't matter how. They're coming.

Her pulse quickens. It's not a natural acceleration, but a clenched-fist gear shift, the gas pedal pressed straight to the floor. What did he say to her? What was it? She tries to picture his face, picture him saying the words, but all she can think of is him nodding at her, the snow through the driver-side window white streaks on black, and the cold-water sensation as he jerks the wheel and the traction goes from under her. All she can think of are the questions she wants to ask him. *Why did you do it? What did you see coming that I didn't?*

'Cameron.' Ray leans hard on her name. 'We've got to go.' There's a stairwell ten steps away. She knows they could make it if they go now. They could give up, and disappear, and that would be it.

Why did you do it?

Cameron has no intention of giving up.

'Ten seconds,' she says.

'We don't have ten seconds.'

Her hands are shaking. She grips the phone hard to keep her fingers steady. They're coming. She can't keep her mind on the task. All she can think about is the car. *They'll want to pull up close*, she thinks. *They don't know we aren't armed. They'll use the car to give themselves cover, use the size and speed to intimidate. They'll stay in the car as long as they can.*

'We have to get out of here,' Ray says.

The words stick, like she's heard them before. She can hear Nate saying them. 'That's it,' she says. She starts typing.

Youhavetogetoutoftherejustgo

She types it in as one long string. *Do you understand?* That was what he had said.

The car engine revs, deep and muscular. Close. It's on the ramp to their level now. Cameron hits the accept button as the tires squeal, spinning as they fight for a grip on the concrete.

The file transfers.

She looks up to see the BMW speeding along the garage towards them. Collision course. An intimidation play. They'll stay in the car as long as they can. She's already running as she pulls the phone free from the dead drop. Not sideways, away from the threat, but straight at them. When they rush you, you rush them right back. *Break their rhythm. Take back the initiative.* The hood of the car looks like it's an acre across. There's no room to dodge it. If it doesn't stop, she'll have to try and jump high enough that it doesn't break both her legs.

The guy behind the wheel panics. No time to confer, no time to decide. Only room for reaction. His eyes go wide and white and he stamps on the brakes. The nose of the car dips sharply as it shrieks to a stop.

The passenger-side door is already opening before the car is stopped and Cameron takes the jump anyway, a tiny shift in direction all she needs to launch herself over the bonnet and catch the door two-footed, all of her weight behind the kick. One foot connects with a gun hand, and the guy holding it pulls the trigger in reflex. The crack of the gunshot is loud in the enclosed space, a bark of noise that rings in Cameron's ears and makes her skin prickle with fear and anger. She doesn't feel the jolt and scrape of landing, all of her attention focused on the gun hand. He's pulling it back inside the car and she aims a kick at it, right leg cocked up towards it and hammered out with vicious quickness. The door frame catches him square across the back of the hand and he drops the gun. Cameron scrambles after it, throwing herself forward on forearms that feel like they're on fire and lunging to catch the gun before it can skitter away behind the rear wheels. She gets it, letting her momentum carry her forward and over, rolling on to her back and bringing the gun up two-handed as the driver rounds the front of the car.

He isn't well trained, and that's what saves her. Her gun isn't centered on him when she brings her arms up in front of her. Her aim is about twenty degrees out of line when he clears the bonnet. But then neither is his. Instead of coming round the corner with his gun already aimed down the length of car, he arrives facing the way he's moving, arms long and rigid like he's at the shooting range. He starts the long right-angle turn to bring his gun to bear, and Cameron has already got him clean in her sights, arms braced against the angle of her knee. He sees it, knows that she cannot miss him at this range, and makes the wrong choice. He pulls the trigger, too early to ever have a chance of hitting her, blind panic making him desperate, and Cameron fires in answer.

The shot kicks high and right of center mass, catching him a hand's breadth below his left collarbone. The shot goes straight through him, the bullet barely slowed by layers of skin, muscle and lung. Cameron sees the bloom behind him, the spray of blood that mists the air in the bullet's wake as it exits, and the stunned look on his face as the first wave of realization hits him. He goes slack-jawed at the jolt, and Cameron can almost see the wheels turning in his head.

All he has to do is fall. Let gravity and fate's good graces take over. His friend in the car can help him, hold the wound closed while waiting for help to arrive. Emergency services will be on high alert, so it won't be long. All he has to do is let go, and fall. For the second time in as many seconds, he makes the wrong choice. His hands tighten on his gun and he lifts it back into line, seeking vengeance.

Cameron's second and third shots are not off-center. The second bullet flies past the top of his gun and hits him dead in the center of his chest, shattering the sternum and collapsing the ribs inwards, burying itself in the meat of his heart. It does not come out of his back. Her third bullet goes higher, her aim kicking upwards with the recoil of the gun. It hits him under the chin, the entry hole a dark spot of color, and travels up and through his head, tumbling as it hits the bone at the base of his brain. The spray that fills the air behind him is pink-red, blood and brain matter, his medulla oblongata reduced to liquid by the passing bullet, the shards of bone that spin in its wake. It's the part of the brain responsible for the reflexes. Responsible for breathing. If putting a bullet in his heart wasn't enough to stop him, then this makes it a certainty.

His body falls, the slack weight of his arms pulling him forwards, crumpling at knees and waist and neck. His face sags, already empty of life. It's not like seeing someone fold up after a knockout, or feeling them slip away in a submission hold. There's no return from this.

Cameron struggles to her feet, tries not to see the look of open-mouthed shock on Ray's face as she catches sight of him standing off to the side, caught halfway to the stairwell because he was already running the second she pulled the connection. She turns on the balls of her feet, the gun heavy in her hands, and levels it at the passenger window of the BMW. She doesn't need to aim at this distance, but she does it anyway, her eyes focused on the front sight, the tiny stub of metal pin-sharp in her vision.

'Get your hands up and get the fuck out of the car!' She bellows it at the window, her voice raw, cracking on the swear word. The guy in the passenger seat is an out-of-focus blur, his hands two pale patches either side of his face. His voice is high, muffled by the car door.

'Don't shoot. Please. I'm coming out. Don't shoot.'

Cameron pops the door handle, hauls it open. Swung fully out, the bulk of the door means that she doesn't have to look at the dead man, the blood pooling around him. She can smell it, the air thick with a coppery tang that lies like a blanket under the acrid taste of gun smoke that swirls blue-grey in the draft of the door opening.

'Get the fuck out!' Cameron yells it in his face. He's wearing a tactical vest, black webbing, radio kit, pouches bulked out across the front of it. Black shirt underneath. She grabs him by the vest and hauls him out of his seat, one foot braced against the side of the car. He sprawls on the garage floor face-down, and Cameron aims down at him, the gun pointing directly at the back of his head.

'Cameron.' Ray's voice breaks her aim. 'Put the gun down.' She looks up and he's standing right next to the dead man, a gun in his hands, angled downwards. Not aiming straight at her, but held in such a way that he could be, very quickly. 'Put it down, Cameron. Now.'

Chapter 15

Ray knows that he should arrest her. He should take her back to the precinct, process her, and let the system do what it was built to do. Find the truth. That's what he believes in. *Believed in.* Ray can feel the gun twist in his hand, the grip slick with sweat. Cameron doesn't move an inch, her own gun still aiming downwards, only her gaze lifting in response to his challenge. Her gaze is like a rock. No twitching, no nervous sideways flick. She looks straight at him, and Ray can read nothing in her eyes. No remorse. No rage. In the space of three breaths, she is completely in control of herself. He has the drop on her. She knows it. She also knows he's not going to shoot her. That he can't. Because his faith – his faith in the system he swore to uphold – has been shaken.

Ray feels a tremor building in his left thigh, his nerves and his body betraying him, giving way under the pressure. He knows for certain now: he was never ready to come back to active duty. They rushed him back. His mouth feels like it has been pasted shut, and he has to work to regain his voice.

'I know what it's like,' he says.

'Know what?'

'What it's like to kill someone.' He lowers the gun a few inches, edges forward. 'This is the first time, right?'

Cameron blinks, a rapid flutter of eyelids. 'What?'

She's not processing. Confusion is a common symptom. The first crack in your armor. Everything moves so fast, it's hard to catch up.

'This is the first time you've killed someone.' He thinks about stepping closer, and decides against it. He remembers how fast her kick was. Out of reach is a good distance. 'Cameron, I need you to take your finger off the trigger. Keep it on him, by all means. Keep him covered. But I need you to take your finger off the trigger.'

Her head jerks almost involuntarily and she grins, a terrifying flash of even, white teeth. 'You afraid I'm going to shoot him?'

'I'm afraid that these are exactly the type of assholes who'd modify guns to fire on a hair trigger, and that if you don't, so much as a cough is going to kill him.'

Cameron nods and eases her finger out of the trigger guard, laying it flat along the line of the gun. The movement pulls the gun to one side, and she's no longer aiming directly at the man's head.

'Thank you.' Ray flicks the safety on his own gun, and lowers it completely. A show of trust. A de-escalation. He feels the stickiness of the blood pool reaching his sneakers, steps away a shade too slowly to avoid getting it on them. A de-escalation. Try telling that to the dead guy, see what he thinks.

'You said you know what it's like.'

'I do.'

'So tell me what it's like.'

Ray takes a deep, shuddering breath. 'You try and justify it. You never stop trying to justify it. "It was them or me", or "It was just bad luck."' He pauses, finds the words ready to be spoken without even trying to recall them. '"The panel concludes that in the time between the officer's reaction, the pull of the trigger, and the bullet's impact, the suspect was able to turn sufficiently that the fatal wound was sustained to the rear portion of their right lumbar region. The panel concludes, therefore, that this was a clean shoot."' He's shaking by the time he's done saying it.

'Doesn't sound like you agree,' Cameron says. The guy lying on the ground at her feet moves his arm, a slow but very deliberate attempt to get his hand closer to his side. Before Ray can call it, Cameron moves her foot and steps on his hand. 'Don't think I've forgotten you,' she says. The noise he makes when she rocks forward and puts her weight into it – a scream through gritted teeth – makes Ray go cold.

Ray takes a deep breath. 'I don't.' It's the first time he's ever said it out loud. When they investigate a shooting, they make you go over it again and again. They reconstruct the scene, using computers and math and angles to build back from a body, a brass casing and a handful of bullet fragments to model an event that stands free of any witness interference. They show you it, show it to your lawyers, your co-workers, and they say to you, *walk us through it, one more time*. The scene they built absolved him in the eyes of the law. And by the time they were finished running him through it, he could almost accept that was how it had gone down. Enough that he breezed through the mandatory therapy sessions, enough that he was given a clean bill of health and put back to work. 'It wasn't a clean shoot,' he says.

He would have missed the reaction if he hadn't been looking straight at her. Something in Cameron's face gives, and he sees that swell of pity pass across her face before she smothers it down, her brow creasing with the effort.

'Why are you telling me this?'

'Because I didn't want to see you kill a man in cold blood,' Ray says.

'I wasn't going to shoot him,' she says. 'Not without a good reason.'

'You were close,' Ray says. 'I could see it.'

Cameron shakes her head, but Ray knows what he saw. Her blood was up. He knows what that does to a person when they've got a gun in their hand.

'That's not why you told me,' Cameron says. 'You knew he was safe. What else is going on, Ray?'

Ray can't find an answer. When he caught the smell of gunpowder, saw the blood pooling, it took him back to something he thought he had managed to put behind him. He'd realized that he wasn't ready. Cleared in the eyes of all the experts, the tribunals, the counsellors, his colleagues, but he still wasn't ready. They should have seen it.

Maybe they did see it, and they sent you back out anyway.

He pulls that thought tight to his chest, like he's gone all in on aces and eights, and there's only the river to come. A dead man's hand. They put him back on duty when they knew he wasn't ready for it, and every cop in the precinct knew it: the captain, Bulwell, even Kaz. Ray takes a deep breath, holds on to it. *You knew they were covering something up*, he thinks. *Maybe it wasn't duty they thought you couldn't handle.*

The feeling is like discovering a tick burrowed in tight under your skin: that there's something rotten in the department, and everyone knows it but you. Dispatch had tried to wave him off responding to the call-out to the apartment, but he'd been on the end of the block when it came through. Silicon Valley had been keen to fit Cameron King up for a murder with a broken timeline. Was someone else meant to find Sam Gorton's body first? After he died, did they wait for her to show up before calling it in? Even if it means turning a blind eye here, he's going to find out who the hell is pulling the department's strings. Until he can, the precinct is burned. A no-go area.

Ray gestures to the man stuck under Cameron's heel. 'We should see what he has to say. If they know we're here, they won't be the only ones sent after us. We need to get moving.'

Cameron looks down at the man on the ground, then up at the car. 'Hey.' She addresses it to the captive. 'You come kitted out for a kidnap?'

He stays silent until she leans on his hand again. 'Yes! Yes! Christ!'

'Back seat? Trunk?'

'Back seat. Look, jus—' He loses his voice. Ray hears something pop: maybe a knuckle, maybe the scaphoid bone. Six months to heal, if he's lucky.

'Shut up,' Cameron says. 'Ray, check what they've got in the back seat.'

'We're taking the car?'

'We're taking the car.'

'You want me to drive?'

She gives him an unreadable look. 'I'll drive,' she says.

125

Chapter 16

Cameron drives the BMW out of the garage and on to an empty street. The car judders as she peels out, lurching hard enough that the rear end scrapes on the ramp upwards. She bites down on a curse, the sort of thing she would have yelled in private, a curse aimed at all things four-wheeled and dumb as shit. It's a stick shift, and while she knows how to drive one in theory, it's been a long time since she had to do it in practice. Ray is sitting in the back of the car, and Cameron is amazed at how loud someone can be when saying nothing. Their would-be kidnapper, now prisoner, makes the sort of noise that suggests he was the one that signed off on the rental. He's in the passenger seat, zip-tied at ankle and wrist, held in place with loops of duct tape. Most of it is across his chest, holding him tight to his seat; the tape around his knees has another length passed down between his legs, securing it to the lever underneath. A final piece is round his neck, loose enough that he can breathe but little more than that. With the back of his head pinned to the headrest, he has to look down his own nose to see ahead. It gives him the air of a man who regrets ever getting on the rollercoaster but can't get off, and Cameron thinks that it suits him, given the circumstances.

For the sake of good road safety, they put his seat belt on for him.

'You okay there?' He doesn't answer. She fumbles the first couple of gear changes, but it's slowly coming back. The light ahead changes to red, and she sighs at having to put her foot back on the clutch. 'How do people cope with this shit?'

'I did offer,' Ray says.

'You did.'

When he told her to put down the gun, she'd expected a stand-off. Instead, she'd looked up into the eyes of someone on the verge of a breakdown. He'd remembered his training, kept control of his voice and his posture, and yet he'd been shaking. His voice had cracked, and when he told her why, she had understood. When she shot the driver, she'd sent Ray back to the moment he shot a man. Three bullets, two casualties. He'd tried to make it sound like he was trying to help her, but he was talking himself down more than her. There was something else. Some question he kept to himself, odd pauses as he worried at it in the privacy of his own thoughts. Cameron hopes that he'll solve it in his own time. The first shots have been fired, and this is far from over. She wants to be sure that if it comes down to it, he won't freeze up.

She turns the corner on to a wider road, signposted towards the outer city limits. She's picking the route by feel, mostly. The car has a satnav, but she's disabled it. Too easy to hijack, to track from a distance, or spoof new directions to it and force them into a trap. Once they realize their team hasn't picked her up, they'll send back-up. When they find the body, they'll go straight for the car. As long as they are in it, she has to assume that they're on borrowed time. No dead ends, no stops, no doubling back. A wide loop that swings out and round, and they can ditch it somewhere and double-time it on foot to a BART link to vanish back into the heart of the city. Leave their passenger somewhere where he'll be found. Eventually.

'How did you find me?'

'What?'

'Sorry, weren't you paying attention?' Cameron jerks the wheel, making the car swerve suddenly. She glances across at her would-be kidnapper, sees that he has gone grey in the face. She knows how terrifying it is to be helpless. 'Maybe you should be. How did you find me?'

'I didn't.' It comes out in a rush. He's breathing hard and tight with panic, and it makes him speak in staccato fragments. 'I didn't find you. We were given— we were given a location. Told to pick you up. They said,' he shakes his head, as much as the tape will allow, 'they said it'd be an easy job. Said you were running scared.'

'How'd they contact you?'

'R-radio.' He drops his chin towards his chest, to where the earpiece is hanging by its cord. She took it off of him just in case he found a way to broadcast an alarm. Some models could be programmed to do it with a channel switch, or the press of a button.

'Channel?' She gives the wheel a nudge as she asks it, to put him off thinking too long on the answer.

'Seven! Jesus fuck!' His eyes are close to popping clean out of his head. 'Seven.'

Cameron checks the radio. It's still set to channel seven. She didn't hear any mayday being sent, but then she'd been half-deaf from the gun going off. 'Who are you working for?'

'I'm with Axion. Axion.'

'Axion?' Ray speaks from the back seat. 'The security company? I thought they worked bank contracts, all that armored van stuff?'

'No, they do lots of stuff. Transplant runs. Personal security.'

'And kidnapping, apparently,' Ray adds.

'Dude, I swear, I didn't think it'd be like this.'

'What's your background?' Ray asks. 'Army? Marine corps? You look young for an ex-cop.' Cameron takes the opportunity to check the road signs ahead, thinks about getting off the 101. They're making good time heading south, but the car will be easy to spot.

Especially if they're airborne.

'I answered an ad. They said there'd be training on the—'

He yells as Cameron turns hard, hauling the car across two lanes to get to an exit. She puts her foot down as they hit the ramp.

'Cameron, what the fuck?'

'They wanted us to take the car,' she says.

'They what?'

'Look out the window, see if there's anything over us.'

'Over us? Like a chopper?'

'Chopper, drone, whatever. Something that can fly and keep pace.'

'Cameron, I—'

'Just look, Ray.' She turns off the ramp and starts off down a road that lies at roughly ninety degrees to the path they were on. She flicks the trip meter to zero. A couple of miles should keep them off the same roads they drove out on. In the back, the electric window whirs as Ray lowers it, and the car's cabin fills with noise and wind. The meter ticks over to one mile before Ray brings his head back inside and closes the window. It's like putting on ear defenders: once closed, the car is silent save for the low rumble of the engine. 'Well?'

'There's something up there,' he says. 'It's not a chopper.'

Cameron shakes her head. 'Drone. I fucking knew it.'

'Like a Predator drone?' Ray sounds doubtful. 'It looks pretty small.'

'It doesn't need to be big,' Cameron says. 'Not if you're tracking someone. You put a mark on the roof of their car, follow the car from the air.'

'Like numbers on police units.'

'Right. Nobody ever thinks to look up to see if they're being followed.'

'There was no mark on the roof of the car.'

'It doesn't have to be visible. You could use ultraviolet or infra-red active paint. Looks like a clear coat to the naked eye, lights up like Christmas to the right kind of camera.' Cameron looks across at her passenger, who is trying to lean as far away from her as his bonds will allow. 'What about your partner? Did he answer an ad, too?'

'I never met him before today. I got a message saying I'd be picked up, he was waiting downstairs. He seemed pretty tough. Said we were on a mission.'

'Who's your manager? You must know someone.'

'I got sent down to Bakersfield on a training course. Full board and pay, maybe fifty other guys on the same deal. I got back two weeks ago. They gave me my kit bag, told me to keep it ready, they'd be in touch.' He bites down on a sob. 'This was my first . . . God. It wasn't meant to be like this. I thought I'd be—'

'You thought you'd be four nights a week on your ass guarding some gate, yeah. Whatever. Let me guess, they told you there'd be simulations, exercises. High-pressure situations that would test how well you'd done at training.'

'They said we'd be assessed—'

Cameron turns back towards the city, leaning back in her seat to address Ray. 'They must have sent out a bunch of cars to different locations. Dead drops, known associates, anywhere they thought we might go. Send out a bunch of rookies, guys who barely know what end of the gun goes bang, hand us a free ride. Put a ring of spotters round the city, see which car breaks from the pattern. Tells them where we are and where we've been.'

'I guess they want to find your brother too,' Ray says.

Cameron nods. 'And what he's told me. This is their plan B. They weren't trying to catch me this time. They're fishing.' She clicks her tongue, frustrated. If they can get under cover quickly, they might be lucky and be able to slip the drone. Throwing a net around the city takes a lot of organization. If they're spread thin enough, she and Ray might be able to ditch the car and walk away.

'At least your brother used a password,' Ray says. Cameron curses. She had forgotten about the USB key. By taking the car, they'd given away the location, and probably what it contained.

'Shit. We need to go back and destroy it.'

'Do we?'

'If they listened in on Nate's phone call, then they could guess—'

Cameron is interrupted by a shadow sliding into her peripheral vision. Her first instinct is to dodge, and she hits the brakes hard. The car that had been coasting in her blind spot lunges past the driver-side door, swerving hard as its driver tries to respond. Cameron keeps her head up, seat belt smarting across her chest as it holds her against the deceleration and watches the other car go past their front bumper and over to the passenger side. She drops into second and jams her foot on the accelerator. The car revs hard, and she is pressed into her seat as it lurches forward. As they come up alongside the other car, she can see the rear windows lowering.

'Ray?'

'I see it.' He doesn't bother with the window. She hears the snick of the safety going off and the rear door opens. 'Brake when I shoot!' She glances back to see him head down, holding the door right-handed, the gun pointed down and back under his right elbow. In the other car the driver is waving at them to pull over, the barrel of a pump-action shotgun visible on the far side of him. The instant they pull level with the other car, Ray fires three times. The rear tire of the other car bursts with a bang as loud as the gunfire, and Cameron hits the brakes a second time.

The other car fishtails, almost recovers, then spins out, doing a one-eighty as it curves back across the front of the BMW. Cameron can see the driver struggling to regain control, his passenger fighting to retrieve a gun that has leapt out of his hands like a live fish. She punches the accelerator again as they clear the driver-side bumper.

'Brass!' Ray yells, and Cameron flinches away as he starts firing through the rear window, arms straight, the spent casings ejected into the front of the car past Cameron's right ear. The window behind her shatters, and in her mirror she catches a glimpse of steam rising from the other car. It struggles to move forward, a groggy final effort to try and beat the ten-count, and falls away, unable to give chase. The car is quieter than she expects with the window gone, and she realizes that the sound of gunfire behind her head has left her half-deaf.

'Motherfucker.' Cameron can barely believe what she sees in the street ahead. Bullet Head is standing in the middle of her lane, not two hundred yards away. He doesn't have a gun: he's just standing there with his arms loose at his sides, shoulders hunched forward, daring her to hit him. He's standing like he has faith in human nature, that she will brake or swerve to avoid hitting him. Maybe he thinks it's instinct, or that she has somehow forgotten how clearly the stakes have been laid out. Cameron keeps the car in a low gear and puts her foot on the gas. Next to her, their duct-taped prisoner starts yelling, an incomprehensible rush of words.

Ray grabs the back of her seat, by her shoulder. 'Cameron, you're not going to—'

'If he doesn't move, it's his own fault.'

She braces herself for the impact, back glued to her seat, arms braced against the steering wheel, elbows and knees bent. They're almost on Bullet Head, and he hasn't moved. This isn't the same as the garage. There's no gun, no threat. Just a man in the street, waiting for her to mow him down.

I know what it's like.

Cameron can't do it. She swerves, tries to jink across to the other lane to pass him, but the car is going way too fast for her to correct and the rear end slides out, the cabin filling with the smell of burnt rubber as the car goes from forwards to sideways. The front end is still on a collision course with Bullet Head, but it doesn't matter. As they scythe towards him, all hope of avoiding impact gone, he springs up and forward, laid out horizontal in the air as he clears the hood of the car. Cameron watches him pass, her hands steering into the skid on autopilot, and as he rolls into a landing she sees his arm unfurl, hand opening as he flings something after them. She can only think of one thing it can be.

Grenade.

Chapter 17

Cameron has her arms tight across her chest and her feet free of the pedals when the grenade goes off underneath them. Between the skid and the explosion, it's like a giant hand comes up under the right-hand side of the car and flips it, sending them tumbling. They go up and over, and Cameron holds tight against the weightless feeling that comes with it. She knows what's coming.

The car lands three-quarters of the way through the flip, the corner of the roof catching the first impact. The airbag goes off in Cameron's face and her window implodes at the same time. As they go over on to the roof, the frame on her side buckles awkwardly. Everything in the car's frame is built to take a head-on collision, to crumple and fold neatly about the driver without flinging the engine into their lap or putting the steering column through their chest like a lance. All that weight on the roof, on the columns that are meant to stay rigid around the driver, is too much for it to take. The force goes into the door, which folds like paper and pops clean open.

As the car slides the last few feet, the scream of metal on tarmac so loud that she can feel it trying to turn her bones to powder, Cameron is already scrabbling to find the release on her safety belt. Upside down, she's half hanging out of it, pinned in place by the two lengths of strap that are bunched together across her waist. She can see Bullet Head's feet and legs, the angle of her head making it look like he's standing balanced on a sheer cliff. She doesn't know what's happened to Ray or their prisoner, doesn't dare look away from the waiting figure outside the car. She can't hear anything but the pings and creaks of settling damage, the metal ticking like footsteps on a hard wooden floor. The car reeks like a mechanic's workshop, of oil and grease, and over it all is the distinctive cut of gasoline. Cameron finds the release, braces with her bad arm and her knee under the steering column, and presses it.

It isn't until she gets right side up that the dizziness hits her. She turns round to get out of the car, and the pavement keeps on turning under her hands, far enough round that she has to brace herself against the car to keep from falling sideways – or down, she can't quite tell – into the steering wheel.

Cameron almost loses her footing as she climbs out of the car, her feet sliding on the broken glass. She catches herself on the buckled remains of the door and is struck by how heavy her arm feels, how hard it is to close her hand on the metal. She can't decide if it's the shock of the crash or the fatigue piling up that's most responsible, but she knows that she doesn't have much left in the tank. Bullet Head is just standing there, waiting for her. It's only a matter of time before he gets bored and stops gloating – any sensible thug would've kicked her in the face before she could climb out of the car – but she'll take all the rest that she can get.

'You look like shit,' he says, and something in his voice brings Cameron's head up fast, twin spikes of pain shooting up the length of her neck as the muscles there spasm, still stiff from the crash impact. She ignores them. She's heard his voice before.

'What did you just say to me?'

'I said you look like shit, Cameron King.'

'You motherfucker.' She knows exactly who he is. *Ho-ho-holy shit.* An arm pushing past her, the flash of a photo being taken. When she woke up in the hospital, her lawyer was the first person she'd called. He'd sat on every news outlet and photo agency for a full day afterwards waiting to find out who had taken that picture of her. It never showed, and she'd assumed that either no one was willing to touch it, or he'd not got a shot worth selling. 'It was you that took that photo.'

He snorts in disbelief. 'You remember that?'

'Hard to fucking forget.' If she had felt drained when she climbed out of the car, she didn't feel it now. The anger is burning through layers of fatigue like a blowtorch on full blast, fueled by the immediate need to tear this guy's boiled-egg head off his steroid-swollen neck and take a steaming shit down the neck hole.

He searches for something clever to say. She can see the change in his expression as he thinks it up, like watching a light go on in the echoing void where his brain should be. 'You know,' he says, 'we should really stop meeting like this.' He gestures at the car, like he's not sure she'll get it.

'Yeah?' Cameron pushes herself up off the door and stands tall. Her hands lift into a guard on instinct. 'I got an idea of how I can make that happen.'

'Oh?' He feigns surprise, but his stance changes. He starts rolling his shoulders, loosening them up for the fight. *Boxer?* Cameron can't help but think it. 'You want a fight now?'

'There's not going to be a fight, dickhead.' Cameron watches him limber up, watches as he punches the air in front of his chest. Short, choppy arm movements, each one coupled with a quick turn at the waist. She knew a boxer who did the same thing. In front of a heavy bag, at the start of fights: always the same kind of movement. But this guy's feet are all wrong. He's standing flat-footed, feet almost a yard apart. Like he couldn't care less about moving them. *Not a boxer. Arrogant, in good shape, swings like a boxer: he's probably military. Don't need to be able to throw a punch well if you're pulling a trigger.* She takes a careful step forward, away from the glass, towards him. He doesn't adjust. Doesn't seem to care how far away she is. Cameron speaks low, keeps the anger tight and focused. 'I'm going to kick your balls straight into your brain pan, and then I'm gonna have a sandwich.'

'Is that right?' He keeps punching at the air, less a warm-up and more an intimidation tactic. He's got long, muscular arms, and each swing is like a challenge, a reminder. If he gets a clean hit on her, if he gets a good grip; either way, she's fucked. Cameron doesn't recall the arm that pushed past her being like a tree trunk, but then she'd had other things on her mind at the time. 'Come on, then.'

Cameron takes another step forward.

Time and distance are everything in a fight. It's why his stance, his apparent unwillingness to move even an inch, is strange. He's a big guy with a long step and a longer arm. He could be on her in two steps if he wanted to. He's got one hell of a reach, and Cameron is right on the edge of it.

She wants him to move. Wants him to take the bait and launch a big, fight-ending right so that she can slip it and kick his knee clean out of joint. He isn't taking the bait, though. He just waits, and he looks as though he's happy to keep waiting. Cameron doesn't like it much, but she's going to have to go to him.

She gets up on to the balls of her feet, her calves protesting every bounce, and starts moving round him. The way he's standing is an invitation to kick him square in the crotch, but a shot in the balls isn't going to stop him straight off. Big guys don't fold up that easily. It takes them a long time to realize what's happened. All it will do is set him up to grab or punch, and piss him off into the bargain. So she goes round him instead, and though she has further to go, the stupid way he's standing makes him slower on the turn.

The instant the weight shifts on his feet, Cameron changes direction and skips in, kicking hard, her foot swinging round at ankle height to scythe one of his legs out from under him. Break his base, put him off-balance. *Wipe that grin off his face.*

Her kick misses. Quick as a snake, he lifts his foot just far enough that the kick goes under it. He sets his foot back down and keeps on turning to face her. He's fast. He's really fucking fast and when he sees Cameron's surprise it makes him grin even more. *Maybe you're just slow.* Cameron crushes that thought the instant it appears. Doubt will end the fight for her if she lets it.

She speeds up, keeps going round him, watching the shuffle of his feet as he follows. He's lighter on his feet than she thought, and that makes her cagey. Still, he doesn't chase her, doesn't capitalize on the opening she gave him, and even if it's a choice born of mocking confidence, it's still a mistake. He might be fast, but that cockiness makes him a rookie.

She feints with the low kick again, turns her hip and lifts it into a high kick at the last moment. There's not a great deal of power in it, it's not hard to block, but it's something fighters can walk straight into if they're not watching for it. The sort of thing you throw at a promising beginner, or a sparring partner who thinks they've seen everything you've got.

It doesn't land. He almost catches it full in the face, his feet planted square on to her, but at the last second he jerks his head and neck back. He's shit-quick, but the movement is awkward as hell and even though the blow doesn't land it still rattles him. His smile vanishes and his whole face flushes red. She can see a vein in his forehead bulge, pressing hard against the skin. He lifts his fists, holding them up six inches from his own face. If he wasn't so quick, she'd kick his forearm or elbow and he'd punch himself and break his own nose.

'Come on, then.' She taunts him as she moves, circling round behind him. 'Move your fucking feet, you pussy.'

She only dodges the punch because she knows it is coming, sees the decision being made long before he starts to move. It's a straight right, something she should be able to get past and build on, but his arm is like a steel girder, fist thrust forward with so much momentum that it's all she can do to get clear of it by ducking on the blind side of his arm. She senses the follow-up coming more than sees it, and dives forward as he stiffens his punching arm and swings it like a log through the air where she was standing a moment before. She bangs her forearm hard on the road when she lands, but she rolls through it and is back up and facing him again.

He charges at her, launching forward in a lumbering run that she answers with a kick, a big step in and a kick at chest height, the full force of her weight behind it. Anyone else running on to it would have caught her foot in their sternum. He shifts as it comes in, feet sliding as he turns around the kick, catching hold of her leg in both hands. He pulls, and Cameron's head snaps back as he uses his grip to throw her past him. It's pure rage – if he had kept his cool the fight would have been over the instant he got a hold of her leg – and while she lands badly, it isn't the end of the world. When she gets her feet under her, one of her ankles is so painful to stand on that she sees stars bursting in her vision.

Cameron knows that she's going to lose the fight. It's a hard truth to take but it's better to accept it. Nobody ever got out of a chokehold by denying that it was happening. It's not that he's big. She's trained with big guys before. Beaten them, on occasion. It's not that he's better than her, either. From what she's seen of him so far, she's surprised he can make a fist. It's their difference in speed that's going to win it for him. He's fresh, and she's not. To beat him, she needs an opening to bridge the gap between them. Each time she's tried to close it, she's moved so slowly his reactions have been able to save him. He's too fast and Cameron is too tired, and in recognizing it she accepts that there's no way she can win this. And if she knows she can't win the fight, there's not much point in prolonging it.

She closes with him again, hands up in a guard, and feints another kick at him. He doesn't flinch for it, or when she switches her stance and feints off the other foot. He doesn't even blink, and Cameron realizes that he's trusting his reflexes entirely, only moving when a blow gets close enough to hit him. *This is it.* She comes in a third time and throws a high kick with her left foot that whiffs short of target, the motion turning her so far that she ends up facing the opposite way. As soon as she loses sight of him, she pulls the same foot in and kicks back and up towards head height. It almost hits Bullet Head in the face: coming forward after the first kick he walks straight on to the second, and he leans so far back to avoid it that he stumbles away from her.

Cameron takes the opportunity to sprint for the car. There's a gun in there, and if she can get to it then his speed won't matter. Fast as he is, he's not going to dodge a lump of copper-wrapped lead travelling at nine hundred feet per second.

She ducks as she reaches the car, catches the upturned frame with one hand and turns on her back as she slides in the driver-side door. The inside of the car is hot and close, and the smell of petrol is very strong. She looks at Ray in the back seat – he's still upside down in his seat belt, knees trapped by the seat back in front of him, his head pushed over to one side hard against the roof. There's no blood, and no gun in sight. Cameron paws round the roof, feeling for it. No luck. *No fucking luck.* She tries to work herself forward on her elbows to check the roof behind Ray's head, but a hand closes around her ankle and pulls hard. She cries out, gets both arms round the driver's seat, kicks at the hand that's pulling at her. He's going to drag her out of the car, and there's nothing she can do about it. Cameron fumbles for the phone in her pocket, tosses it into the back next to Ray. All she needs to do is make sure he doesn't come looking for it. Bullet Head's fist interrupts her train of thought by coming down like a hammer on her injured ankle. White specks burst in her vision as her grip fails, and the pain is so intense it feels as though everything below her knee has been flash-frozen. Bullet Head hauls her out of the car, and the bump of her head against the door frame jolts Cameron back to her senses. She pushes off the ground with her hands, not caring what the glass does to them, and climbs the arm that's holding on to her, hauling herself up on two fistfuls of shirt. He tries to peel her off, his other hand coming across her back and grabbing the crappy-quality shirt she's wearing: it gives way before she does, tearing at the shoulder as Cameron gets her hands to his face.

She forgets about the pain in her ankle, the glass cuts in her hands, the bruising echo of falling that lies like a mantle across her shoulders. Her whole world, her universe, shrinks down to her two hands, and his head. She gets her right arm round his head, her elbow locking right where the back of the skull meets his neck, and grabs hold of her left hand before sinking her left thumb into his eye and pressing as hard as she can.

Her thumb goes in a long way. She feels something give way, a hot rush of fluid, and crooks her thumb to try and lock it hard against the inside of his skull. Bullet Head is screaming now, shrieking in horror and pain, and the hold on her ankle gives way as he lets go to thrash at her with his hands. Every time he pulls at her, it jerks her thumb and he shrieks even louder.

Cameron's hand slips a little, her grip loosening. He's thrashing around too hard for her to do anything now but hold on until she can't any more. She knows she's going to lose. At the very least, he'll have paid dearly for it. Her hands slip more, the pressure coming off of Bullet Head's eye socket, and he reaches up with both hands and peels her free, lifting her over his head with a roar of pure animal rage.

Cameron knows what's coming. In spite of herself, she laughs.

'I got you, you bas—'

He throws her, one step and a heave, and she folds into a V-shape as she flies clean over the crashed car and bounces off the tarmac on the far side. She's still conscious when she lands, but the world is fuzzy, out of focus. She tries to say something, to prove to herself that she's still there, but the words won't form in her mouth. She can hear a car coming, rolling up to a stop, and for a moment she feels something that's uncannily like hope. *Here comes the cavalry.*

A pair of shoes appear in her vision, someone standing over her.

'Miss King.' It's not a comforting tone, but Cameron can't bring herself to feel much about it either way. She feels numb. 'You've given us quite a chase.'

'What should we do, sir?' Another voice, off to her left.

'Get her in the van. Prep her.'

A pause. 'And the rest, sir?'

The first speaker sighs. 'Get Samson up and get someone to look at that eye. Torch the rest.'

Cameron blinks, and she comes to, flat on her back on a gurney. She can't lift her head. Someone leans over her and a needle pierces her arm. 'This'll help you rest,' they say. They're not kidding. When she closes her eyes, she sinks into total darkness.

Chapter 18

Ray doesn't come to slowly. He jerks awake like he's just been shocked, flailing his arms up and trying to push away the roof where it is pressed against his neck and cheek. It takes him a second to realize he's upside down, pinned by his own weight, his inner ear and brain compensating to try and make sense of an inverted world.

He's still in the car.

He remembers the crash. The drawn-out feeling of it lifting underneath him, a rollercoaster gut-drop as it turned over and then the hammer of his cranium pounding hard on the anvil of the roof. Unconsciousness was like blinking. He's tensed up like the car is going to turn again, his whole body tricked into waiting for an impact that has come and gone while he was out. Ray doesn't know how long it has been, but the smell and the hot, close feel of the car tell him that it's been long enough.

He does a quick inventory of limbs. Both arms, still with hands; legs cramped tight against the back of the seat in front, but otherwise whole. There's a sharp pain along the outer curve of his right elbow, an old strain pulled fresh, but it's almost a comfort to know that's the least of it. Ray puts one arm up over his head, forearm braced against his weight, and feels for the seat belt release with the other. It doesn't budge. He thinks it might be his weight on it and jumps, legs pushing hard against the seat back, but it does nothing except dislodge the gun that was caught behind his knee and send it rattling past his face, making him flinch.

'Did you hear that?'

Ray hadn't made sense of what he could see through the windows, but as soon as he hears the voice, the two gray pillars on the other side of the car resolve themselves into legs, calves turned away from the car.

'Hear what?' Another voice, behind him. He can't turn enough to see where exactly they are standing, but he can tell that it's close.

'I'll take that as a no. You think there's enough fuel to burn all this?'

Ray hangs frozen in place, waiting for the other to answer.

'Nope. Tank must've been pretty empty. Most of it ran down the chassis, dripped off the front. I'll grab a can and we can splash it up inside the cab, toss in a road flare. Do it once, do it right.'

'Cool.'

The guy behind him walks away, and Ray reaches to get a hold of the gun. The scrape as he lifts it feels loud enough to echo inside the car. He watches the other man's legs, the impatient twitch in one of them as he waits for his buddy to get back with the petrol. They probably checked him already, crouched down and told themselves he was out or dead, and not likely to wake up soon. Ray eases the slide back on the pistol just enough to see the gleam of brass from the chambered round, and lets it slip forward before taking aim at the weight-bearing leg. One shot. He knows he kept count when he fired at the other car, but the numbers escape him. He knows he went down to single figures, but the crash has taken the exact number from him. Even if he could pop the clip in silence, he can almost hear the thump of a trunk closing, the other guy coming back to throw gasoline in through the broken windows. Ray mouths a prayer to Saint Jude, his father's favorite, a prayer for lost causes and the fate of all gamblers, and thumbs the hammer back to cock the gun.

'What the fu—'

The shot takes Grey Pants high in the meat of his calf and he drops with a yell, not enough weight on his other leg to keep him standing. He grabs the popped driver's seat door and catches himself, his back blocking out all but a wedge of light. Ray aims past the driver's headrest – *at least Cameron got out* – and shoots center of mass. Spine, heart, lungs; whatever it hits, the guy's grip on the door slips free and he goes down on his face and doesn't move.

A shot hits the door behind him, a hailstone smack against the metal as it ricochets off at a shallow angle. Rather than struggle to turn, Ray hooks his feet under the seat in front and heaves, pulling himself up with his legs and pushing with his left arm until he's sitting upside down in his seat. He arches his back as far as he can, head tilted right over, trying to catch the other guy coming through what he can see of the cut-off, crumpled wedge of glass that was the rear windshield. His gun hand is shaking as he tries to get it over to aim, and he almost drops it when his hold slips, smashing his face hard against the car roof. Another pair of shots smack the door, and a third takes out the window. Something jolts hard against Ray's calf, and it feels like someone has drawn a line on his leg with a hot coal. He yells out loud, a quick, panicked bark, and puts the barrel of the gun over his right shoulder to fire off three shots blind, as fast as he can fire them.

His gambler's luck holds, the shots rewarded with a yelp – not pain but shock – and he takes the opportunity the other man's distraction gives to hammer the seat belt release with the butt of the pistol, roaring as he lays into it.

The belt comes free and whips across his chest, setting him free to fall down and sideways just as two more bullets bite into the seat back where his legs were a moment before. Ray turns and pushes himself backwards on his elbows, away from the window, aims the gun towards the back of the car. There's a shape that could be a man, crouched, and Ray puts his sights on it, not willing to wait for a muzzle flash and a bullet in his face to confirm it. The front sight comes into sharp focus, centered on the bulk of the shape, a clear shot. He pulls the trigger.

Nothing happens. The gun is empty. Normally the slide would have stayed back, but when he hit the seat belt release it had sprung forward again, and he had missed it.

'Shit.' He pops the clip, finds it as empty as it seems. 'Shit.'

The rear windshield shatters, and Ray throws himself sideways as though he can somehow dodge the gunfire, burrowing tight against the driver-side door, trying to present as small a target as he can. 'Jesus Christ.' More shots, and he puts his head down. *This is how you die, shot and incinerated in a crashed car.* The thought has him hyperventilating, his skin too tight and too hot. He thrashes his free hand around, looking for something – anything – to hold on to.

He finds the phone, the one Cameron had in her pocket, and his panic doubles at the realization that she's gone, and he doesn't know where. As he pushes it away, his hand bumps into a clip, still heavy with bullets.

Everything he has focuses down on this one thing. He sucks in a shuddering, swift breath, holds it tight. The clip comes up as the gun turns to meet it; it slides into place with the oily resistance of metal parts machined to a close tolerance, accelerating home as their precise, matching nature irons out the fractional misalignments that human hands cannot avoid. He jerks the slide back to chamber the first round, feels the whole gun kick in his hand as it returns, signaling its readiness as weapon and savior. He turns the gun and takes aim, only to realize that the kneeling human shape he could just make out is now prone, and there is no more gunfire.

'Officer . . . Perada?' A new voice, male. Higher than the other two, and hesitant, as though unsure of the name.

Ray keeps his gun trained on the figure. 'That's right.' He shouts it, and is surprised to hear how raw it sounds. His jaw won't keep still, not without him clenching it, and he feels suddenly very cold.

'The man who was firing at you has been neutralized. I, uh . . . I mean you no harm.'

'Right.' Ray can't keep the skepticism from his voice.

'What I mean is, I would like to help you. And I really don't want to get shot.'

'How do you plan on helping me?'

'Well, I would say I can get you out of the car—'

'I got that covered. What else?'

'I have some medical supplies. Sounds like you're hurt.'

'You just happened to have those.' The sights of the gun blur a little, then jump with the effort of bringing them back into focus.

'I do. And I have a good reason for it.'

Ray sniffs, wipes at his face and realizes that he is weeping. He rubs the heel of his hand over his eyes and takes a deep breath. 'Okay,' he says. 'Okay.'

'I'm going to come over to you,' the voice says. 'Like I said, I don't want to get shot.'

'Hold up.' Ray thumbs the magazine eject, catching the magazine as it falls free of the pistol. Racks the slide back all the way, and as the bullet clatters off to the side, locks it in place. Last of all, he flips the gun over and sticks his little finger into the chamber, making sure it is clear. 'There,' he calls. 'Safe as I can make it.'

'Thank you, Officer Perada.' Ray starts as the man speaks just next to him, and he realizes that he walked over while Ray was dealing with the pistol. Either he is very quick and quiet, or it took Ray a long time. He makes a fist of his trembling hand and suspects it to be the latter.

The door opens with some effort from the man pulling on it, a screech of metal before it springs open and he staggers back to avoid being hit by it. Ray looks up to see a tall, skinny figure with long, sun-blond hair and a familiar-looking face. He's wearing a light grey suit, powder-blue shirt, and no tie, and looks like he has just strolled out of a meeting populated entirely by people who make million-dollar cell-phone apps. In one hand he's carrying a black duffel bag.

The man offers him his hand. 'I'm Nate, Cameron's brother.' Ray clasps it, and finds himself holding a hand that feels fragile, like it could shatter under his grip. Cameron's brother might look like her, but that's where the resemblance ends. Something shifts down by Ray's waist, and he puts his free hand on the door frame, stopping Nate from pulling him out.

'What's wrong?' Nate asks.

'These medical supplies you mentioned,' Ray says, 'they come with a pair of pants?'

Nate frowns, confused. 'I don't . . . no, they don't.'

'Can you pull a pair off the other guy for me?' Ray tips his head in the direction Nate came from. 'Because I'm pretty sure I just pissed myself.'

Chapter 19

Nate King makes Ray walk a forced march for two whole blocks before letting him change his jeans. Ray can hear the sirens and knows that he should be happy that they're not currently being arrested and that none of his peers are going to see him like this, but he can't shake the indignity of waddling in the other man's wake or the feeling that having to endure it is somehow Nate's fault. His wet jeans cooled fast, faster than he'd thought they would, and the fabric clings to every inch of skin it touches, pulling at it as it dries, and by the time they stop Ray feels as though he will never be able to get clean again. He's got them halfway off when Nate starts talking. He's wheezing from the walk but he pushes the words out anyway, impatient to question Ray.

'Have you been to the hospital recently?'

'What?' Ray doesn't look up at him. As the jeans crumple round his ankles, drops of cold piss bead on the inside seam and Ray almost falls over trying to keep it from touching his leg.

'A hospital.' Nate shifts his feet, impatient. He coughs once, a convulsive, wet sound that makes Ray feel like backing away from him. 'Or a doctor's appointment. Or the dentist. Any medical appointments in the last twelve months, you need to let me know about it.'

Ray had needed a full work-up before going back to active duty, but between the piss and Nate's tone, he doesn't feel like sharing. 'Fuck you, man, you want to check my credit score too?'

'That's not a denial, so I'll take it as a yes,' Nate says. 'You get a shot any time you were in?'

'You want to know if I got a shot?'

'Did they give you a vitamin shot, an anesthetic, something like that? Any injection at all.' Ray thinks about it, and while he's thinking Nate puts the bag he's holding down and steps closer. 'Ray. This is important.'

Ray worries the corner of his mouth. They did give him a shot, not that he thought anything of it at the time. 'Flu shot. Said it was city-funded, part of a new initiative to help lower the amount of hours lost to sick leave.'

'When they waived the insurance, they made you sign for it.'

It's not a question. 'Yeah.' He frowns. 'Standard procedure, they told me. Part of the insurance fee waiver.'

'Did you read the fine print?'

He hadn't even thought about it. They'd held the clipboard out with a fluorescent orange sticker on the page to show him where to sign. 'Does anyone? Hospital charges twenty bucks for the shot, eighty for the needle and another hundred for the nurse to stick it in your arm.'

'Yeah, that's how they get you.' Nate squats down and opens the bag that's in front of him. 'Which arm was it?' Ray points to his left arm, just below the shoulder. 'Thanks. Can you hold it out for me?'

Ray holds his arm out, and Nate pulls a handful of circuitry and wiring from the bag, resting it on top as he lays it out and checks it over. Ray isn't an expert on these things, and the sight of a circuit board connected by colored wires to a hand-sized rectangle wrapped in black tape makes his stomach go cold.

'Is that a—'

'A bomb?' Nate laughs, and picks up the black brick in one hand. 'Battery pack. Need to keep the power supply separate as it can interfere with the signal.' He puts it down and with two fingers follows the line of the cable up to the circuit board. 'This is basically a small computer. Cost you twenty bucks, you could watch movies on it if you set it up right. And on the other side' – he flips it over to reveal an eight-by-eight grid of off-white squares – 'we have a very basic display.' There is another cable snaking away from the board, slender and red-coated, and at the end of it is a flattened black egg of plastic. Nate picks it up. 'And this is where the magic happens. You ever build a crystal radio when you were little, Ray?'

'I used to beat up kids who did,' Ray offers.

'Right. You got one of those cards where you can pay for your coffee just by holding it near the magic money box?'

'You went a bit too far the other way on the example, but yeah, I do.'

'Right. It uses a thing called RFID.'

'Like FasTrak.'

'Just like that. The chip passes within range of a reader, it can read it.'

'You're saying there's a chip in my arm?'

Nate pauses, tilts his head in a way that suggests he wants to fire up a set of slides and give a twenty-minute primer on the topic. 'I suspect there is, yes. Arm up, please.'

Ray's arm had dropped while they were talking. He held it up and out, and pointed right where the injection had gone in. 'That's where she got me. If they put a chip in, I'd be able to feel it, right?'

'Not this type of chip. The case has a biocompatible mixture of organic and inorganic compounds which when combined with a living substrate . . .' Nate's head twitches again, like dumbing the answer down pains him. 'It's built to feel like living tissue. It beds in after you inject it. And it doesn't necessarily stay at the injection site.' He presses a button on the circuit board and the LED grid floods green.

'Green is good, right?'

'Green is good.' Nate waves the plastic egg in Ray's direction, and the outer ring of LEDs shift to a bright pink color.

Ray sniffs. 'And I'm guessing Unicorn Shit Pink is bad.'

'Magenta. And you're two for two.' Nate doesn't look up from the screen. He pulls his hand away until the board is full green again, and edges it towards Ray until the color appears again. 'Would you like to go for Double Jeopardy where the scores can really change?'

Ray stiffens. 'Range is about four feet. Which means unless they've laid down a carpet of readers this chip they put in me is pretty fucking useless.'

Nate tips his head. 'Not useless. They did a trial in Europe a couple of years back, a tech company fitted all their staff with them. Wave your hand at a locked door, the door opens. No need for ID cards. These ones are the next generation. Try making a fist for me.' Ray closes his hand into a fist. Nothing happens. 'Now flex your elbow?' As he does, the whole board turns pink for a moment, then falls back, ring by ring, to the resting state.

'What the shit? Did I do that?'

'Yes, but not voluntarily. The chip in your arm piggybacks off of muscle motion. It goes from being passive – pretty fucking useless, as you put it, except that's not remotely the truth – to being active. The more you move, the bigger the signal.'

'So what's the active range?'

'Ten feet? Twenty? Maybe more. We could measure it but it'd be a waste of time.'

Twenty feet. A thrill of panic makes Ray shake himself uneasily, and he jumps outright when the reader flushes pink in response. 'This is some fucking bullshit, man. You're saying they low-jacked me? Like I'm on fucking house arrest?'

Nate stands still, coughs into his fist as he waits for Ray to calm down. It isn't easy, but Ray takes some deep breaths, puts on his best parade face.

'Twenty feet,' Ray says. His chest feels tight as he says it, but he keeps it together. 'So they have, like, chip readers installed in all the buildings? How'd they sell that?'

'They don't just install them in buildings,' Nate says. He pauses, and takes a deep breath. 'Do you know how many homeless people there are in the city, Officer Perada?'

Ray shrugs. There's an official figure but the numbers slid right past him at the last department presentation. 'Four thousand,' he says.

'Closer to seven thousand, officially,' Nate says. 'The real number is higher. And while many people see them as a problem in the city, Carrington came to see them as an asset.'

'They've been putting this shit in all the homeless people, too?'

'Actually, a great deal more than just a simple chip.' Nate waves his homebrew electronic, and the LEDs flicker in response. 'Imagine this reader, but about the size of two half-dollars stacked. Small enough you could install it in a person. Cut a little notch in their abdomen, slide it in with the subcutaneous fat, they might even forget it was there.'

'You're shitting me.'

'Readers installed in thousands of people,' Nate says. 'A flexible, mobile and virtually undetectable network, relaying information from all across the city back to us.'

Ray feels sick at the thought. 'What'd you hand out to get them to sign up for that?'

'Whatever they wanted,' Nate says. 'Nobody asked for anything substantial. It's amazing what people will sell their souls for.'

Ray simmers at how casually Nate talks about it. Like seven thousand people on the streets were an untapped asset. The flesh of his arm itches, like the memory of a mosquito bite. He draws in a long, tight breath through his nose. 'Switch that off and get this thing out of me.'

'I told you, it's biocompatible. It's made to—'

'They made it hard to find. I get it, Nate. I do. Now get it the fuck out of me.'

Nate makes no move to switch off the machine. 'It's not as simple as that.'

'What, you need to dig it out or something?' Ray is breathing hard now, chest forward, his whole body in full fight response and nothing in him trying to hold it back. He can feel the scale of the betrayal like a chasm opening up at his feet, his anger the last thin bridge keeping him from falling head first into it. 'You got a knife? Find wherever the signal is strongest. We can do it right here.'

'It's specifically designed to avoid detection and removal.' Nate sweeps the detector the length of Ray's arm demonstratively. There's an even signal. 'Once it's injected, it stops being an implant and starts being . . . you.'

Ray looks down the length of his left arm and finds that he can't feel it, can't move it. It hangs there like a prosthesis, an immobile and completely alien lump of flesh. The feeling passes after a moment – he flexes his fingers and feels the alternating tension of tendons in motion, the skin of his fingertips against the ball of his thumb. He tries not to look at the readout on the LED screen, and realizes that Nate is talking to him.

'—take the idea of mimicking biological systems to the next step and just bootstrap off the cells that are there already. So over the course of a few weeks your body absorbed the casing and built a new one itself.' Nate coughs into his hand. 'Yourself, I should say.'

'That is some fucked-up space-age bullshit,' Ray says.

'It's the truth,' Nate says. He crouches again to put the detector away in the bag at his feet. 'Carrington are on the bleeding edge with this stuff. All of their embedded tracking technology? It's the tip of the iceberg.'

'How do you know all this?'

'I was wondering when you'd ask.' Nate grins, a quick, nervous flash of even, model-white teeth. Seeing them makes Ray really aware of how unwell Nate looks. They're the healthiest thing about him. He's gaunt, and even with the fake tan his color is off, like he's been ill a long time. 'There's no easy way to say this. I helped develop the technology.'

Ray points to his arm. 'You did this?'

That earns a scoff. 'No, not by myself. In fact the tracker itself was almost finished when I was recruited. I was hired because I was good with programming distributed systems . . .' Nate trails off and tilts his head to one side, hands still hidden in the bag at his feet. 'Look, do you want the chip disabled or not? We don't have a great deal of time before they realize you're not dead or in police custody and start looking for you.'

'Of course I want it ou—' Ray's voice fails him when he sees what Nate is pulling from the bag. It's a portable defibrillator, one of the automatic ones that gets packed into high-end first aid kits to justify the price point. It's a bright orange plastic box with a built-in handle, and two buttons on the front. One is green, circular, and is marked with the universal power symbol. The other is a red triangle with a lightning bolt. As if the meaning is somehow unclear, it also has *SHOCK* written on it in bold letters. Ray works his mouth for a moment, finding it suddenly dry. 'What are you gonna do with that?'

'One pad on your shoulder,' Nate says. 'The other on your hand. The electricity will route to the shortest path, which will be the biotracker.'

'Hold up. Can't those things kill you?'

'Absolutely. We're lucky it wasn't injected into your side or chest, or else surgery would be the only option.'

'Woah, okay,' Ray holds his hands out to ward Nate off. 'So you're saying surgery is an option?'

Nate shrugs. 'It is, but I don't have the equipment or the expertise for it. I mean, I could saw your arm off if you want.' He is opening the defibrillator as he talks, and Ray can make out the cartoon diagrams on the back of each pad – red under the left armpit, yellow high on the right side of the chest. 'This is the best and quickest way, Ray. Believe me. It's going to hurt a lot, and you're probably going to struggle with that arm for a while, but if we don't do it? I walk away. I can't let them find me. You'll have to take your chances with them, and Cameron . . .'

'What about her?'

'I was hoping you could help me get her back,' Nate says.

'You know where she is?'

'I know where they've taken her.'

That swings it. Ray swallows hard, holds his hand out for the pads. 'I'll do it,' he says. Nate passes them over, and Ray is surprised by how flimsy they feel, how thin the cables are. In his mind they should be substantial, as though the weight of them slamming into someone's chest after the yell of 'Clear!' is an essential part of the procedure. 'One on my hand, one on the shoulder?'

'That's right.'

The pads have an adhesive layer on them, and Ray peels off the cover before sticking one to the back of his hand. It feels tight on the skin, tighter when he pulls his arm across his body to stick the other pad high on his left shoulder.

'You think this will leave a scar?'

Nate gives him a blank look. 'I'll be amazed if it doesn't.' He passes over the defibrillator. 'Green for power, red for go. I've set it to full power, so it might take a second to hit full charge.'

Ray feels the weight of the case in his hands. It's a lot heavier than he expected. 'How much power is full power?'

'It's best not to think about it.'

Ray presses the green button. The power light jumps on, startling him, and there's a faint flashgun whine from some-where in the middle of the casing. The note rises out of hearing, and a second green light flickers on next to the word *READY*. He looks up at Nate. 'You might want to back off for this.'

Nate nods, but doesn't move.

Ray takes a deep breath, closes his eyes, and jabs the red button. Nothing happens. He opens his eyes again and frowns down at the green *READY* light. 'I think it's bro—'

Ray's entire left side goes rigid, and the jolt that follows is like being drop-kicked. There's a surge of pain unlike anything he's ever felt, and his mouth fills with a strong metallic taste. The paralysis drops as fast as it came on, and Ray's legs fold underneath him. He lands on his right side, muscle spasms making him jerk like a landed fish. His field of vision feels narrow, and he can just make out Nate coming over, holding something near his arm.

'Looks like we got part of it,' Nate says. Ray tries to speak, but the best he can manage is halfway between a grunt and a moan. 'But not all.' Nate fishes the defibrillator box out from under Ray's right side, and Ray's world tightens down to the sound of it charging. 'We'd better hit it again to make sure. Are you ready?'

Ray can't find voice enough to protest, or even swear at him. The ready light comes on, and Nate hits the button.

Chapter 20

Cameron and Nate are sitting on a porch watching the sun setting over water, passing a beer back and forth between them. They stole it from right under Pop's nose, Nate distracting him with a question about electronics while Cameron eased the fridge open to keep the bottles from clinking. He'll be mad as hell when he finds out about it, but right now they have a beer, the porch, and what feels like the whole world spread out in front of them.

She's sixteen. Nate is back for the summer, his first college year under his belt. Neither of them know it, but this is the last summer they'll spend together as a family. Nate got placed in a summer program: advanced coding, or some other nerd bullshit. Industry money putting the best and brightest on the fast track to grad school. If Cameron had sensed it, even a little, she would have said something to him.

They drink in the grinning, companionable silence of a brother and sister until Nate has a coughing fit. Chronic organ dysfunction, the doctor called it. Mom says it's like he's got a cold that never goes away, but Cameron knows it's worse than that. He's stick thin, like he struggles to put on weight. She's seen what he coughs up from time to time. Nate sticks his hand out and she passes him the bottle: he makes a face as he takes a long pull from it, like the beer has gone sour. He throws the bottle, beer and all, into the lake and Cameron watches it vanish with a sound like a trout snapping a fly off the surface.

There's a jug on the table next to the bed they've put Cameron on. It's full of water cold enough that the plastic has beads of condensation gathering on it, and yet Cameron can't help but feel it's only been put there as decoration. With the restraints pinning her arms to the bed rails and the broad strap across her chest holding her down, there's little chance of her ever reaching it to pour herself a drink.

It looks like a private room in a hospital: peach-colored paint on the walls, fluorescent lighting, the hum of an industrial ventilation system circulating dust- and allergen-free air around the room, but really she could be anywhere. She missed the journey, the indignities of being put in a gown, bandaged up, and strapped in. There's no clock, no natural light, no indication of time passing other than her own growing discomfort. Sometime after she noticed the jug of water she stopped being directly angry at her situation and more concerned about how thirsty she was, how dry her lips and mouth were because of the air conditioning. She'd have yelled in protest, but for the mile-wide stubborn streak that she's clinging on to. Cameron has deep reserves inside of her dedicated wholly to digging her heels in. Instead of yelling, or whimpering, or wasting energy trying to reach that water, she tries to take stock of her situation.

There's an intravenous line running into her right arm. The plastic tubing runs up to a bag hanging from a metal stand, already empty. Whatever was in it has run completely into her: she can see blood backfilling into the plastic tubing, her body pushing back against the weight of fluid. She hopes it was just saline that was in the bag.

On her left, near where an intravenous line would go, is a small, circular patch of flesh-colored Band-Aid. If she turns her arm in the restraint, she can see another applied to the outside of her arm. There's one on the back of her hand, just visible. They stitch a line down her arm, following the lightning-strike path of her surgical scars. Just seeing them focused around her wound makes the skin on either side of it itch.

Cameron kicks off the covers to see her legs. The crash and the fight have not been kind to her, and both shins are covered from knee to ankle with purple-black bruises. She tests the flexion in her knees, and turns her ankles from side to side, testing the range of motion and feeling the tension of a strain in both of them. Nothing broken, though. *Small graces.* She frowns, and feels the tension of a bandage tight around her brow. The touch of it on her face – near her eyes – is disturbingly personal, and it feels like more of an insult than all the rest.

'Hey!' she yells, and her voice comes out clear and loud. 'What the fuck are you doing to me?'

There is a click, and the soft buzz of a loudspeaker on the wall up and to the left of where she is lying. Cameron doesn't doubt that there's a camera next to it. 'Please remain calm,' the voice says. It is a woman's voice, and the toneless, practiced neutrality of it only serves to make Cameron even more angry.

'Bitch, you unstrap my hands I'll show you how fucking calm I am.'

The voice continues, undeterred. 'You have sustained multiple severe injuries and have been restrained to keep you from any risk of making them worse. If you cannot control yourself, you will be sedated.'

That gives Cameron pause. Whatever is happening to her, she doesn't want to sleep through any more of it. Information is key. The more she can get, the better her chances are of getting out of this. Even bruised to shit, Cameron's certain she can give whoever has to come in to sedate her their worst day at work, ever, but as tempting as that is it would be a hollow victory. Better to keep a clear head, so that when she comes back to burn all this down she doesn't leave a single thing standing above ground level. 'Who are you?'

'We are here to help you,' the voice says. 'We are here to help everyone.'

The loudspeaker clicks off, leaving Cameron with the air conditioning and the odd stress on that last word. *Everyone.* The only people who say they can help everyone are zealots and used car salesmen. If this is leading up to her being offered a dented Pinto on layaway, Cameron is impressed. Kidnapping and private medical facilities are a real step up from filming an ad on the lot and running it hourly on the local cable channels.

She lies still, thinking it over. The dead guy in the flat, the cop, the assault team, the chase, the fight. All to get a hold of her. Could have sent a private jet and a check if they wanted an after-dinner speaker, but instead . . . they'd played this *game* with her. They'd known where she was every step of the way. It was the only way they could have gotten ahead of her like that, kept the pressure on her. She hadn't slipped them at the parade; they had let her go. Waited until they were in a quieter spot, away from the crowds. Like a cat batting a three-quarters dead mouse into one final dash for freedom, the chase had meant more to them than the capture, and that meant that they hadn't really wanted to catch her at all.

They wanted Nate.

It was why they'd brought her here to do it. Because they knew Nate was here in San Francisco, so close that they could almost touch him, and the threat against her might be the tipping point they needed to draw him out of hiding. And yet he hadn't taken the bait. The call, the dead drop: he had something on them, whoever they were, and he had tried to pass it on to her. Some kind of leverage that would hold them at bay. And Cameron knew then why he'd crashed the car with her in it, why he'd disappeared that night. Why she'd recognized Bullet Head's voice when he spoke. Nate had been working for them. And now he'd gone and pulled another disappearing trick, and they were casting about for anything they could use to get him back.

The door, on Cameron's left as she lies in the bed, opens and a man walks in. He is dressed in a tan blazer and gray tie over a white, high-collared shirt, and navy pants. He's very tan, with thick-rimmed glasses, and his brown hair is long and slicked back from his forehead. *Silicon Valley*. Maybe this is the same guy Ray mentioned before, the one who'd been in the van outside Sophia and Ophelia's house. He's put a great deal of effort into his look, and Cameron wonders if his personal shopper knows that he doesn't quite have the build to carry it off. He's handsome enough, but he has a very thin neck that the stark wedge of collar does nothing but accentuate.

Whatever position he holds, no one has had the stones to tell him that it looks as though a strong wind would decapitate him, and it's a hint of weakness that makes Cameron feel a little less scared of him.

'Miss King.' He gestures towards the jug by her bed. 'Would you care for a drink of water?'

'Not right now.'

'My name is Miller. I won't insult you by saying these are pleasant circumstances, but I have to say I'm very pleased to meet you.'

'Pleased enough to take these restraints off?'

'Eventually, yes.' He tilts his head like a bird watching for worms in the long grass after rain. 'Although I would like to talk to you a little first.'

'About Nate?'

He doesn't even blink. 'About what we do here.'

'Which is where, exactly?'

'This is a hospital.' He shrugs. 'Not general population, but a hospital nonetheless. Mostly research and drug testing, but they do have facilities for some private patients.'

Cameron leans her head back, looks up at the ceiling. 'Carrington Medical,' she says.

'You've heard the name.'

'The name was on one of the banners at the protest.'

'We at Carrington are pleased to support both the city and the values of its residents. We even have a float for Pride, when it comes round.'

'Hiding in plain sight.'

She hears him laugh at that, a dry, brief noise. 'I think they prefer to call it "Public Relations".'

Cameron lifts her head again. 'You're not from public relations, though.'

'No.' He shakes his head. 'I'm not. But their involvement is important. They do excellent work in letting the public get used to our research in the fields of rapid wound recovery and muscle repair. We've had so many wounded soldiers thank us for our efforts.'

Cameron waves her left arm as much as the restraints will allow. 'Is that what all these Band-Aids are for? Wound recovery?'

'Band-Aids.' He gives her a tight, humorless smile. 'Actually, each one of them is a microneedle applicator, a polylactic acid polymer that delivers—'

'Hey!' Cameron barks the interruption at him. 'I don't give a fuck what they are, I want them off me.'

He clasps his hands together and gives her that sharp, white-lipped smile again. Whoever Miller is, he doesn't like being interrupted. 'Very well. Do you have any idea why you are here?'

'I'm here because my brother either double-crossed, stole from you, or straight-up quit, and you baited me down here to try and find him.'

Miller's smile warms up a little. 'You're almost right,' he says. 'Except we didn't set you up.'

'You're saying Nate did?'

'We're almost certain that is the case.'

Cameron shakes her head. 'He called me. He tried to warn me.'

'Exactly. He called you, and in doing so triggered our surveillance of you.' Miller's hands tighten momentarily into fists, as though the memory annoys him. 'We had been keeping tabs on you ever since he went rogue, in case he tried to contact you.'

'You're saying he knew that this would happen?'

'As I've said, it's our best approximation. It is the first time he's surfaced since he vanished three months ago. From what we know of him, it would be foolhardy to think it was anything other than intentional.'

'And so you sent your goons after me.'

Miller nods. 'We created a high-pressure scenario with the intention of drawing your brother out of hiding. We hoped he would attempt to rescue you.'

'Motherfucker, I don't know if you're up on your recent history but my brother once crashed a car with me in it on purpose.'

'Yes, we know all about that,' Miller says. 'We asked him to do it.'

'You did what?'

'We headhunted your brother to work for us on a very special project,' Miller says. He gestures a lot, like he's giving a TED talk. 'One that requires absolute internal secrecy. When we spoke to him, we found that he talked about you a great deal. Enough that even though he was enthusiastic about coming on board, we proposed a test. Something to clear away the doubts we had regarding his loyalty.'

'You told him to crash the car.'

'We told him to kill you.'

Cameron feels fear settle like a blanket thrown over her. Miller says it like he's recalling his coffee order from this morning. All of a sudden Nate's strange behavior that night makes sense. The way he'd looked at her when she popped his seat belt. *Fair's fair*. She works her dry lips, trying to find something to say.

'But he didn't kill me.'

'No, he didn't,' Miller says. 'In fairness, the crash left him a little too disoriented to check for himself. In any case, the attempt itself was proof enough for me. When he walked away and left you, I was convinced.'

There's more to come. Cameron can tell from the way he's standing, waiting for her to prompt him onwards. 'But you were wrong.'

'I was wrong,' Miller says, nodding in agreement. 'Not only has he betrayed us, but the first sign of him resurfacing has been to contact you. And so, here we are.'

Cameron shrugs. 'Where the fuck are we?'

'I'm going to be straight with you, Miss King. We wanted your brother, but instead we got you. You may not agree with us, but we feel that it's actually turned out to be a positive outcome.'

'You're damn right I don't.'

'Your brother was – is – a very talented man,' Miller says. 'He helped this company make great forward progress, and we expected a great deal more from him. Until three months ago, when he left our employment.'

'He quit?'

'He disappeared, Miss King. No phone calls, no ATM withdrawals, no bus tickets, no security camera footage, not even from the lobby of his building. It was like he simply ceased to exist. We even entertained the possibility that he might have been killed, until he called you.'

171

'Who would want to kill him?' Miller rubs his hands together and looks away, and Cameron bristles at his reticence. 'Hey. You said you were going to be straight with me.'

Miller nods. 'I did, yes.' He looks past her and takes a long breath, like a pitcher on the mound waiting for the catcher's call. 'We do a lot of sensitive work here at Carrington,' he says. 'Sensitive enough that it has gained the attention of several government agencies. Foreign and domestic. They are all very keen to retain exclusive rights to it.'

'You think he's gone over to one of them.'

Miller tips his head again, like he's about to guess her weight or her star sign. She knew a fight manager just like him, the kind of guy who could tell you to the nearest thousand dollars how much a fighter's career was worth. Cameron wouldn't have trusted him as far as she could throw his deadbeat ass, and so far Miller has shown he deserves less than half that. 'Do you know who the dead man was?' he asks.

'He was a finance geek. Wanted for fraud. The bounty on him was worth half a million.'

'Ah yes, the bounty. Would it interest you to know that it was faked?'

'Faked?' Cameron doesn't trust Miller an inch and yet she knows that right now he's telling the truth. He wouldn't be enjoying himself so much otherwise.

'Faked. By the US government. He wasn't wanted for fraud, I can tell you that for certain. There was a kill order on his head. He was an arms dealer operating within the US military supply chain. Weapons being marked in their crates as damaged goods and instead of being destroyed, sold on to foreign powers.'

'How do you know that?'

'Because the military came to Carrington first.'

'They came to a medical company?'

'I think you understand already that we're more than a medical company.'

'So why didn't you find him?'

'They wanted us to do it for free. As a "show of good faith".' Miller shakes his head. 'Absolutely no understanding of modern business.'

'So why farm it out as a fake bounty?' Cameron shakes her head. 'All it would have taken was for one person to slip up and it would have been a huge scandal.'

'They weren't looking for Gorton anymore,' Miller says. 'Or, perhaps I should say, they found him and then they used him as bait. For whatever reason, Miss King, what they really wanted, was you.'

Cameron remembers catching sight of her gun on the floor in the apartment. The strap across her chest flexes, following the motion. 'I was never going to get paid, was I?'

'I doubt it,' Miller says. 'But there is a way to salvage this.'

Cameron sighs. 'Man, I've had the shit kicked out of me, I'm tied to a fucking table and now you're telling me I'm never getting paid. If you've got a way to salvage this, I'm all ears.'

Miller grins at that. 'We want to hire you to track down your brother.'

Chapter 21

It's a close-run thing, but Cameron is certain this is the strangest way she's ever been offered a job. Maybe the second. There was that one time a TV producer thought that getting his dick out halfway through a meeting was a good move. It wasn't a good move. Cameron looks from one arm to the other, making a show of it as she turns her wrist against each of the restraints. She looks up at Miller. 'If you want to talk business,' she says, 'then take these off.'

Miller rolls his shoulders, bobs his head about as though thinking about it. 'And you promise to behave?'

Cameron has zero intention of behaving. Even with a grab bag of injuries courtesy of Bullet Head, she's fairly certain she still has the strength to tie a knot in Miller's pencil neck. 'Call it an act of faith.'

He offers the same thin, humorless smile as before and reaches for a buzzer set in the wall by the door. It occurs to Cameron that Miller isn't comfortable unless he gets the last word in, and that smug-ass smile is the only thing he has to cover the fact he can't think of anything smart to say.

A nurse comes in, and Cameron recognizes her for the real

deal. Petite, with swimmer's shoulders, she looks as though she's turned enough patients to last her two lifetimes. For a moment Cameron wonders if she's going to be bad cop to Miller's hands-off and smug cop, but it's unfounded. She's polite and businesslike, and has the restraints off in short order. She reaches to support Cameron's neck as she sits up, and Cameron waves her off. 'Thanks. I'm okay.'

Sitting up, Cameron feels a million miles short of okay. Without the bed to hold the lion's share of her weight, it feels like her ribcage is going to peel free of her spine and drop clean out of her ass. There's a lot of tension on her right-hand side when she breathes, and her hand goes to it automatically.

'Be careful,' the nurse says. 'You bruised a couple of ribs.'

Cameron nods, holds her breath as she walks the very tips of her fingers along the bandages she can feel under the gown, feels the shift as they find the injury, a sensation of ultra-awareness that makes her eyesight go pin-sharp. 'Not broken?'

'I can show you the X-rays, if you like. You were lucky.'

'Yeah, I'm real lucky.' Cameron laughs, and it really fucking hurts to laugh. 'You want to go half and half with me on the Powerball?'

The nurse suppresses a smile, and Miller coughs, keen to be the center of attention again. 'So, you have your act of faith,' he says. 'Shall we talk business?'

Cameron takes as deep a breath as her ribs will allow, and reaches for the water by the bed. She doesn't make it. She winces when her arm is halfway extended, and by the time that passes the nurse is already putting the plastic cup, three-quarters full, in her hand. 'Thanks again.' Cameron tilts her head to check the nurse's name, but she has no visible ID. 'You, uh, don't have a name tag.'

'Terri.'

'Thanks, Terri.'

'No problem.'

Cameron takes a long drink of water. It's cold enough to make her teeth ache, and the only thing more pleasant is enjoying the sight of Miller simmering as she makes him wait. She holds on to the empty cup. 'I have a question,' she says.

'Go on.'

'What do you need me for? You tracked my ass down like it was child's play.'

'We had something of an advantage,' Miller says. 'The project your brother was working on for us? Subdermal tracking chips.'

Cameron looks at the Band-Aids that are running down the length of her left arm. Subdermal. Under the skin. 'You fucking piece of—'

She is off the bed so quickly that her feet go from under her and she almost falls on her ass. She catches hold of the railing on the bed and the pain that jumps from her right hip up to her shoulder is so sharp that she yells out, the sound raw with anger. Terri moves to help her up and earns a snarl for her efforts.

'You put a fucking chip in my arm?'

'Actually, we put several chips in your arm.' Miller clasps his hands together. 'The pins they used to hold your bones together gave us a unique frame to work with. A test bed for our new prototypes.'

176

Cameron steadies herself on the side of the bed. As her weight shifts, she can feel stitches pull on her side. *Surgical stitches.* 'What have you done to me?'

'Faith only goes so far, Miss King.' Miller dips into his pocket with one hand and comes back with a thin, black rod, like a TV remote. A tiny red light shows on one side of it. 'I have no doubt you'd have tried to attack me, if you could stand.'

'I would kick your ass into orbit if I could.'

'Which is why we put this in, too.' Miller presses a button on the remote, and all the muscles down Cameron's left side go rigid. Her mouth floods with a metallic taste, and all she can think of as she falls is the time that Nate dared her to touch her tongue to a nine-volt battery and how the flavor of it had lingered for hours. She can't lift her hands to catch herself, and the fall ends with her smacking face-first into the floor. It's not the first time she's had her nose broken, and the fire of it – a sphere of pain in the center of her face – is at least something familiar to cling to. *You're still you. No matter what they do to you.* She tastes blood, and – even as she realizes how pointless a worry it is – hopes that her teeth are all right.

Miller tuts aloud. 'Sorry. I thought the bed would . . . Terri, would you, please?'

Terri turns her over with the brisk efficiency of someone who's done it a lot, and she has, at least, the decency to look embarrassed while she does it. Miller is grinning, his mouth a wide slash of unnatural brightness, veneers so bright they look luminous in his face. He waves the remote at her.

'We developed a new kind of pacemaker several years ago,' he says. 'Much smaller than a standard one, programmable via wireless connection. You'll find it halfway down your left side. It's not subtle, I'll admit, but it gets the job done.' Miller waves the control at her, making sure he has Cameron's full attention. 'Let me lay it out for you. Your brother has some plan, some scheme that somehow involves you. You can either choose to help us track him down using the resources we will provide, or we can dump you back in the city as bait. You try to run, go to the police or the press, then I will tape this button down and you will get to discover how much fun permanent nerve damage is.'

Cameron wants to tell him to go fuck himself, but her jaw aches and her teeth feel like they've been glued together. She makes do with hissing at him, the sound coming out as a bubbling whistle through her inflamed sinuses. He tuts again, unimpressed. 'Fix that for me, would you?'

Terri's forearm blocks the view of his face as she grabs Cameron's nose and re-aligns it with a single, crisp motion. The crunch of shifting cartilage is loud in the room, the sound of fresh snow trod underfoot, and the pain sends a thrill of sensation through Cameron's whole body, a flashgun blast of feeling that silhouettes the numbness that still fills her left arm. She lifts her head and looks at Terri. She doesn't seem the evil corporation type, and yet here she is.

'How'd they get their hooks in you?' Cameron asks.

Terri meets the accusation in her gaze with a flat look. 'Hey, my rent went up four times in two years,' she says. 'And there aren't any apartments going on the moral high ground.'

Cameron shakes her head as Terri helps her back on to the bed. She doesn't have the strength to do anything else. It's the hardest thing to give in, but sometimes you have to tap out.

You take that loss, and come back when you're stronger. 'You should get out of here,' she says. She doesn't care that Miller hears. 'Before it gets bloody.'

'Bit late for that,' Terri says.

Miller taps the railing at the bottom of the bed with the remote control, and it sends a note ringing through Cameron's whole body. She feels like throwing up, and would if she had the strength to do it.

'Get some rest,' Miller says. 'You look like you need it. We'll get started in the morning.'

Cameron seethes, the anger boiling up from deep inside of her, filling her with a sudden burst of energy. Ludo would be disappointed – you don't fight sad, you don't fight scared, and you never fight angry – but Ludo isn't here. 'Hey Miller,' she says.

'Yes, Miss King?'

Cameron knows that it's a mistake, but she doesn't care. 'Someday I'm going to take that little box off you, and I'm going to make you swallow it.'

'Hm.' It's not an unhappy noise. Miller sounds like a mechanic, all patience and abstraction, watching as the flaw in a running engine reveals itself. Like he doesn't mind the work it will take to fix, because half the battle is knowing that it's there. He brandishes the remote, and Cameron braces herself as a light on the side of it flickers back into life. 'Let's try that again, shall we?'

Chapter 22

It's hard to see, but if Ray turns his arm at just the right angle the scar is visible again. He should feel good that it's so hard to see, but instead it unnerves him. Knowing that it's there, even if no one can see it – especially if no one can see it – makes his skin itch so bad that he wants to claw it out.

Ferning. That's what it's called, or the closest thing to it. When lightning strikes you, the electrical discharge works its way down your body seeking out the path of least resistance, burning as it goes. The scar it leaves behind looks like a fern growing under your skin. Ray's scar has the same characteristics but looks like anything but a fern. The faint lines that hang subdermal and indelible are more like the lines on a circuit board, tight grids of right-angles and the long, straight roads that chain them together. The scarring runs along the outside edge of his bicep, snakes round behind his arm above the elbow and reappears on the inside of his forearm, fading as it heads down towards his wrist. Nate has told him it's a good sign that it didn't get as far as his hand and that Ray shouldn't expect any loss of sensation, but it's zero comfort. The marks are alien, obscene in their electronic likeness, and the revulsion he feels borders on mania. There's a distant voice screaming in the back of his head that the current from the defibrillator didn't get it all, that something is left, that it's growing back. *Cut it off. You won't be rid of it otherwise.* He knows where to get a knife. Alcohol, dressings, drugs for the pain. *It'll come back if you don't.* Ray takes a sharp breath, surprised that he's even thinking of something like that, and feels a spike of pain high in his chest. *Maybe even that wouldn't be enough.*

Congratulations. That's what Nate had said when he came to. *You're off the grid.* It was a half-truth, if even that. He'd explained how there were systems in place to support the implant program, systems like cell phone tracking that would eventually be superseded but for the moment were maintained to catch and monitor failures and build a list of unregistered assets. Ray catches himself on that one. People. Not assets. There was something in the way Nate had talked about it that marked him as one of the same breed as Silicon Valley. The kind of asshole who saw people as units instead of humans, a morass of data and variables to be corralled and categorized.

Still, Ray couldn't deny the sense that gave shape to the other man's cold disregard for mankind. *Off the grid* was something that took real effort. Traffic cameras. Phone networks. Automated turnstiles on public transport. ATMs. Anything that could be used to pick you out of a crowd and log your location was a potential threat. That other people simply couldn't bring themselves to accept that these things even counted as a threat, that they handed over everything about themselves so freely, put them below Nate's contempt. Ray took the point even as he felt the weight of his own ignorance settling on him like guilt: people were becoming property not because their rights were taken from them. They had handed them over freely.

Nate coughs, a wet, ugly sound, and Ray's head comes up. They are sat on a piece of plastic sheeting, unfolded so the clean inner surface lies uppermost, in the corner of an industrial warehouse. They'd dodged a security guard to get in, which had been as easy as waiting for him to go for a piss and walking in through the unmanned guard station, and found the long, low building crammed with the detritus that followed in the ebb of a brief surge in infrastructure development. Inside, mildewed pallets are stacked high about machinery just starting to show the first fringes of rust; oversized wooden bobbins half-spooled with cable and sprayed with arcane identifiers; a tar-spreader laid to rest in the center of it all, reeking of burnt coal and sweet bitumen, shovels and brushes like insects caught in the hardening black amber, fossils to be cut out and marveled over in a future where all roads are past. Ray can't help but wonder what the air in here is doing to Nate's lungs when he has a cough like that.

'Man, are you okay?'

Nate coughs again, fist over his mouth, and nods with his lips pressed tight together. He digs around in his bag for some paper to spit into before he speaks. 'I'm okay,' he says. 'I've had this a long time.'

Ray watches as the paper goes away and Nate goes back into the bag for a clear plastic pipe with a nasal cannula on it, two tiny pipes that fit into each nostril. Ray has never seen one on someone as young as Nate before. 'You need oxygen?' he asks.

'Only on the bad days,' Nate explains, hooking the pipe over his ears and fitting it to his nose. There's a short hiss of gas and Ray sees Nate's posture ease as he breathes in.

'You get bad days often?'

'More than I'd like.'

'There a cure for what you've got?'

Nate looks straight at him. 'Yes,' he says.

'So what are you taking for it?'

'I'm not.'

'Expensive?' Ray asks.

'Hard to get a hold of.'

Ray finally takes the hint and backs off. Nate goes back to flicking through a stack of handwritten notes, ciphered text from what Ray can see of it, and occasionally glancing at an impossibly new-looking laptop by his side. The computer is connected to a router directly, the wireless aerial removed completely, and the router itself is plugged into a long piece of telephone wire that snakes off across the plastic and up the near wall to disappear through a hole. The hole looks recent to Ray's eye, a comet's tail of white dust still fresh on the wall beneath it, and he wonders when Nate found time to drill it, and why the security guard has never heard or spotted it. All that cement dust in the air wouldn't have helped Nate's cough much. Someone is backing Nate King, and it sets alarm bells ringing in Ray's head that he hasn't said anything about it.

Ray clears his throat. 'So this is what off the grid looks like.'

Nate bangs his hand flat on the pile of notes and looks up at Ray sharply. He smothers the look quickly and follows the line of Ray's gaze to the hole in the wall, the wire vanishing through it. 'Internet access and air conditioning,' he says. 'That has to be worth two stars at least.'

It's a weak deflection, and Ray isn't going to let him have it. 'You've been set up here for a while?'

Nate shakes his head. 'I have a bunch of places set up around the city. Some are more permanent, others' – he gestures around them – 'are little more than an access point. No more than two trips before I change. No more than thirty-six hours in one place. Never use them in the same sequence. And I always check before approaching. If anything seems off – anything at all – I consider it burnt.'

'Well, that doesn't seem paranoid in the slightest.'

'You've experienced their attention, so you have an inkling of what they're capable of. What you call paranoia, I call caution.' Nate puts the paper he's holding down and rolls up his right sleeve. His arm is thin and so white his veins show through the skin. There's a blue tint to the base of Nate's fingernails that makes Ray feel uneasy, and he tries to focus on what Nate is showing him. As Nate turns his wrist in the light, Ray sees the same criss-cross scarring that marks his own arm. 'If anything, staying here is reckless. But I have to see this finished.'

Something in the declaration rings false to Ray's ears. It's a gut feeling, the sense you get when you go to canvass the neighbors and one of them answers every question a little too readily. Like he's practiced for this moment. *Pour a little cold water on his moment. See how he takes it.* 'And this is how you're going to finish it? Running jackrabbit from cover to cover, hoping the hawks don't notice you?'

Nate doesn't even flinch.

'If that's what I need to do, then yes. Hit and run. Survive to keep fighting. Guerilla tactics are the only course when you're an army of one.'

'Two, now,' Ray says. Nate gives him a tight, non-committal smile. Ray can feel his hackles rising, even as he recognizes the manipulation. *He's waiting for something.* An act of faith, something given freely. Instead, Ray pushes him again. 'It would have been three, if they hadn't taken Cameron.'

'I couldn't have stopped them.'

'You could have tried,' Ray says. 'You know why they want her?'

'I know why they want her.'

'They're trying to get to you.'

He looks away. 'Yes.'

'And you know what they'll do to her.'

'Hold her. Wait for me to make contact.'

'Bullshit they will.' Ray leans closer. 'They're not going to wait. They'll torture her, and they'll make sure you know about it. Audio, video, whatever. They'll record it and put it up online somewhere you're sure to look. They won't strike up a rapport, get her talking with a beer and a pack of cigarettes. I've met their new hires. All that kind of guy knows is how to follow an order and which end of a knife to use on someone.'

Nate's eyes dart to the laptop and back, his mouth set in a tight line, lips white. 'That is a possible outcome,' he says. The prospect of Cameron being tortured seems to have troubled him more than anything else so far.

'So what the fuck are you going to do about it?' Ray asks. 'Keep moving every six hours in the hope that if we run in circles fast enough they'll get dizzy trying to follow us? Keep picking cowardice and calling it caution?'

Nate doesn't look at him. 'I'm doing what I can,' he says, quietly. 'It doesn't look like it, but I have . . . something.'

Ray digs in his pocket for the mobile phone Cameron left in the car. 'We've got this,' he says. 'Whatever it is.'

Nate sits up straight, staring a hole in the phone Ray is holding. 'What is that?'

'The dead drop,' Ray says. 'Cameron knew she wasn't getting away. She didn't want them to find out what you had.'

Nate slaps the laptop shut and swears, then bangs his fist on the closed lid of the machine. 'You didn't think to tell me you've had that all this time?'

Ray waits, trying to weigh up the situation. Whatever Nate had left for Cameron, it wasn't dirt on Carrington Medical. He hadn't seemed too upset that she'd been taken, and everything since then has lacked urgency. Until now.

Ray takes a quick stock of their surroundings. No gun in reach of Nate's hands, and although Ray is sitting awkwardly, he's damn sure he can be faster than an invalid if he needs to be. 'What's on this phone, Nate?'

He can see Nate visibly trying to calm himself, to regain control. He's not flushed, but given the guy looks like a waxwork Ray can tell that he's still panicking. 'It's a back-up plan. Something I left for Cameron, in case the worst happened.'

'I asked what's on the phone, man,' Ray says. 'Don't make me ask again.'

'It's a virus. One that, if it gets plugged into a computer on Carrington's network, will shut down their security systems.'

Ray is gripping the phone so tight he feels like it might crack in his grip. 'You knew they were going to take her?'

'I made sure that if they did, she would have a way out,' Nate hisses, pointing at the phone. 'But she doesn't have it now, does she?' He looks around, like he's lost something, opens the laptop and taps at the keys. 'I've wasted all this time waiting for it to activate and you've had it in your fucking pocket this whole time.'

'You've been waiting.' Ray looks around. 'That's what we've been doing? You think Cameron was just going to walk out by herself?'

Nate shakes his head, agitated, ignoring the question. He gets up on to his hands and knees and reaches for the phone handset connected to the router. It's an all-weather handset built for construction use, the hard plastic angles and oversized rubber keypad refugees from somewhere in the mid-eighties. He's breathing hard, a wheeze catching at the back of his throat, but he forces the words out. 'We're going to have to move. I need to call in a favor, but first you need to call your family.'

'My family?'

'Your parents, your ex-wife, any kids you have.'

'Where'd you get the idea I have an ex-wife?'

Nate nods towards Ray's hand. 'No ring. Cops either stay married forever or collect messy divorces like baseball cards.'

Ray snorts dismissively, but Nate waits him out. Eventually he cracks and reaches for the handset. 'Never got as far as the wedding ceremony,' he says. 'I think she'll be just fine on her own.'

'I'm sorry. Phone your parents.'

Ray's hand stops short of grasping the telephone. 'And tell them what?'

Nate sits back. His expression doesn't change, but Ray can feel the shift in the air between them, the sudden tension that tightens across the gap.

'It's very important,' Nate says, 'that we don't waste time playing games with one another. I know where my sister is being held. I need your help in getting her back. I can't do that if your family could be used as leverage. You already know what you're going to tell them.'

Ray knows. He's known ever since he saw his mother getting spat on in the line for groceries, his father punched and told to go back where he came from. His whole family has known there might come a day when the whole world would go mad, and they would have to vanish before someone else turned up with a black van to make sure they vanished for good. He nods and looks down at his palms. Smooth. No calluses. Nothing like his father's. 'You know, I saw a program once about all these doomsday preppers, all these rich white boys getting tooled up so that when the world ends they're ready for it.' He turns his hands over and closes them into fists for a moment, imagining a black bag going over his father's head. His mother's. 'They never stopped to think that maybe rich white boys *were* the apocalypse.' Ray takes the handset.

He knows what surveillance means. An automated system, the successor to PRISM or whatever else the NSA was low-jacking the whole country with, lines of code running phone calls, texts and emails past a line of trigger words that flag individually for more direct action. He can't shake the image of an insertion team sitting in a cramped van across the street from his parents' place, itching to breach.

He's been on one of those teams himself. You gear up in a hurry and get briefed on the way. If you're lucky, you get to glance at a floorplan. It's a box full of sweat and nervous fear, because when you breach there could be anything waiting for you on the far side. Some deaf old grandma with her TV too loud and thirty cats in lieu of friends, or an LMG bolted to the floor and loaded with armor-piercing rounds. It's a pressure cooker, and there isn't a cop or operator alive that doesn't feel it crawl under their skin and make them want to shoot first. Ray swallows hard, and starts dialing.

'How long have I got?'

Nate shrugs. 'Twenty seconds, maybe thirty.'

'That's a lot of leeway.'

'Depends on what you say. Even the best software can't be everywhere at once. The more you give yourself away, the more it will shift resources towards pinning you down.'

'Right.'

The phone rings once and Ray's father answers it. He must have been sitting right next to the landline. Ray can see him in his mind's eye, snatching the phone up so that he can get the conversation over with. He can hear the sports channel in the background.

'Yeah.' For the longest time he thought his dad couldn't speak English. Turned out he just didn't like talking much.

'Hey.' Ray reflects his curtness back at him. 'Got a bad line here. How about you?'

His father doesn't answer. Ray hears the TV noise cut out as the old man switches it off. They'd talked once, before Ray left for the police academy, about what they would say if the time came. What had been a faint, awkward memory was now a thunderhead darkening the horizon.

'Clear as day here. What you selling today?'

'A better America. You know, like it used to be.'

'Yeah, when's that happening? Tomorrow?'

'Today.' Another silence. Nate holds up a warning, finger to wrist, and Ray nods at him. 'You understand what I'm selling.'

'Yeah. I hear you.' His father's voice sounds strange, like it's the first time Ray has ever heard it. It's because he sounds scared. 'How long for delivery?'

How long until the all-clear, is what he's asking. Ray's mouth feels like it's gone bone dry. The way things are going, he could be dead tomorrow.

'Call it a week,' Ray says. 'We'll let you know if it's longer. You take care of yourself.'

'You too.'

His father hangs up the phone. Ray stares down at the handset as though he's holding a detonator. His father. His mother. His sisters. Their kids. For as long as this lasts, they'll be running. The shock of it almost sees him dial the number again, to take it back, but instead he thinks of the scarring on his arm, about the thing they put in there. That grew inside of him. The world is ending, or at the very least changing beyond his ability to recognize it. At least his family has had some warning of it.

'Is it done?' Nate asks.

Ray nods. 'They're in the wind.' He stands and stretches, brings his arm up and massages the residual pain of the electric shock out of his bicep with his thumb. 'Now if I heard you right, you said you know where Cameron is?'

Nate has already gathered up his papers. 'I know where they're keeping her.'

'Great.' All of a sudden, things feel simpler. For many reasons, he really, really wants to find that Silicon Valley asshole and punch him so hard that the next time he takes a shit it'll have teeth in it. And Nate knows where to find him. 'So what are we waiting for?'

Chapter 23

They don't restrain her anymore. It's not a show of respect. With the bullshit taser they've buried in her side, they don't need to. From the moment Cameron wakes up, coming out of a dreamless dark into pin-sharp, panicked clarity, she is keenly aware of the stitches in her side, and the tingling sensation that swept from her wrist up to her shoulder a split second before the paralysis hit. She can feel the implant in there, an alien presence that in her lowest moments makes self-mutilation seem like something she'd sign up for.

She moves carefully through the facility, between the rooms they've assigned her, wary of the nurses and handlers who move freely in and out of the space, taking measurements, making notes, always watching her. They're not interested in breaking her. They seem perfectly happy to accept her anger, as long as it doesn't turn into action against them. Terri tried to get on her good side by pointedly taking the batteries out of the remote Miller had left with her, but Cameron chalks that up as another trick and ignores her.

A meal comes, one of the eight that appear in every twenty-four hours. There are no clocks and no natural light, but

Cameron has an instinctive feel for the time passing which is reinforced by the staff rotation. They aren't disciplined about covering their watches and phone screens, for one thing, and the night shift is perceptibly lighter and less responsive than the daytime workers. All of them complain about the air conditioning, the constant running of the fans like a ferryboat hum, making everything vibrate softly and drawing a chill into the air. Two days have passed, and she's already tuned into their rhythms.

Cameron drew up the diet plan herself. It's halfway between a fighter's diet and a bodybuilder's. There's a lot of protein in it. A lot of fish. Apparently someone in the building feels bad about cooking meals with an offensive level of blandness and has included a slice of lemon, which she dutifully eats with the same mechanical action as the rest of it. Every meal comes with a pint flask of cold protein-rich slurry that she chokes down in a single effort. It is chalky to an extreme, and drinking it leaves her mouth feeling as though it's been lined with aluminum foil for hours afterwards. It is without a doubt the single most disgusting thing Cameron has ever drunk, beaten only by the faint memory of finding an ancient bottle of cream liqueur as a teenager and, in spite of the fact it had split into two layers, declaring it *still good.*

She eats it – all of it – because it's one thing she can control. *They asked him to kill you, and he tried.* Nate has pissed away every good memory she had of him, every good moment they shared. Carrington have taken everything else. All Cameron has left is this one sliver of opportunity: that they are keen for her to recover. She runs through her physiotherapy exercises to warm herself up, and pushes on into a basic workout. She knows it won't keep her mind from racing, won't dull the pain of betrayal or hold back the rage she can feel fizzing up inside of her, but it does give her focus. An opportunity will present itself, given time. All she has to do is be ready for it.

Cameron is in the ad-hoc gym they've provided when she realizes that Miller is on his way. It's like instinct: the subconscious register of a footfall outside, or the first faint smell of coffee and tobacco and body wash combined in such a way that the hairs on the back of her neck stand up. She looks up to the door in expectation of his arrival, and for a moment she considers the possibility of putting the barbell she's holding clean through his head before he can drop her. She wouldn't even have to run over there. She could throw it like a spear, and hope her sore ribs don't put off her aim. Cameron can feel a tension gathering at the top of her spine – the adrenaline building, ready to flood through her – as she weighs up her chances. They aren't good. *Not yet.* She lets the bar drop back on to the rack, and steps clear of it as Miller enters the gym. *Don't give him anything to work with. No sign of weakness.*

Miller comes in smiling, the air of a professional PR bullshit artist about him. 'Cameron. How are we this morning?'

Cameron wipes her face with a towel, using it as cover, time to master her expression. 'Is it morning still?'

'You can't tell?' There's a sour edge to it, and when he looks aside Cameron struggles not to smirk. He's a constant source of questions, a walking progress survey, and it annoys him when every answer she gives is vague enough that he can't be certain she's lying.

'You're the ones with battleship grey walls and no clocks,'

Cameron says. 'Did you run a casino in a previous life? Because I judge these things by the same signs that everyone else does: sun rising, birds tweeting, presence of coffee. Oh yeah, and not being held prisoner. That's a big one.'

Miller gestures at the weight bench. 'You seem to be adjusting well.'

Cameron sniffs. 'The sword is the soul.'

'What?'

'Body and mind,' Cameron says. 'They're all linked.' *Christ, this is the sort of shit Ludo spouts.* If it means getting back to being fit enough to make a run for it, Cameron is happy to go full hippy. 'You want me sharp, this is how I get sharp.'

'Hm.' Miller sounds doubtful, but doesn't argue. Instead he hefts a laptop bag, holds it out to her. 'I would have thought this would be of more use to you,' he says.

Cameron takes it, and finds her laptop inside. It is suspiciously clean, like someone has taken a pack of wet wipes to the casing. 'I bricked this,' she says.

'Actually, you bricked some of it,' Miller says. 'You burned out the USB port and a significant chunk of the motherboard, but the hard drive survived. We got one of our tech guys to fix it. He says it took five hours, which probably means it took two and the rest he spent staring at a vending machine trying to decide which snack to get.'

Cameron opens the laptop, powering it on, and lets out a low whistle when it takes ten seconds to boot up instead of ten minutes. 'Tell him thanks for the upgrade.'

Miller frowns. 'He did say something about it being an insult to his sensibilities.'

'So what's the WiFi password?'

'Your computer will connect to the internal system, but for security reasons we keep our building's server physically separate from the outside world. Whatever information you need you can request, and we'll upload it as necessary.'

'Your building's server isn't connected to the Internet?'

'Correct.'

'So . . . you have someone who actually lifts the memory from one computer and plugs it into the server when you need it transferred?' Cameron mimes the action, stunned by the madness of it.

'We have a robot.'

'That's handy,' she says. 'Keeps it from telling you how dumb that is all day.'

'Miss King, when I said that more than one government agency is interested in our work, I was not boasting. You'd be surprised how much more effective a computer system can be when it is not constantly fighting off attempts to hack into it.'

Cameron waves away the explanation, and looks at the handful of tools she has sitting on her desktop. Links to financial tracking services; real-time transaction monitoring; a search engine that runs down aliases and returns a value for how complete they are: all of them are useless without the Internet. Facial recognition, though, will run just fine on archived footage. *And what about unsecured camera access?* Cameron smothers the smirk that comes on the tail of that thought and tries to look businesslike. 'Fine, whatever. Get me everything you collected from back when my brother "vanished".'

'You think we missed something?'

'I know you missed something,' she says. 'People don't just disappear. They leave a trail.'

'I don't see how going back that far helps you find him.'

Cameron sighs. 'You want me to find Nate?'

'Yes. But—'

'Then take your twenty questions, and push them all the way up your ass,' she says. 'If he found a way to get off your grid that works, then it stands to reason he's still using the same method. So when I get out of here and start looking for him, I'm not just looking at random.'

Miller nods. 'You're right. I'm sorry.'

'You're sorry? Take this fucking implant out of my side, I'll show you sorry.'

'No,' he says, and Cameron stops fiddling with the laptop to pay attention to the tone of his voice. 'I am sorry, but you won't be leaving here to hunt your brother.'

The anger in Cameron's gut flares up, but she keeps a lid on it. It's exactly the kind of bullshit she expects from Miller. 'You don't want to risk him getting his hands on me.'

'His actions suggest you have value to him, and as such that makes you an asset,' Miller says. 'Once you've completed your preliminary report on how your brother got away, you'll be advising Samson in the field.'

'Samson?'

'Our prodigal son. You came close to blinding him.'

Bullet Head. 'Hell of a name to give to a bald guy.'

Miller shrugs it off. 'We can't be blamed for the choices our parents make,' he says. 'But he has made a very quick recovery. He won't recover the eye you took, but he'll be back on his feet in a few days.' The offhand way Miller talks makes it sound like they're discussing a lab rat. Samson could be his first or his last name; it doesn't matter to Miller. All he's lacking is a clipboard and a pen to take down notes. 'What did you think of him?'

'You want me to give you feedback on the guy who tried to beat me to death?'

Miller waves the question away. 'Just your general impression of him.'

'Was he meant to be your headliner?' Cameron laughs. 'What was he, army?'

'Special Forces, originally,' Miller says. 'He left under some unfortunate circumstances and we picked him up not long after. I take it you weren't impressed.'

'No, no, I was impressed. Your boy was faster than shit through a tin horn, but he wasted every opportunity to end the fight for the sake of showing off.'

'You felt he was overconfident.'

'Overconfident? Look, whatever shithole barracks you found him in, you should send him back. Whatever you're paying him, it's not worth it.' Cameron clicks her teeth. 'As soon as he lost his temper, he stopped being an asset and became a liability. If I hadn't got a hold of his head, he probably would have killed me.'

Miller coughs and looks away, shooting his cuffs as though his shirt isn't sitting right inside his suit jacket. Cameron sees it, and pounces.

'You can't send him back, can you?' Miller doesn't answer, but a muscle in his jaw twitches, betraying him. 'What was it? Dishonorable discharge? Drugs? Did he kill someone?'

'Your assessment is very close to the truth,' Miller says. 'He has some issues with holding back.'

'Your asset couldn't control himself.' Cameron shakes her head. 'You're a business guy, right? Don't you spend millions on risk analysis?' Miller shrugs. 'Didn't you stop and think that maybe putting an arrogant man-baby on point was a bad idea? All I had to do was embarrass him and he lost his shit.'

'He almost killed you.'

'Yeah. Your first-in-class prize specimen almost took out someone half his weight and a foot shorter than him after she crawled out of a car wreck.' Cameron slow claps it out, and Miller's expression is like sour milk.

'If you'd been fully fit,' he asks, 'would you have beaten him?'

'Fully fit?' Something flares inside Cameron at that. An old pride, something that she had almost forgotten. 'If I was still fighting?'

'Yes.'

Cameron wants to shake her head and say no. He had been damn fast. Even at her best, she wouldn't have wanted to fight him. Fighting outside your weight class was dumb enough without picking a heavyweight as your opponent.

'I would have destroyed him,' she says.

Miller falls silent, runs his thumb along the line of his jaw, then looks up at her. It's as though her answer confirmed something, answered a question that he had held back from asking. 'Excellent,' he says. 'Perfect, in fact.' He rubs his hands together and they make a dry, papery sound, like he's spent too much of his life in air-conditioned rooms. 'We had conceived of your pursuit as a milk run for Samson. A simple exercise to demonstrate his field-readiness. And yet it proved to be the exact opposite. You are correct about his limitations, and our part in creating them.'

'What are you selling, Miller?'

He spreads his hands wide, palms open, the picture of innocence. 'I was hoping you might agree to replace him.'

'You were hoping?' Cameron holds up her left arm. 'Spare me the soft sell. Try some honesty for once. Take your boy's place or you'll zap me so hard I'll spend the rest of my days eating through a tube, right?'

'The implant in your side is for your own safety.' Miller says it with complete conviction, the kind of sales-floor firmness that comes from long practice. Cameron can sense the edge to it, the admonishing, predatory tilt in his expression that makes her keenly aware of what a single press of a button can do to her, and that Miller could, if he wanted to, press it on a whim. 'When our business with your brother is concluded, when we find out what he wants with you, then there'll be no need for it to remain active.'

Cameron bites down on an insult and stays quiet. He can have his power trip. Miller doesn't realize it, but he's given her a spark of hope in the shape of her laptop. If he's too busy talking shit to notice, then all the better.

'If we were to go out and recruit someone, we would be looking for a candidate just like you,' Miller says. 'Martial arts training from childhood. A successful fighting career. And after it a second career that – while less profitable – has broadened your range of skills. Skip tracing, surveillance and pursuit, subterfuge . . . not to mention your obvious knack for improvisation.'

'I'm not interested,' Cameron says.

'We're changing the world, here, Miss King,' Miller says. 'Once we roll out our program nationwide, we will be in a unique position. Everyone who accepts Carrington as their care provider will be willingly opting to become a living part of the largest monitoring and surveillance network ever built. The losses we make on their insurance will be insignificant in comparison to the value of the information it generates.'

'What are you going to do, lease it out to the NSA or something?'

Miller grunts in disgust. 'The government is a shambles. All of them scrambling to try and climb a little higher than the person next to them. They don't protect the people. Not like we would. Once it goes national – once it goes global – Carrington will be able to completely and genuinely ensure the safety of every man, woman and child in the United States.'

The scale of it is beyond what Cameron expected. He sounds insane. 'All safe under your watchful eye. So what do you need me for?'

'A ground team. To protect our assets and, where necessary, identify and neutralize any attempts to bypass or imitate our system.'

'You want me to crush any resistance.'

'Right now, you're part of the flock,' Miller says, sidestepping the lethal implication. 'How would you like to be one of the shepherds?'

'I'm not interested.' Part of her wants to show willing, string him along, but her instincts tell her he would sense the feint. *Keep him at arm's length*, she thinks. *Make him reach for it, until he thinks the tiniest amount of give is a breakthrough.*

'You don't want to think about it?'

'Look, Miller, you can either stay and give me the hard sell, or I can get to work.' Cameron gestures at the laptop screen. 'Do you want me to find Nate, or not?'

Miller nods, his mouth a tight little line, like she's hurt his feelings. Cameron doesn't buy it for a second. 'I'll leave you to it.'

Cameron ignores him until he goes. When he's out of the room, she finds the program she's been waiting to activate since the laptop booted up. *Access Unsecured Cameras.*

Chapter 24

It's the way nobody secures their phone or their watch that gave Cameron the idea. Carrington putting their server offline might have fixed one potential weakness in their security, but it makes them lazy about others. If your employees can't grasp the point of taking down the clocks and blocking up all the windows, then it's just as likely that they've never even heard of the first rule of owning a laptop: you put a sticker over the camera. There's a moment of doubt when Cameron starts the program running, a lean little bloodhound of code that sniffs out cameras on a network and, if possible, turns them on, but when the first images flicker up she almost punches the screen in triumph. It's the first taste of victory.

Flicking through them, Cameron makes a quick note of anything that looks useful. Several have doors visible in the background, and she catches a man in shirt and tie just as he punches in a code on the keypad next to it. *Nine eight six*— The last digit is obscured, but his hand goes fractionally up and left when he presses it which means it's likely a *one* and possibly a *two*. The doors slide open to reveal an elevator, and Cameron grins at the sight. Jackpot. *Nine eight six one. Nine eight six two*. She chants them silently in her head, committing them to memory. The less she writes down, the less she records, the less likely it is anyone will see what she's doing.

She can't really hide the fact she's accessing cameras via their internal network, but she can keep everyone who could be watching her too busy to dig in and check. Nate is the key to that. Treating the job of tracking Nate down like any other skip would be too simple – you set a bunch of searches running and sift through the hits you get looking for leads – so it's up to her to get creative.

She opens the internal email they've added to her laptop and puts in a long request about the data from Nate's disappearance. She asks for everything they can put their hands on from six weeks prior to that date, including internal surveillance and traffic cameras from the city. *He didn't just vanish at the drop of a hat*, she writes. *There would have been changes, and a signal to start him off.* She puts in a demand for a floor plan like it's an afterthought, piled in amongst a barrage of questions about Nate's routines, where he worked, where he had access to and how much time he spent off-site. Elevator Nine Eight Six One/Two is a good start, but it won't be of any use to her until she can work out where it is. She signs off with a reminder to send her some headphones, and access to the police band. If nobody in the building is covering their camera up, they sure as shit aren't muting their mics, either.

For the first time, Cameron feels like she's pulling ahead of Miller. The nutrition plan and the workouts were just the foundation, something to keep her anchored. Now, though, she has purpose. Direction. Something to work towards. You don't win a fight by being the strongest or the quickest. People think you train hard, you hit the heavy bag a whole bunch of times, skip rope, maybe spar some and that makes you ready. It doesn't make you ready. All it does is make you fit. What they don't see is the prep work. The research, the frame-by-frame breakdown of their fights and your own, the creation of a strategy that you carry into the ring. You don't win fights with your fists. You win them with your head. By knowing more than your opponent. Cameron knows what Miller is missing. She knows why Nate pulled her into this, what he wanted her for.

He wanted her in here with Miller.

That was what his song and dance routine with the pass-word and the dead drop was all about. He knew she was looking for him, had been looking for him ever since the crash, and he played her with it. By baiting her with just enough information to put her on his scent, he had tricked her into downloading the data off of a USB stick without thinking twice about what it was and why he had left it for her to find.

In the heat of the moment, she had thought it was some great secret waiting to be spilled, the truth of where he had been all these years, something so hot that he could not possibly deliver it in person. The whole thing is like a bitter taste at the back of her throat, that she had been holding so tight to the hope of seeing him again, she'd walked right into it. It only struck her when Miller boasted to her that their servers were completely cut off from the outside world, rendering them immune to cyber-attack.

Nate had known that calling her would set Carrington on her heels. Since she was the one he was meant to kill, the one he'd left alive, it would be impossible for them not to come after her. The data on the USB stick – the data she had downloaded – was meant to be in her possession when they caught her.

It's a virus.

Nate isn't working for a foreign power. Cameron can picture what it is like: a virus like a warhead, a sleek mass of code designed to inject itself into the Carrington system and start shutting down vital components without damaging the bulk of the system's code. A smart-target missile that takes down the security systems, but leaves the rest of the server complete. Vulnerable, ready to be salvaged.

Cameron has heard of that kind of virus before. Stuxnet was a cyber-weapon created by the US government to derail the Iranian nuclear program. Nate is working for a US agency. Whatever Carrington did to piss them off, it must have been really bad. Instead of dishing out a fat government contract, they've flipped Nate and given him the means to hobble his former master. He was never trying to help Cameron. He needed to inject the virus into Carrington's system, and Cameron was his route to making that happen.

Except he hadn't counted on Ray helping her, and that she would leave the data with him.

A chill floods her gut thinking about that. If Ray is alive, then he's in danger. And Cameron has no way of warning him.

Someone clears their throat to get Cameron's attention. She looks up a shade too quickly, closing the laptop on reflex, and curses herself for being so obvious. Thankfully, it isn't Miller. It's Terri, and she is standing in the doorway with a blood-pressure cuff in one hand and a metal tray in the other. Blood tests.

'Is this a bad time?' she asks.

Cameron stares at her. 'You want to take a wild guess at the answer to that?'

Terri takes that without blinking and walks over to where Cameron is sitting. She puts the tray down, pulls up a chair, and sits. Cameron holds out her left arm, and Terri inspects it briefly before slipping the cuff on.

'How does it feel?' she asks. 'Any numbness? Tremors?'

Cameron takes a deep breath in and lets it whistle out through her nose. The swelling from the break has reduced, but isn't completely gone yet. 'If I say yes, does that mean I get all the shit you've put in me pulled out?'

Terri takes her blood pressure in silence, and Cameron wonders why she doesn't do it on the right arm as well. If she was worried about circulation in the limb, it would be one way to check it.

The blood test comes next, and Terri turns the crook of Cameron's arm upwards and slips a tiny needle into a vein with quick, professional ease.

'Ten out of ten,' Cameron murmurs.

'Sorry?'

Cameron shakes her head. 'Old habit. You wouldn't believe how many times someone has missed that vein,' she says. 'I used to give a score out of ten.'

Terri nods, understanding. 'Not everyone has the knack. They've got these new needles that are meant to make it easier.'

Cameron looks at the needle in her arm. 'It doesn't look special.'

'I don't use them,' Terri says. 'It feels like cheating. Like if I used them, I'd forget how to do it properly.'

Cameron watches the vial filling with her blood and feels an odd kind of pride in that sentiment. It sounds a lot like something Ludo would say. *Stick to the fundamentals. You can't build anything if your base is weak.*

'What is it?' Terri asks.

Cameron realizes she is smiling, and smothers it. 'Nothing. Something an old friend told me.'

Terri pauses, on the verge of saying something, then busies herself drawing out the needle and putting a folded wad of dressing in its place. She holds the dressing in position with her thumb, pressing hard into Cameron's flesh.

'You know I saw you fight once.' Terri speaks in a low voice, not looking at Cameron. 'At the Oracle, five years ago. Got my brother some great seats for his birthday.'

Cameron knows which fight she is talking about. She'd been talked into filling a card against Susan Monroe after her opponent pulled out with a training injury. With a weight deficit of almost ten pounds and two inches of reach on her, Monroe had not anticipated a tough time. An excellent grappler, she came close to pulling a submission out of Cameron in both the first and second rounds. In the first round the bell had saved Cameron; in the second, Cameron had held the fraction of an angle against a hold that should have put her out of the fight. Instead, she had held it, getting angrier and angrier at herself for being so dumb as to wind up in the same situation twice in ten minutes. Three seconds into the third round Monroe had rushed her, greedy for the win, and Cameron kicked her in the head so hard that the whiplash tore a muscle in Monroe's neck. She went down and didn't get up until the medics lifted her on to a gurney.

'Must have been a hell of a show.'

Terri grins, but doesn't look up. 'He still talks about it. Says it was the best fight he's ever seen.' Cameron almost says something sarcastic, but bites down on it. This has the air of a confession, and she can sense Terri is building up to something.

Terri reaches for some tape to hold the gauze in place, and Cameron sees her slip something else off of the tray, palming it into her gloved hand. 'Never been a big fan of fights, but I did take one thing home from that night,' she says. As she fixes the gauze in place, she takes whatever it is she's holding and presses it hard against Cameron's skin, just below the edge of the tape. 'You never gave up.' It's barely a whisper. She sits back, pulls Cameron's right hand over to cover her own, and speaks in a normal voice again. 'Keep pressure on that until you get sick of holding it.'

Cameron presses down on the gauze and the packet beside it, the desire to peek making it feel hot against her fingertips. 'Is that a real length of time?'

'Proven science,' Terri says. She gathers her stuff and gets up, ready to leave.

'Hey, Terri?'

'Yeah?'

'You sound rough.' It startles her, and Cameron makes a point of holding her gaze, of not looking down at her arm. 'If you've got a cold coming on I don't want you coughing your germs at me. Take a day off or something.'

Terri's eyes widen, but she recovers quickly. 'I'm fine,' she says, waving it off as she walks to the door. 'It's just a sore throat.'

'I'm serious,' Cameron says, her voice rising as Terri leaves. 'You make me sick I'm gonna sue.'

When she's certain that Terri has gone, Cameron takes her hand off the gauze and tape, and transfers the package to the keyboard of her laptop. It's a square of film, no more than an inch across, and trapped inside it is a spiral of wire with a tiny metal dot at its center. It's an RFID chip. There's a sticker on the other side, and Cameron turns it over to find written in tiny, cramped capital letters: *CHIP CLONE: T. JOHNSON* and below it, in another hand: *9861*.

Nine Eight Six One. *Jackpot*. It didn't occur to Cameron that doors might need a chip as well as a keycode to open them, but if they put a chip in her it makes sense that they're doing it to everyone else on staff. Cameron wants to run after the nurse and hug her. It doesn't fix the problem of the taser buried in her side, but it's a start. On the laptop screen, the active cameras are arranged in a grid, waiting to be picked.

It's a start, but it's not enough. You win fights with your head. By knowing more than your opponent. Cameron clicks on the first camera, and gets to work.

Chapter 25

Ray wasn't sure what he expected. A glistening skyscraper, maybe. A polished crystal shard driven like a spike into the ground, indomitable in its glass-clad armor, deflecting everything, even light. Or a military-style compound complete with high razor-wire fences and a watchtower, jeeps endlessly patrolling, weaving and circling their way through the pattern of telephone poles set in the ground to keep helicopters from landing.

The home of Carrington Medical, Axion, or whoever their enemy is, looks like neither of the scenarios he imagined. What it looks like is a cluster of cement blocks that were dropped in the middle of a scrub patch of abandoned industrial real estate, and have slowly clumped together to keep themselves warm through the night. It looks like the kind of place your uncle would drive an hour out of town to so that he could load up on discount house paint, and not even offer to buy you a soda from the dust-clogged vending machine by way of an apology.

There's a cursory attempt at a fence, loose squares of galvanized mesh hanging limp from battered-looking metal posts that sit too awkwardly to have been set in concrete. It's the sort of thing that keeps most of the big animals out of the trash cans at night, and little else.

All told, it looks like the least secure location in the world, and Ray feels like an idiot for having bought into Nate King's insistence on a cautious approach. They're sitting far enough out that they need binoculars to really add some detail to how unimpressive it all is, and Nate is still twitching like a cat at the sound of distant cars passing.

'Are you sure this is the place?' Ray asks. 'It doesn't look like much of anything.' Nate says nothing, so Ray starts to get up, making to stretch out some of the road-tired feeling that has crept into his lower back. Nate catches hold of his side and drags him back down to ground level.

'This is the place,' he hisses. 'Keep your head and your voice down.'

'What, you worried the two-man team of rent-a-cops they hire to look after the place is going to come point a flashlight at us?'

'You don't see it?'

Ray sighs. 'What I see is a waste of my fucking time.'

'And you call yourself a cop? Look at it. Look how inconspicuous it is. You think that's an accident? It doesn't just blend in. It's genuinely, completely uninteresting. Your gaze slides off it looking for something better to see.'

'I noticed that.'

'Yeah, well that should start your alarm bells ringing. You ever see a place that shabby that didn't have some story hanging off of it? Someone's bankruptcy, some local family feud, the whole business written off. Here? Nothing. The whole thing is just camouflage.' Nate pauses, waiting for a reaction, but Ray gives him nothing. It's all conjecture. Maybe somebody local could point to the place and tell you the story; it's far enough off the beaten path that it's more likely than not people just forgot about it. Nate presses on. 'Look again. You see any birds down there?'

Ray pauses, lifts his binoculars, and looks again. It's not something he ever gives much thought to, but there are always birds. Little ones, dipping low to the ground, chasing down insects or interesting scraps. Big ones, attracted to anything above a storey in height, craning their necks as they search for anything they can grab hold of. Raptors, riding the thermals upwards, hanging casual in the air as they wait out their prey. Here at Carrington there's no sign of any of them, no signs of life at all. It is as still and as silent as the grave.

Ray takes another long look at the site. He's still not convinced. It's just another shit-smear industrial lot rotting at the edge of the city. Not even the birds give a fuck about it. 'Nate, this is a waste of time. The biggest secret they've got down there is a filing cabinet full of sales receipts from 1972.'

'I thought you'd say that.' Nate turns, looking down the length of the access road, the long dusty strip of nothing that leads down from a freeway turn-off. A battered car has turned on to it and is making its way towards the site. 'Here he comes now.'

'Who the hell is that?' Ray asks.

'Pizza delivery.'

Ray looks down at the car in disbelief for a moment before checking through the binoculars. On the sky-blue panel door a faded pizza store decal is just visible. 'You ordered a pizza. Unbelievable.'

'You need to see this,' Nate says. 'You need to see what we're up against.'

Ray's fingers brush the spot where faint scars mark the ghost of his implant. 'I know what we're up against,' he says. 'I just don't think this is—'

'Look.' Nate is pointing, and as Ray follows the line of his finger he sees a black minivan, windows tinted, accelerating down the site road towards the car. Ray didn't catch which building it came from, and it's almost as though it just sprung up out of the earth.

'Who is that? The fucking A-Team?'

'Site security,' Nate says. 'Watch.'

The black van brakes in a cloud of dust, swerving to block the road, and men with assault rifles pile out of the side door, leveling them at the beat-up car. The pizza guy slams on the brakes and stops about a hundred feet short of the van.

'This shit can't be happening,' Ray says. There's enough firepower down there to kit out a SEAL team. 'I'm going to call it in.'

'Call what in?' Nate asks. 'Even if your colleagues would listen to you, it's private property. As far as the law is concerned he's trespassing.'

It's the first time Ray has thought of it as that. *The facility.* There's a palpable air of danger to its blandness now, an edge he hadn't felt before. The pizza delivery guy, now out of the car and waving his arms in surrender, could disappear into those cement blocks and no one would ever think twice about checking for him. The thought lies heavy and cold in Ray's

214

gut. Nate might well have condemned an innocent man just to make a point.

'What will they do with him?'

'Standard procedure with strays is to stick them in a dark room and threaten the shit out of them. They'll turn his life inside out just to make sure he isn't anyone important, and when they confirm the only danger he presents is being too high to beat the thirty-minute promise they'll make him sign a non-disclosure the length of his arm and take him home.'

'They going to chip him, too?'

'If he wasn't already, he'll walk out of there with a chip in his arm or thigh. They'll make it seem like they're doing him a favor.' Nate nods towards the wreck of his car. 'Maybe even offer to get that fixed up if he takes something more substantial. They fit homeless guys with signal repeaters in exchange for food, shelter, healthcare. Whatever they need.'

Ray bristles, his voice rising. 'You let an innocent man get Gitmo'd just so I'd believe you?' Nate doesn't react to it. Ray stares at him for a long time, and Nate sits there watching the black bag go over the pizza kid's head, the restraints go on, and the van door closing with the same cold expression. 'You know, I'm starting to wonder why the fuck your sister would ever want to find you.'

That gets a reaction. Nate turns to look straight at Ray, his expression tight with anger. He coughs in spite of himself, fighting to try and keep it down. 'You don't know a thing about me, Ray Perada.'

'Yeah?' Ray says. 'I know a piece of shit when it stinks up the place.'

'You think I threw that guy to the wolves?' Nate asks. 'Wake up. People have been getting chipped in this city for months, willingly. You think this is a problem? This is a dry run for what they plan on doing. Imagine this: a nationwide rollout of Carrington Medical's new medical aid program. Agree to have a chip installed, and they will beat down any insurance roadblock that stands in your way. Agree to the advanced chip – the one that collects and passes on signals – and you don't worry about insurance again. How many people are going to say no to that?'

Ray shakes his head. 'That won't happen. People will see through it.'

'They won't. They haven't. Ring up every family that's had a cancer death in the past five years and promise them free screening for life if they use our new easy-testing subdermal implant. They'll queue round the block.'

Ray knows the kind of person he's reminded of when Nate speaks. There are guys on the narcotics task force like him. All veterans of the much vaunted and ultimately futile war on drugs, burned out and cynical, their morality worn thin by decades of exposure to the very worst of human nature. The sort of cop who thinks the ends justify the means.

Ray swallows hard. Nate is playing him. *Right now, you're the pizza guy.* He wants Cameron, but it sure as shit isn't to help shut down his old boss's surveillance network. There's something else, and for all his prodding Ray can't get it out of him. *If you don't do it, he'll send someone else.* 'I understand.'

Something down on the access road catches Ray's attention and he lifts his binoculars to see it. The rendition-in-progress has halted momentarily as one of the crew has gone back to the ruined delivery car to fetch the pizza. They're taking it with them.

'What did you order?'

'Double pineapple, arugula, anchovies,' Nate says. 'No cheese.'

Ray lets out a low whistle. 'Shit. You sure they're not going to kill him after he turns up with the pizza?'

'Not unless they make him eat the pizza.' Nate shuffles back down the rise, putting himself out of line of sight of the access road and the buildings. 'Come on. We've seen enough, and there's a lot still to do before tomorrow.'

Chapter 26

Ray adjusts the bag in his lap, shifts in his seat, and looks out of the window. Nobody on the bus is talking. They were expressly told not to. A pinch-faced bus guard, skin so tight over the bones of his face it made him look like he was wearing a mask, had laid it out for them. He'd opened with an appetizer of human resource welcome-speak, *we know it's a great opportunity, we know you're all excited*, and followed with the meat-and-potatoes main course: *in the interest of security you are not allowed to speak in transit*. Between the threat and the group of lantern-jawed men watching them board, it felt more like a prison detail than a new-hire induction day. Ray always wondered what it would be like to be on the receiving end of that treatment, and now he knows: it turns people into livestock, and the short ride out to the Carrington Medical buildings is made long by the attention of the guards. Each boring moment stretches out with the threat of dismissal, and as they turn away from the bustle of the highway and down on to the access road an unpleasant sensation rises in the back of Ray's throat. Do cows know when they're being taken to slaughter?

He plays along with the others, acts curious about the landscape. He can see an abandoned shack, whitewash peeling, and another in the distance. They look identical, and when he looks across the aisle he can see others dotted about the landscape. Camouflage, or something like it. This is the most uninteresting place in the world, and Ray finds his focus drifting.

Cameron. Ray can remember waking in the car now, a gap in his memory filling with a hazy recollection of half-grasped moments of awareness. He remembers seeing her crawl from the car, getting up and standing on legs that looked ready to collapse out from under her to fight Bullet Head. Big bastard. There's a gap in what he recalls of the fight, but he knows he saw her land, ragdoll-limp, at the very end of it. He thought she was dead. With all the shit she's brought down on him since they met, Ray could be – should be – anywhere else. But she got out of the car, and she didn't run, even though she could – should – have. She fought, and Ray owes her for that.

Don't get caught. Don't get shot. Don't get lost. Ray takes a deep breath and smothers the sigh that threatens to follow it. *Simple enough.* Find Cameron and work out who her brother is working for, and what they want with her. *Less straightforward.* Oh yeah, and escape.

He can feel the sweat making his shirt stick to him already.

They pass the point where the pizza guy got stopped, and Ray tries not to look too much like a man about to vomit. Up by the driver, a panel lights up green and the guard next to him visibly relaxes, clipboard lowering from where he was clutching it like a shield. He gets to his feet and clears his throat, as though he doesn't already have everyone's full attention, and offers the seated rows the most insincere smile Ray has seen short of the SFPD public relations department.

'Thank you, everyone, for your patience. We apologize for the strict security protocols. We've had some information about our products and services slip out through leaks, so an ability to be tight-lipped is a quality we cherish in all our staff.' He looks at the driver again, who nods in confirmation. 'You may now talk amongst yourselves, if you wish.'

There's a long silence as the bus absorbs the sudden freedom before a soft murmur of introductions begins. The guy sitting next to Ray is wearing a suit that probably cost the same as Ray's rent and is groomed in that exact, polished way that suggests he either has a team of stylists to hand or got up at four a.m. to get started on it. When he turns to Ray he extends one tanned hand, turned slightly to show off the Ivy League ring he's wearing.

'David Farrow, Strategies. I used to be in Assets, but I divested.' He smiles, his straight, even teeth so white they almost glow. Ray tries to suppress the cop instinct – *what is this guy hiding?* – and puts on a grateful-for-the attention face.

'I'm George. Perez.' Ray says it like he's apologizing. 'My name is George Perez.'

'What do you do, George?' It's both question and threat, the old high school leveler carried up to the corporate world. *Which group do you belong to?* and *Am I ruining my reputation by talking to you?*

'I work in data entry and compliance.'

It's not bad work, according to Nate. Spend your days looking at code, spreadsheets, making sure everything is complete, hunting down discrepancies. It's well-paid and rewards a certain level of concentration and analytical thought. In a crowd where everyone wants to be a world-changing innovator you might as well say you catch other people's shits for a living. Farrow's smile doesn't drop, but he does withdraw his hand with haste and turn away to find someone worthier of his time.

By the time they get through the chain-link fence, draw to a stop and line up to get off the bus, word has spread of Ray's status at the bottom of the programmer food chain. He stays in his seat as David slips out ahead of him into the aisle, and then waits quietly for everyone to filter past. They close ranks to make sure he ends up at the back. Nobody asks his name. They barely even look at him. Ray is musing on the idea of a computer tech as the ultimate undercover role until one of the others mutters 'George' to himself, shaking his head as he passes. *Oh yeah, there is that.* Every other person on the bus is white, and his low-level job isn't the only prejudice here. *We'll see how fucking clever you are when I come back and arrest every one of your asses*, he thinks.

Inside, the building is massively more hi-tech than the exterior implies. The lobby they walk through is a kaleidoscope room of granite and steel, dominated by security screening apparatus. There's a metal detector and a body scan to go through, and more than one person has their bag confiscated. Ray's lunch bag and thermos, the latter three-quarters full of a clear beef soup from a pop-up place on the way to the bus, are given a quick once over and handed back without incident. Ray is almost suspicious until he glances back and catches sight of the monitors: there's security camera footage of him from this morning, the girl behind the counter caught freeze-frame pouring soup straight into the thermos for him. On the screen next to it, there's a string of ID photos: Ray's, the girl's, the guy behind him in the queue, the woman leaving with her dog tucked under one arm. Everyone that is in the shot is listed on the second screen, and all of them have a green border. *Safe*. One of the staff catches Ray looking and he moves on quickly.

More surprising than the fact they have access to all this information is that George Perez gets a green flag. Nate King couldn't have known they would meet, and whoever is bankrolling him must have either built a new identity from the ground up in days, or found funds enough to buy one off the shelf. They must have some serious pull to make that happen, and not for the first time Ray wonders who Nate King is working for. They want this incursion to happen, and Ray knows he's being thrown into a meat grinder as part of some grand plan they have, but he owes Cameron too much to walk away.

They filter out of the lobby and are escorted by a team of six handlers along a battleship grey corridor to a warehouse space, an open floor with a high ceiling bounded by wide doorways, built to allow heavy plant to move in and out. Ray is struck by the livestock comparison again. Like the first cows to arrive at market, all the new hires huddle together in a tight group, not quite in the middle of the space. The floor is clean enough that whenever someone moves their shoes squeak. Overhead, six massive vents are pulling air fast enough that the whole room seems to tremble with their thrumming.

Ray raises his hand. One of the handlers lifts his chin in acknowledgement, but otherwise does not move.

'Hey, you know where the toilets are?'

That gets the handler moving. He walks the space between the door they came in and the group with a deliberate slowness, not obviously armed but making a big show of how badly his suit jacket fits him, how awkward it is for him to move his left arm while walking. *Maybe you can wait to go to the toilet*, is the message. Ray can feel the rest of the new hires silently urging him to drop it.

'What?' The handler stands too close, deliberately. Ray can tell that he's a smoker from his breath.

'The toilets,' Ray says. 'That morning coffee really loosened things up, you know what I'm saying?'

The handler's eyes go distant as an instruction is relayed to him through his earpiece. He nods once, to himself, a firm, militaristic jerk of the head as though his unit has been ordered to move out. Ray guesses that he spends a lot of time imagining what it would be like to shoot someone. 'Fine. Does anyone else need to use the head?'

'I could use a break,' Farrow pipes up, and Ray curses inwardly as he steps forward.

'No one else?' The handler makes a challenge of it and everyone else catches on. It's just Ray and David. The handler jerks his head at them. 'This way,' he says, walking them off to one side of the warehouse and out into another anonymous corridor.

Ray walks straight past the bathroom, as it resembles every other door that they pass on the way: a plain panel of wood painted the same color as the walls and fitted with an electronic keypad instead of a lock. The handler calls him back and punches in a four-digit code that opens the door to a small, sparse and very, very clean bathroom. There is a single stall, and two urinals. Ray steps across the threshold as though stepping on to the surface of the moon: it's the first men's room he's ever seen that doesn't smell of week-old piss. Either their cleaning staff is round the clock on call, or he's about to christen the porcelain with its first ever use.

'Be quick,' the handler says.

'Don't burst a valve.' David grins companionably at the man and is met with a stone-faced response. Ray is already heading for one of the urinals. He'd planned on getting rid of the handler, but the Strategies hire tagging along makes things a great deal more complicated.

Come on, Ray. Think.

He gets to the urinal and hears a burst of static from the doorway, someone talking so loud down the radio channel that the handler's earpiece is audible to both him and David. The handler mutters something into a mic sewn into his cuff and almost leaves before realizing that Ray and David are still at the urinals, both of them half-turned to see what the fuss is.

He scowls. 'Finish up, both of you. You need to go back.'

Ray doesn't even start, let alone finish. David, as he pisses, leans over to whisper conspiratorially, 'Are you the plant?'

Ray's jaw locks tight for a moment, every muscle in his body keying up for fight or flight. 'What?'

'The Carrington plant.'

Ray realizes why the Strategies hire followed him. It's an old urban legend that sometimes filters down to rookie cops: that the brass put a mole in with interviewees and new hires to see which of them really has the right stuff. An idea occurs to him.

'Good job, Farrow.' Ray uses his most serious, most official voice, and David beams at the validation. 'Now phase two begins. Are you ready?'

David nods at him like a puppy, and Ray shoves him, hard. He bangs off the modesty panel that borders the urinal, and the push is enough to spoil his aim and make him piss on the floor between them.

'Hey!' Ray yells, his voice rising. He switches tone again, going for the most aggressive gangbanger accent he can muster. 'The fuck you think you're doing?'

The handler is at his shoulder in an instant, but the spilled piss does its job. He ignores Ray and stares down at the floor, his face twisted in disgust.

'What the fuck is this?'

David, too shocked to do anything other than stand there with his pecker hanging out, holds his palms up in the universal symbol for innocence. 'Look, I can explain—'

Ray interrupts by punching the handler in the gut. It's not a department-sanctioned control maneuver, the sort of thing they teach in the academy as an eight-week course before giving you a semiautomatic handgun to use instead. It's quick and nasty, the kind of punch you learn from long experience of punching people and being punched in turn. It's a tight, fast hook, elbow out, turning through the hips and coming up on to the balls of the feet to really drive the blow deep into the soft mass of the man's midriff. All of the air goes out of him in a great huff of breath, his eyes popping as though they're about to jump straight out of his head, and Ray capitalizes on that moment of surprise. He steps in, grabs the handler by his jacket front and with a grunt of effort that rings off the walls throws him up and over his hip, the kind of clumsy-ass throw that's only useful if the other person is too willing or too winded to stop you doing it. There's no space for him to land neatly, so instead the handler smacks face first into the urinal, bounces off of the wall and Ray gets the hell out of the way as gravity takes him all the way down to the floor.

'Fuck!' Ray can't tell if David says it, or if he says it himself.

Ray hauls the unconscious handler away from the broken urinal and into the middle of the room before turning him over and checking his pulse. He's still breathing, and after a moment Ray finds his heartbeat. His face is a mess, but Ray tries not to think too closely on it. *You were always going to get your hands dirty doing this*, he thinks. It was never going to be bloodless. There comes a time when you get so far, turning back would be just as bloody. Ray shakes his head as he opens the handler's jacket and starts an inventory of his stuff. Baton. Taser. Gun. Radio. Mobile phone. Zip ties, bundled in a loop on the side of his belt. For a guy working internal security, he's tooled up for some serious work.

A glance up at David tells Ray he's not coping too well. He's managed to zip himself up, but is backed up into the corner and looks set to bolt.

'Hey, Strategies? Farrow!' Ray snaps his fingers and the other man jumps. 'You still with me?'

'Y-yeah.'

'I really am a plant,' Ray says. 'Genuinely. Good spot. But here's the thing. I'm not a plant for Carrington. I'm a cop.' For a moment Ray thinks David really is going to run, so he stays very still and lays it out for him. 'You've fallen in with some bad people.' Ray gestures at the gear, all laid out on the floor. 'Look at all this crap. You think he was carrying all this around because he likes the look? These guys are fucking crazy.'

'I don't think . . . I didn't . . .' For a guy that claims he specializes in strategy, David is taking a long time to process it. Time that Ray doesn't have.

'Into the stall, David.'

That puts some life into him. 'No way. If you're a cop, you have to—'

'I don't have to do a damn thing other than offer you one of two options. Sit quietly in that stall with a zip tie round your wrist and what's left of my soup until someone comes to find you, or I Taser your ass and leave you spooning with Chuckles McSquarejaw here.'

David thinks about it. The safe territory of a multiple-choice quiz seems to ground him. 'What kind of soup is it?'

Chapter 27

Cameron can feel trouble coming as though it is rising up through the Earth's crust, a seismic tilt of tectonic plates that begins low in her hips and rises up through her spine, her center of gravity shifting to cope with the new normal. With that sensation is the dread that everyone who's ever been on the West Coast feels when the earth starts to move under them. It's not a fight-or-flight fear, not an instinct. It's the cost of self-awareness: that some dangers are unknowable, and just too large to fight against. It's knowing that everything is about to go to shit, and that there's not a great deal you can do about it.

Ever since Carrington picked her up, Cameron has been well acquainted with that sensation.

She's sitting cross-legged on her bed with the laptop balanced on one knee, much as she has been for the past twelve hours, flicking between the data they've gathered on Nate and the internal cameras that she has been able to connect to, her fingers running on automatic as she switches between the two, eyes taking it all in, waiting for aberrations to leap out at her. Meditating is not the word for what she's doing. *Simmering* would be closer to it.

There's nothing on the Nate side of things. No change in his routine, no sudden shifts in behavior. He was chipped, just like the rest of them, and yet even with all that extra data available, Cameron can't figure out how he escaped. Whatever game he was playing, it was well hidden. He must have been so careful, the whole thing orchestrated in the tiny gaps where his signal stuttered or jumped. She'd queried that, and there were dead spots in their coverage, kinks still in the process of being ironed out. Nate had known all about where they were, and how to exploit them. He was always the smartass, full of schemes to get them both into and out of trouble. Knowing that he'd turned that talent against her sits sour in her belly.

The internal cameras at Carrington are what get Cameron's attention. She can tell from the expressions on people's faces alone that something is happening, and that it isn't good news. People talk out of frame, check their phones and are frustrated by what they find. In the background of one, what looks like a security detail comes into shot, moving with purpose. Cameron catches sight of a few employees putting their things together, and then shutting down their computers. Getting ready to leave, or maybe to evacuate. Something big is going down, big enough that it has filtered down to the rank and file. There will be a lot of confusion right now. A lot of chances to slip away.

The chip in her side – the leash they have her on – is a problem that still needs dealing with, but she's not going to solve it sitting on her ass. Out in the world there are doctors, vets, surgical tools, X-rays. Hell, a roll of Reynolds Wrap and a cell phone signal jammer might do the trick. It's probably how Nate managed to drop off their system until he could get his own dealt with permanently.

She flicks from camera to camera, trying to follow the security team that she saw. Three men, in full tactical gear, with automatic weapons. She catches them once or twice as she works her way through, then loses them completely. Cameron can see the security cameras, but she can't move them. She can't pause or wind back the footage. In her head she's been building a picture of the building's layout, trying to link together camera ID numbers with the floors she sees the same people on. The team are moving on the ground floor, or maybe the first. It's hard to tell.

A flicker of movement on the grid of active cameras catches her eye, and the picture goes dead, a flash of white and then static. *Weird.* She scrolls down the list of cameras and finds a couple more are already dead. They're all ground floor, from what she remembers seeing on them. She scrolls up just in time to see a figure taking aim at another one, and before she can click on the picture it dies, too.

Cameron's pulse picks up. Someone is inside Carrington, and they are taking out cameras as they go. She closes the dead camera feed and tries to find the next one in line, taking a guess at which direction they're headed in.

She guesses right. Just as they appear in frame to take aim, she automatically hits the button to take a screenshot.

'Holy shit,' Cameron says to herself. She only saw his face for a fraction of a second, and has to go back and look at the picture she took before she can convince herself she actually saw his face.

Ray Perada.

He's sporting a weak mustache and a haircut that suggests the barber was blind or in a hurry, but it's definitely Perada. Cameron finds that she is grinning at how impossibly good it feels to know that he's alive, and that he's here for her. That he found her, that he got in at all . . . It means that he's not alone, and there's only one person she can think of that would help him.

Nate has sent him in. He must have tracked him down after Carrington took her, found out that the data had stayed behind. And now Ray is his back-up plan, another pawn pushed across the board to set off whatever he wants the virus to do. Ray probably thinks that he's here to get Cameron out. Cameron knows that he's been set up to fail.

She is off the bed and into a pair of sneakers before she even knows it. She pauses a second, instinctively looking for her wallet, keys, phone, but none of those exist here. Sweatpants, vest, shoes. That's all she's got.

She goes back to the laptop, and back to the grid of cameras, looking for the security team. If she could work out where Ray is from that, then security can too. In her head, Cameron tries to plot the course Ray is following, using the cameras he's taken out as reference points. Without a map of the building it's guesswork, but it's all she has. *Where's he going?* He's coming for her, so she guesses down into the basement levels is his rough destination. The lifts are coded, so he'll be heading for any stairwell he can find that will take him down to where she is being held captive. She wonders if Nate knew where they'd hold her, or if Ray shook it out of someone.

There's just one problem with the stairwell: the three-man security team is headed that way as well. Even if Cameron could reach them, they can just zap her with the pacemaker before she can do anything to back Ray up. Still, he's going to be three on one if she doesn't do anything about it.

Nine Eight Six One. Terri's cloned ID chip. Ray has to go past a lift to get to the stairwell. If Cameron can be quick enough, she just might make it.

She picks up the laptop, tucking it under her arm before she opens the door, and sets off at a sprint. No one has been sent to check on her yet, but she can't stay put and hope he'll be okay. The chip in her arm is still tracking her and the pacemaker they've put in her side can still be used to disable her, but only when someone pushes the button to make that happen. All she has to do is avoid running into anyone sporting a Carrington ID and she'll stay in the game. And she has to stay in the game. Because if Ray came here to rescue her, Cameron is going to have to rescue him first.

Chapter 28

The handclap displacement of a bullet passing through the air inches from Ray's head is an uncomfortably familiar feeling. For a half-second he's back in the alleyway, listening to the calm discussion of two men who are making their businesslike way along it to kill him dead, before he shakes off the feeling and presses himself back into the broad doorway he's using as cover.

Things are a little different this time. Firstly, there aren't two of them. There are three, if the number of voices he counted was correct. Secondly, there are no exits. Every door he has tried has been locked, and he can't risk stepping out into the corridor to kick one in. If he moves too far out of cover, he'll instantly make a target of himself. Thirdly, he isn't nearly as scared as he was before. He feels numb to it, like the factors weighed against his survival are just a calculation, a sum that he has to find a solution to. *Maybe this is what happens when you know you're going to die. Maybe you just forget to be scared.*

A foot squeaks on the corridor floor. Ray takes the Taser he's carrying and pokes it out past the edge of the door frame.

The point man will be in the middle of the corridor, aiming down sight, waiting for any movement. He angles the Taser slightly, a blind guess, and pulls the trigger.

The Taser launches its probes with a sound like someone popping a bubble of chewing gum. The wires spool out and the grip lights up, crackling in Ray's hand as it starts to discharge through the target. A direct hit. The point man opens up, an involuntary squeeze of the trigger on his automatic weapon as bullets fly down the corridor before stitching a line along the ceiling as he falls. There are shouts from his back-up, keen to offer supporting fire but unable to shoot past for fear of hitting him. There's a solid thump as he lands and a grunt as his friends pull him back down on to the stairs. One of them is panicking, and Ray grins as he puts his arm round the door to throw the Taser grip towards them.

'Fire in the hole!' He yells it just as the grip clatters off of the floor and there is a flurry of sudden movement as the men try to get away from what they think is a grenade. Ray is about to duck and run when more fire opens up from the stairwell, a man's voice yelling in defiance over the report of his weapon. *Trust my luck to find the one gung-ho asshole who won't put his head down*, Ray thinks.

This is the only way down. Ray pulls the pistol he took from the handler and checks that the safety is off. It's a compact Ruger LC9, a slim piece chosen to fit under a suit jacket. Ray's not a fan, but he'll do what he can with it. Lethal force is a big step, but he can't avoid taking it. He only knows one route down to Cameron, and that's the stairs. He only has Nate's word on it, but considering how everything seems to revolve around getting to her, it's one word he can trust. Ray closes his eyes and tries to think, to find anything that he can use to get out of this. *At least they don't have grenades of their own.*

There's a crisp ripping noise, like someone peeling off a length of Velcro, before something small is slid along the length of the corridor floor towards where Ray is hiding.

They have grenades of their own.

Ray has no answer to this realization other than to stand frozen in place as he waits for the flash and the blast to hit him. He can't even find his voice to swear one last time.

And then he's falling, stumbling sideways as the wall slides away, turning as something takes hold of his shirt and hauls him backwards so suddenly that the heels of his shoes scream as they are pulled along the floor.

Ray hits the back wall of an elevator just as the flashbang goes off, the ice-white flare of burning magnesium silhouetting a figure against the open door for a moment before his body reacts to shield his eyes from damage. Painted in purple and blue across the back of his eyelids like an inkblot test, the figure is unmistakable.

'Cameron?'

'Shh.' He hears the doors sliding shut. Then, closer, a whisper. 'We're waiting them out,' she says. 'Don't make a sound.'

What Ray thinks is blindness is simply darkness: there are no lights in the elevator. He blinks away the last of the after-images to discover only black, although after a short time his eyes adjust and he can make out the faint impression of light from the corridor creeping in under the door. After a minute of waiting, shadows move along the bottom of the elevator door, stop in front of it. *They're outside*. Ray tenses, sits up with his gun in line, arms braced against his knees, ready to open fire. The instant the door opens, they're going to walk into a full clip.

Cameron's hand settles on his shoulder, urging him to wait. On the other side, he can just make out the sounds of a muffled conversation.

. . . think he has the code for this?

. . . doesn't have a chip. Must've run for it—

A fist bangs against the elevator door, making Ray jump, but the footsteps move on. Cameron's hand stays on his shoulder for a full count of ten before relaxing.

'They're gone,' she says in a normal voice.

'How do you know that?'

'All the elevators are coded,' she says. 'If they weren't, they'd be opening the doors with a crowbar to see if you were in here.' An oblong slice of blue-white light illuminates the elevator as she opens up a laptop. It lights up her face from below as she works on it, as though she's about to tell a scary story. Instead, she nods to herself. 'Looks like they're moving on.'

'If the whole floor is locked down how do we—'

Cameron holds something up to the elevator panel and the lights in the elevator go on. Ray doesn't cover his eyes fast enough, and the after-effects of the flashbang make the experience painful to the point that he feels close to vomiting.

'Sorry,' Cameron says. 'I should have told you I was putting the lights on.' As she pulls him to his feet, he can't suppress a burp of gas, the sour acid stench of it rising in his throat. Cameron steps neatly to the side, supporting him with one hand holding the back of his shirt. Ray shakes his head.

'Some rescue mission this turned out to be,' he says.

Cameron gives him a smile and a thumbs up. 'Better than none.' She lets him go and turns to punch in a code on the elevator keypad. After a brief pause, the elevator starts to descend. After all the evasion he's put up with from Nate, seeing her punch in that code like she's been here forever makes his hackles rise.

'They give you a key to the front door, too?'

Cameron has the good grace to look uncomfortable. 'Not exactly,' she says. 'I got some help with the elevators.'

'Wait, there's people on our side in here?'

'Not really,' Cameron says. 'She's a fan.'

'Well, whatever you got, I hope it's enough to get us past these guards,' Ray says. 'Your brother said light security, not three-man roving teams with automatic weapons and flashbangs.'

Cameron doesn't look at him. 'I hope so, too.'

Chapter 29

Cameron is wary of Ray on the way down to the basement. It's not the gun he's holding. It's the way he's watching her. Like a lion tamer edging round the bars of a cage, trying to get to the door. She can feel his suspicion like a wall between them. When she first saw his face pop up on the laptop, she had wanted to hug him. The urge to do it had withered the moment she punched that code in and saw his expression shift. He thinks that she's betraying him, that he's being toyed with. She knows that feeling all too well: to come so far, only to find the person you were looking for is long gone.

Ray looks away. 'So I guess your brother fucked us both over.'

The relief feels like a wave cresting. 'Yeah. When did he find you?'

'He pulled me from the car wreck,' Ray says. 'After you were gone.'

'I thought they killed you.' Cameron doesn't apologize. She hadn't expected to live, either, once that fight was done.

Ray swallows, his throat working as though he's choking down the worst-tasting mouthful of his life. 'I saw you fall,' he says. 'I was certain . . . I knew for sure you were dead. I knew it. And then your brother told me that you were alive, and that he had a way to reach you . . .'

'It smelled like bullshit.'

He nods. 'Reeked of it. But I had to come. I saw you fall.' He doesn't need to say what that looked like. Cameron can see it in his face. 'I thought maybe if I found you . . .' He trails off, embarrassed.

Coming in after her was the wrong call. He knows it, probably suspected it from the get-go, but he'd still gone ahead and made it. That was worth a lot to Cameron. 'Thank you, Ray. It's good to see a friend again.'

Ray holds his hands out as though trying to grab hold of something, trying to find its shape. The truth, perhaps. Or, from his perspective, a betrayal. 'You know, I thought when I found you – if I found you, you'd be . . .'

'Starved? Tortured?'

'In a body cast, at least.' Ray gestures towards her. 'You look like you've stepped off the cover of a workout plan for people who hate carbs.'

'They didn't torture me,' Cameron says. It feels like she's pulling the words up out of a well, they take such a long time coming. 'They . . . put a chip in my arm. Told me they wanted me to find Nate for them.'

The elevator arriving is a relief, the jolt of tension in the cable offsetting the silence that follows. As the doors slide open, Ray unbuttons one shirt cuff and pulls up his sleeve. High on his arm, running from the elbow up along his bicep, is a burn pattern that looks like someone once pressed a red-hot circuit board to his arm. The shape of it, the thin spiral of an aerial running down towards a thicker central core, looks familiar to Cameron's eye.

'You had a chip in you?'

'A tracer,' Ray says. 'They scammed me into it through my medical insurance. Didn't know about it until your brother told me. Probably how they tracked us.' He doesn't apologize, either. They're beyond that now. 'But I burned it out. We can burn it out of you, too.'

The scarring is an electrical burn. Nate must have hooked him up to a defibrillator or something and burned the tracer out of him. At the very worst, he's lost a little sensation in his hand, maybe even some fine motor control. A small price to pay for freedom. Cameron suspects that in her case it's impossible. Even if they could find enough power to burn all the chips they've implanted, she has pins and screws embedded in the bones the entire length of her bad arm. Put enough current through it and she might lose the whole limb.

'I don't think that will work for me,' she says. She starts out of the lift and into the corridor beyond. Down in the lowest basement level, the neutral lighting and blank walls have given way to painted mesh and open pipework. There's no aircon down here, and there are patches of damp where water has pooled on the bare cement. 'What's your plan to get out of here?'

Ray starts. 'Oh,' he says, patting at his pockets as though searching for his keys. Whatever he's looking for, he finds it in his left pants pocket. 'Here.' He offers her a lump of plastic and metal, something that was once part of a thermos flask lid. In the center of it, there's a tiny memory card. She knows immediately it must be the one from her phone. The last time

Cameron saw her phone, she was throwing it at Ray's head in the hope that he would be able to do something with it. She is shaking as she takes it out and holds it carefully between forefinger and thumb, wary of breaking it with the pressure of her grip. 'It's not information. It's a—'

'A virus,' Cameron says. 'Military-grade software designed to target Carrington's server. They keep it offline, disconnected from the Internet. That's why Nate set me up in the first place. He wanted Carrington to find it on me.'

'Nate came up with a plan,' Ray says. 'Something about a diversion to keep security occupied, and that he would pick us up as soon as we cleared the building.'

'Motherfucker!' Cameron almost throws the memory card, but instead turns and kicks out at the wall, her heel catching a section of pipework hard enough that the welded joint holding it in place breaks and the whole thing springs loose from its bindings with a squeal of metal on metal.

Ray is looking at the pipe with a look of horror. 'What the hell, Cameron?'

She can't think of anything she can say that will put him at ease. All she has is the truth. 'My brother betrayed me,' she says. 'He betrayed us.'

That seems to bring him back to himself. 'Yeah. I can believe that,' he says. 'Your brother was very keen to keep me in the dark about who he's working for and why he needs you. The only thing I learned for certain is that you are really, really important to him.'

Cameron nods slowly, taking that in. He'd crashed the car to please Carrington, and now he was playing games to please someone else. *Why are you dragging me into this, Nate?* Had he always just hated her, or something? She tries to speak, but her throat feels suddenly tight and she has to cough to find her voice. 'When he realized I'd left it with you,' she says. 'He didn't plan to send you as a back-up. This isn't a rescue. He's thrown you to the lions, too.'

'Wolves.'

Cameron comes to a dead stop. 'You want me to kick you again, Ray?'

'No, ma'am.'

'He wanted this virus planted,' Cameron says. 'And that's all. You and I were never meant to walk out of here.'

She starts walking again. After ten more paces, Ray plucks up the courage to speak. 'Where are we going?'

'Regrouping,' Cameron says. 'There should be a place for us . . .' She turns a corner and sees a shabby-looking door in one wall breaking the flow of pipework. 'Right there.'

'What is it?' Ray follows her towards the door. 'Looks like storage space.'

'Kind of.' Cameron tries the door. It's locked, but it also trembles in its frame when she rattles the handle. Deep in the heart of their own building, why pay money for a secure door? 'Back it up a sec.' She lifts her right foot and kicks the door once, smartly, just below the handle. Something metal pings off into the room and the door pops open.

Inside, the room is bigger than Cameron expected. The majority of the wall space is taken up by tall panels filled with lights and gauges, and most important of all: switches. All of the building's systems are computer controlled, but Cameron knows what people are like. You go into any office, big or small, and even if they're rocking the most cutting-edge accounting and cost efficiency software, they'll still have a folder full of receipts tucked at the back of a cupboard just in case the auditor comes knocking. You don't pull all the switches out of your walls just because you can turn the lights on from your phone.

There's a table to one side, and when Cameron puts her laptop down it raises enough dust to make Ray start coughing. 'You think this counts as archeology?' he asks, slapping himself on the chest to clear it.

'Close enough.' Cameron finds the power for the building's elevators and turns them all to off, flicking the switches up as she counts them off in her head. The last is marked *EXECUTIVE SUITE*, and she leaves that one alone.

'So what's your plan for getting us out of here?'

'Try to shut the building down,' she says. 'Lights, elevators, computers, everything. Once I get rid of all that, they'll be as blind as we are.'

'So we'll all be fumbling in the dark.'

'Country of the blind,' Cameron says. 'It's not a great plan, but it'll buy us some time.' She stands back from the board and folds her arms. 'What do you think, Ray? Turn them all off, or hit the master switch?'

Ray doesn't get a chance to answer. There's a burst of radio static from the corridor, and Cameron feels her blood freeze.

'Fuck,' Ray says, looking towards the door. He's holding his gun in both hands now, ready to bring it up into line. 'You think they know we're here?'

Cameron thinks of the chip in her arm. 'Yeah. Wherever I go, they'll know.'

Ray nods once, a crisp, nervous motion. 'Okay,' he says. 'Okay. So we have a three-man team coming, yeah?'

'Most likely.'

Ray nods at the panel. 'So we pull out a few pipes, fill this place with steam, kill the lights. Make a fight of it. We can still get out of here.'

It feels tough to swallow, to find her voice. 'There's something else, Ray.'

'What?'

'They put another implant in me. A modified pacemaker. They can give me a shock with it. I brought us down here to get as much cement between me and a kill signal as I could.'

'A shock. Like a smack on the wrist?'

'A bad one,' Cameron says. 'You'd have to wheel me out of here on a gurney.'

Ray's face falls, all of the fight dropping right out of him. 'Shit,' he says. Out in the corridor, there's a faint ringing sound as something metal is kicked aside, clattering along the floor ahead of the security team that has come down several flights of stairs to reach them. They're out of options, and out of time.

The memory card in Cameron's pocket feels like a lead weight. Her fingers have already found it, got hold of it before she could even think that far ahead.

'Hey, Perada,' she says, and the sound of his last name brings his head up like he's coming to attention. Cameron holds up the card to show him. 'We're not beat yet.'

Chapter 30

Cameron heads out of the control room with Ray in her wake. She isn't sure where they're going, but away from a dead end feels like the right call to make. She needs to find somewhere with a lot of cover to hide behind. She just has to hope that Nate's virus can infect the system before they get close enough to activate the implant and drop her.

The air cools perceptibly, and Cameron notices the density of pipes and vents increasing towards their destination. It puts her in mind of every spaceship she's seen in movies or on TV. Nothing is hidden: every pipe and lever, every button and switch is immediate and accessible.

There's a plastic-sheet curtain across a doorway up ahead, thick opaque strips glowing nebulous from the harsh lighting beyond it. Cameron pushes through, and shudders as the temperature beyond drops so much it's like walking into a wall. Her breath plumes in the air in front of her as she surveys the emptiness beyond.

No cover. The room is circular, about forty paces across, the floor tilted on a few degrees of slope so that anything spilled runs down into the drain in the center. It is almost completely empty, save for a tall metal tank marked *DANGER: CRYOGENIC FLUID*. It's mounted on four metal legs that lift it up past waist height and give access to the five connecting heads that are fused into its base.

Cameron looks at the tank, turns and looks back at the plastic sheet doorway they've come through, trying to judge the angles between them. 'Ray,' she says.

'You got a plan?'

'You won't like it.'

'Didn't get where I am today by following plans I liked the sound of.'

She waves her hand towards the far wall. 'See if you can find any hose or connectors for this tank. Failing that, something big and heavy.'

'Got you,' Ray says. 'What are you going to do?'

Cameron holds up the memory card. 'I'm gonna give Nate his wish.'

'Is that wise?'

She shrugs. 'Didn't get where I am today by—'

'Yeah, yeah,' Ray waves it away as he heads off across the room.

Cameron opens up her laptop and breathes a sigh of relief to see that it's still connected to the network. She doesn't have access to the cameras, the signal is so weak, but it's unlikely to matter. Whatever Nate's backers have cooked up is probably sophisticated enough to make use of any signal it can get. She comes close to putting the memory card in, and pauses.

For a brief, beautiful moment, Cameron imagines a different world, one where she cracks the memory card in two and goes to work for Miller and his friends. With Carrington's tracking system and their manpower at her back, hunting down Nate would be simple. And as a special thank-you for all that he has done for her, she would get to pull his spinal cord out through his asshole.

And everyone else would lose. Carrington would develop their surveillance net until it covered the state, the country, the world; and Miller would have it all at his fingertips. He'd have Cameron and whoever else they could recruit acting as enforcers, assassins. The corporate will made manifest. Manipulation, intimidation, and fear would be their choice of tools, and they would circle the world with a constant, controlling gaze. A hostile takeover, except Carrington wouldn't be gaining control of another company. They'd be in a position to run the country.

She puts the memory card into the laptop, and it immediately goes to work. The screen stutters, static flickering across it, and Cameron can almost feel the suite of intrusion tools unfold and launch themselves at Carrington's network, slamming into the system's internal security like a stag locking horns at the rut, pressing to seek out the vulnerabilities that will give it a route inside.

The lights overhead flicker, and Cameron's laptop screen goes dark. She can still hear it working, but as far as she is concerned it's a dead weight. She closes it and runs over to the wall, putting it up out of the way, as high as she can reach.

'Did it work?' Ray asks.

She lifts her left arm and presses gently at the lump under the skin on her side, down near the floating ribs, as though she could somehow tell by touching it that the implant has been disabled. 'I guess we'll find out. Did you find any hose?'

She turns to find Ray holding the biggest wrench she's ever seen.

'Couldn't see any,' he says. 'I got this, though.'

Cameron takes the wrench, and hefts it two-handed. It's even heavier than she thought. 'That'll do nicely.'

'What now?'

'We need this,' Cameron points at the liquid nitrogen tank, 'pointing there.' She pivots, pointing past Ray's shoulder to the door they came through. He frowns and looks at the base of the tank.

'I don't see any wheels on that thing.'

'No,' Cameron says. 'I'm going to have to push it over.'

'You mean we,' Ray says. 'There's no way you can—'

'I need you to buy us some time,' Cameron says. 'If they've lost their tracking signal, they'll be in a hurry. I need them to not be in a hurry.'

Ray shakes his head. 'This isn't going to work.'

'Ray, even if they can't zap me, there are still three of them. There's no cover here. Please.'

'Look,' Ray says, 'I'll go take a look. Maybe if this virus has worked, they'll be pulling back.' He goes out through the plastic curtain and then with a whoop of surprise comes barreling back through. There's a shouted command – stop, halt, freeze, a monosyllabic bark that could be any or all three at the same time – and the report of a gunshot. Ray pulls the pistol he is armed with and points it out through the plastic curtain to fire blind along the corridor towards wherever the challenge came from. It might have bought them a minute, maybe a little less.

Cameron puts the wrench down and stands very, very still,

reaching down inside herself to try and find a spot of absolute calm, a point she can use to focus. She's never trained for this. Never prepared. Her recovery has been limited to the weights they brought her, and a handful of physiotherapy exercises. She's never been tested like this, not even in the ring, and has never felt less ready for it.

From somewhere above, the dull crump of an explosion interrupts her train of thought. The concussion reverberates down through the building, and makes concrete dust fall in a fine shower from the ceiling.

Cameron realizes that the virus has found its way in, and has shut down the building's security systems. Every lock opened, every door breached, no automatic defenses. Perfect conditions for an assault team to carry out an insertion and take everything that isn't nailed down. With the computer system compromised, whatever arm of the military Nate works for will be facing only the lightest resistance. It's just a matter of time before they get their hands on the server, and on Miller.

She takes a deep breath and sizes up the tank again. *You can do this*, she thinks. Up on those stilts, the tank has to be top-heavy. They don't look like they were built to handle anything but weight coming straight down on them, either. All she needs to do is get high enough, and push. Cameron can feel the scar running down her arm like it's dragging at her every second she waits, sapping her strength.

She takes a run up, past the tank and up the wall, one high step and a jump up and round, turning back the way she came, arms reaching up to catch the top edge of the tank. She catches a bolt with her left hand, her right not so lucky but still holding on to the metal collar as the rest of her body touches the metal side of the tank. Even insulated, the tank is very cold to the touch, and Cameron can feels the cold burning from her forearms all the way down to her thighs.

Cameron hears a pistol shot, Ray trading her a bullet for a few more seconds, and she kicks off the tank with one foot, reaching for the wall behind her. Her heel finds it with a jolt, striking against steel with a deep ringing sound, and she turns, putting her back to the tank and her feet flat against the wall, sitting on nothing. Her knees have a ninety-degree bend in them, and she bears down into the brace, feeling the tension build in her thigh muscles.

She takes a final glance back to check she's got the angle right, but can't see anything past the bulk of the tank. Even if she is in the wrong place, there's no time to do anything about it. *Here goes nothing.* She rolls her shoulders once, feels her shoulder blades grind against the cold metal of the tank. She puts her chin down and pushes as hard as she can.

Cameron pushes so hard it's beyond any feeling she has ever experienced. No leg press, no deadlift, no workout has ever been this hard on her. Her jaw is clenched so tight, it feels as though her back teeth are going to force themselves up into her skull. The tendons in her neck are painfully tight, as though they are about to pull free of her collarbone. Her back pops with the strain, an uncomfortable shift of vertebrae as they realign themselves and settle against the unnaturally flat surface of the tank. Her ankles feel as though they're being ground to a paste, and her thigh muscles, for all the work she ever put into them, shiver with the effort of trying to push the tank over.

You can do this. She says it even though she knows she can't, that all that weight is just too much for her to move. *If you don't, Nate wins.* Cameron roars with the effort and leans into the push again, driving deep into it.

There is a crack, a thunderous release of energy, and Cameron half suspects that it is the sound of her thigh muscles tearing, the fibers detaching themselves to roll up the length of her upper leg like a roller blind snapping open. Instead, the legs on the far side of the tank have popped their welds, and the whole thing starts to shift. Cameron scrambles for purchase as her feet come away from the wall, but there is none and she puts her palms flat on the side of the tank and pushes off in the hope she'll fall clear.

Timber.

Chapter 31

The tank lands with a deep, concussive ringing sound that fills the room and kills all other noise. Cameron can feel it shudder through her even as she lands hard, trying to roll through it like she's just walked into the worst throw in history. The skin on her back feels like it's on fire, and her legs are shaking with every step, but she makes it to the wrench before Ray can get over to her.

'You okay?' He yells it, and yet to Cameron it sounds like he's shouting through an inch of bulletproof glass. She nods, not because it's true but because it gets him off her case, and drags the wrench back to the fallen liquid nitrogen tank. The angle it's landed at isn't perfect, but it's good enough: the row of valves are pointing roughly towards the plastic hanging over the door, and there's going to be a lot of spray when Cameron pops it. She puts the head of the wrench just behind where the valve is attached, a seam of gold against silver.

'Ray!' He's standing in the line of fire, holding his pistol like he's been trained to: barrel down, finger off the trigger. There's a team coming down the corridor and they're not shy about dropping automatic fire, and yet here he is trying not to escalate the situation by keeping his weapon down. Trapped, surrounded, about to get shot full of holes: his first instinct is hope. Cameron loves him for it. If she had any doubts about him before, she's got none now. 'Get out of the fucking way!'

Cameron visualizes the breach team setting up outside, the whisper of cloth on cloth as they communicate through gestures, getting ready to move in. She gets up on the balls of her feet, bounces some life back into her legs. She's going to have to be quick once this valve breaks. *If it breaks at all.*

A noise cuts through the buzz of the tank falling, something sharp and metallic, like a metal clip snapping shut. They're readying a grenade. A flashbang, like the team upstairs used on Ray. They're working off the same playbook, their tactics a to-do list that they tick off one by one. Cameron counts in her head, just like he will be doing.

Three. She looks down at the valve and tries to picture the pressure it must be under. *Hit it right, it'll break.*

Two. She takes a step back, clearing her swing as she lifts the wrench up over her head and brings it down two-handed, an executioner's axe aimed not at the neck it's going to cut through, but the block on the other side.

One. The valve cracks clean across the seam, and as Cameron turns to run it explodes with a sound like a cannon firing. A wall of cold washes up from the breach, the water in the air hissing as it turns to mist. Spray from the tank catches Cameron's left arm and leg as she sprints for the back of the room, the fluid sticking her clothes to her like water, burning so cold that she stumbles and screams, pulling at her sweatpants in a panic as it bites into her skin.

Ray grabs her, grunts as he half-carries, half-drags her and

Cameron wants to kill him because it's still burning her and she needs to get free of the clothing. It's only after he puts her down that she realizes the floor is awash with liquid nitrogen, and he had saved her from being covered in it. He's pulled her all the way back into one of the access corridors: a draft of warm air from the freight elevator is holding back the cold, the mist it makes as it hits the cold air a curtain that shifts like liquid. She tries to stop herself from screaming, the burning already beginning to fade, and realizes that she isn't screaming at all. The sound is coming from someone else.

It takes a minute for the mist to clear enough that Cameron feels safe walking into it. The screaming dies away long before she takes her first, hesitant step back into the room, and she and Ray make their way across the cambered floor in silence. The air is freezing cold – breathing it is an effort – and although the floor is dry again, the drain in the center of the floor has given way, collapsing under its own weight, and a white cloud of water vapor is pouring out of it, filling the room past knee height and slowing their steps. The plastic sheet curtain is almost entirely gone, frozen solid and shattered by the force of the blast hitting it, and only shards of it remain hanging in the frame. The walls have survived undamaged save for a grey-white discoloration where the liquid nitrogen caught them directly. Cameron doesn't touch it as she passes, but suspects the concrete would crumble beneath her fingertips.

Out in the corridor, there is carnage. Two of the three men are down: one is curled tight against the wall in a fetal ball, clutching his right arm and keening in pain. The other is flat on his back, with the third man trying to perform chest compressions on him. Cameron can see that it's a lost cause.

Most of the dead man's face and neck are gone, and his chest has collapsed inward on one side. He must have stuck half his upper body round the door frame to get a good swing on the flashbang, and caught the liquid nitrogen full-on.

Cameron reaches out to put a hand on the man's shoulder, and stops when she sees that he still has his gun slung across his chest. 'Ray?'

Ray nods as he passes her, lifting his gun a fraction higher as he comes, not quite pointing at the last man standing but close enough that he can beat any attempt at a draw. He cocks the gun, the sharp, distinct click enough to gain the man's full attention. He sits straight up off the last compression and doesn't move.

'Hands,' Ray says, no room for argument in the way he says it. The man complies immediately, arms coming up on each side, palms forward, fingers spread. 'Cameron, take his gun and sidearm. The same for the others.'

Cameron does as Ray asks, unclipping the guns from where they hang across each man's chest, the pistols from their hip holsters. The guns from the dead man have got an odd look to them, like they've been splattered with whitewash, and she doesn't trust either of them not to fall apart or misfire. She slides them back into the room, where they vanish into the fog.

While she does it, Ray talks the uninjured man through removing his tactical vest and having his wrists cuffed. Cameron keeps an eye on them, but realizes there'll be no trouble. All he can do is stare at the fallen point man, the ruin that the liquid nitrogen has made of him. Cameron doesn't share the same urge. She's trying not to look at the dead body,

255

trying not to close the circle of cause and effect that started with her swinging a wrench at a valve and ended with a man being killed in the worst way she can think of. Ice crunches underfoot, and when she looks the sole of her shoe is red and pink. They're walking around in what once was his face.

'Oh fuck me,' Cameron says. 'Fuck this bullshit.'

'Cameron,' Ray says, a warning in his voice.

It's too late. Her reaction sets the other guy off. He struggles against his cuffs, tries to get to his feet. 'Fuck you! You killed him.' He looks from Ray to Cameron, his face wild with fear and hatred. 'He had a family. A family.'

Cameron can't find words, can't find the strength to reply. It's Ray that answers.

'Hey! We all got family.' He nods his head towards the guns that Cameron has taken. 'You sure as shit weren't thinking about what my mom would say when you were putting rounds past my ear.' He steps closer, his voice falling. 'You knew the risks when you took the job. You knew the risks coming down here.'

He shakes his head, not looking at Ray. 'I never—'

Ray doesn't give him the space. 'Hey.' He pushes out, bumps the other man's chest, makes him look up. 'Someone told you this would be easy? This would be a walk in the park? They lied to you.' He points at the corpse. 'Did he call the shots?'

The man sniffs, red-eyed, and nods.

'Yeah,' Ray says. 'He walked his team blind into an ambush. You heard the fucking tank go over, right?'

'We heard it.'

'You know what it was?'

'No, sir.'

'Then you should've backed off.' Ray shakes his head. 'You made the wrong call. Get your man on his feet, and get the fuck out of here.'

Cameron watches as the man scrambles to comply, waiting for Ray to chew her out, too. When he does turn, his face is drawn, ashen, like he hasn't slept in a week. All of the cold, parade-ground fury has drained out of him, and she realizes it wasn't for the other man's benefit that he turned it on. He did it because it put him in control, and that control was what kept him from falling apart. He looks down at the dead man, shakes his head. 'This isn't your fault, Cameron.'

Cameron tries to take that in, but can't. All she can hear is her own heartbeat, heavy in her chest, the sound climbing up through her neck and into her head until it is roaring, smothering every other sensation. The point man is dead, and she killed him. It is her fault, no matter what Ray says. She let Nate get into her head. She never once stopped to think that he was playing her. Had always been playing her.

'FUCK!' Cameron's yell is like an explosion. She turns on the ball of her foot and slams both fists into the wall behind her. She doesn't notice the damage, doesn't care what it does to her hands. She staggers back until she hits the opposite wall, bouncing off the pipework, a ragged edge catching one of the cold burns and sending a deep spike of pain through her. As suddenly as it came, all of the rage just drains out of her, like a valve has opened somewhere and it all floods out, leaving her completely empty. 'Look what you've done to me.' She knows that Nate can't hear her. That even if he could, he wouldn't listen. That is the worst of it. He never cared at all.

'Cam.' Ray isn't holding his gun anymore. He's there at her elbow, not touching her at all but *there*, warm and human and alive. He speaks with a calm, steady voice, not talking her down but talking *to* her. 'You can't blame yourself for this,' he says. 'He made a choice. Just like the guy in the garage did.'

'I didn't have to kill him, Ray. It's not the same.'

Ray looks as though he's about to disagree, then thinks better of it. Cameron wonders how many cops he's talked to after a bust went wrong and someone died. She wonders who talked to him, the first time. 'Maybe,' he says. 'And I ain't gonna lie to you. You won't ever stop thinking that.'

Cameron looks down at the dead point man. She can't imagine what it would have been like for him. *Was it over in an instant? Or did he have to stare up at the ceiling as his body fell apart?* Something shifts inside of her at the sight of the corpse, at the realization that whatever happened, there's no one left in there to think about it. She clenches both hands into fists, tight enough that it feels as though they'll start bleeding.

'We're getting out of this,' she says. 'We're getting out of this and I am going to find my brother. And when I find him, I'm going to kick his ass clean off the planet.'

Chapter 32

Ray goes through the pile of gear he stripped from the men seeing what he can find, what he thinks he will need. All three of them were carrying way too much for the job they'd been given, and even once the stuff that's been damaged by the liquid nitrogen has been put aside, it still looks like he's been handed the keys to an armory.

He feels oddly conspicuous shouldering his way into a bulletproof vest in his shirt and suit pants. There's a ritual to gearing up. The all-black outfit, the heavy boots and the helmet are part of it. The rest is that the whole team changes together, the conversation giving way to operational silence. It's how you put your conscience to one side and become part of the thin blue line. Without it, Ray feels exposed, unready; the bulletproof vest sits loose on his chest and no amount of fiddling with the straps is going to fix it.

They have automatic weapons but Ray sticks with his pistol. He's got more than enough ammunition for it and he's not planning on ventilating anyone as a first choice. He takes their flashbangs, though. Every. Single. One. The radios are silent: he's guessing the panic has caused security to switch channels at some point, and not even Cameron's knowledge of the facility can come up with the code to find it.

A pull at his side makes Ray look up to find Cameron taking the stack of cable ties off of him and clipping them to a loop of cord she's using as a makeshift bandolier. She's holding an extendable baton in her other hand, a collapsible steel tube with lead shot weighting the tip. She swings it experimentally, flicking the tube open and holding it vertical to let it fall shut, and Ray knows from experience what she's finding out from doing it – the lead shot puts the balance point further up the baton's length than you'd think. It's not the sort of thing you twirl around and look fancy doing it: it's built for short, brutal arcs, each one capable of breaking a bone.

Cameron throws it upwards, giving it a flick so it tumbles in the air, and catches it without looking.

'Is that all you're taking with you?' Ray asks.

'I've had enough of guns,' Cameron says.

'Easy to say,' Ray says, 'but they might not be done with you.'

Cameron nods. 'I'm not running into the crossfire,' she says. 'There's only one fight I'm looking for.'

Ray doesn't doubt it. He saw the way she climbed that tank, put everything she had into a plan that he wouldn't have thought possible. She put it over like she was knocking a glass of milk off the table, and walked off a handful of burns like they were nothing. If anything, he's not convinced she even needs the baton. Part of him doesn't want to know what she's going to do, but he still has to ask. Even without his badge, he still has a duty.

'What are we going to do, Cameron?'

She looks up at the ceiling. Through the ceiling. 'You heard that explosion, right?'

'Yeah.' Ray remembers the tremor, a God-hand punch to one side of the building. 'A big-ass breaching charge, or something like it.'

'The virus my brother gave us shut down the security system. I think they coordinated a physical attack with you coming in here.'

'So we've got a bunch of CIA dudes running around upstairs?'

'I thought military. Special Forces, maybe.'

'They're here to pull out everything Nate couldn't give them himself,' Ray says, and Cameron nods.

'High-value targets,' she says. 'They want physical access to the server and the staff. Team leaders, researchers, anyone with expertise that can help them replicate Carrington's work.'

'They've got some balls coming to grab them here,' Ray says. 'US citizens, US soil? That's free tickets to life in prison for everyone if word gets out.'

'To them, it's worth the risk.' Cameron flicks the baton open with a snap. 'If they get their hands on this tracking system that Carrington have built, they'll be able to roll it out nationwide. Call it an immunization drive, make up a scare that means everybody gets a chip. Total surveillance. Total control. We have to stop them.'

Ray feels like spitting. His arm feels hot with the memory of what was burned out of him. He knows Cameron has more than one in her, chips bound to the pins running all the way down her scarred arm. They've buried it in her bones, and that means she likely won't ever be rid of it. It's in so deep no amount of burning or cutting will be able to dig it out. Somehow, she's dealing with it better than he did with his. 'Your brother put all this together, yeah?'

She nods. 'Yeah, he did.'

'That is some fucked-up kind of family you have.'

'Tell me about it.'

Ray looks down at the gun he's holding, the vest hanging awkwardly off of him. He looks back up at Cameron. He knows why she has to do this. If she doesn't, the chip in her arm is a leash that will follow her the rest of her life. Destroying the thing that can access it is the only way she can be free. But her baton and his pistol aren't enough to take down Carrington, let alone Carrington and a government assault team. 'How are we gonna do this? You think I'm going to arrest them all?'

Cameron shrugs. 'You're a cop,' she says. 'Call nine-one-one, get some back-up.'

Ray shakes his head. 'Cops are on board,' he says. 'Carrington bought a lot of loyalty, and they'll sure as shit cave if any of the agencies lean on them.' He laughs at how stupid it is. 'I couldn't even get a squad car out to help your friends.'

'Shit.' She paces back and forth across the corridor in front of Ray, tapping her leg with the baton. 'We're gonna have to try and stop them ourselves.'

'I was just thinking that,' Ray says. 'I mean, we're stuck in the basement, I've got a pistol, you've got a stick, and there's a good chance one or both of us is going to get shot. Not getting the fuck out of here is the obvious choice.'

She ignores the sarcasm. 'The server room is on the ground floor. We need to destroy it, or any part of it they try to take out of the building.'

'Or get shot,' Ray says, in spite of himself. 'Anything else on that list?'

'Head of the snake,' she says. 'Top floor, executive suite. They want Miller.' Ray sees something shift in Cameron's expression, like for a moment the mask of calm has fallen away and he can see how much cold rage is driving her.

Miller. *Silicon Valley.* Ray wants to ask how she plans on keeping Miller out of their hands, but doesn't want to hear the answer. Instead, he steps carefully round it. 'How are we going to get up there?'

'There's an executive lift.' Cameron worries at her lip. 'The keycode I have might not work for it.'

'Are there stairs?'

She thinks about that for a second. 'That's like ten flights, Ray.'

'We're both gonna catch a bullet, you're worried about some cardio?'

'Worried I'll be too busy puking my guts up.'

'Doubling over makes you a smaller target.' Ray grins at her. 'See? I'm helping you out.'

Cameron doesn't look encouraged. 'We'll hit the server room, see where that gets us.' Ray takes a breath and she keeps talking. 'Aside from a trip out of here on a gurney.'

'Now you're talking,' Ray says. 'We can take the elevator up to the server, though, right?'

'Might not be the best idea to go up that way.' Cameron points in the opposite direction to the way they came.

'Maintenance stairwell. It runs up one corner of the building. Right to the roof.'

Ray gestures towards the pile of gear they'll be leaving behind. 'You sure you don't want a gun?'

Cameron crouches by the pile, and for a moment Ray thinks she's going to take one. Instead, she picks up two of the radios. 'I'll try and find an emergency band,' she says. 'If there's a news channel eavesdropping, it might force the cops to show their face.' She holds out one of the radios to him. 'If we get split up, I'm on channel two.'

Ray takes the radio. 'If this goes south on us . . .'

'Then we get the fuck out of here.' Cameron looks straight at him, and he knows she doesn't mean it. She's not leaving until this is done. Even trying to joke about it, Ray can feel the cold forming in the pit of his stomach. *You could die here, and no one would ever know the truth of it*. He swallows that thought down and buries it deep. That's the job. You wear a shield, you make the choice to accept the risks it brings with it. You could get shot by a perp on your first shift. *Hell, you could get hit by a fucking bus directing traffic*. Ray had always known it was part of the job, what you accepted if you wanted to make the world a better place.

He offers Cameron his hand. 'I'd say good luck, but . . .'

'Break a leg?' she offers, taking his hand.

Ray smiles at that. 'We're gonna break all their fucking legs.'

Chapter 33

Cameron takes the stairs two at a time, her steps as light as she can make them. Ray falls behind on the first flight, weighed down by the vest, and it is a relief to leave him behind. The look on his face after she broke the tank was something like awe, as though he couldn't believe she was still standing.

Cameron can barely believe it herself. The burn from the liquid nitrogen on her back is wet, like a scald, and she can feel the vest she is wearing sticking to it, the rest moving freely about that fixed point. The one on her leg is throbbing with every step, and she suspects that it's the tight fit of her sweat-pants that is keeping her thigh in one piece. The effort of springing up the stairs is painful: she can feel it spiking in her calves, the hammer-blow beat of her heart, but there's no way left but forward. She's been forced right into a corner and all she can do is put her head down and charge, hope there's a way out on the far side of it.

The ascent is terrifying. There's no real telling what she'll find on each landing before she hits the turn. Looking up the height of the railings might let her spot someone looking down, but that would let them see her too. Setting up an ambush would be as simple as aiming down the stairs. She's light on her feet, but nobody alive is light enough to dodge a bullet.

The first person she sees is up on the ground floor. He's not dressed for an assault; he's dressed for bomb disposal. Full body armor with an armor-plated apron that hangs down to his knees, a high-angled neck cuff that obscures half his face, and enough helmet that she can barely see the man inside the suit; he's on his way out to the stairwell through an access door from the main corridor. Incongruous against the suit, he has a submachine gun slung across his chest, and as his head comes round Cameron grits her teeth and accelerates, flinging herself up the last few steps with a grunt before he can get his hands to it.

When he sees her he realizes she's too close, and tries to backpedal the way he came. Cameron flings her hand out and gets a grip on his right arm, the padding soft under her fingers, and yanks him forward into the stairwell. The door swings shut with a bang as he staggers, taking two long steps to recover, pulling his arm from her grip and fumbling for the sidearm at his hip. Cameron is already there, though, stepping in close to keep him from turning the barrel on her, flicking the baton open in her left hand. As he twists round, she takes his gun arm by the wrist, jerks it straight, and swings the baton as hard as she can into the gap in his armor over his elbow. With the leverage on his wrist and the swing combined, there's enough force in the blow that something snaps in his forearm. He makes a noise like he's just burned his hand, drawing in a huge, shocked gasp of air, and as he does Cameron throws him, the body armor just giving him more momentum as he goes over her hip, the impact with the ground knocking all that air back out of him before he can cry out for help.

He's not Carrington. Cameron takes the gun and does a quick check for identification. No rank, no numbers, no insignia. Through the visor, she can make out the expression on his face as he looks at her. Recognition. *He knows who I am*.

'Who are you?' she asks. He doesn't answer. Instead, he makes a move with his good hand for the push-button mic clipped to his chest armor. He isn't fast, not with the pain of a broken arm to deal with, and Cameron gets there first, pulling it free and tossing it down the stairwell. 'Special forces? CIA?' It gets no reaction.

She searches him as best she can for weapons and finds nothing more than the submachine gun and the pistol. Once they are safely away she hustles him to his feet and forces him to the railing by the scruff of his neck. He bangs his broken arm on the way, making a noise that lands halfway between a groan and a whine, and Cameron sees his eyes go wild with panic. 'You've got to give me something,' she says. 'Seeing as there's not a lot of space between the railings.' She leans him forward, making him look. 'Three flights, give or take. If I was to push you over, I reckon you'd hit every single one of them on the way down.' She makes a show of looking herself, clicks her teeth. 'All that body armor, a few bounces to slow you down? You'll survive. Won't be worse than, say, a car crash. Took me two years to get full use of my arm again.'

'Homeland.' It comes out thick, and he swallows hard after saying it.

'You work for Homeland Security?'

'ICE. I'm with the intervention team.'

Cameron frowns. 'Well isn't that something?'

'Cameron?' Ray is at the landing, looking up towards her.

'They're not Army,' Cameron calls down to him. 'They're Homeland Security.'

Ray stomps up the stairs, breathing heavily. He probably picked up the pace when he heard the fight. 'You sound surprised.'

'I thought they were . . . you know.'

'Glorified customs? Border patrol?'

'Something like that.'

'Biggest police force in the country.' Ray looks the man she's holding up and down once, as though to confirm his suspicions. 'No oversight, virtually no jurisdictional limits. Twenty billion dollars in funding.'

Cameron lets out a low whistle. 'Twenty. Billion. Dollars.'

Ray raises an eyebrow. 'To keep us all safe,' he says, sarcasm dripping from every word. 'What's with the bomb squad? There something we need to know?'

Cameron gives the Homeland agent a shake. 'You heard the man.'

'Fuck you.'

'Ah.' Either he's found a fresh stash of balls somewhere inside his armor, or he's worked out that Cameron has no intention of throwing him down the stairwell. She presses the Homeland agent down on to his knees, and pulls a cable tie free from the bundle. 'If you know about me,' she says, 'then you know about my brother. And if you know about my brother, you will know that he is a straight-up son of a bitch.'

He doesn't answer. Cameron sighs and holds the cable tie

up so he can see it. 'We're going to leave you here without your radio. There's no two ways about that part of the deal, but I am going to give you a choice. You can tell us why you're dressed up for Halloween and I put this on your good wrist, or you can keep quiet and discover exactly how painful that broken arm of yours can get.'

There's a mist forming on the inside of the man's visor, sweat and breath trapped inside an outfit that must be sitting north of one hundred and ten degrees inside. He's staring Cameron out, like he's daring her. *Bring it on.*

Ray draws level with Cameron's shoulder and slowly pushes her to the side, out of the Homeland agent's field of view.

'I know what you're thinking,' Ray says. He speaks with a low, even tone. 'You're thinking you'd rather die a hero than live out the rest of your days thinking you sold your buddies out.'

The agent shudders, and Cameron can just make out his face twisting, angry at being confronted. 'You don't know a thing about me.'

'I will always place the mission first.' Ray says it like a mantra. 'I will never accept defeat. I will never quit.'

'Hey,' Cameron says, resisting the urge to elbow him. 'Are you trying to fuck us?'

'I will never leave a fallen comrade.' The agent finishes for him.

'Your mission has changed,' Ray says. 'Is any of this what you signed up for? Taking on American citizens on American soil?'

'My orders—'

'Your orders are bullshit,' Ray says, his voice suddenly full of venom. 'You think this operation is on the books? You think there's going to be a medal and a parade? This whole thing is bullshit, and you and I are buried in it up to our necks.' He plucks the cable tie from Cameron's hand, throws it out into the stairwell. 'What's it going to be, soldier? Do you even remember the oath you swore?'

Cameron watches as the agent straightens, turns to face Ray, and for a moment she thinks he's going to try and rush him. Instead, he sighs, the armor settling awkwardly as he slumps inside of it.

'There's a bomb in the server room,' he says. 'Wired up to all the computers. If we try to take anything out, it'll blow. We've got a team inside trying to disarm it now.'

'And if it goes off?' Ray asks.

The agent swallows. 'The walls are load-bearing. If it goes off, it will level the building.'

'Fuck.'

'What about Miller?' Cameron asks. 'What about the executives?'

It takes a moment for the agent to reply, like he's embarrassed to talk about it. 'We had a team insert from the roof,' he says. 'We . . . lost contact with them shortly after. Orders were to take the server, then after extraction to . . . detonate the bomb remotely.'

Ray snorts, disgusted. 'So much for never leaving a fallen comrade.'

'Sir, I—'

'Don't tell me,' Ray says. 'Your orders.'

'Yes, sir.'

Cameron takes his good hand and binds him by the wrist to the railing with another cable tie. She crouches, gets hold of his opposite ankle and does the same to it. 'Look,' she says. 'Here's the deal. You get out of these as fast as you can, and you get the fuck out of here. Understand?'

'Yes, ma'am.'

Cameron stands. 'Second time I've been called that,' she says. 'Not sure it fits me.' She grabs hold of his neck armor, pulls his visor round to face her. 'You see anyone else on your way, you tell them to get the fuck out, too. If all that's true, I can't promise you this building will stay upright. You get me?'

'Yes, ma'am.'

'Good.' She stands back, and checks that the baton will close. The blow that broke his arm has put a bend in it, but it's slight enough that it still collapses down into the handle.

'You sure that's enough to hold him?' Ray asks.

'I don't want him dead,' Cameron says. 'Speaking of which, we need to move. Come on.'

She's at the door when the agent speaks.

'Wait,' he says. 'There's an eight-man team in there. You can't take them on.'

Cameron doesn't look back at him, feels an old pride burning up inside of her at the challenge. 'You bet your ass I can,' she says.

Chapter 34

Ray follows Cameron's lead through the ground floor of the Carrington building. The lobby could probably win awards for interior design: it's all glass and exposed steel, with a mezzanine deck branching across the space overhead. At least it would have done before the gunfight that destroyed it had taken place. There are at least twenty security personnel laid about the room, and all of them are dead. Ray goes to check one man that might not have lost all the blood in his body; Cameron just shakes her head and moves on. The skin of the guard's neck is cold under Ray's fingers. No pulse.

In spite of the thought that a bomb big enough to take the building out is being messed with, Ray makes the rounds to check as many as he can. All of them are Carrington, from their uniforms and weaponry. It feels odd that they are the only ones that got killed until Ray starts paying attention. There are other blood pools, mostly close to the doors, and long drag marks where bodies have been removed. The Homeland team are making sure that no one is left behind. Surrounded by dead bodies, it feels less like a code of honor and more like a cover-up in progress.

'I thought these guys were private military,' Ray says.

Cameron doesn't look at him. She's bobbing her head left and right, looking straight ahead, like an owl sizing up a distant field mouse. 'They were,' she says, as though answering him is an afterthought.

'Seems a little one-sided for private contractors,' Ray says. Even adding up all the drag marks, he still counts a loss of fewer than ten on the Homeland side. 'They were torn to pieces.'

'Carrington use a lot of surveillance tech,' Cameron says. She climbs past a body to get an angle on a set of double doors ahead and cranes her neck to try and see through the thin windows set high in them. 'I guess they were depending on it.'

Ray doesn't need to guess. He can see it. The Carrington security team, stripped of their eyes and ears when the security system failed, panicked and fell back to what they thought was a defensive position in the heart of the building. With all the locks disabled, the single path to their location had turned into multiple paths, and they found themselves engaged from three different directions, one of them being overhead. The crutch they had been leaning on was kicked out from under them, and they had been annihilated. 'No substitute for real training, I guess,' he says.

Cameron looks at him like he's just grown horns. 'We did this,' she says.

Ray takes a deep breath in and feels the weight of that settling on him. The air is heavy, thick with the smell of blood and spent brass. There's just too much for the air conditioning to clear. He can picture exactly how it went down. They had fought a cursory rearguard down the main corridor, enough

273

to make it feel like they were worth chasing, and set up in a loose arc behind every available inch of cover to focus their fire on that entrance. The Homeland team had worked their way round to the sides, and up to the mezzanine deck. From the pattern of fire on the floor and the broken glass above he can see they had managed to spread out on the mezzanine, looking down on to the waiting Carrington crew. All they would have had to do was call for weapons down, drop a couple of stun grenades. Instead, they had turned the room into a killzone. No mercy, save for the bullet. He blows out a sigh and looks at Cameron. 'We opened the door,' he says, 'but this isn't on us. They could have taken them without casualties.'

'Maybe.' Her answer is a long time coming, and Ray can tell she doesn't believe it. Hell, he barely believes it himself. All those lives ended by a memory card no bigger than a fingernail. The only thing he can take from that is a real need to see the people who did this paying for it. An eight-man team.

Ray's hands are tight on the grip of the pistol, and it's an effort for him to ease them free. 'So these are the people who are bankrolling your brother?'

'Looks like it.' Cameron is looking at the far doors, towards the server. She's keen to move.

'You think he's here?'

She shakes her head. 'He won't be. He wants to be the one pulling the strings, not the one dancing along.'

'Shame.' Ray snorts, trying to clear his head of the smell. 'When we find him, I'll wait until you finish kicking him down a flight of stairs before I arrest him.'

Cameron jerks her chin forward, directing his attention to the doors ahead. 'Don't get ahead of yourself,' she says. 'We have to get through the rest of them first.'

'The server is that way?'

'Yeah,' Cameron says. 'It's that way.'

Ray looks at the double doors. 'We got any room to maneuver?'

'I think so.' Cameron shrugs. 'How would you set them up?'

Ray thinks back to his training, to the tactical exercises they played out at the academy. There's no exact model for it, but he can make a guess. 'If they're defusing a bomb, two of them will be in the room. Point man and someone to assist. The rest will be set up to keep them from being interrupted. Either four close and two roaming the perimeter, or a three-three split.'

Cameron makes a face. 'Let's hope for four and two,' she says.

Ray is surprised. 'You got a plan or something?'

'They know something is happening,' she says. 'But they haven't come looking for their man. We should expect them to be on high alert.'

'You're reaching for that four and two, aren't you?'

'It'd make my life a hell of a lot easier,' she says.

'Make my life easier if you told me what the plan is,' Ray says.

Cameron takes a quick breath, as though she's going to say something and thinks better of it at the last second. 'You'll see,' she says, and ducks to begin searching the first body her hands reach. 'Come on. We need to see if any of the Carrington security have keys or tools.'

Ray sighs and points across the room. 'You want that guy,' he says.

Cameron gives him a look, but goes anyway. She's barely crouched down before she holds up a bundle of keys. 'Bingo. How'd you figure he had them?'

'I'm a cop,' Ray says. 'Better quality uniform, more body armor. He's the leader.'

Cameron looks around, judging the distances. 'He was in the middle of the fight when he died,' she says. 'Would have put the boss in the back.'

'Yeah.' Ray can see the dead man from where he's standing. He was tall and athletic, but by no means a young man. His hair is grey and cropped short. Ex-military, maybe. The sort of guy who takes a security detail because another tour might see his luck run dry. 'My best guess? He did the best he could for his team.'

'Wasn't enough, though.'

'No, it wasn't.' Ray can't stop looking at him. All he can think is that the poor bastard had probably never heard the name Carrington until he saw they were hiring. He just picked the wrong people to sign up with. 'What are you planning, Cameron?'

'Call it restorative justice,' Cameron says. She's going through the keys at speed, looking closely at the bow on each one as she goes. 'Homeland cut the security system, used the building against them.' She peers intently at one of the bunch, holds it up in triumph. 'We're going to give them a taste of their own medicine.'

Chapter 35

Cameron moves as quickly as she can from corridor to corridor, trying to get as much information as she can before making her move. Ray pings her on the radio twice before she is forced to acknowledge that she's already seen everything worth seeing, and the real reason she's still circling the perimeter is that she really, really doesn't want to go any further.

They've done a great job of digging in. With the electronic locks disabled, they have barricaded most of the routes leading to the server room with furniture, enough that anyone clearing it is going to make a hell of a noise in the process. The route that they've left is basically a shooting gallery, a section of lobby with a door at one end and enough distance to cover that even surviving the first three seconds of an engagement would be nigh-on impossible.

They know Cameron is there. She tried to draw them out of cover by kicking a blockade until it drew fire, but couldn't make out if it was two or three men covering the server room. They haven't sent anyone to investigate, and she hopes that's because they don't have a man to spare rather than the fact that they hold the superior position and there's no need for them to give it up.

Eight men, at least three positioned defensively, all of them armed with automatic weapons. She weighs the baton in her hand and wonders if she shouldn't have opted for a gun after all. Leaving them untouched had felt like the right thing to do. She'd left a man dead, killed in the heat of the moment, and she'd promised herself that she'd do everything in her power not to repeat that mistake.

Eight, though, is too many for her to think about holding back over. When you pull a punch, you don't have your mind on the fight: you're thinking about how not to hurt the other person, and that slows you down, leaves you open. It's part of the reason why fixed fights are always so hard to spot: all you have to do is think about losing and it'll happen.

Cameron crouches behind the door, making sure she doesn't touch it. It would be a hell of a shame if one of them fired at a twitch of movement and killed her before she could even get started. She pulls out the baton, eases it out to its full length, then brings out her radio and keys the mic.

'Ray?'

There's a long pause before he replies. With the volume way down, his voice is tiny. 'Here, and ready. You need to let me know when you finish speaking. Over.'

'I'll bear that in mind. Give me a three count, then go for it.' She waits for a second, then remembers. 'Uh, I have finished speaking.'

'Acknowledged,' Ray says. As he speaks Cameron puts the radio on the floor and braces herself, like a runner getting ready to come out of the starting blocks. 'Going in three, two, one . . .'

She doesn't speak for the go signal. Instead she rams the baton through the door handles and puts every ounce of strength she has into bending it. The metal resists for a second, a long strip of pain peeling horizontally across her shoulder blades as she pushes, and with a creak of metal fatigue gives way, the slight bend becoming a tight curve.

Carrington don't have sprinklers anywhere near their server room. Spraying water over their central asset would be as bad as letting it burn. Instead, they use inert gas suppression, a mix of argon, nitrogen, and carbon dioxide that is pumped rapidly into every room to starve the fire of oxygen and heat and leave all of the delicate electrical components untouched. It's expensive and tricky to manage: if the oxygen gets too low, people start to faint; if the carbon dioxide gets too high, the air becomes toxic; if they pump too much gas into the room the barometric pressure can burst everyone's eardrums. When Cameron counted down, Ray was at the control box shorting the fuses on the feedback control for all three gases and before setting the system off. In the server room and the lobby beyond, all eight Homeland agents will have found themselves surrounded by jets of gas so cold that they freeze all the moisture in the air, the vast white plumes dropping from the ceiling like eager hands reaching out to grab them. The overpressure of the gas pumped into the room bangs the doors hard against the baton holding them closed, and Cameron ducks in case the noise is really panic fire chasing her down the corridor. An alarm is blaring, a pair of discordant klaxons so loud the noise is physically uncomfortable. If Cameron could have had Ray cut the lights, she would have, but deaf, half-blind, choking and confused will have to do.

Cameron counts to ten, forcing herself to space each number out. There's a sweet spot in the chaos she's created, a point where their concentration breaks. They'll be expecting an assault: they'll hold fast until the last second, and by the time they realize the air is no good to breathe, they'll panic. She hyperventilates, cycling as much oxygen as she can into her system before she goes in there. They looked for an oxygen mask near the control box, but there was nothing to be found. Whatever she can hold in the tank will have to do. She takes one last gasp, heaving in as much air as her lungs can hold, and starts back down the corridor towards the doors.

Cameron has the baton out from the handles and is through the door as fast as her legs will carry her. She doesn't have time to duck low or look for cover. Instead, she just runs flat-out at the first person she sees. He's got an assault rifle pointed straight at her, but he's not paying attention to the door at all. Instead he's staring straight up at the ceiling, and it gives Cameron the seconds she needs to cross the distance to him without him opening fire. She goes right, not willing to risk taking the gun straight on, and as she runs past lashes out with the remains of the baton left-handed, catching him hard across the visor. He goes down with a yelp, his finger pulling the trigger as he falls, and the sound of his gun firing is a staccato rattle over the sound of the alarms.

Shit.

The next one is standing behind the cover of an upturned desk, and his confusion evaporates when the gunfire starts. He's caught half-standing, his mouth opening as he witnesses

Cameron knocking his teammate to the ground, and she's covered half the distance to him when he changes his mind about shouting and decides to fire at her instead. His gun comes up, and even though he's molasses-slow in all his armor, Cameron knows that she isn't going to make it. She has to clear twelve feet of space, while all he has to do is shift the barrel of his gun a few more degrees.

She throws what's left of the baton, little more than the handle, sending it flying end-over-end straight at him far faster than she can sprint. He flinches, his reactions good enough that even in body armor he dodges it, and in the fraction of a second it buys her Cameron vaults the desk and launches herself two-footed into him, her full weight catching him mid-chest and bearing him to the ground. He lands badly, no hand thrown out to catch his weight, and his helmeted head smacks off of the floor with a sickening crack. Cameron gets on to one knee, but thinks better of getting up when bullets tear through the desk just next to where her head is.

Shit.

Five must have stayed in the server room, not six like she hoped. One to go, and he knows where she is. Cameron scrambles on her hands and knees to get away from the desk, heading for a column that will offer a lot more protection. The gunfire starts again, chasing her, and she goes full-out, rolling to the side as she clears the column. The space where she'd been a moment before hisses as bullets pass through it.

Shit shit shit.

More fire opens up on either side of the column, the stop-start rhythm of suppressive fire, not aimed to kill but to keep her pinned in place while the gunman moves to get a better angle on her. The fire suppression system is still pumping out gas: she can feel the chill of it and the weight of the pressure building up. Cameron closes her eyes and tries not to think about words like *oxygen debt* or *asphyxiation*.

The klaxon is still blaring at full volume, and Cameron can hear the Homeland agent gasping for breath over it. He's close. She keeps her eyes shut focusing all her attention on listening to him struggle for oxygen. A yelp of pain, probably at a burst eardrum, and more gasping. She ignores the tension building in her chest, the horror of what will happen to her if she tries to get her breath back by filling her lungs with air you can't breathe. *Like drowning on dry land.* Gunfire peppers the column she's hiding behind, one last defiant burst, and then footsteps as he turns and makes for the door, giving in to the need for fresh air.

Cameron breaks cover at a run. All of her limbs feel as though they are burning, the weight of them suddenly working against her, pulling all the momentum out of every step she takes. The last man standing is out of cover, his gun swaying this way and that as he staggers for the door that Cameron came in through. If he turned, he'd have a clear shot at her, but his focus is escape: she cuts across the width of the lobby space without a shot fired.

He knows she's coming. He doesn't look back, but there's a desperation in the way he moves that puts Cameron in mind of every horror movie she's ever seen. *And that makes you the monster.* She doubles down on the pace, ignores the spikes of pain that are climbing her shins and forearms. She knows what they are. It doesn't matter how stubborn a fighter you are, but when you get that feeling, when the edges of your vision turn blood-red, you better tap out. They reach your head or your heart, it won't be the hospital they take you to. It'll be the morgue.

The klaxon cuts out leaving a silence that's almost as painful as the noise itself, and the aircon shudders into life, fans rumbling like an earthquake as they try to cope with the overpressure in the room. Cameron doesn't dare breathe. Not yet.

The Homeland agent is at the door now, his helmet gone, black hair plastered flat against his skull with sweat. He's clean-shaven, square-jawed, and looks like he's in his mid-twenties, if that. Cameron takes this all in along with the fact that he's made it to the doorway. The drag from the air conditioning has pulled both doors open, breaking the gas seal, and he's sucking down one lungful after another of oxygen-rich, hypoallergenic, server-safe air. Cameron tries to put some power into her legs, to make one final spring at him, but their roles have been switched. He lifts his gun to make sure of his aim, and Cameron stares down the mouth of a barrel that suddenly looks wide enough that it could swallow her whole.

Three shots ring out, and Cameron falls forward, the anticipation of impact making her trip over her own feet. She catches herself awkwardly, arms braced, and as the rush of air washes over her face, finally takes a breath.

In front of her, the third Homeland agent falls, dropping through a fine red mist that used to be part of him to land face first on the floor. He's missing an eye, and as Cameron looks up past him she sees Ray standing in the corridor beyond, feet wide in a classic shooter's stance, shoulders square, arms straight, hands doubled over the grip. His aim has followed the agent to the ground, and it doesn't waver when he calls to her.

'Did we get them all?'

Cameron nods, swallowing hard, trying to find her voice between breaths. 'We got them,' she says. 'No one came out of the server room.'

Ray lowers his weapon and steps forward into the doorway. 'How many outside?'

'Three.' Cameron wants to get up, but is willing to give it a moment rather than try to push her weight upon leaden arms.

Ray lets out a low whistle. 'You took out two of them by yourself?'

Cameron doesn't reply, and coughs both to clear her throat and to cover the silence. One on three, and she'd come damn close to getting herself killed. Dumb-ass plans that work are still dumb-ass plans, and Ray's admiration sits uncomfortable on her.

'Wouldn't have been able to if they'd stuck with sprinklers. Thank whatever asshole architect got a free pass on his budget for this place.' She coughs again and spits out what comes up. The gases aren't meant to be harmful, but the mouthful she spits out has an unsettling metallic edge to it. She waves Ray inside. 'Thanks for the save.'

He steps over the body as he walks into the room. He doesn't even look down, his eyes fixed on a point somewhere a hundred yards past the back of the room, and his face looks as though it has been cut out of rock. Cameron knows what it is. It's what you do before a fight, when you're alone in the dressing room. You cut out the part of yourself that feels fear, sympathy, compassion. You take all the friendships you share in the business, all the goodness you have in you and you push it down into a box and you lock it up tight. You do it before you go in the ring so that you can win. Ray's doing it to survive. He didn't want to kill that man, to pump a near-lethal mix of gas into a room to disable seven more, but he knows that right now he has to, because hesitation will get him killed. What happens after, when he unlocks that box, Cameron doesn't want to think about. Just making it out will be enough.

Chapter 36

The server room is at the far end of the lobby. There's no sound save for the whir and tick of the computers running, no lights except the electric-blue glow of LEDs flickering on and off, streams of data chasing one another between the banks of machinery. Cameron lets Ray go first, gun ready, and she limps in his wake trying to stop herself from wheezing. Her chest feels tight, like she can't breathe deep enough to get all the air she needs, and only the thought of Miller's smug-ass face keeps her anchored. He would love for her to panic, to run, to let him go without a fight. She can't give him that victory, and her determination is the tether that holds fast against the waves of panic that crash into her every time she takes a breath.

Ray edges the server room door open, and leans back once he takes a look inside. 'Nothing,' he says.

'No one at all?'

'Looks like it.' He holsters the pistol and hauls the door open. The dull throb of the server room gets louder, the neat racks of computers humming away, completely undisturbed by the gunfire or the fire suppression system. Cameron feels something like dread stealing over her at the sight of how clean it all is. She expected them to be piled up against the door, half conscious from a lack of oxygen.

Between the blue lighting, the black racks of computers linked with cables that glow like they're under a blacklight, and the last wisps of mist from the lobby that chase after Cameron as she walks in, the server room feels like walking into a music video from the late nineties. All it needs is a shirtless dude in leather pants to swagger in and the image will be complete. Instead, she gets Ray Perada ducking past her.

'You see a bomb anywhere?' Cameron asks. 'I'm not exactly sure what I'm looking for.'

'If it's built in, we might not be able to see it at all,' Ray says. 'I'll go look.' He walks down the length of the first rack, ducking his head to check between the computers as he goes. When he gets to the end he turns back to give Cameron a shrug before heading on. She taps her foot, impatient. Miller is up there somewhere. She can almost feel him waiting.

'Hey, Cameron,' Ray's voice rings off the metal panels, giving it a weird, distant feel. 'You should come see this,' he says.

The remaining members of the Homeland team are laid out in a rough arc near the back corner of the server room. They're all dead, but it isn't from asphyxiation. They've been shot, the spiderweb cracks caused by a bullet passing through their visors masking what's left of their faces.

'What the fuck?' Cameron picks her way past the bodies, stepping round a blood pool that looks black under the lights, to where Ray is standing.

'They're not the only problem,' Ray says. He points up at

a display that is screwed into one of the racks at head height, the numbers on it presented in a stark white that stands out clearly against the flickering blue background.

9:38

9:37

9:36

'Ray, what did you press?' Cameron asks. He holds his hands up, innocent.

'It was like this when I got here, I swear,' he says. 'They must have triggered it when the shooting started.'

Cameron remembers the sound of the klaxons, too loud and too discordant to ignore. *It wasn't a fire alarm. It was an evacuation warning.* There's something about the bodies that doesn't add up, and even though the timer is counting down to a detonation, she finds herself standing over them.

'We should get out of here,' Ray says.

'Ray,' Cameron says. 'What's wrong with this picture?'

Ray joins her and tilts his head, looking down at the dead Homeland agents. 'They're all facing the same way,' he says, then lowers his voice. 'Someone else killed them.'

'Someone with an oxygen mask,' Cameron says. 'They wouldn't have been able to breathe otherwise.'

Ray's eyes go wide as she says it. 'Nate,' he says. 'Nate has an oxygen tank.'

Cameron almost slips on the blood pool, she turns so fast. *Nate is here.* He must have snuck round the other side of the room when they came inside. She hits the turn so fast she bounces off of one of the server racks and sprints for the door.

'Nate!'

When Cameron pushes through the door, Nate freezes. He's halfway across the room, his back to her. He's wearing a suit – no demolition armor or tactical gear – and in one hand he's got a small oxygen cylinder. In the other, a gun. He's hunched over, like walking is a labor, and Cameron is struck by how gaunt he is. Like a skeleton walking.

'Nate.' She doesn't shout. She knows he can hear her just fine. 'Look at me.' Nate straightens up, and slowly turns to face her. When Cameron sees his face, it feels as though someone has stabbed her just below her heart. He's so ill. The skin under his eyes is so dark it looks bruised. His lips are blue. He barely looks like her brother anymore.

He coughs once, a thick, pitiful sound, and looks down at the gun in his hand. At Cameron's side, Ray cocks his own gun.

'Don't even think about it, man,' Ray says.

Cameron can't stop herself. She pushes Ray's gun down out of line. 'Ray, don't,' she says. Ten paces away, Nate makes a sound that could almost pass for a laugh.

'You should just let him shoot me, Cam,' Nate says. 'It'd be quicker.'

'What are you doing here, Nate?' she asks.

Nate lifts his chin. 'Pulling out,' he says. 'Homeland have ditched the mission. Burned it.' He shakes his head, like he can't believe what's happening to him. 'I should have known you'd find a way to fuck me over.'

'Fuck you over?' Cameron can barely find words, she's so angry. After a few moments, they come. 'You fucking crashed a car with me in it. You ended my career. You almost killed me!'

'Almost,' Nate says, nodding grimly. 'I tried my best, though. Miller was too chickenshit to hold up on his end of the bargain. You both fucked me.'

'What the fuck are you talking about, Nate?' Cameron is yelling now, ready to start slapping it out of him, gun or no gun.

'He's dying,' Ray says, and it's like a needle piercing the bubble of Cameron's anger. She can feel it draining out of her, and the hollow feeling it leaves in its wake. 'He can't breathe. He wanted you here, because you're the one that can cure him.'

Chronic organ dysfunction. That was what the doctor called it. She'd looked it up, asked her own doctors about the outcomes. Total systemic collapse had been the most likely prognosis, with every major organ failing one after the other. He'd seemed almost healthy when the car went over, but now Nate looks like he's about to collapse. 'There's a cure?'

'He needs a transplant,' Ray says. 'Lungs, at least. My guess is you're a match.'

Nate coughs again, his face twisting with anger. He always hated being caught out. 'You're the only one that is,' he says. 'Thank Mom and Dad for their unique genetic markers.' He waves the gun he's holding at the servers. 'Carrington checked. I went to them because they had access to medical files in every developed country. Over two billion people on their books, and only you were a match.' He laughs at that, and the effort sets him to coughing, a wet, heavy sound that cuts deep. When he recovers he looks straight at her. 'Look at you. Healthy as a goddamn horse.' His jaw works for a moment and he spits a lump of phlegm to one side. 'You don't deserve it.'

Cameron feels lightheaded, like a balloon with a cut string. She can feel the hate coming off him like a heat haze. She just about manages to shake her head. 'That's not how it works, Nate. You don't get to decide.'

'The fuck I don't. Do you know what it's like to be shown a chart that tells you how little time you have left to live?' Nate asks. 'I do. Do you know what it feels like to have that timer running in your head?'

'I might have,' Cameron says. 'You could have talked to me.'

Nate ignores her. 'And all the time I get to watch you piss your life away. Punching people for a living. Every time I saw you fight, all I could think was, "what a waste". I used to dream you'd get hurt, end up in a coma.'

A flicker of anger, deep in Cameron's gut. *I used to dream you'd get hurt.* 'But I won.'

'You won.' Nate nods. 'Again and again, you won.'

'So you took matters into your own hands.' The words feel cold in her mouth as she says them.

'I did what I had to do. I told Carrington they could have their precious project if they got me what I needed.'

It feels like a light going on. Carrington played him, like they tried to play her. Crashing the car hadn't been a test of his loyalty. He'd planned it. 'And Miller strung you along.'

'The crash didn't work out. They were meant to take you, too. Keep you stable until I was ready for surgery,' Nate says. 'They told me it was too risky, that they needed more time. I could feel myself dying, and all he could say to me was, "wait".'

'So you went to Homeland.'

Nate looks up at that. 'I went to Homeland. And they told me if I could get them exclusive access to the server, then I would get what I want.'

'Me on a slab,' Cameron says.

Nate nods so fast he starts shaking. 'Couldn't wait around for someone with a matching set to just fall off their motorbike,' he says. 'You know twenty people die every day, waiting for that to happen? Wishing that someone out there will die in just the right circumstances to help them out? I couldn't do that, Cam.'

Cameron bristles. 'You don't get to call me that, Nate. Not anymore.'

Nate sags, looking down at the gun in his hand. He's so thin, it looks as though his arm is about to snap under the weight of it. 'I don't want to die, Cameron.'

'I can't think of anyone who does,' Cameron says. She wanted to beat him to a pulp, but all she can do is stand there, held fast by the weight of knowing what her brother had tried to do. He'd crashed a car trying to create the conditions for a perfect donor. He'd built the whole system for Carrington thinking they'd come and get her when it was done. And when they hadn't come through on the deal, he'd cut a deal with Homeland that made them dance to his tune, brought her all this way himself, engineering one last-ditch attempt to save his own life. 'Why didn't you just ask?'

'What?'

'What, you needed a lung off me?' Cameron's voice rises, hot with anger. 'You think I wouldn't have given it to you? Is that what you thought?'

Nate's head comes up, and she can see the old Nate still in there, his eyes fixed on some far point. Always looking ahead. So fucking clever, but just like her dad had said, not an ounce of sense in him. 'You wouldn't have thrown away your career,' he says.

'Bullshit,' Cameron says. 'You were there for me. I would have dropped it in a heartbeat.' She laughs, and feels a bitter spike of pain shoot down her scarred left arm. 'Hell, I started a whole new one just to find you.'

'Mom and Dad wouldn't have let you,' Nate says, and he's floundering, casting about for an excuse. 'They wouldn't have—'

'FUCK you, Nate.' Cameron yells it over him. 'Don't even try to lie to me. What's the real reason? Why the fuck would you do this?'

Nate drops his head, and Cameron watches as he takes a long breath, gathering himself. When he looks up, it's like a mask has fallen away. He hates her. And the anger on his face is a mirror to her own. 'You win, Cam,' he says. 'Just like you always did.' He peels the nasal tube from his face, and drops the oxygen bottle at his feet. 'Always first. For Mom. For Dad. You got everything you ever wanted.' The gun follows, hitting the gas bottle with a hollow, ringing noise. 'And I got to watch.'

'Nate, you know that's not true.' Saying it breaks her heart, because she knows it won't reach him. For the first time, she can see how deep that hate goes. She can't think how long he must have been holding on to it for it to turn out this way.

'I put all this together,' Nate says. 'I broke every rule, burned every bridge. I killed people, Cam. I did all of it, just to take you down.' When he breathes in, there's a crackling sound that makes Cameron wince. 'Just this once, I wanted to see you lose.' He shakes his head. 'Why couldn't you just lose?'

Cameron's voice comes thick, when she finds it. 'I couldn't lose,' she says. 'Because if I did, I'd be losing my big brother.'

Nate's mouth works as he takes that in, but he doesn't answer. All he does is turn, a painful half-circle, and start to walk away.

'Nate!' Cameron calls after him. 'You can't walk away from this.'

Nate doesn't even look back. 'Watch me.'

If he'd just fucking told her. There might have been something. A lung would have been the end of her career, it might even have killed her, but it would have meant his life in return. He'd been too proud to say it, too stubborn – driven by the same bone-deep pride that had kept her moving all these years – and it had twisted him into a monster.

Cameron knows only one thing for certain. She has never in her life wanted to punch someone more than she does right now.

Ray clears his throat. 'Six minutes, Cameron. We have to go.'

'He can't just walk away.' Cameron isn't sure who she's trying to convince. 'Someone has to pay for this.'

'If he lasts six months, I'll be surprised,' Ray says. 'Besides, he's not the only one.'

Cameron nods. Miller is still up in the executive suite. On the top floor. He has to be. She knows he won't leave until the last moment. 'You should get out of here,' she says.

Ray takes a moment to figure out that she means to go after Miller alone. 'Are you sure you want to go up there?'

The executive elevator isn't far from here. Cameron can imagine what it would be like to be trapped inside as it falls. She reckons there's enough time to get up to the top floor. It's unlikely that she'll come back down, though. The need to dish out some pain over this shit is under her skin, itching away. There's only one way she can think of to scratch it. *Miller.* The server will be gone, but it's Miller's dream. If he gets away, Carrington will just start again and there's no promise that anyone will be there to stop them.

Total surveillance. Total control. Three hundred million people shackled with a tracer in their arm; three hundred million points of data waiting to be harvested by Carrington. The population of the United States, turned into a corporate asset.

'I have to go,' she says. Cameron can think of at least three ways Ray can get out of here. Even if he has to clear a barricade, he should be able to get clear. 'When you get outside, stick to your new-hire cover story. Maybe they'll let you go.'

He stands for a long time looking down at the pistol in his hands. The moment only lasts a few seconds, but Cameron knows how long seconds can be when you're holding on for the bell to ring to mark the end of a round. 'Getting out of here would be the sensible thing to do,' he says. He pops the clip, and racks the slide to eject the bullet that was waiting to be fired. He stands there weighing the mag in his hand. 'You remember when I tried to arrest you, and you kicked me in the head?'

Cameron nods. 'Yeah, I remember.'

Ray tosses the clip to one side and pulls a fresh one from the belt he's wearing. He loads it into the pistol, snapping the base of it flush with the grip with the heel of his hand. He racks the slide, chambering the first round, making it ready to fire. 'Can't say I've had much sense in me since,' he says. It forces a grin from her, and he offers her a smile in return. 'Let's go finish this, Cam.'

Chapter 37

Ray watches as Cameron punches a four-digit code into the keypad by the elevator door. There's a long silence filled with the dread of trying to take ten flights of stairs in eight minutes or less before the elevator kicks into life and starts its descent.

'Your code worked?' he asks.

Cameron shakes her head, looking up at the ceiling as though she can somehow see through concrete and watch the elevator coming down. 'I don't think so.'

'They know we're coming, don't they?'

'They know someone is.'

Ray backs off. He doesn't like the idea of standing square on to an elevator door that has the potential to open with a bullet. 'I'll just be standing over here while we wait,' he says.

Cameron doesn't move. 'If they want to kill us they could just drop a grenade on top of the elevator. Or fire down the shaft. Or riddle it with bullets once we're up there.'

Ray knows what concentrated automatic fire does to targets. He tries not to think what the same kind of firepower would be like in a closed metal box. *People soup with ricochet croutons.* 'You know, it's your cheerful outlook on life that really makes you fun to be around,' he says. He hears the elevator stopping and draws his pistol, leaning slightly to aim past Cameron's right shoulder.

The doors slide open to reveal an empty elevator.

Not quite empty. Ray can't see it directly, but Cameron reacts to something on the floor. She steps inside and lifts it. A business card, folded once across its width to make it stand up. It's a note, left for her to find.

'What does it say?' Ray asks.

Cameron is frowning as she half-turns, leaning to the side so he can see the writing. 'It says, "COME UP".'

'Now I really am suspicious,' Ray says, shaking his head. 'Dude with a gun, fine. I can handle that. Half-pound of plastic explosive with a bunch of wires sticking out of it? I get it. It'd be messy, but I'd get it, you know? This? This is some bullshit.'

Cameron laughs, a short, dry sound. 'They didn't need to send down a guy with a gun, Ray. Sounds like they just kicked your ass with a business card and a marker pen.'

Ray gets into the lift. It takes him a moment to swallow down that bitter pill of truth she's just served him, and he spends it looking at his own reflection in the mirrored back wall of the elevator. His face looks strange, stress and fatigue hidden behind a mask made of sweat and dust. He looks as though he's been just been rescued from a cave-in at a mine after three days of digging. 'I deserved that,' he says.

'No,' Cameron says. 'You're right. They wouldn't send down an invite unless there was a world of shit waiting for us at the top.' Compared to Ray, Cameron looks as if she's just getting warmed up. Her clothes are in a shit state, and her hair is almost flat to her skull with sweat, but her expression is wide awake. She catches Ray looking at her in the mirror and rolls her shoulders, like a prizefighter itching at the mark. 'Best not keep them waiting. They might change their mind about that grenade.' There is a single button set in a panel at chest height on the left-hand side of the elevator. Cameron presses it, and the plastic strip around it lights up blue. The doors close behind them.

Ray's reflection swallows hard, adjusts its grip on the gun in its hand as though holding it that little bit tighter is going to make a difference. He's put himself on Cameron's right shoulder so he can shoot the instant the doors open. *And push her to the side if you need to.* He thinks about offering her the vest, but before the question can even get past the thinking stage he knows she will decline. He knows she's psyching herself up for a fight, and this is the long walk to the ring. You don't take anything with you.

A speaker pops somewhere in the elevator ceiling, making Ray jump. Cameron doesn't move, save to look up in curiosity. After a moment, music begins to play. Guitar, double bass . . . and a saxophone. Ray bursts into laughter as he recognizes the song: 'On Days Like These.'

'What the fuck is that?' Cameron asks.

Ray raises his eyebrows at her. 'You don't recognize it?'

'Am I supposed to?' She frowns. 'Sounds like shit off an infomercial.'

'It's Quincy Jones. He used to score films in the sixties.'

'So about twenty years before you were born?'

Ray grins. 'I pulled the short straw on stakeout duty about ten months back. You see a lot of old movies at three in the morning.'

'Huh,' Cameron offers before lapsing into silence. Ray can tell she's not done. After five more seconds of it, she shifts her weight from one foot to the other and points upwards. 'Do you think you could shoot that speaker out?'

Ray feels the lift slowing. 'Sorry,' he says. 'Heads up.' He sets his feet as the lift comes to a halt, giving himself a stable base. It's what you do at the range, it's what you do in real life. It's not just good practice. It's what takes your mind off the fact that you've voluntarily gone up ten stories to the top of a building that is very shortly going to be demolished, and that the only comfort to be found in that decision is that you're more than likely going to get shot long before the floor falls out from under you.

The doors slide open to reveal the penthouse office, and Ray is relieved to discover that they aren't immediately shot.

The reason they aren't is because every person holding a gun is dead. The office is a wide open, airy space, with long windows that sit entirely in opposition to the rest of the building's concrete slab aesthetic. On two sides, the windows have been smashed completely, shards scattered on the floor about the open frames. Ray can guess at what happened to them. The incursion team came down from the roof, abseiling in on either side, using small charges to blow out the windows. What happened to the incursion team is less clear. There is gear all over the floor: webbing, ropes, harness. There are at least eight men stacked like firewood, leaning against a console that is covered in monitors, all showing security cameras still active inside the building. There aren't many of them live. *I shot a few*, Ray thinks, *Nate's virus blinded the rest*. The monitors are undamaged, as is the rest of the computer equipment that makes up the bulk of the room's furniture. If there was a firefight, it was a short one.

Silicon fucking Valley is standing dead center, about twenty-five feet away, looking straight at Cameron with a shit-eating grin on his face. In front of him, just to the right, is Bullet Head. He's not looking his best – his skin is so pale he's practically glowing, and his bad eye is covered by a bandage that is soaked through with blood – and yet he still looks like bad news. Neither Bullet Head nor Silicon Valley have a scratch on them. It isn't a big deductive leap for Ray to work out why Silicon Valley let them come up. He knows what Bullet Head is capable of, and yet the same guy lost an eye fighting Cameron. He wants to see them fight. He wants to see how she did it.

Fuck that, Ray thinks. Fucker probably has a vest on, but even a straight hit to a vest is going to wipe that smile off of his face. He takes aim – rear sight and front sight aligned over the center of mass – and Cameron's hand comes out, pressing the barrel of his gun downwards, spoiling his shot.

'Ray,' she says. 'Put the gun away.'

Ray looks at Cameron like she's gone mad, then realizes what he missed when the doors opened. There's a green box on the floor in front of them, standing on four thin legs. On the curved surface he can make out the words *FRONT TOWARDS ENEMY*. It's an M18 Claymore mine. Inside, there are several hundred steel balls and a wad of explosive capable of turning every single one of them into a bullet. If it fires, what's left of him and Cameron will drip out of the colander that was the elevator long before the building comes down. Suddenly he knows how the entire assault team died and why every single window is gone.

'Toss it.' Silicon Valley gestures with the detonator he's holding. Ray puts the safety on and tosses the gun forward and away, over to one side of the room. 'Thank you. Now, shall we get started?'

Chapter 38

There are ten paces between Cameron and Miller. Five if she runs it. It would only take two tenths of a second for him to detonate the mine and kill both her and Ray. As much as she wants to put her fist through Miller's head, there's no point in trying.

Miller rubs his hands together with the kind of oil-slick, uninhibited glee that is the sole preserve of fight promoters adding up pay-per-view revenues and casino pit bosses the moment a whale goes under at the high rollers' table. 'It is not often that I am surprised,' he says.

Cameron doesn't say anything. She can't find the stomach for it. Not with Samson there. His one good eye is fixed on her, and he looks furious. All he has to do is take the detonator off of Miller and press the switch to kill her. She's amazed that he hasn't already.

Miller keeps talking, like she somehow gives a shit. 'I was expecting to see your brother when those doors opened.' He gestures towards the mine pointed at the lift doors. 'As you can see, I was all ready for a reunion. I have to ask, did you kill your own brother?'

'Fuck you, Miller,' Cameron says. She looks at Samson. 'How's the eye, asshole?'

Samson's cheek twitches, but he stays put. Miller glances up at the back of his head, and says something that Cameron doesn't catch. It's short and terse – a warning – and she suddenly realizes that Miller himself is the source of Samson's new-found self-control.

'This building is coming down,' Cameron says.

Miller shrugs. 'It was always a possibility that we would have to activate the contingency plan,' he says. 'As my father always said, don't put all your eggs in one basket.'

Ray pipes up next to Cameron. 'Your daddy used really common sayings? That's a fucking revelation, man. You want to talk surprises, you should see your boys downstairs. Homeland spanked them without breaking a sweat.'

That gives Miller pause. Samson glances back at him, and Cameron can guess the question: *do you want me to deal with it?* Miller is vulnerable without him, and Cameron knows what his answer will be long before he gives a tiny head shake, *no*.

'You brought this on yourself,' Cameron says.

'I rather think your brother brought it on all of us,' Miller answers. 'He betrayed you, and us, and in the process betrayed you again. And yet, you let him use you.' He nods carefully. 'Yes. I know the virus came from you. It wouldn't have done the damage it did unless you let it out.'

'You know why I let it out, right?'

'You wanted to create an opportunity for yourself,' Miller says. 'A way out.'

Cameron is only half paying attention to what Miller says. Her mind is racing. There's no way Miller would have someone like Samson around if he didn't have a leash on him. An ex-soldier with nothing to show for his service, he's bitter and impulsive. Cameron pushed his buttons with a single kick; Miller would have needed an implant to control him, to let him know who the boss is. Cameron looks from Miller to Samson and back again. *He has a pacemaker implant, and he thinks Miller can still zap him with it.*

'. . . that it matters.' Miller is still talking, oblivious to the fact that Cameron is ignoring him. 'You were doubtless coming up here to silence me, maybe force me to authorize a complete system wipe?'

Cameron came up here to beat his ass like a drum, but she's not going to tell him that. There's no guarantee Miller won't press the detonator the instant she says it. If she can get past the mine and keep him busy there's a chance that Ray can make it out of this. Cameron looks past the two men, trying to pick out details. Every hold has a counter. There has to be an escape route. Miller wouldn't have stayed if there wasn't a way out. 'That was the plan.'

'Then you weren't paying attention. The central control program started a full system wipe the instant the virus went to work. Even if any code remains, it will be too frag-mented to salvage.' Miller smiles thinly. 'You should have run.'

There's a roof view visible on one of the security cameras. Cameron can just make it out on one of the monitors. In the corner of the picture, a black bar is flickering. Cameron realizes that it's a rotor, and that there's a helicopter up there. A way out. 'I had to come,' she says, 'because I have something to say.'

Miller scoffs. 'What could you possibly say to me that—'

'Not to you, dick.' Cameron looks straight into Samson's one good eye. 'Him.'

Samson lifts his chin, and speaks in a thick voice. 'What is it?'

'I let the virus loose so Miller couldn't shock me anymore,' Cameron says. 'I bet you any money he can't shock you, either.' Samson's eyes widen, and Cameron's question is answered. He'd been bearing the weight of an implant so long that just the threat of it had been enough. And now Cameron was calling Miller's bluff.

Miller tries to grin, but Cameron can see it doesn't reach his eyes. 'That's not going to change a—'

Samson turns with a roar and catches Miller by the shirt front. Miller starts to shriek as his feet leave the floor, but it is cut off when Samson heaves him up past head height before throwing him back down on to the floor. The impact flings his arm out wide, and Cameron takes a deep breath as the detonator flies out of Miller's hand. Ray almost runs for it, but it bounces once and is gone, skittering through the broken glass from a window and falling out of sight. Miller isn't conscious when Samson lifts a booted foot and brings it down on him heel first and he's probably no longer breathing for the second, third, or fourth time, but Samson doesn't seem to care. He beats Miller's corpse until it's no longer recognizable as Miller, then stamps a triumphant foot in the bloody mess that's left.

Samson turns back to face Cameron and Ray, his face half-obscured by the blood on it, a trickle of red-black gore dripping from his right fist. He looks feral, and Cameron has a sinking feeling that killing Miller isn't going to be enough for him.

'Bet you've been wanting to do that for a long time,' she says.

'Since I met him.'

The floor shudders underfoot, and one of the surviving panes of glass on the far side of the room shatters with a crash. Ray jumps and yells out, thinking it's the claymore going off. The mine sits inert between them, and Cameron edges into the room, out of its arc of fire. Another tremor ripples up through the floor, and Cameron feels the shift that comes in its wake, like a wrecking ball dropping loose from its moorings. A moment after, a dull rumble far below their feet makes the room shake. Something – a ceiling, a stairwell – is collapsing down there. Ray's face goes blank. He knows what an earthquake feels like, knows what it can do. There's no faking that fear. 'So we all friends here or what?' he asks. 'I mean, this building is coming down on us, so now would be a good time to decide.'

Samson lifts his bloody fist and extends a finger to point straight at Cameron. 'We have some business to settle.'

'Okay,' Ray says. 'So it's "or what". Just glad to see where we stand on that. Cameron?'

Cameron doesn't look at him. 'There's a helicopter on the roof. Get up there, get on it, get the fuck out of here.'

'What, and leave you with fucking . . . Prom Night Carrie over there?'

'He's going to be busy. Now get out of here.'

The floor moves underneath all of them. It's probably only a few inches at ground level, but here on the top floor it's closer to six feet of sway. Behind them, the elevator lets out a screech as the shaft warps around it. Ray puts his hand on Cameron's forearm. 'Cameron, if you don't make it out—'

'Ray, there isn't time for this.'

'There has to be another way,' he says.

There probably is, but they're out of time. 'If you think of it,' Cameron says, 'let me know.'

On the last word she launches herself at Samson, going from standing to sprinting as fast as her aching muscles will let her. It's not impressive, but it does get his attention. He grins, opening his arms as though welcoming her, and Cameron can see blood on his teeth. *Just hold him off until Ray is clear.* She promises herself that's all she needs to do. Even though it sends a spike of pain through her side, she puts her foot flat in front of her and changes direction, moving sideways so she's going round on Samson's blind side.

Samson lunges, the movement fast but inaccurate – his hands grabbing the air where Cameron was instead of where she is – and Cameron darts past his shoulder to end up behind him. She squares off to his back and kicks up between his legs, a hard, quick blow that connects with enough force to make her foot hurt.

Samson doesn't even flinch. He turns, the same grin spreading wider on his face at her having tried. He takes a step forward, and Cameron tries to convince herself that he's a little slower on his feet for having just been kicked in the balls.

No such luck. Samson comes at her, fast, and she bolts to get away from him, his fist slamming into the drone console as she scrambles up and over it, landing hard and rolling on the far side.

A gun fires, and Samson ducks faster than Cameron ever thought a person could move. Ray fires again, emptying his magazine as Samson takes cover behind the console.

'Cameron, come on!' He's yelling at her, but all she can think is how easy it would be for Samson to get over the console and run them both down if she tried to run now.

Cameron puts her hand out to push herself up on to her feet and finds a stick lying on the floor. It's a nightstick, two feet of black polymer with a handle sticking out at right angles down by one end. She picks it up and climbs to her feet as Samson comes round the side of the drone console.

'Is that it?' Cameron rolls her left shoulder as she brings her baton up in a guard, feeling out for gaps in her range of motion. 'That all you got?' The burn on her back has opened completely, and she can feel her vest sticking to the wound. Her right arm has a numb patch running from the peak of her elbow to her right pinkie, and she tries to put the thought of it giving out on her out of her head as she circles around the room, drawing Samson away from Ray.

Samson follows, his fists held up in a ragged guard, and starts swinging.

Cameron only ever took up stick fighting for the novelty of it. Timing and distance are everything in the ring – they're the difference between a clean takedown or walking face first into a right hook – and any excuse to break up the routine with something that helped you focus on it was welcome in her book. She was never great at it, but she has training enough to know that Samson is missing chances left and right to close on her and do some damage. He's throwing punches that would finish her if any of them landed, but every time she blocks him there's an opening that he isn't taking. It takes five of them for Cameron to realize what's happening.

He's afraid of her.

He's already lost an eye when she grappled with him, and that's the reason he's not comfortable closing. If she gets a hand to his other eye, she can blind him. It shouldn't matter – the floor is shaking under them like it's a drum skin instead of concrete – but in a fight fears aren't rational. They come from the gut. And if Samson is afraid of her, it doesn't matter how strong or fast he is. Cameron can beat him.

Fuck this guy. I'm gonna win. Cameron steps into the next blow when she should step out, angling herself into Samson's blind side, and when he veers away from her, trying to make some distance, she kicks away his lead foot and sends him stumbling backwards. She can feel her whole body surge with a kind of excitement, the fighter's pride waking, every wound and ache forgotten as she warms up to the challenge. She steps back for a beat and looks around, and sees that Ray has vanished out of the room. *Good.*

She dodges to the side on sheer instinct, and a chunk of metal torn from the drone console goes past her nose so close that for a fraction of a second she can see every line and curve in it like she's looking at it through a microscope. Samson charges after it, and instead of trying to dodge, Cameron stands her ground, lunging forward with the nightstick held straight out, a blunt spear for him to run himself on to. Samson jerks to the side to avoid it, off-balance, and Cameron grabs hold of him as he goes past, turning her body in time with his to throw him cleanly over her hip. She puts every ounce of strength she has into it, and Samson goes over like a

310

whip being cracked, landing with a thump that makes the floor shake. Something in Cameron's back goes tight, and instead of following him down to crack his head open, she is forced to limp in a circle, trying to walk it off.

Samson gets to his feet, but doesn't attack. The building sways again, and he and Cameron both stare at the long, lightning-strike crack that is forming across the floor between them. Cameron grimaces as the pain in her back spikes, then eases, and lifts the nightstick up into a guard. She couldn't bring herself to punch her brother, but this guy will do just fine instead.

'Let's finish this.'

Chapter 39

Ray finds a set of metal steps leading up to the roof at the far corner of the room, and takes them on legs that are shaking so hard they feel ready to collapse under him. He took a clear shot at a target standing side-on to him, and missed. Too keen to take Bullet Head out, he couldn't calm down enough to line up the sights and ended up shooting high. Bullet Head didn't even look pissed about it, either, just crouched out of the fucking way and let Ray empty his mag into the console he ducked behind like some kind of idiot. Cameron was not impressed, and he'd beat feet out of there to keep from being a distraction. Get to the roof, secure the helicopter, make sure they both get an exit before the building falls out from under them. Simple.

Ray takes a deep breath as he hits the top step. *Get your shit locked down. You can do this.*

He comes out on to the roof through a maintenance door that is so flimsy it warps when he pushes it open. There isn't a lot of wind, but without any railings on a flat roof, it feels like a lot more than Ray is entirely comfortable with. The door is close to a corner, and his first steps take him straight for the center of the roof.

The drones are sitting docked in a nest that fills the center point, the nest a dark hump of black plastic and pipework that sits almost ten feet square and comes up to chest height on Ray. There's a canopy over it of corrugated plastic sprayed silver, a deliberately shoddy roof that hides the drone site from aerial and satellite view. On the far side of the nest, a helicopter perches on the roof like a giant insect, a touch of iridescence to the sky-blue airframe putting Ray in mind of a dragonfly. It's a Super Huey, loaned or appropriated from the Marine Corps, and Ray is only slightly relieved to see that there isn't a door gunner sitting waiting to open fire on him. Its rotors are turning, beating the air with the characteristic overpressure *whomp* that feels loud even with the wind noise. Ray can't see into the cockpit from this angle, but it doesn't look like it's getting ready to take off. It's making a hell of a noise, but if he was asked to guess, the helicopter is the equivalent of a getaway car left running outside the bank.

Ray ducks into the cover the drone nest offers and works his way round it to try and get a better angle on the cockpit. If he can work out where the pilot is, it gives him the best chance of getting across the open roof and into the helicopter before he can take off. *Or return fire*, Ray thinks. *Because pilots, especially Marine Corps ones, carry sidearms.*

There's the scuff of a footstep behind him, and Ray manages a quarter turn before he hears the hammer being pulled back on a pistol. 'Don't even try it, son.' The voice is even, measured, but far from calm. It's the voice of an experienced soldier standing in a world of shit. 'Two fingers only, pistol at arm's length, and drop it. Once that's done, put your hands behind your head.'

Ray does as he is told. The pilot must have been behind the flimsy structure where the door comes out on to the roof, standing with his heels over a sheer drop. He must have stayed there even when the bomb went off and the whole building started to shift. Ray can tell this isn't someone he can fuck with.

'Identify yourself.'

'Officer Ray Perada, SFPD.'

'You got a badge?'

Ray jerks his head towards the helicopter. 'Your helo's registration numbers are sprayed over and you want me to pull a badge? We're all off the books here, marine.'

There's a pause before the pilot snorts in agreement. 'You got that right. Turn around, Officer Perada.' Ray turns, and finds himself looking at a silhouette with the sun at his back. It takes a moment for his eyes to adjust, and in that time the pilot lowers his sidearm. He's not a young man, and his mouth is set in a thin, serious line that Ray suspects is a permanent fixture. He wears no rank or insignia, but from his age and demeanor Ray can tell he's in a command position. 'You can put your hands down,' he says. 'What's the word on those Homeland boys I brought in?'

Ray doesn't sugar-coat it. 'All dead.'

'Damn it.' He works his mouth for a moment, as though trying to build up the spit to get rid of a sour taste. 'I take it their insertion went to shit?'

'You could say that. They walked straight into an ambush.'

'Well, that's a peach,' the pilot says. 'How'd you get past it?'

Ray isn't that great a liar, but he knows all about talking round the truth. 'The foundations are compromised. This building is coming down.'

The pilot gives him a long, considering look. 'And everyone is running from it.'

'Everyone that can,' Ray says. 'Look, Major—'

'Major?' The pilot sounds offended.

'Wow,' Ray says. 'Too low?'

'Just an inch.' The pilot shrugs. 'How'd you call it?'

'Forgive me for saying it, but you aren't exactly a spring chicken and the armed forces aren't in the habit of keeping second lieutenants on to retirement.'

The pilot nods. 'No, they are not.'

'This is how I think it went down,' Ray says. 'ICE turn up at your base demanding an unmarked helo and a pilot to deliver ten men to a civilian building under radar and assist in the extraction of a valuable asset. It stinks to high heaven, especially when the crew turns up looking like they're inserting into Afghanistan. You try to pull the plug, but the call comes down to make it happen. So you take the helo yourself, because you know that no matter how the mission ends it's going to be a long walk off a short plank and you sure as hell aren't going to do that to anyone in your command.'

The pilot grins suddenly. 'I like you, Officer Perada,' he says. 'You got some good insight. And while I can't imagine how or why you managed to walk through a paramilitary black op without a scratch to show for it, I feel it is my duty to offer you a lift off of this building before it falls out from under us.'

'Colonel, that sounds like a great offer, but I've got one request to add to it.'

Chapter 40

Samson comes at Cameron with his fists high, taking a long step forward and lashing out with a jab that moves like lightning. There's no way to dodge it but to go backwards, and Cameron deliberately shortens the step and brings up the nightstick, bracing the length of it against her forearm and letting his punch hit it.

His punch is like a sledgehammer, and the force of it is enough to send Cameron stumbling back, taking long steps to keep herself from falling. If she'd blocked it with her arm alone, it probably would have broken something. The hardened polymer of the nightstick is strong enough to take it, and as Cameron recovers she sees Samson frowning at his hand, his fist opening and closing like he's testing it. *Probably broke a metacarpal.* It's a common fighter's injury: part of the reason why you strap your hands up and put on the biggest gloves you can get away with. It's hard to keep fighting when every punch you land makes the damage worse. Strong and quick aren't the same as smart, and if she's lucky he'll punch his own hand to pulp.

Samson shifts his stance, puts his other hand forward, and gestures for Cameron to come and get him. He's not that stupid. She knows she can't turn her back on him, can't run for the roof while he's still able to run her down. And she can't stay put. The building is collapsing. She can feel it going, the cement floor shuddering beneath her feet as more and more walls give way. The explosion wasn't big enough to take it all down in one go, but the building is, bit by bit, falling out from under them. Cameron doesn't have the time to string this out. She is going to have to go to him.

She takes a step closer, and another, the stick ready, her stance loose, ready to dodge out of the way. Samson waits her out. Cameron is wheezing in spite of herself, her chest still tight from the fight downstairs, and it pisses her off that he can see how tired she is. Already her legs are burning, the lactic acid making them feel they're pressed hard against the very edge of failure. Like if she stops now, even for a moment, they're going to fail her.

You won't win this by dodging, Cameron tells herself. *He's afraid of you getting close. Use it. You can beat him.*

With a grimace, she gets up on the balls of her feet and starts moving laterally, back into Samson's blind side. He turns awkwardly, nervous of losing her, and she lashes out at his lead arm with the nightstick.

He takes a step back.

He's still got that speed. He takes the step so quickly that Cameron is half-convinced he slides back like he's on skates, and she isn't nearly quick enough to capitalize on it. Still, his reaction is to retreat, when he could have just pulled his arm back, and Cameron reckons she's got at least one more before he realizes it, too.

She moves in again, working on the blind side, waiting for him to lift his lead foot to follow her round. Some fights you win without ever taking a hit. Cameron knows they exist, but she's never seen one close up. She knows what she's going to have to do to beat Samson. *You're dead anyway. Get on with it.*

Samson's lead foot comes up and Cameron throws the nightstick up into his face, ducking and slipping past his blind side as he reacts on instinct, stepping back and slamming into the drone console. Cameron gets a hand to Samson's shoulder, a foot up on the console and kicks off to get as much height as she can to leap on to his back. The instant she's up, Cameron snakes her right arm around Samson's tree-trunk neck and catches hold of her left bicep to apply the oldest and simplest hold she knows: a rear naked choke.

Samson responds by going insane. He charges in circles, flailing his arms up and over, hands trying to grab her, but she brings her free hand up to his face and it drives him into a panic. Cameron bears down on the choke, the bone in her forearm a hard edge across his throat, and his bald head turns brick-red as he hisses and grunts, trying to suck in a breath through the windpipe she's holding shut.

The floor goes from underneath them. One whole half of the room drops a clear foot lower than the other, and Samson loses his footing, stumbling once and falling backwards like a tree being felled. Cameron has to let go of him before he crushes her, and as she hits the floor a big chunk of the ceiling cuts loose and drops, forcing her to roll away as it smashes the drone console into scrap metal.

The floor is tilting underneath Cameron as she tries to get to her feet. She doesn't know where the roof access is from where she is right now. She doesn't even know if it exists anymore. *This building is going to fall, and you're going with it.* Her entire right side feels cramped with pain, and she takes a faltering step away from the pile of rubble, hoping it's in the right direction.

It's instinct that makes her duck more than anything else. A chunk of concrete the size of her fist whips through the space where her head was a fraction of a second before, and she turns back to face Samson. His face is crimson, a sheet of blood washing down his cheek where the bandage has been torn aside, his ruined eye bleeding freely. He's up on one knee, and as Cameron watches he drags his other leg out from the rubble as he climbs back to standing.

'You think we're done here?' he asks.

'Yeah,' Cameron says. 'I'd say so.'

'I'm going to kill you, bitch.' He says it slowly, like he's taking an oath. 'I'm gonna kill your family. I'll kill everyone you ever dared call a friend.'

Cameron knows he means it. Samson's good eye is shining with the kind of madness that would drive someone to fight even after a roof fell in on them, give them the will to survive the whole building falling down.

She takes a deep breath, feels every muscle sparking with pain as she does it. 'No,' she says, and lifts her hands up into a guard. 'You're going to try.'

Samson charges at her, coming up and over the rubble like a linebacker charging the quarterback, all fear and hesitation gone. There's nothing left in him but rage. Cameron watches him come, sees the hitch in his gait that wasn't there before, and makes her decision. She drops low into her stance and breaks into a run, kicking off the concrete to head straight for him.

The physics of a collision are simple enough that even a fighter can understand them. Two objects coming together at speed will collide with a force determined by the sum of their speeds. Even though she ducks down at the last moment, sliding under his arms to try and tangle up his legs, running into Samson's midriff is like headbutting an anvil. As he goes over, Cameron's head snaps back and to the side, and her vision is filled with purple-black bursts. Samson's momentum keeps him going, falling past her, and Cameron brings her legs up and over, years of practice turning it into muscle memory more than intent, tangling round Samson's right leg to trap the thigh and calf. As he bounces off of the concrete, Cameron's hands close around his foot.

There's no quarter here. No rules. There's fighting, and then there's survival.

The ankle lock is meant to be a submission move, but Cameron knows Samson isn't going to tap out and shake hands. He may be bigger and stronger, but Cameron has the advantage of biomechanics and a lifetime of training. With her whole body leaning into it, she turns his ankle the wrong way, the foot bending back at an impossible angle. She feels the tendons shudder, and there's a pop deep within the joint as Samson's ankle gives way. Something warm spills over her hands, soaking into her chest, and Cameron looks down to see a shard of bone has broken the skin, and he's bleeding all over her.

Samson roars with rage and pain, jerks his foot loose of her grip with a titanic effort, and pushes himself up and round on to one side to punch down the length of his body at Cameron, the blow catching her clean in the midriff. The force of it sends Cameron flying sideways, skin and clothes tearing on the concrete, her gut spasming with the shock of the blow. She lands on the gap in the concrete floor, bounces hard against the sheared ends of the steel rods that were buried inside it, and there's a terrifying flush of fear as she feels the back of her neck go cold, the sensation of all that air underneath her.

Samson is on her before she can get her bearings, looming over her, fist raised, his face twisted in fury, and Cameron rolls away from him as his fist smashes into the floor where her head was. He's screaming, bellowing at the top of his voice, and she rolls again as more blows land, showering her in dust and making the floor shake under them both. There's no way out. Cameron feels like she's standing to one side, watching it happen to someone else.

He's going to beat you to death, and all you can do is sit there letting it happen. Cameron can almost feel Ludo's disappointment that it's come to this. She can hear his voice, somewhere over to her left telling her to breathe. That this is easy. That all Samson's got is that hammer-blow punch of his, and without it, he's done.

Samson swings another punch and Cameron rolls, but instead of away she rolls inside it, feels it whip past her head as she rolls into his supporting arm and pulls it out from under him. He's still yelling on the way down, and only stops when his face smacks into the concrete with an audible crack. Cameron turns, the movement automatic as she controls Samson's wrist with one hand, wraps her other arm around

321

the back of his elbow and closes the lock by grabbing her own wrist. He groans as Cameron levers his arm back against its natural rotation, and she can feel him straining to hold her off. She leans hard into the hold and feels the man's shoulder giving way, the rotator cuff tearing under the strain. He's screaming now, helpless to stop her, but Cameron presses on until she feels the elbow separate: tendons tearing, cartilage shorn free of the bone. When Cameron lets him go, his arm is destroyed.

She rolls away from him and gets to her feet. Samson is still down, clutching at his useless arm, eyes closed, spine straight, every cord and tendon in his neck standing out, the fight forgotten.

'You walked away with one good eye last time,' Cameron says. Her voice is shaky, but she can keep it together long enough to let Samson know he's lost. 'You got one good leg and one good arm left. You come after me again, I'll take the rest.' The floor shudders underneath her and Cameron steps away from him, from the crack that's starting to widen. 'Enjoy the express elevator.'

She isn't sure that Samson can hear her, but Cameron knows he'll understand. There's no surgery, no steroid in the world that will fix that arm. If he even survives the building coming down, he'll struggle to lift a bowl of soup, let alone punch anyone.

She walks in a circle, trying to get her bearings. She knows that the building is coming down, that she has to get to the roof, but now that the fight is over it feels like someone has put a blanket over her head. Every part of her hurts. The building is going to fall, and part of her is tempted to just let that happen. Only the anger, the stubborn *fuck you* that still burns white-hot in the very center of her chest, is holding her upright. *You die, and even in Hell Miller can still call this a win.*

'Cameron!' She can hear Ray's voice, but the sound doesn't connect in her brain. Ray is long gone. 'Cameron! Come on!'

She can barely see, and the sound of Ray shouting is difficult to hear. She shuffles left and right, head cocked, trying to listen past the thrumming beat that fills her head.

The sound isn't in her head. It's a helicopter. It's flying lined up with the broken windows on the uphill side of the building, the broad side door fully open. Hanging out of it on a tether is Ray Perada. His face splits into a grin when he sees her looking at him. 'Come on, Cam! You got a fucking death wish?'

Cameron breaks into a run, stumbling at first and gaining speed as her stride lengthens. For the first time since waking up strapped to a table in Carrington's basement, she can feel a spark of something other than anger ignite inside of her. *Hope.*

As she runs, the building goes down.

It's the other half of the room that goes first. The floor jumps like a sheet snapping in the wind as the far side of the room tears free and drops, the noise a screaming wind that pulls at Cameron as she runs for the open window. Ray's eyes are so wide she can see a perfect circle of white around the pupil, and that is all Cameron can think of as she takes the last long step and launches herself out into thin air. Whoever is flying it knows their stuff, and as she stretches out her arms knowing that she will never be able to reach, the helicopter sways up and sideways, tilting the landing skid towards her.

Cameron catches it with both hands, and there's a stomach-dropping lurch as her weight on the skid pulls the helicopter off-balance and over towards the falling building. The engines scream, and Cameron swears she can see the rotors bending when they dive down and past the top three floors as they fall. The helicopter peels away from the building, and she gets her legs up and wraps them around the skid with the firm intent of never letting it go. A loop of rope is lowered past her face and bumps against her shoulder. Looking up, she sees Ray hanging over her, his hand braced against the winch.

'I'd offer you a hand up,' he says, 'but you have to promise not to break it first.'

Cameron stares at him for a long moment before she reaches for the loop of rope. 'Has anyone ever told you your sense of humor sucks?'

'Yeah, I've heard that,' he says. 'Here.' Ray reaches down and grips her wrist, holding her in place while she gets the loop under both her arms. Once she's safe, he lets go and uses the winch to pull her up into the crew space. 'I think it's the stress, you know?'

Cameron looks back as they fly towards the city. The Carrington facility is gone, the rubble obscured by a cloud of grey dust that is spilling out across the flat landscape that surrounds it. Something is burning in there, the orange-red flicker of flames like a heart beating in the middle of the cloud. On the highway, four police cruisers and a fire truck are speeding towards the scene, slowing to turn on to the access road. She turns away from the sight. They're not going to find anything there. Not now.

'Let's get the fuck out of here,' she says.

Chapter 41

One week later

The diner isn't doing a fast trade. It's the sort of place that has been around forever, sporting the same red and cream upholstery and the same gingham check tablecloths since the day it opened. It's a place that lives off its regulars, people who've been coming through the door every day at the same time for most of their professional lives, stopping off for pancakes or eggs and a straight gallon of coffee before they have to clock in.

Ray walks the length of the counter, a nod to the waitress as he goes, and slides into a booth on the far side, taking a seat across from its sole occupant.

'Bet you never had lunch with a dead man before,' he says. Across from him, Nate King's eyes go wide and he comes damn close to spitting his coffee straight back into the mug. He takes his time swallowing, hands fidgeting on the table like he's wondering if he can get one down into his lap without Ray noticing. 'Maybe just keep your hands on the table, keep this whole thing civil.'

'Are you here to arrest me?'

Ray gives the waitress a wave, and she signals back: *one*

minute. 'I'm not here to arrest you, Nate.'

Nate shifts uncomfortably in his seat, palms flat on the table. The waitress comes while he's squirming.

'What'll it be, hon?'

Ray gives her his best public relations smile. 'Pancakes would be fantastic, thank you.'

'You want butter with them?'

'You got syrup?'

'Sure thing.'

'I'll have syrup. And some of that coffee too?'

'Coming right up for you.'

'Thank you, ma'am.'

Nate leans forward the instant she steps away, his voice low and urgent. 'So why are you here? And how did you find me?'

Ray twirls a finger in the air. 'We'll take those in reverse order. Firstly, I didn't find you. Cameron did.'

'She's alive?'

'Your sister is definitely alive,' Ray says, 'and boy is she pissed with you.'

Ray watches Nate's face change, twisting into something like hatred. 'Figures,' he says. 'Fucking golden child. Drops a building on herself and walks out without a scratch.' Ray had hoped for some remorse, some kind of contrition from him, but all he can see is Nate's bitterness.

'You still holding that grudge?'

'You have any idea—' Nate says, a cough overtaking him. It goes on for a long time, and Ray watches him swallow before he speaks again. 'You have any idea what damage a chest infection can do to a growing boy?'

Ray looks at Nate's thin frame, his hollow cheeks. That

326

heavy cough. 'I can probably guess,' Ray says. 'You blaming that on Cameron?'

Nate spreads his hands. 'She's the one who made me like this. Hating her is all I have left.' Ray sees the tremor in his hands, and Nate quickly clasps them to cover it. 'Where is she now?'

'Not here,' Ray says. 'And she isn't coming. Considering what you did to her, you should consider yourself lucky.'

'I don't get what you mean.' Nate's face pales, then goes red like he's having a hot flash. He knows he's being played, but he can't work out how, and that's making him nervous.

'You didn't let me finish telling you why I came here.'

Ray's coffee arrives. He nods at the waitress but doesn't touch it.

'I came to bear witness,' he says. 'I came to let you know that if there was anything you wanted to say, I'm willing to hear it.'

The silence lies heavy across the table as Nate takes that in. Ray watches as he works his mouth, his chin jerking as the internal dialogue plays its course. He knows as well as Ray does that there's no way out. All he has to do now is come to terms with it.

'Homeland?' Nate asks.

Ray says nothing. Standard cop procedure.

'I can still be useful to them.' He can't hide the edge of desperation in his voice.

'No, you can't,' Ray says. 'You sold it to them as a quick, quiet snatch and grab with minimal resistance. What they got was a dozen men killed, another dozen injured, an official complaint from the Marine Corps about requisition of resources, and the uncontrolled demolition of a building on the edge of the city that put every emergency service on terror alert for two days straight. You're not useful, Nate. You're persona non grata.' Ray lifts his coffee and thinks better of it, setting it back down perfectly on the pale coffee-circle mark it had left on the table. 'That's Latin for a fuck-up.'

Nate's expression twists into one of disgust. He's brick-red in the face now, and he works a finger into his shirt collar, trying to ease it loose. 'So fucking proud of yourself. You think you'll come away clean from all this?'

'I don't think,' Ray says. 'I know I will. They did a sweep through the precinct, interviews for everyone who might have seen or heard something about what happened out at Carrington. I mentioned your name and all doors were opened. I cut a deal: help them find you, and everything goes away. My family get to go home, and I can go back to work with a clean sheet.'

'They won't let you go that easily.'

Ray shrugs. 'See, I thought that too, but they really, really want this to disappear, and as far as my part in this is concerned, sending me back to my captain with a vague but glowing commendation was their preferred outcome.' He leans forward.

The waitress comes with Ray's pancakes, and she looks down at Ray's full cup. 'Something wrong with the coffee, hon?'

'Not at all.' Ray keeps his eyes on Nate as he talks. 'I just wanted to check with you to make sure I'm not getting poisoned into the bargain.'

The waitress sighs. 'We're the FBI, not the CIA.'

Across from Ray, Nate splutters and jumps in his seat. The waitress has a gun in his face before he can do anything else, and three more guns appear seconds later, all trained on him.

'Nathan King,' the waitress says. 'You are under arrest for the murder of Sam Gorton.' She steps aside as one of the men pulls Nate out of the booth, and instead of standing he simply falls sideways out of the booth and on to the floor with a crash. None of the other diners react. As the man kneels on Nate's back to cuff him, they stay on their marks, going through the motions of a normal morning routine of eggs and coffee and idle conversation.

Ray doesn't move from where he's sitting. He stares straight ahead, picking out the tiny cracks in the upholstery as he listens to the waitress read Nate King his rights, feeling the weight of the badge in his pocket. Homeland washed their hands of the whole thing. Carrington Medical's stock took a hit at the news of a terror attack, but their global brand had bounced back stronger for it. Nate's arrest is the best he could get, and for all the satisfaction it gives him, Ray can't help but feel like he's been thrown the smallest fish in the sack to keep him quiet. He sighs and picks up his fork, digging into the first of the pancakes. 'Never knew the FBI did breakfast,' he says.

'That's eight ninety-five,' the waitress says.

He stops digging with the fork and looks up at her. 'You're shitting me.'

'Plus tip.' She's probably been in that get-up since seven a.m. to keep the pretense up, and looks like she wouldn't be above calling in the CIA to poison Ray for stiffing her on the bill.

'I didn't bring any cash,' he says. 'You take cards?'

The waitress turns and looks back at the counter. Ray follows her gaze to where a large cardboard sign proclaims *CASH ONLY*. She turns back and shakes her head at him.

'The dishes are in the back, Officer Perada,' she says.

Ray sighs, nods, and steps out of the booth, rolling up his sleeves as he heads for the back.

Chapter 42

A cathedral is as good a meeting place as any. Cameron isn't worried about being followed or cornered. Not anymore. She let Ray pick the place, and he chose one on California Street, a red-brick spike of worship sticking up out of the street, dwarfed by the office building next to it. She can see all the way down to the Bay Bridge from the street, and as she goes up the steps Cameron reads the words mounted underneath the clock on the cathedral's facade.

SON, OBSERVE THE TIME AND FLY FROM EVIL

Cameron stops and takes that in. A great piece of advice, delivered way too late. Two broken ribs, a concussion, and enough grade two and three sprains that the hospital recommended a combination of casts and a wheelchair too late. She adjusts the sling on her arm and picks a slow path up the steps, watching where she puts her feet. Ray probably thinks bringing her here is hilarious.

Inside, she makes her way up along the nave to the altar, where a golden Christ hangs flattened against a field of yellow and orange as though his crucifixion burns like the sun. One of the murals catches her eye – an angel kneeling before Mary, one hand pointing to heaven, the other holding a flower between them. The angel's face and chest are delicate, as frail as they are human. The rest of it is not. Its legs are vast, hidden to Mary by the folds of its robes; its wings stand proud behind it, half-obscured by the angel itself, reaching far beyond the limits of the frame. Clouds roil around it, surrounding its feet, framing it as something wholly other than the human face it shows to the world.

Cameron closes and opens her left hand, feeling the tendons shifting beneath her skin. The chip Carrington put in her – the tracer – will never come out. All she can do is hope that all the data on how to access it was destroyed along with Carrington's server. Carrington Medical still exist as a company, but their brush with Homeland has blunted their ambition. Their stock rallied in the wave of support that followed the 'attack' on their building, but it doesn't look like they're going to rebuild anytime soon.

Sometimes when she sleeps, Cameron imagines that she's still stuck in that basement, with Miller's grinning face hanging over her as he presses the button on a remote control over and over, the paralysis creeping across her chest, suffocating her. She has nightmares about being caught in the collapse, Samson's weight holding her fast as his fist comes down on her hard enough that it drops the building around them. Tracking down Nate was hard work, even with the FBI's help, but it gave her something to do when she couldn't sleep anymore. Cameron looks up at the storm clouds that surround the angel's head, and wonders if maybe they're not his wrath at all. Maybe they're haunting him. Mary's face is enigmatic, making no promise of sanctuary. Or forgiveness.

She hears Ray coming, his footsteps unmistakable on the flagstones, and Cameron lets him walk all the way up to her before turning to acknowledge him. He's got a bag from a bakery in one hand, and coffee in a disposable cup in the other.

'I don't think you're meant to have those in here,' she says.

'That's the joy of confession,' Ray says. 'God forgives everything, even the little things.'

'Does he?' Cameron looks up at the angel standing over Mary again, and feels nothing but a coldness, as though the peace they both offer isn't intended for her.

'More than man, at any rate.'

'They picked up Nate?'

'This morning.'

'What's going to happen to him?' she asks. She could have let Nate go. It wouldn't have been impossible. Here at the altar, that thought feels like a lead weight on her soul. Even though he'd come close to killing her, she still feels guilty.

'Twenty to life in supermax,' Ray says.

'He won't last five,' Cameron says.

'You ask me, he still lucked out.'

'How'd you figure?'

'Between you, me, and this bag of Danish?' Ray leans closer, his voice dropping. 'Homeland wanted him gone. Erased. Boston PD would have found a partial skeleton near where your car crashed. Bleached, broken, covered in tooth marks from scavengers, but they'd have been able to identify them. Coroner would have ruled that he was thrown from the car and killed instantly, that the snow prevented the search from finding him.' He stands straight again. 'Spend the rest of his days on a bed in an infirmary watching daytime TV? He got off light.'

Cameron can feel tears prickling at the corner of her vision. They're unexpected, but not unwelcome. She can imagine the relief her family would have felt if that had happened. Grief is easier to recover from than betrayal.

Ray waits until she recovers before offering her the pastry and the coffee. 'I thought you might need these,' he says.

Cameron laughs and wipes at her eyes. 'Thanks, Ray.'

'So what are you going to do now?' he asks.

'I could go home.' Cameron says it, just for the feel of it. She misses her friends. She misses the training, the life she had. She even misses the physiotherapy, God help her.

'You could stay here.' Ray says it simply, a statement of fact. A possibility.

'I could do that.' Cameron takes a deep, shuddering breath. She feels lost, like every tether that had held her life in place has been torn loose.

'Split the difference,' Ray says. 'Buy a field in the middle of nowhere. Build a ranch miles from the nearest phone line and raise cattle.'

'Make a good show of staying out of things, you mean?'

'It's just one idea.' Ray looks at her. Neither of them says it, but she knows that someone from Homeland or the FBI has been shadowing her. There's one of them in the church right now, sitting at the back, incongruous with his close-cropped hair and designer peacoat.

'Can you imagine them allocating satellite time to a patch of nowhere? Keep me pinned in the dirt like a bug mounted for show.' Cameron goes to take a swig of the coffee but the figure of Christ catches her eye and she lowers the cup, feeling guilty for trying. 'No thank you.'

'You planning on disappearing, Cam?' Ray says it softly, as though Cameron's shadow can hear him.

'I was thinking about that,' she says. 'But nobody can disappear forever. Nothing gets lost that can't be found again.'

'So what's the plan?'

'It's Saturday,' Cameron says. She sees Ray's confusion and throws him a wink. 'It's fight night.'

It's tough work getting past all of the layers of security that keep fans and creeps clear behind the scenes, but where Cameron's name falls short Ray's badge picks up the slack. There's a final hurdle as Ophelia's team try not to let her past the door of the locker room she's using, but Ophelia herself deals with that by hauling them out of the way and dragging Cameron inside.

'Cameron King,' Ophelia says. She's not started her warm-up yet, still dressed in loose sweatpants and a top with her own name plastered across it. Her hands are taped up, ready for the gloves. 'Look at you. You look like you got a building dropped on you.'

'You say that . . .'

Ophelia's eyes widen. 'You didn't.' She walks Cameron away from her entourage, her voice dropping low. 'That shit with the building going down? That was you?'

'It was the people who shot up your house,' Cameron says, 'but I was there.'

'You kicked their asses, right?' Ophelia nods, a smile breaking wide on her face. 'Right? You kicked their asses, didn't you?'

Cameron shrugs, feels suddenly shy in the face of her friend's enthusiasm. 'Yeah, Ophelia. I did.'

'YES!' She runs to the far wall, and hammers on the broad white tiles with her fist. 'Pickaxe! Hey! Can you hear me through there?' She waits, listening carefully, and a faint voice answers with something that sounds like '*What is it?*'

Ophelia pounds on the wall again. 'Cam's here!'

'*WHAT?*'

There's a lot of noise from the corridor, and then Sophia barrels in through the door, trailing a handful of outraged officials, to cross the room and haul Cameron off of her feet and crush her with a hug.

'Hey,' Ophelia says, 'be careful with her sling.' Cameron tries to agree, but all she can manage is a groan. It's like being crushed by a hydraulic press of affection.

'Fuck the sling,' Sophia answers before putting Cameron down and grinning at her like the devil herself. 'Which one of us are you walking down to the ring, Cam?'

Cameron looks from one fighter to the other. Both of them are smiling expectantly at her. *Shit.* She holds up her good hand, backing out of the stand-off. 'Look, I just wanted to come by and say good luck—'

'You should hand over the belt!' Sophia says, almost shouting in her excitement. 'It's here in the building! We can get you down in the ring and make a whole thing of it.' Cameron never lost to either of them, and when the crash took her out of the business she still held it undefeated.

Handing it over won't mean anything officially, but it's a great piece of theatre. Cameron isn't keen, but if it goes viral, then both women will likely see a better payday off of the back of it.

'I do owe you a new door.'

Sophia nods. 'Damn right you do. You need a change of clothes?'

The walk down to the ring is chaos. Ophelia okayed it with the fight promoter, but they agreed not to tell the announcer that Cameron was coming out to the ring. The instant she clears the doorway she can hear him yelling into his mic – '*Ladies and gentlemen, it's the champion herself, it's Cameron "The Hunter" King*' – and the crowd starts cheering and whistling like she's never heard before in her life.

By the time she gets to the cage doors, Cameron is dizzy with the sound of it, the noise giving way to stamping feet and a chant of her name – '*King, King, King, King*' – over and over, filling the arena to the roof.

She's got the belt over one shoulder, and when she gets to the center of the ring she knows what she is meant to do: lay it on the mat and step back from it, leaving it for Sophia and Ophelia to fight over. Both of them are standing watching her, warm now for the fight, skin shining with sweat, bobbing light on their feet and itching to go. Sophia grins, her mouthguard a wedge of blue smiling at her, and Cameron looks the other way to see Ophelia sporting the same in red.

You pair of bitches. They knew what bringing her down here would do to the crowd, and what it would do to her. It's fight night, and she can feel the excitement of it like adrenaline coursing through her. She motions for a microphone, and the ref brings it to her.

'You want this?' Cameron asks the question, looking from one woman to the other. They both nod, as keen as she is. For the first time since the building came down, Cameron knows who she is. Who she has always been. She's a fighter.

Cameron drops the belt off her shoulder, slipping free of the sling to catch and heft it in her right hand. 'Then come and get it.'

Acknowledgements

It takes a lot of time and effort to make a book happen, and a great deal of that is provided by other people. First among all of them is my agent, Juliet Mushens. I signed as her client hoping to develop a strong professional partnership. Instead, I gained an amazing friend who has worked tirelessly to champion my writing to everyone who will hear it. None of this would have been possible without her.

A massive thank-you is due to my editor, Toby Jones, whose boundless enthusiasm has made working with Headline a genuine joy. Thanks also to the rest of the Headline team for both their warm welcome and for putting their collective shoulders to the wheel to turn out an amazing book.

Thank you to Jen Williams, my writing BFF, for always being there when I need a hand shoveling in the salt mines.

Special thanks go to Alasdair Stuart and Den Patrick for being relentlessly upbeat and always ready to enable my wildest ideas, and to the rest of Team CaskieMushens for being the greatest support network and hype team an author could ever hope for.

A huge thank-you to my brother, Alistair Reid, for being a

razor-sharp alpha reader, an endless idea generator, and a literal lifesaver. Thank you to my beta readers, Emma Maree and Rob for taking the time to read an early version of the book and drop some truth on me about it.

Thanks to my parents for all of their support, and for putting up with my childhood habit of buying every withdrawn library book I could find, and to Eva-Britt and Toshihiro for all of their patience with a son-in-law who spends most of his time staring at a notebook.

Finally, thank you to my children, Aoife and Eilidh, for reminding me that there is always more than just the book, and to my wife Lisa, for telling me to stop talking about the idea of a book and try writing one instead.

THRILLINGLY GOOD BOOKS
FROM CRIMINALLY
GOOD WRITERS

CRIME FILES BRINGS YOU THE LATEST RELEASES FROM
TOP CRIME AND THRILLER AUTHORS.

SIGN UP ONLINE FOR OUR MONTHLY NEWSLETTER AND BE THE FIRST
TO KNOW ABOUT OUR COMPETITIONS, NEW BOOKS AND MORE.

VISIT OUR WEBSITE: WWW.CRIMEFILES.CO.UK
LIKE US ON FACEBOOK: FACEBOOK.COM/CRIMEFILES
FOLLOW US ON TWITTER: @CRIMEFILESBOOKS